When
Upon a Duke

"Would you allow me to pretend to kiss you?"

Isobel Tinker stared at him from deep within her hood.

"It's an old trick," he whispered, "but it can work if you keep your face averted." He held his breath, waiting for her answer. He hadn't lied; it was an old trick, reliable too. It also happened to be his most fervent wish at the moment.

Still, she could say no. She could slap him. She could call for the watchman and claim abduction. He put his odds at fifty-fifty.

Do it, she mouthed. *Hurry. Do it, do it, do it.*

Right, Jason thought. He bit the notebook and pencil in his mouth to free his hand and reached for her.

In one, cloak-fluttering movement, he scooped up Isobel Tinker and plunked her into his lap. She settled on his thighs in a puff of green skirts and emerald cloak. She weighed almost nothing. She stared over the notebook into his face, her blue eyes huge.

He removed the notebook from his mouth and whispered, "Sorry." He settled his hands on her waist.

"I say, who's there?" the night watchman called again.

Isobel's eyes bored into his.

Jason mouthed, *We needn't really—*

She kissed him.

By Charis Michaels

Awakened by a Kiss
A DUCHESS A DAY
WHEN YOU WISH UPON A DUKE

The Brides of Belgravia
ANY GROOM WILL DO
ALL DRESSED IN WHITE
YOU MAY KISS THE DUKE

The Bachelor Lords of London
THE EARL NEXT DOOR
THE VIRGIN AND THE VISCOUNT
ONE FOR THE ROGUE

CHARIS MICHAELS

WHEN YOU WISH UPON A DUKE

AWAKENED BY A KISS

AVONBOOKS

An Imprint of HarperCollinsPublishers

WHEN YOU WISH UPON A DUKE. Copyright © 2021 by Charis Michaels. All rights reserved. Printed in the United States of America. No part of this book may be used or reproduced in any manner whatsoever without written permission except in the case of brief quotations embodied in critical articles and reviews. For information, address HarperCollins Publishers, 195 Broadway, New York, NY 10007.

First Avon Books mass market printing: September 2021

Print Edition ISBN: 978-0-06-298497-5
Digital Edition ISBN: 978-0-06-298498-2

Cover design by Nadine Badalaty
Cover illustration by Chris Cocozza
Cover photograph by Shirley Green Photography (couple)
Compass art © Channarong Pherngjanda / Shutterstock

Avon, Avon & logo, and Avon Books & logo are registered trademarks of HarperCollins Publishers in the United States of America and other countries.

HarperCollins is a registered trademark of HarperCollins Publishers in the United States of America and other countries.

FIRST EDITION

Printed and Bound in Barcelona Spain by CPI BlackPrint

21 22 23 24 25   CPI   10 9 8 7 6 5 4 3 2 1

For Cassidy
My favorite book for my favorite girl.
"If I only had one helmet I would give it to you."

WHEN YOU
WISH UPON
A DUKE

Chapter One

Mayfair
1817

Does this man think he's invisible?

Isobel Tinker stared out the window of her Mayfair travel shop. On the sidewalk outside, looming with his face to the glass, a tall man stared back.

The window was several yards away and the man's features were obscured by a hat, but she could see the shadowy outline of his eyes through the *a* and *n* that spelled "Everland Travel" across the pane.

She raised her brows in an expression of, *Yes?*

No reaction.

She gestured to the door. *Come in?*

Nothing.

She gave an elegant, two-finger wave.

He remained expressionless, as if he couldn't see her at all.

"Samantha?" Isobel called to her clerk. "There's a man standing at the window. Can you see him?"

"A man?" Samantha asked, sorting folios behind the counter.

"There. To the left. Purplish greatcoat, high collar, highwayman's hat."

"Oh yes, I see him," said Samantha, cocking her head. "Shall I get the saber?"

Isobel swallowed a laugh. "The saber, I hope, would be precipitous in this moment. He appears simply to be—"

"*Stalking*," Samantha said knowingly. "Or is he more . . . casing? Calculating?"

"I was going to say 'standing,' " said Isobel. "He has the look of a man who wishes to come inside but for some reason . . . cannot. Perhaps he has a diametrical opposition to . . ."

"Rule of law?"

"Travel agents," finished Isobel.

"Well, I've set the locks on the windows and he's far too broad for the chimney. So if he will not use the door, never you fear—"

"I'm not *afraid*, Samantha. I simply wished to confirm that he isn't an apparition. If *you* see him, and *I* see him, then he must be there."

"Oh, he's there, to be sure," said Samantha. "And I don't mind saying, I don't like the look of him. Too tall by half. I cannot abide tall men. Never have done."

"And why is that?" Isobel learned a new thing that Samantha could not abide nearly every day.

"They can see over the heads of crowds."

"And this is a problem because . . . ?"

"Stampedes," said Samantha. "Started by tall men, one and all." Samantha's fierceness was matched only by her deeply held suspicions. Never had a spectacled vicar's daughter indulged such robust bloodlust.

"Right," said Isobel, looking again to the window.

And now the man was gone. Of course.

Isobel muttered a curse. "I need fresh air," she said, shoving from her chair. "I'll take a turn around the block."

"The saber is in the bureau by the alley door," Samantha called, not looking up.

"I shall risk Lumley Street with no weapons today, save my parasol." She took her umbrella and gloves and was halfway to the door when she paused.

"What is it?" asked Samantha.

"Nothing, I'm sure." Isobel looked right and left out the windows. "It's just that . . . this isn't the first time I've seen this person. Do you think that's odd? To see the same lurking man three times in one week?"

Samantha's head popped up. She glared at the spot where the man had stood, narrowing her eyes as if she was taking aim.

"Do not overreact," said Isobel. "I've noticed him here and there. He's committed no offense."

"That remains to be seen. Where 'here and there'?"

"Waiting to be served in the tearoom on the corner. Leaning on the wall behind the flower cart. With a horse in the hostler's yard at the end of the street. He appears one moment and is gone the next."

"I knew it," said Samantha, her voice filled with excitable dread.

"I really do think he means no harm," repeated Isobel. "I'd not bother to challenge him, except for today. Of all days. He must not—"

"Hunt for unsuspecting women—"

"Loiter around the shop," corrected Isobel.

"And your plan is—what? Stern words and a formidable look?"

"I'm hoping a simple introduction will suffice. Ask him how we can help. Request that he call another day. How long before Drummond Hooke arrives?"

"An hour. At most."

"Right," Isobel sighed, making a face. "An hour."

Drummond Hooke was the disaffected and mostly *absent* owner of Everland Travel. Barely twenty-two years old, his parents had died three years ago and willed ownership of the shop to him. Drummond was lazy by nature and a miser by choice, and if left to his own devices, he would have driven Everland Travel to bankruptcy within months.

But he had *not* been left on his own; his parents' will had wisely left ownership of the shop to their son, but *management* of Everland Travel to their most valued employee, Isobel Tinker.

Drummond accepted his parents' terms so long as the shop succeeded—which Isobel made certain it did. She also indulged him as the unseen mastermind of the success, which he most certainly was not.

Isobel and Samantha devoted hours to preparing for each Hooke visit. The office and clients must appear prosperous and esteemed, while Isobel must appear humble and matronly. Meanwhile, Drummond's role—despite being five years Isobel's junior—would be critical and patronizing.

If Isobel made everything appear immaculate, the young man would return to the Hooke estate in Shropshire and not be seen for another six weeks.

But lurking men were not immaculate. At even the slightest whiff of irregularity or alarming behavior, Hooke would usurp Isobel's management role, relocate to London, and ruin everything.

Isobel was *determined* to outpace ruin by Drummond Hooke.

In fact, Isobel's true goal was to save enough money to *purchase* Everland Travel from him and become not only the manager but the owner, free and clear.

She needed only five more years of savings. Ten at most.

Now she pushed out the door into Lumley Street, motivated to dispatch the Lurker well before Hooke's arrival. The August sun was bright today, illuminating Mayfair with sparkling light. It would be impossible to hide in the brightness, and Isobel didn't try. If the Lurker had come to seek her out, well—here she was.

But he wasn't stalking or hunting her, no matter what Samantha thought. The man didn't feel dangerous to Isobel, merely out of place. Honestly, he seemed little more than curious. Isobel was accustomed to curious. She was a young woman who operated a successful business. Female businesswomen were unexpected at best and scandalous at worst. This was not the first lurking husband or brother she'd encountered.

Isobel Tinker designed seamless holidays for women and girls. Her voyages were safe, respectable, and luxurious. They offered the finest destinations in Europe with white-glove service. A lady's world broadened. The envy of her friends.

It was why Mr. and Mrs. Hooke left *her* to run the agency instead of their prize-idiot son.

It was how she'd taken Everland Travel from a struggling budget holiday packager to its current premier status: "Travel agent to the most esteemed women in England," as read her favorite quote in *The Times*.

It was her life's work. If she was also a bit of a curiosity—well, she was a *successful* curiosity.

And if she could achieve her dream of purchasing the agency, she would not simply elevate Everland Travel to new heights; she would *own* it too.

"I don't have time for this," Isobel grumbled, glancing

up and down the sidewalk. She turned left, eyeing the pedestrians of Lumley Street.

Despite the Lurker's great propensity to disappear, his other distinguishing quality was his considerable height and breadth. He stood out like a professional boxer. The tearoom, in particular, had framed his size in striking contrast; its spindly tables and chairs seemed to bow and creak under his weight. The flower cart, which was an immovable rattletrap with warped wheels, wanted only his strength to be rolled spryly away. The horse he stabled at the hostler's yard looked like a mythical beast. The Lurker himself, who'd been instructing a stable boy on the horse's care when she'd seen him, had made Isobel think of . . .

Well, the phrase that'd popped into her brain had been *Greek god*.

Now she turned the corner at Brown Hart Gardens and pressed toward Duke Street. Here, too, the sidewalk was devoid of professional boxers or Greek gods. She was just about to turn into Duke Street when she saw movement in the alley behind her shop.

Isobel slowed, squinting into the dim, crooked passage. She tilted her head and listened. Footsteps crunched from the murk, the heavy footfall of godlike boots.

Isobel sighed, glanced at her timepiece, and followed the sound. Drummond Hooke was due in forty-five minutes. If the Lurker was in the alley, she had fifteen minutes to learn his business and dispatch him, and a half hour to settle at her desk.

Who's the lurker now? she thought, picking her way around alley debris. A cat leapt into her path, and she jumped. She unhooked the parasol from her arm and held it perpendicular like a handrail. The rear door to her shop came into view. She saw her back steps. The rusty railing. Her mop bucket. And—

Him.

The Lurker stood on her back door stoop, his back turned.

She took a silent breath and flipped the parasol so that the pointed tip faced out. Her heart beat faster, but she felt no real fear. She'd traveled the world, for God's sake. This was *Mayfair*. She'd yet to see anything in Mayfair, night or day, that rivaled her life before she'd returned to England. And anyway, what choice did she have but to confront him? Drummond Hooke frequently smoked in this alley when he visited. Discovering a giant man loitering on their back stoop would be unacceptable.

"I beg your pardon?" she called, staring at the Lurker's broad back.

Her tone was sharp and demanding and the man tensed.

"Turn 'round, if you please," she commanded. "Slowly."

Obligingly, the man raised two giant gloved hands and slowly pivoted.

Isobel held her breath and watched him turn. She straightened to her full five-foot-two-inch height. His large shoulders were smoothly encased in gray-purple wool; his profile was chiseled, just peeking from a rakish, wide-brimmed hat. His greatcoat hung open, whirling slightly when he turned.

At last, he raised his head and she saw his face.

Isobel blinked.

His eyes were amber-hazel, the color of dark caramel. His mouth was . . . well, *perfect* was the only word that sprang to mind, as useless as it was. His nose (who noticed noses?) was not unlike his height: Greek-god-like.

Isobel took a deep breath.

Of course, the nature of his nose or mouth made no difference. What mattered was that he was ever-so-slightly *smiling*. Just a quirked uptick at the corner of his (perfect) mouth.

It was the smile of someone who'd staggered from the pub and eaten the Christmas pudding the night before the feast.

"Hello," said the Lurker.

His voice was casual. Playful. Confident.

Isobel felt an intermittent shimmer at her wrists and throat.

No, she thought. *Oh no.*

She'd left Europe seven years ago with only the clothes on her back and two solemn vows: never to return to Europe and *never, ever* to engage with playful, confident men.

The word *danger* began to burn in the back of her mind like a pillaged farmhouse.

The Lurker continued, full of innocence and good humor. "Do you happen to know if this door is always locked?"

It was a ridiculous question, which they both knew. Either he was trying to distract her from his larceny or catch her off guard to commit some worse crime.

Isobel was, to her extreme irritation, both distracted and caught off guard.

It had been so long. So very long.

"I *do* know that this door is always locked," Isobel said, "as it is my door, and I lock it."

"Always?" he wondered.

"Stop," she said, unwilling to play along. If Isobel Tinker understood nothing, she understood the easy currency of flirtatious, handsome men who "played" at everything they did. She'd learned at the foot of a master, and it had nearly destroyed her. She'd survived instead, and now she was immune.

Or mostly immune.

"Who are you?" she demanded, tapping the parasol in her palm. "And what is your business at the alley door of my shop?"

"I was . . . hoping to come inside?" Another joke.

"Why not use the front door?"

"Why not have a back entrance?" he suggested. "Double your traffic?"

"Because this is an alley, and no one travels here except rats and men trying to pick the lock."

"Well, there you have it—two potential customers at your disposal."

"I'm sending for the constable," she said.

"No, wait." He reached out a hand. "I am a customer. I need to book passage. Truly."

"Passage for whom?" The words were out before she could stop them. She gritted her teeth. If he'd been old, or wretched, or spotted, or anything but handsome and dashing and jocular, she would not entertain this conversation. Not for *One. Second. More.*

But he was handsome and dashing.

And she'd learned nothing at all.

Obviously.

"For myself," he said. He leapt from the stoop and landed in the alley with a *thwack.*

Isobel took a step back. "Everland Travel provides holidays and travel services primarily for *women*," she informed him. "I'm sorry, Mr.—"

"Northumberland," he provided. "The Duke of North-umberland."

Isobel let out a laugh. "The *Duke* of Northumberland?"

She shook her head. "Charming. A stalker and an imposter."

"Heard of me, have you?"

Isobel stared at him, taking in his posh accent, his finely crafted boots, his easy confidence.

Surely not.

He added, "I prefer to be called 'North.' "

Surely, surely not.

He finished with, "I'm only now becoming accustomed to the title. It's . . ." a sigh, ". . . new. To me."

Isobel opened her mouth to challenge this preposterous misinformation. A duke, new or otherwise, lurking in her alley? Highly unlikely. But something made her stop short of saying the words. There was no time for preposterous misinformation or challenges. There was only Drummond Hooke, *due any minute.*

"I'm forced to ask you to leave, sir," she said. "And also, you really must cease your lurking."

"My lurking—"

"The alley, the window, the businesses up and down Lumley Street? Today of all days, to be sure. Although I prefer a neighborhood devoid of lurkers on any day. So if you could simply . . ."

She walked her fingers through the air, the gesture of something small and invasive skittering away.

"Wait, but I—" he began.

"You're mistaken if you think I haven't noticed. You're also mistaken to claim business with Everland Travel. And if you try to pass yourself off as a duke again, I really will call the constable. The Duke of Northumberland, as anyone knows, is a national hero. *And* he's mourning the loss of his brother, the previous duke. May God rest him. Let us show respect for families who suffer such great loss. If we do nothing else."

The man tried to interrupt, but Isobel pressed on. It was all coming back to her now—how to manage imposing men who exuded playful charm. You called them out and sent them on their way. You kept your distance.

She made a twirling gesture with her parasol. "You're handsome and dashing—I'll concede that—but I've not the time nor patience for lurkers or liars, no matter how they appear. In less than an hour, I'm convening a very important meeting inside the shop. There can be no interruptions or irregularities. Now." Deep breath. "Please, sir. Be gone."

She hooked the handle of the parasol over her arm, brushed her hands together, and began to stride away.

"Miss Tinker, I presume?"

Isobel faltered. She turned back. "I beg your pardon?"

"You are Miss Isobel Tinker?"

Many people know my name, she reminded herself. *I've sold holidays to half the heiresses in London.*

She stared at him, not confirming or denying.

"I thought you'd be older," he said. "Considerably older. You're not yet thirty. I'd put money on it."

"What business is it of yours, my age?" She was seven and twenty as of last week.

"I was led to believe you were a cynical, gray-headed matron, running this shop behind spectacles and a stack of dusty travel books."

A vision of Isobel's future flashed before her eyes, and she wasn't certain she liked it.

He went on. "*And* you're shorter."

"Led to expect by whom?"

"The Foreign Office." He stepped up and gestured to Lumley Street with an open arm. "After you."

Isobel's feet moved of their own accord, walking toward the sunlight. "What foreign office?"

"The one that serves the interest of His Majesty King George outside our United Kingdom."

"You're lying."

"The governmental office where *national heroes* mill about, doing their duty. For Crown and Country."

Isobel's brain began to spin. On leaden feet, she walked into Lumley Street. She blinked. She took a step toward her shop. And another.

"I'm sorry our first encounter was in the alley," he said. "I'm not a thief, I promise you. I was doing a bit of reconnaissance, although very poorly, I'm afraid. I cannot account for the debacle of this introduction."

"This is not an introduction."

"I was being obtuse, and there's no excuse, although I do have one." He flashed her a heartbreakingly handsome look and Isobel turned away. She felt a *ping* inside her chest like a reverberating chime.

He went on. "My file on you and this shop was riddled with bad intelligence. Obviously."

She looked back. He was staring in open assessment, his gaze methodical, like he was in the business of studying people.

"Deuced unprofessional," he continued. "Amateur, really. No wonder you don't believe I'm a duke."

"I've asked you to go," Isobel said weakly. No matter who he was, *he had to go*. Drummond Hooke, the meeting. She reached for the door—

"Not before," he said, taking hold of the door above her head, "we discuss this journey."

"But you cannot mean . . ." Her brain swam with the highly unlikely (and yet very small possibility) of dukes and foreign offices and national heroes and a file about *her*. She drifted to her desk.

Behind the counter, Samantha looked up. She stared

at the Lurker with narrowed eyes. "You've found him, I see," she said, her tone suggesting that a snake had been found beneath the barn.

"How do you do?" the Lurker asked pleasantly.

"Managed to find our door, did you?" Samantha asked.

"Indeed," said the man.

"Did you tell him?" Samantha looked to Isobel.

Isobel stared back, her brain going almost entirely blank. Her only thought was, *I'll tell him nothing.*

Samantha said to the man, "Please be aware, sir, that we've an important meeting in ten minutes' time. The owner of this agency has traveled from Shropshire for a review. When he arrives, all customers will be asked to—"

"He's not a customer," corrected Isobel, her heart thudding in her throat. "Samantha, can I trouble you to prepare tea? Mr. Hooke relishes little flourishes."

"The kettle is on," said Samantha, looking back and forth between Isobel and the man.

"Go and check it," Isobel bit out.

"It's not whistled."

"*Please.*"

"*Right*," drawled Samantha. "*Now* may I get the saber—?"

"*Samantha!*" breathed Isobel.

Samantha backed from the room with exaggerated stealth. When she was gone, Isobel hurried behind her desk. With the safety of the familiar oak between them, she took a deep breath and turned to the Lurker. In two frustrated yanks, she pulled off her gloves.

He exhaled. "Can we begin again?"

"Can you be gone in ten minutes?"

"My name is Northumberland—North, if you prefer—

and I've come to book a journey." He approached her desk in two easy strides.

Isobel braced against his proximity. The alley was one thing, dark and easy to flee. Now sun through the window illuminated him like an angel and she was trapped behind her desk.

She checked the clock. How had he evaded her for days but now trailed her inside? Perhaps if she changed tack. What if she simply went along?

"This trip is for yourself?" she asked. She took up a pen.

"Yes."

"As I've said, Everland Travel primarily arranges holidays for *female* clients."

"But are you capable of booking passage for a man? It's *possible*?"

She sighed heavily and sat down. She scooted her chair behind her desk. She hovered the pen over a blank piece of parchment.

"Where do you wish to go?" She looked up with faux professional interest.

"Iceland," he said.

Her professionalism and detachment dissolved. Isobel blinked. She squeezed the pen. A single drop of ink dripped to the sheet.

"I beg your pardon?" she said to the drop.

"Iceland?" he repeated. "Nordic island? Recently ceded to Denmark? Covered with volcanoes and, one would assume, ice?"

Isobel felt the blood drain from her face in the same moment her cheeks caught fire.

"Why?" she rasped.

"I've business on the island," he said simply.

"And your business is . . . shepherding?" she asked, her voice strange and high and breathy. "Goat shepherding? The only work to be had in Iceland at the moment is goat farming and agronomy."

"*No,*" he said carefully, "I'm on assignment for the Foreign Office. As I've said."

She closed her eyes. *This* again. "And why hasn't the *Foreign Office* booked this Foreign Office–related travel on your behalf? Surely if the Crown dispatches you to . . . foreign shores, they manage the details of the journey."

"My office *could* arrange it," he said, "but it would take time I do not have, and the nature of the mission is particularly delicate. More secret than most. I've come to you because my *file*—that is, the background information on this mission—pointed me in the direction of a woman called Isobel Tinker in a travel agency in Lumley Street. It's been suggested to me that you might know a devil of a lot about Iceland, more than anyone on the travel desk at the Foreign Office. And so here I am."

"You're joking," she said, dropping the pen. She'd never had a conversation that sounded so patently false but also so terrifyingly possible.

If he *was* some sort of governmental agent, and he *did* have access to information ("files"?) on private citizens, was it possible his office *knew* something? About *her*? Isobel Tinker? After years of being so very good and so very stationary and so very . . . so very—

Isobel closed her eyes. Was it possible that her uncle had left a trail of documents when he'd extricated her?

Could this strange man possibly know anything about the time she spent in *Iceland*?

"It is *not* a joke," he said easily. "And by the look on your face, I'd say you're not entirely surprised that I've sought you out."

"I am wholly surprised," she whispered. "I am in shock." The truth.

"Why?"

"Because Iceland is an obscure island that is impossible to reach seven months out of any year and difficult to reach the rest. The least traveled destination in all of Scandinavia, to be sure." This was also true, but only a fraction of why she was surprised.

She managed to add, "It's sparsely populated by common laborers and a handful of landowning families. There are no trees. To say that it is *remote* is an understatement."

She scooped up the pen and jabbed it back into the inkpot. She shoved back from her desk. "That is really all I have time to say on the matter, Mr.—"

"It's 'North.' The Duke of Northumberland."

"Please stop saying that."

"It's my name."

"You are *not* a duke . . . you do *not* work for the king . . . you are not standing in my travel shop asking to book passage to an island that I—"

She couldn't say it.

"You don't sell holidays to Iceland?" he asked. He looked so very confused.

"No."

"Really?"

"*Really.*"

"Why not?"

"Because I do not *believe you* when you say you wish to travel there." In her head, she thought, *Because I was utterly destroyed in Iceland, and the memory of it is too painful to bear.*

"Well," he sighed, shrugging giant shoulders, "it's where I'm going."

"Then you'll have to find some other travel agent, because it is out of my realm of expertise."

"But the file—"

"Do not mention 'the file,' or the Foreign Office, or your identity as an alleged duke again," she said.

He blinked at her. His handsome face was creased with innocent confusion.

Isobel narrowed her eyes and planted her fingertips on the desktop, leaning toward him. "I'm sorry that I cannot help you. You'll need to find someone else. As I've said, I have a very important meeting. Now . . ."

A deep breath.

". . . I'm afraid I must ask you to—"

She was cut off by the arrival of Mr. Drummond Hooke sailing through the door.

Chapter Two

*J*ason was confused.

Jason was confused, and irritated, and extremely pressed for time, and no one in the hallowed halls of Everland Travel seemed to care.

Miss Isobel Tinker had gone from dismissing him and dodging him and moved to simply ignoring him.

She *ignored* him.

Even before he'd become the Duke of Northumberland, Jason "North" Beckett was not accustomed to being ignored. Or dismissed. And certainly not dodged, not by a woman.

"If you'll excuse me, sir," she'd said, evading him smoothly when the little bell on her door jingled. "My meeting. It's happening. Now. I'm afraid we'll need to postpone your . . ."

She'd stopped talking, seemingly at a loss about what she might do for him.

At a loss, after he'd clearly said, "Please sell me passage to Iceland," at least five times. It was almost as if she knew what he really wanted was not a holiday package at all. It was almost as if she knew what he really needed was a *guide* inside Iceland.

Jason looked again at the man who'd breezed through the door. He stood in the center of the agency's small lobby and turned a slow, deliberate circle, assessing the room. He was of medium height, thin, with a patchy beard. Small eyes, like a subterranean creature prone to burrow. A mole? He wore the ostentatious greatcoat and voluminous cravat of someone far older, a country squire on his first trip to London. He carried a gold-tipped walking stick and teetered on high-heeled boots. And he looked at Miss Tinker like a puppeteer looks at his favorite marionette.

Miss Tinker, in turn, greeted the man with the bracing smile one reserved for pushy vicars.

Jason tried to remember if she'd flashed that smile at him. He'd tailed her for three days. She'd demonstrated polite cordiality to neighbors and crisp helpfulness to strangers, but she did not waft about with a freewheeling grin. In the alley, her pervading expressions had ranged from irritation to impatience. There had been no smiling.

The alley had been a turning point. Jason had realized that his file was all wrong; the profile of Isobel Tinker bore little resemblance to the Isobel Tinker of life.

Generally speaking, diminutive women did not interest him, but Isobel Tinker was very pretty. Although not sweet-pretty or fancy-pretty; more unpredictable-pretty, exciting-pretty. Like a baby snake. Or a lit fuse.

There was something about her that reminded him of a demonstration he'd seen in a chemist's lab at Oxford: a luminous burst of electrical current flickering inside a tiny glass orb. She *strummed*. Her bearing suggested coiled energy. He was afraid to look away for fear of missing the explosion.

Ducking into the alley had been, quite literally, the act of "looking away." He'd hoped to learn more about the shop; instead, she'd materialized behind him. She'd been direct and articulate, calling him out for the dark-alley marauder he'd been.

And she was so bright. Big blue eyes, swinging umbrella, pale hair in a bobbing bun on the top of her head.

He'd spent fifteen years in the Foreign Service and seen mortal combat, but in the alley, he'd had to work to keep up.

He was working still.

"Samantha?" called Miss Tinker now. "Can I trouble you to provide this gentleman with literature about our Scandinavian destinations? And to set an appointment for another day?"

She meant him, of course. *He* was the gentleman. *He* would receive literature about Scandinavia and be sent off until another day.

Surely not. He looked at Isobel Tinker.

Surely yes, Miss Tinker said with her eyes.

The clerk called Samantha bit out the words, "Right this way, sir." She pointed a sharp finger to a desk near a window.

Given no other choice, Jason went.

At the desk, Samantha thunked down a stack of travel guides and slid them to him. *"You,"* she whispered, "must go."

"Who's the bloke?" Jason whispered back, flipping open the topmost book.

"Who are *you*?" the clerk countered.

"I'm the Duke of Northumberland," he said, enunciating the words with tight poshness, perhaps his first time ever to emphasize the title.

"Why have you been stalking Miss Tinker for a week?"

"I—"

Jason stopped. Wasn't the title enough? For his father and brother, the title had always been enough.

He tried again, speaking like the foreign agent he'd been long before he was a duke.

"I'm not stalking Miss Tinker," he whispered. "I'm *appealing to her*. On behalf of the British Foreign Office."

"Appealing for what?"

"Information. About the island nation of Iceland. And possibly a booking. Although she seems very young to be an expert on foreign destinations. She seems too young to be an expert on anything at all. I was led to believe she was . . . older and, er—Older."

"She's seven and twenty," the clerk said slowly. She glanced at Miss Tinker and back at Jason, the movement of someone who knew she was speaking out of turn.

"Miss Tinker has assured me," Jason lied, "that she can provide information about Iceland. She said she's spent a considerable amount of time there. She was an expatriate, I understand, some eight years ago?"

The clerk bit her lip. She glanced again at her employer.

Jason flipped a page and tried again. "But can you tell me how often she *returns* to Iceland?"

"Miss Tinker will never return to Iceland."

"Why is that, do you think?"

The clerk gave a slow shake of her head.

"Right." Jason fell back. "But how long did she live there? Two years? Or was it three?"

"She does not discuss Iceland with me," said the clerk. "Or anyone."

Jason nodded and returned to the truth. "Well, she was very shrewd to have spotted me these last few days. I was only surveying the shop to get the lay of the land. I had no idea she was the owner. Or is she simply the manager?" He eyed the girl.

"Miss Tinker is the manager," informed Samantha. "But she might as well own the shop. She *should* own it."

Jason shut the book, filing away this bit of information. "This book is written in Dutch," he said. "Which I cannot read. How long will she meet with this person?"

"With Mr. Hooke? They will meet for hours. At least."

"*Why?*"

"He is the owner of Everland Travel."

"*This man* owns the shop?"

A nod. "He inherited it from his parents. Most of the year, he lives in Shropshire and Isobel manages the business. When he travels to London, he must be included. And validated." Another frown. "He must *bask.*"

Jason made a grunting noise. "Bask?"

The clerk inclined her head, indicating the ongoing conversation in the center of the room.

"I see you've worn the dress I enjoy so very much," Hooke was telling Miss Tinker, his voice a singsong.

Irritation flared and Jason stifled the urge to join the conversation. His skin buzzed with the familiar, jumpy energy that tormented him whenever he was forced to sit idly by and wait. He reached into his pocket for a coin and flicked it into the air. He caught it, spun it in his palm, and flicked it again.

"Was this a favorite?" Miss Tinker asked her employer.

"But you've not worn the pinafores, I see," said Hooke.

"Oh yes, the pinafores," hedged Miss Tinker. "I'll need to call to the seamstress's. There was some issue with the embroidery, I believe."

"Oh, the embroidery must be perfect," said Hooke.

"Please remember, the tailor in my village can do up the confections I have in mind—"

"Do not trouble yourself, Mr. Hooke," soothed Miss Tinker. "We shall have them for next time . . ."

Jason caught the coin and whispered to Samantha, "Pinafores?"

"He wishes for us to wear ruffled yellow aprons with the words 'Hooke's Everland Travel Lass' embroidered on the bib."

"No."

The girl nodded. Jason made a coughing noise and flicked the coin again.

"I was surprised," Hooke was saying, "to see you've not *closed* the shop for our meeting. We've so much to discuss. Ideas and directives. Money-saving measures . . ."

Now the man looked pointedly to the desk by the window. Jason stared back, flicking his coin into the air.

Miss Tinker rushed to say, "Oh, this gentleman was just on his way out." She shot Jason a pleading look.

"A drop-in client, I assume?" Drummond Hooke said, studying Jason.

"Indeed," said Miss Tinker.

"How often," Drummond Hooke now asked, "do lone gentlemen come to us without wives or sisters in tow?" He puffed up, inhaling deeply. "I cannot say it's—"

"Oh, very rarely," assured Miss Tinker. "In fact, I cannot remember the last time we've served a gentleman without his family. The ladies wish to be involved in each step of the planning. Anticipation is part of the holiday."

She rushed to appease him, signaling to the clerk. "Samantha, perhaps if you bundled up the guidebooks for—"

Enough.

Jason flicked the coin once more and caught it. He shoved up and crossed to the younger man.

"Northumberland," he said, giving a slight bow. "The *Duke* of Northumberland. How do you do?"

Twice in his life now, he'd proclaimed the title with the intent of impressing everyone in the room.

"Northumberland?" gasped Hooke, clearly impressed. "But, Your Grace!" Hooke swept his hat from his head and bowed with exaggeration. "Isobel?" scolded Hooke. "Why didn't you say something?"

"I—ah . . ." began Miss Tinker.

"What an honor to have you in my shop, sir," continued Hooke. "But how similar you look to your portrait in the papers. Wait! I've today's edition here."

While the room stared, Hooke pulled a broadsheet from his greatcoat and unfurled it.

"Aha, there 'tis!" Hooke shoved *The Times* at Jason, but only Miss Tinker and Samantha leaned in to see.

The headline "Northumberland Departs Foreign Office to Assume Dukedom" shouted from the page, accompanied by a rather constipated-looking etching of Jason's face.

The sight of the headline invoked a now-familiar burn in the lining of his stomach, and Jason looked away.

"Let me guess," boasted Hooke, "you intend to pack away your mother and sisters on holiday so you may enjoy peace and quiet as you settle into Syon Hall?"

"Mr. Hooke," said Isobel Tinker in quiet shock, "the Duchess of Northumberland and His Grace's sisters have suffered a great loss."

Hooke ignored her. "You could not have chosen a more reliable, respectable, and, dare I say, *esteemed* travel agent for the ladies! And what luck, you've called on a day when the owner—that would be me, sir—is in the office to manage every detail. Samantha?" he barked to the clerk. "Bring chairs so His Grace and I might sit."

Jason held up a hand. "If it would be agreeable to you, Mr. Hooke—it is Mr. Hooke, isn't it?"

"Drummond Hooke, at your service," said Hooke, bowing again.

"Right," said Jason. "If it would be agreeable, I'd hoped to finish quickly and be out of your way. I've already given my details to your Miss Tinker here. I understand that you're in town on important business and I'm loathe to intrude on your meeting."

"'Tis no intrusion," tried Hooke.

Jason gritted his teeth. "Miss Tinker and I were nearly finished, and I've my own demanding schedule."

Hooke looked uncertain.

Jason finished it. "Honestly, these are the sort of secretarial notes that are surely below the notice of the owner." He gave the younger man a knowing look. "The girl will do for this."

Hooke nodded, mimicking Jason.

Miss Tinker cleared her throat. "Perhaps I can see the duke on his way while you review the ledgers with Samantha, Mr. Hooke?"

The younger man glanced first to Samantha, then to the open ledger on the counter, then to Miss Tinker. It occurred to Jason that Drummond Hooke had been looking forward to crowding over that ledger book with Isobel.

"It's all settled, then," Jason said quickly. "I'll not take more than five minutes of Miss Tinker's time."

He scooped up a second chair and plunked it at the desk. Meanwhile Samantha darted behind the counter, flipping pages in a ledger.

"Here you are, Mr. Hooke," the clerk called. "In fact, we have a question on the profits for this quarter. Higher again, you'll see."

"So you say," said Hooke slowly, watching Jason flick his coin again.

Isobel Tinker slid into the chair. "You have three minutes," she whispered.

"I said five." Jason sat across from her.

She closed her eyes and drew a deep, calming breath. When she opened them, she said, "Why didn't you tell me you were a duke?"

"I did."

"Dukes do not lurk about in alleys. They do not book holidays at small travel agencies for women travelers."

"Well, I haven't been a duke for long," he said offhandedly. "Now, about Iceland—"

"Stop." She raised a small hand. "I'm at a loss to make myself clearer: *no one* travels to Iceland. It's simply not done. If it's your intention to waste both of our time on a lark, you've come on a terrible day. Dealing with my employer is both delicate and taxing. My livelihood depends on accommodating him in a hundred different ways. Mitigating your odd requests is not one of them. I cannot tell you again that there are no holidays to Iceland. Iceland is many glorious things, but it is *not* a holiday destination."

"It's no lark, Miss Tinker," he said.

"Then what's the meaning of—?"

"Pirates," he said plainly. "Nordic pirates. It's why I came, and it's why I cannot leave until we speak."

Her blue eyes widened. "What of Nordic pirates?"

He exhaled deeply and glanced toward the duo at the counter. He looked back at Isobel. "A band of Nordic pirates has taken capture of a contingent of English merchants."

"Oh," she said, a hollow sound. "How? Why?"

"We cannot say for sure. The merchants were trying to establish some unofficial arrangement for trade between the east coast of England and Iceland. They set out to speak to civic leaders in Reykjavík about importing goods, but they were taken captive by pirates instead."

"But the merchants should have sailed to Denmark, not Iceland," Isobel said. "Denmark controls trade in Iceland." She reached for a pamphlet entitled *Tour Majestic Denmark*.

"They should have," Jason acknowledged, "but they did not. The merchants sought to circumvent the Danes and trade directly with Iceland."

"To escape the Danish tariffs," she guessed.

"Yes," Jason said, his heartbeat kicking up. This young woman knew far more about Scandinavia than he'd been led to expect. But perhaps she could be of significant help to him.

"The merchants were, in essence, setting up a smuggling route," he said. He'd never intended to reveal this much. But he'd also not expected her to *know* this much.

"They would not be the first English smugglers to Iceland," said Miss Tinker. "England and Iceland are neighbors that have been either fighting or trading—or both—for centuries."

"Indeed. And our government might allow the merchants to simply languish in captivity—pirates are, after all, a consequence of smuggling—but one of the captured merchants just happens to be a . . . relation of mine." Another deep breath. "A cousin. His father, my uncle, has appealed to me for help. In doing so, I should not rattle the Minister of Trade in Denmark. In fact, none of the leadership in Iceland should be invoked. It's a colossal cock-up and has the potential to be a diplomatic nightmare."

"Oh," she said again, barely blinking.

Jason continued. "The recovery of my hapless cousin and his townspeople is to be my last assignment before I retire to Syon Hall in Middlesex and assume my duties as duke."

Jason heard himself say the words, his voice remarkably steady, his body relaxed. He was getting better at concealing the gut-rolling dread.

He forced himself to finish. "My brother's been dead almost a year. I've put off my family responsibilities long enough. My resignation has already been announced, but I should like to restore my cousin before I go. He is not the . . . shiniest marble in the pouch, but we were close in boyhood and I'm fond of him. And anything I can do to keep England on the up-and-up with Denmark is advantageous. The relationship between our two countries is tremulous at the moment."

Miss Tinker nodded. "They sided with France in the war."

"Indeed they did." Denmark's alliances were hardly obscure, but he couldn't name another young woman who could readily spout off the contents of Napoleon's dance card. She surprised him nearly every time she opened her mouth. He waited to hear what she might say next.

"I . . ." began Miss Tinker, and then she paused and

closed her eyes. She looked so anguished Jason thought it could've been *her* cousin taken by pirates.

He offered, "Not to heap you with reasons, Miss Tinker, but also there is some urgency on the part of the captured merchants. They hail, primarily, from the coastal town of Grimsby, in Lincolnshire. The lot is made up of unknowing townspeople who were, in a manner, convinced of the endeavor by an ambitious town council that misled and bullied them—my cousin included. The captured merchants, by and large, are innocent of the aspiration of smuggling and likely terrified."

She opened her eyes, shot him a look of something like desperation, and then stared at the ceiling.

Jason went on. "One man is old and frail; still another has a sick child at home. They were only meant to be gone for a month, and now it's been nearly three. I must go after them, but Iceland happens to be a gray void in my realm of experience. I've been a lot of places, Miss Tinker, but never there. However, I understand that *you have*. And I need your help."

Now she nodded and glanced at her employer behind the counter. When she spoke, her voice was unsteady. "Look, you appear to be everything you've said. I'll grant you that. And the situation you describe sounds both believable and . . . pressing. But *why me*? You claim to have information on my experience in Iceland but you don't know me—not really. Meanwhile, there are Norse scholars and North Sea adventurers and even Icelandic immigrants in England to whom you could appeal for information. I am . . . I am nobody. I'm also distracted and reluctant. *Why me?*"

"Ah, yes," he said. "That. I need *your* help in particular for precisely those reasons. You happen to be the very best source of information because you are obscure in identity and, by all accounts, discreet by nature. You are a young woman who lives a quiet life in Mayfair and wants nothing to do with international diplomacy."

"Meaning, I won't tell anyone, and if I did, no one would listen?"

"Yes," he said. He thought, *And very, very clever.*

Isobel Tinker nodded, more to herself than him, and looked away. This afforded him a prolonged view of her profile. Delicate nose, a swoosh of lashes, a fringe of soft blond wisps against her forehead. She was lovely. A bit unexpected. Different. Fiery and tightly wound. He found himself wondering what it would take to unwind her.

He wondered why she was unmarried. Why spend her days toiling away in a travel agency, enduring the scrutiny of its petty owner? Most bright and pretty women of seven and twenty were married and had begun a family by now.

"What if I tell you I cannot help you?" she asked softly. "What if I said that I know nothing about Iceland or pirates."

"Then I'd say you were lying." He watched her carefully. Her heart-shaped face tightened but she didn't deny it. Something about the tenseness and the dread gave him pause. Her expression said, *Anyone but me.*

"Lives are at stake, Miss Tinker," he said lowly, speaking to the coin in his hand. He wasn't immune to silent pleading but he truly needed help. And she was proving herself to be a very promising resource.

He looked up, hoping his face conveyed the same plea. "Will you not help us?"

She said something under her breath. A curse? A prayer? He couldn't be sure. She glanced over her shoulder at Hooke.

"Likely my contributions will be of no help at all," she said, turning back, "but I'll share what very little I . . . I remember." She shot another look at the counter. "Only, *not now*. And not here."

"Fine. Meet me tonight?"

"Mr. Hooke will wish for me to accompany him to dinner and some diversion."

Jason felt a twitch by his left eye. "Diversion?"

She shook her head and held up a hand. "It's nothing . . . amorous. Let me be clear."

"You said you would accommodate him a hundred ways."

She gave one, curt shake of her head. "Not *that* type of accommodation. It will be dinner and a concert in the park or similar."

"I believe you," he said. He hadn't meant to embarrass her, but he'd wanted to know. It felt very important, for some reason, that he know how she accommodated Drummond Bloody Hooke.

"My job depends on indulging him in this," she said. "But I cannot say when I will be home."

"You live here?" he asked.

She nodded. "Upstairs."

"Alone?" he confirmed. This also seemed important. A nod.

Jason felt himself breathe. "Fine. I'll wait for you. Check the alley when you return."

"I am not in the business of creeping around in alleys, Your Grace. This afternoon notwithstanding."

"Don't disparage alley creeping," he said. "It's one of the many things I'll miss about this job when it's gone."

Miss Tinker stared at him with an inscrutable expression. As a rule, Jason had no time for inscrutable women, not when there were so many demonstrative women. But he'd not sought her out because he had *time* for her. He'd sought her out because he needed her help.

"Fine," she began, "meet me in the street—*not* the alley—at ten o'clock. Surely I will be home by then. I'll give you half an hour on a park bench in Grosvenor Square. But no more."

Chapter Three

Osobel's evening with Drummond Hooke ended with a single thought: *If this man touches me one . . . more . . . time . . .*

She squeezed the ties of her reticule and gave it a perfunctory swing. She'd sewn a fishing weight into the lining for the purpose of uninvited touching, and wouldn't Samantha be proud. If swung at the knuckle between wrist and thumb . . .

She mustn't, of course. Just as she hadn't driven the heel of her boot into his instep nor jabbed him with her umbrella.

If she couldn't contradict Drummond Hooke, how on earth could she injure him?

Her only hope was to escape, and thankfully they were half a block from her door.

"What a lovely way to review this quarter's earnings, Mr. Hooke," she said lightly, stepping around a puddle and out of his reach. "It's never necessary to squire me about, but I do thank you. The meal was very generous."

The meal had been tepid stew and hard bread in a tavern some two miles from Lumley Street. He'd ordered one tankard of ale and suggested they share it. No pudding. They walked because he'd refused to hire a hackney.

"When can we expect you back in London?" Isobel asked, fishing for her key. *Months and months*, she wished silently. *Please say, "Months and months."*

She was just about to unlock the door when something across the street caught her eye. A thick, hulking presence where there should have been only potted geraniums.

She squinted. Yes, there. A tall smudge that sharpened into a man-shaped density in the dark. She could just make out a wide-brimmed hat, long greatcoat, and heavy boots.

Northumberland.

She sucked in a breath and looked away, fumbling again with the key. If Drummond saw the duke, his jealousy and suspicion would set her back for months. He would restrict her autonomy and question the propriety of her running the shop. The ramifications could be devastating.

But why had the duke come so early? She had an hour, at least, before their rendezvous. She'd rushed through dinner because she'd wanted time between her employer and her—

And *him.*

Drummond hovered over her now like a damp fog. Isobel turned to the door, desperate to keep his attention away from the street.

She let out a little cough. "Forgive me. The pollen in August has always plagued me. You were saying? About your next visit to the city?"

"Nights like this?" mused Drummond. "I can see never going back to Shropshire."

"Oh, you would miss the countryside surely," she said to the door. "The city has a way of crowding in, especially for an outdoorsman like yourself."

"You think me a bumpkin."

You are an insult to bumpkins, she thought. "Nonsense. I think of you as a gentleman with a fine home in the country. *You* may choose when to subject yourself to the London crush. What a privilege. The best of both worlds, whenever you like."

She shoved the key into the lock. Hooke was so close behind that his breath fluttered the ribbons on her hat.

"What is the progress of your renovations to Crane Lodge?" she asked, pivoting beside the door. She smiled up. It was hardly prudent to back herself against a wall, but she needed Hooke's eyes *away* from the street.

"I could be convinced to show you the new Crane Lodge in person," Drummond said, "if ever you made the journey to Shropshire . . ."

"How can I run the agency," Isobel asked, "if I am in Shropshire? My duty to you and to your late parents, may God rest them, is to be at my desk. Crane Lodge has been remarkably restored, of this I have no doubt."

Certainly she had no doubt of the bills that crossed her desk. Materials, craftsmen, cherry trees imported from the Far East. But she dared not challenge Drummond's renovations. The lodge kept him out of London, and the bills kept her in it.

"Surely the shop could spare you for a fortnight," he cajoled, stepping up.

He put a hand on the wall beside her head and leaned in. Isobel blinked, surprised by his boldness. Over Hooke's shoulder, she saw the duke step from the shadows.

No, no, no, she thought frantically. She made a shooing gesture, low and urgent, with her right hand.

In a calm voice, she said, "The shop cannot spare me. You know this, Mr. Hooke." It was a lie. Autumn was their slowest time of year. She'd had plans to leave Samantha in charge and visit her mother in Cornwall next month.

"Isobel?" Drummond said lowly, his tone suddenly conspiratorial.

"Yes?" She searched the opposite sidewalk. Northumberland had disappeared, thank God.

"*Isobel?*" Drummond repeated.

"*Yes?*"

"I've thought all day about the Duke of Northumberland."

Isobel's gaze shot to his face.

"I know," Hooke soothed, "we were both surprised to serve a duke. Very esteemed patronage indeed. However, seeing him there . . . alone . . . asking to speak only to you? It rekindled my worry."

"Worry?" croaked Isobel, scanning the street behind him.

"Hmm, extreme worry," said Hooke. "About an unattached single woman managing the shop alone."

Not this again. Isobel closed her eyes.

"Is that distress I detect?" he said. "Oh yes, I can see you are so very troubled."

"I am *not* troubled," she assured him. She forced a smile.

He gazed at her with a piteous expression of *Come now.*

"Mr. Hooke, no," she said. "You mustn't devote another second of worry to so-called troubling male clients. The success enjoyed by Everland Travel has been earned, as well you know, by service to the *female* traveler. Men may accompany women to the shop—they pay the bills—but Samantha and I accommodate the ladies. Truly. It's what sets us apart."

"So you say," mused Hooke, "but imagine the earnings if we cultivate gentlemen clientele as well? What then? You cannot discuss hotel suites and Grecian bathhouses with *men*. A single woman alone is ill-suited to discuss most things with men—I don't care if they *are* dukes." His faced dipped closer. "I am thinking of propriety for the shop as well as your own safety."

"My safety," she scoffed. "I assure you I am perfectly safe." This was the truth. Even now, as her heart pounded and she scanned the darkening street, she felt no danger. She felt like a juggler spinning two towers of fragile plates.

"Perhaps," Hooke said, "but it cannot be said enough: it's very strange for an unmarried woman to conduct business without a male superior in the shop. Highly irr—"

"Please remember," Isobel cut in, trying to sound reminiscent, "this was never an issue for your dear parents—"

"But I can think of a solution," he pressed.

Isobel wanted to squeeze her eyes shut. She wanted to dive behind the door and slam it in his face. *Don't say it, don't say it. Please do not say it.*

"If we married," he went on, absolutely saying it, "then you would not be single or unattached. You would be a respectable matron and a member of the Hooke family. If you must invoke my parents, you might as well know that this is what they wanted."

"They expressed no such desire to me," she said, inching sideways.

He stepped sideways too, flanking her. She could smell the herring on his breath and see the barley stuck in his teeth.

"*It is what they wanted,*" he repeated slowly. "And it is what I want too."

JASON HOVERED IN the shadows, weighing his options. He could insert himself into the uncomfortable conversation across the street, or he could leave Miss Tinker be.

In favor: her face was pure misery, Hooke's tone had gone from wheedling to threatening, and he was crowding her like a hungry wolf with a sheep.

Against: she'd waved him off twice already, and she didn't seem like the type of woman who welcomed intervention.

Ultimately, he elected to keep back. For now. Hooke was more insect than wolf and Miss Tinker was no sheep. She'd evaded Hooke three times in the last ten minutes—slick spins and sidesteps—she could handle herself. Her faux smile was matched tonight with a faux laugh, and all the while she was flashing Jason angry hand signals on the sly. He reached into his pocket for a coin, working it back and forth through his fingers.

"Mr. Hooke," Isobel said now, "I've made no secret of my wish never to marry. You know this about me. Marrying a woman against her will is a recipe for misery."

No wish to marry . . . Jason had spent the afternoon wondering a great deal about Isobel Tinker. He'd returned to Whitehall and combed through her file, realizing that the facts had not been wrong so much as absent. He'd not gotten bad information; he'd made up details in his head. He'd thought she'd be older because—why wouldn't she be? What young woman would have already spent years in Iceland, still more years in other countries on the Continent, and made her way back to England to set herself up in a travel shop?

Jason had returned to Mayfair with far more questions than answers and taken up a spot in the shadows to cease the assumptions and start paying attention.

"If you would but *allow me* to demonstrate how I might make you happy . . ." Hooke was saying. He dropped a clawlike hand on her waist, and Miss Tinker jumped. Jason shoved off the wall.

"I can persuade you to *rethink* what you wish," Hooke insisted. "Your stubbornness stands in the way—"

"I am not stubborn, Mr. Hooke," Isobel bit out, all trace of cordiality gone. "I am telling you *what I want*. Please do not contradict me."

She ducked left, slipping from his grasp. The door was steps away. In half a beat, she had her hand on the knob, pushing it open. "Good night to you, Mr. Hooke."

"You insult me with your . . . your rudeness, Isobel," called Hooke. "Of all the ungrateful—"

"Mind yourself, sir," Isobel warned, spinning around. She stood in her open doorway, stance wide, her reticule swinging from her clenched fist. "If it is rude or ungrateful to make choices about my own future, then—"

"It is the very heart of rudeness. Considering who you are and from whence you've come."

"And what exactly do you mean by that?"

"You may speak prettily and serve fine ladies in the shop," he snarled, "but pretty speech can be learned and you are *no lady*."

If Hooke expected her to flinch, he was disappointed. She was as steady as the sun. Her eyes flashed hot, blue rage.

Like an idiot, Hooke continued. "I'd hoped it would not come to this, but you force my hand. I'll say it." A deep breath. "A girl like you is *fortunate* to receive an offer of marriage from the likes of me. Very fortunate indeed. Your age alone puts you at a disadvantage. Most men want a bride closer to twenty, not thirty. Furthermore, think of the many pressing questions about your past—questions that have never been answered. Your well-placed uncle may have impressed my parents, but . . ."

"Questions?" A dare.

"Fine," said Hooke. "I'll say it. What of your father or mother? Who are your people, Miss *Tinker*? Would you be alone in the world without Everland Travel and the Hookes? Taken as a whole, your life's story is a very great mystery."

"What mattered to your parents," Isobel bit out, "was my work."

"Perhaps," Hooke said, "but my parents are dead. And the notion of a person's breeding matters very much to the rest of the world. Especially when it comes to a young woman who serves fine ladies in a shop, who advises them and arranges for their well-being. However, I would be willing to overlook all of it. If you were married to me, you'd not have to think of your advanced age or your parentage or misspent youth ever again."

"I don't think of my—"

He cut her off. "But if you *refuse* to marry me, well . . . I cannot predict the future or your place at Everland Travel."

Isobel was silent for a long moment. Jason was reminded again of a fuse, burning to its explosive fringe. Her anger looked incandescent. Hooke took a small step back.

"Pray, find the words, Mr. Hooke," said Miss Tinker quietly.

He retreated another step. "I should have known

you would force me to phrase it so very frankly. Like a transaction."

"Any union between us has always been, and will always be, a transaction, Mr. Hooke. *Whatever* do you mean?"

"I mean," he hissed, "I cannot allow my travel agency to be run by a lot of single women. If you wish to continue in this job, you will forsake your misplaced pride and consider my offer."

"But what of our collaboration?" she ground out. "The profits? Think of all the money I've made you. If we married, none of that would be the same."

"I've no wish to 'collaborate' with you, Isobel," he said. "I wish to—"

"I do believe I've heard enough," she cut in, holding out a hand. "How long do I have?"

"How long until . . . ?" His strident voice faltered. He sounded as if he'd not rehearsed this bit.

"How long to consider this threat of expulsion?"

"Well, I'd hoped you'd not consider it a threat," he whinged.

"That is exactly how I consider it. *How long?*"

"Well, of course, I'll not name anything so vulgar as a date. When you've had time to think . . . when you can comprehend *my* point of view, I will call upon your uncle and ask for your hand properly. I wish to do this *properly*," he insisted. "If only you would see my intent."

"You've made your intent very clear," she said. "When you decide upon a deadline for my sacking, do let me know. In the meantime, good night."

Slam.

The door closed so suddenly Jason jumped.

Hooke threw up his hands, the reaction of someone who couldn't catch a ball flying at his face. He stared at

the closed door. There was no sign of life from inside—
not a curtain flutter, not a puff from the chimney.

Finally, Hooke made an exaggerated hissing noise,
muttered angrily, and slunk away.

Jason checked his timepiece—they still had nearly an
hour—and looked again to the door.

Well.

Drummond Hooke was controlling and took advantage of Miss Tinker's talent, but this was entrapment.
He wasn't simply insecure and entitled, he was desperate. And cruel.

Even so, she'd not minced words about his chances.
Good for her. She could have feathered him with vague
denials or flirted just enough to put him off; instead,
she'd called his bluff, bold and unafraid. And so proud.
Jason had been transfixed.

Again: good for her.

And good for Jason. Because if she hadn't needed incentive to help him before, she surely needed it now.

He wondered if she would demonstrate that same
boldness and lack of fear with him.

Could she view his work as noble and patriotic?
Could she view their collaboration as (dare he say) ami-
cable?

Was there any chance that she would . . . enjoy it?
Enjoy *him*?

Likely—no. Restlessness overtook him, and Jason
flicked his coin into the air. It landed in his gloved hand
with a heavy *pat*. He flicked it again.

Typically, women did enjoy Jason Beckett, and the
feeling was so very mutual. His job in the Foreign
Office occasioned him to encounter beautiful women
around the world; it was one of his favorite parts of the

job. It was one of the many reasons he hated to leave his post; Syon Hall meant isolation and stagnation.

Jason loved all women generally and quite a few women personally, and it had been a very long time since he'd encountered a woman who was not a . . . a . . . certainty. *Flick.*

So far, Jason knew far more about what Isobel Tinker didn't want than what she did. The list was long. And he was at the top. Well, perhaps Drummond Hooke was at the top. But likely he was a close second.

Meanwhile, he felt confounded by her. He was drawn in by her resistance and prickliness and guarded history. It needled him. It should have increased his restlessness and impatience. *Flick.* Instead, he was *intrigued.*

Dropping deeper into the shadows, he checked her shop again. If she was peeking out of windows, he couldn't see it.

Fine. *Flick.*

He would wait.

He would be needled and restless. He would be twitchy and *speculate* about Miss Isobel Tinker. There were worse things.

And anyway, the point of their collaboration was not his *regard* for Miss Isobel Tinker, nor her regard for him. It was about Reggie, and the mission, and putting off Syon Hall as long as possible.

Chapter Four

Isobel scrawled the word *Alley* on a scrap of parchment and tacked it beneath the knob of her door. Northumberland would understand.

How ambitious she'd been to believe the public street would be an acceptable place to meet him at ten o'clock. She'd come to think of Lumley Street as a safe haven, secure and comfortable, a place she could do as she wished, even after dark. All corners of her new life had felt so very haven-like that she'd forgotten she did not have the freedom to be reckless or imprudent or to meet strange men. How thorough of Mr. Hooke to remind her of all that was at stake.

The sun had only just set when Drummond Hooke had delivered her home and made his ultimatum. She prayed no neighbors had seen. The fact that *Northumberland* had seen her was an outrage for which she was still trying to find the correct words. Inappropriate, for one. Intrusive, for another. Interesting, for a—No. No, *not* interesting. *Unacceptable.*

"You're late," she said ten minutes later. These words took no effort. He emerged from the alley gloom as she waited on her back stoop, her emerald cloak pulled tight.

"Would you believe," he asked lightly, "I've been standing just out of view, watching you?"

Isobel felt an annoying tingle in her tailbone. Cursed stone step, cold even in August. She shoved up. "I *would* believe you've been watching, but out of view? Your boast is misplaced. An hour ago, I saw you clearly lurking about."

He stepped closer, making no response. Just like that, she could see his face. Her first thought was that she had not misremembered. He was—

Well, he was far too much for her already complicated life. A handsome man with a direct, interested gaze and some pressing business that could only be discussed in dark alleys? Too much. The very last complication she needed at the moment. Or ever.

She clipped down the steps. "What were you thinking, turning up in my street when I was . . . was meeting with my employer?"

"Oh, is *that* what was happening? I had no idea the idiot was going to *propose* to you."

"He didn't propose, he—" She couldn't finish. Explaining Drummond Hooke's extortion was not part of her civic duty.

"It makes no difference about my conversation with Mr. Hooke," she finished. "I've agreed to your interview, and so now here I am. Are we meant to talk in the alley? The rats take over after dark, I'm afraid."

"Indeed. I don't suppose you would invite me inside?"

"Ah, no. I do not entertain men alone inside my house."

"Quite so. Which is why . . ." and now he sounded like he was improvising, ". . . I've scouted Grosvenor Square. You'd suggested this, did you not? If we clear the fence and take a side path to the center, we should be out of sight and undisturbed. Well chosen. Very sensible."

"I'm always sensible," Isobel muttered, more to herself. A reminder. She'd taught herself to be sensible. Since returning to England, sensibility had been her guiding force.

Pulling her hood around her face, she picked her way to Duke Street. Northumberland fell in beside her, a large, silent presence over her left shoulder. Before she could stop herself, Isobel asked, "You heard every word, then? With Hooke?"

"I'm a spy, Miss Tinker. Hearing every word is part of my job. It's why I came early to Lumley Street. It's why I was late to the alley."

She glanced at him. He was neither gloating nor threatening, simply stating a fact. She watched him scan the street like a wolf hunting in a dark wood.

Isobel felt the tingling again, this time on the back of her neck. If she hadn't sworn off men—which, absolutely, she had—she might have wondered why her body always conjured tingles for the *wrong* men. Why not tingle for someone like . . . a Boring Rule Follower or Dependable Office Hack? Why not tingle for Drummond Hooke and make life simple for everyone?

Isobel recoiled at the thought. Anyone but Drummond Hooke.

She knew the way to Grosvenor Square and he allowed her to take the lead. She kept to the shadows, head down, cloak barely fluttering. They reached Grosvenor Street, and the square loomed like a black void in the center of torchlit Mayfair.

Northumberland stepped around her, gesturing for her to stay back, but she'd already tucked herself into the recess of a building. She knew how to navigate a dark street, for God's sake.

Go on, she said with a nod of her head.

He considered her a long moment and went, a silent shadow darting into the abyss. The gate to the square was locked at sunset, and the duke didn't try it. He chose the most overgrown stretch of fence and vaulted over it with a swift bounce, disappearing into the trees.

He'd not suggested her next course of action. Isobel had been surprised by this—surprised and a little bit thrilled. She knew well how to slip into a locked park but this would be a secret skill to him.

Shrugging deeper into her cloak, she followed his path to the fence. She detoured slightly to retrieve an empty crate on the corner and propped it against the black iron. Working quickly, her movements small, she climbed first the crate and then the fence, balancing a booted foot between the spiked iron slats. With one hand, she clasped the top of the fence, and gathered her skirts with the other. She was just about to bring her second foot to the fence when giant hands caught her around the waist, lifted, and whirled her over the fence in a smooth arc.

She made only the slightest yelp.

"*Shhhh*," he warned.

This is not exciting, Isobel lectured herself as the duke plunked her down beside a rosebush.

This is not diverting.

He is not exhilarating.

I've been sacked from my job and will be evicted from my home. This man wants to know too much about things I've vowed never to discuss.

I'm having no fun at all.

When she was steady on the ground, the duke ducked between two bushes, signaling her to follow into the foliage. Isobel returned to the crate, reached between the slats of the fence, and tipped it gently away. Without waiting for the *crack* of wood against stone, she hurried after the duke.

When it rains, it pours, she thought unhelpfully, pushing through leafy fronds and low-hanging boughs.

If one trouble comes, wait for the other.

Didn't respectable ladies spout wise-but-baseless idioms during trying times?

Isobel endeavored to do the thing that respectable ladies did, especially if her own instinct was to swear profusely.

How had she managed to imperil her beloved job and be interrogated by a handsome foreign agent *on the same day*?

In theory, she could have dodged Hooke's proposal and bought more time, but she'd lost her temper instead.

She could have told the Duke of Northumberland she had nothing to contribute, but she was following him into a dark, secluded park.

Agues come on horseback, but go away on foot, she recited, although she really had no idea what this one meant.

"Bollocks," she muttered, tripping over a root. Northumberland came to a stop at that same moment and Isobel collided with his back.

"*Oof*," he said, taking a step to brace himself. Isobel let out a little yelp, arms flying. The duke half spun and caught her at the waist.

"Careful," he said, rocking her against him. He was as hard and solid as a tree. For a fleeting moment, she settled her hands on his biceps, pressing her fingers into the fine wool of his greatcoat. The muscle beneath was contoured steel.

"Why are you stopping?" she whispered, snatching her hands away.

"We'll be safe here, I think," he said, watching her. A smile quirked the corner of his mouth.

The path had opened up into a clearing. Two benches sat adjacent in a beam of silver moonlight. A bird-bath pooled black water that reflected the stars. Night sounds of the city could barely be heard through the dense vegetation of the square.

Isobel bit her lip. Mayfair was not meant to offer up secluded moonlit gardens inhabited by handsome men with mysterious half smiles. Mayfair supplied honest work, a cozy flat, and a peaceful new life. How cunningly Mayfair had misled her. Likely, it was all her fault—her past, stalking her to the ends of the earth. How foolish to believe it would not.

The duke, in no way betrayed by Mayfair, drifted away and dropped onto a bench. He leaned back and a low-hanging rhododendron knocked his head and dislodged his hat. Now the brim extended at an angle, low-slung and rakish. He smiled again, and the expression actually stopped Isobel in place. She felt the very first stirrings of a kind of . . . shimmering inside her chest.

He whipped off the hat and dropped it on the bench, running his hand through his hair.

"Do you think he'll really sack you?" he asked, sitting back.

"I beg your pardon?"

"Hooke," he prompted. "Do you really think he'll sack you?"

"Yes—No." She thought a moment more. "I cannot say what he will do. I'll not marry him. If he sacks me for refusing, he will have no wife *and* no business. At the end of the day, he is self-serving. He may keep me on for sheer sloth. He fancies himself a gentleman and does not enjoy work."

"Oh, to trade places," Northumberland sighed. He stretched his legs on the crushed gravel, crossing his Hessians at the ankle. "I'd rather work than be a gentleman."

Isobel was not prepared for the duke to reveal personal details about his situation. But this was a large part of charm, wasn't it? Openness and honesty were like currency for charming men.

In no way was she *intrigued* by his preference for work over a life of gentlemanly ease. But better to indulge his musings than not discuss her future with Drummond Hooke.

"Perhaps," she ventured, "you are a gentleman with the freedom to also work."

"I'm a gentleman, I suppose." A beleaguered sigh. "But the missions I lead for the Foreign Office have been my life's work. There'll be no time for spy craft when I return to Syon Hall. I would never be able to do both—not properly. Who has time to meet informants in dark London squares when they are in Middlesex, minding the smelter?"

"Am I an informant?" Isobel asked. The designation of *informant* sounded impersonal, almost tactical. Maybe, possibly, she could tolerate being something like an *informant*. An informant did not confess their misspent youth to unknown dukes or relive horrible memories. They spoke about harbors and climate and what the locals eat for lunch.

"It is my great hope that you're an informant," the duke said. "Will you sit?" He patted the bench beside him.

"I prefer to stand, thank you very much."

There, she thought. Some good sense prevailed. She would not sit. She would not say more than was strictly necessary. She would not complicate her life more than it already was. She would be a marginally helpful bystander . . . possibly an *informant*, but no more than that.

"Right," he said. "So . . ."

He shot her that half smile again, and Isobel felt the shimmers toss about inside her.

He's just a man, she told herself.

He's just a very handsome, very confident, very charming man. And this is not my first trip around the moon.

He said, "So, you've spent time in Iceland."

"Yes." Denying this was obviously not an option.

"Do you speak Icelandic?"

Isobel weighed her answer. She'd decided in advance not to lie. Withhold, if necessary, but not lie.

"Some," she said. "Before I left the country, I could get by. Now, of course, it will be rusty."

"And when was that exactly? Your years there?"

"When I was younger."

"A child? You are hardly old now."

"I am twenty-seven," she said, giving him something he already knew. "My time in Iceland was . . . years ago. I was younger than I am now, obviously, but not a child."

"But were you in the company of your parents? The file, which I admit is very thin, suggested that an uncle made arrangements to bring you back to England— alone, was it?"

"I would rather not discuss my specific, personal experience in Iceland, if you please. It was some time ago, and the memories are part of a difficult history that I have worked very hard to overcome. My business in Iceland has no bearing on your work, I feel sure."

There, she thought, *I've said it*. She'd alluded to pain and overcoming it. Any gentleman would abandon the topic.

"Was it '08?" he asked gently, abandoning nothing.

She narrowed her eyes. How beguiling he'd endeavored to be. His relaxed sort of *lean* on the bench and his reasonable tone, light and curious. But Isobel was not born yesterday. She'd been born seven and twenty hard-fought years ago, as they'd already established. And on the topic of *when* she was in Iceland, "several years ago" would be all she'd say.

The duke went on. "My notes say that your uncle arranged to have you returned to England in October 1808. That would have made you twenty at the time. Can I assume that voyage, which involved prodigious pulled strings in government—enough to warrant a file in my office—means you were *not* in Iceland in the company of your parents?"

"Ask repeatedly if you must, Your Grace, but my answers to personal questions will remain brief and vague. My time in Iceland is entirely irrelevant to these Englishmen who are currently stranded."

"Held captive," he corrected. "The Englishmen are being held captive. But forgive me, I was hoping for some frame of reference. Authentication is a large part of working with informants. Your personal experiences will inform how current and reliable your information may be."

"And what if I say my information is wholly *un*reliable and *in*authentic? What if I say that I remember virtually nothing about Iceland except how wretched it is? Would we be finished here?"

The duke sighed. "You're aware, I hope, that your denials only make me want to know more, Miss Tinker? Evasive, elusive informants are far more intriguing than people who gush."

"I am not evasive or elusive," she said. "I am private and discreet. I haven't anything to hide; I simply do not relish talking about . . ." here she faltered, as there was so much she had no wish to discuss, ". . . my youth. In any country."

He took a deep breath and nodded. He reached into the pocket of his waistcoat and pulled out a coin; he examined it in his hand and then flicked it into the air and caught it. Isobel had a moment of anxiety, certain his easy manner would now turn nasty and demanding. She'd seen this before—men who reversed their charm into cruelty like the flip of a coin.

But Northumberland did not reverse. He launched the coin again and said, "Would you consider this? You tell me five things you may know about Iceland—*not* including your personal experience there. Just five things that you believe that I might find useful. I will not interrupt, I will not pursue any given point; I will simply listen. After you finish, I will ask you *three* following questions. These will be questions that you may answer or *not* answer as you see fit. Could you abide this exchange?"

No, Isobel said in her head, but that wasn't true, not really. It was a perfectly reasonable proposal. She hesitated. She was unprepared for reasonability from a man as attractive as the duke. Attractive men didn't have to be reasonable. The world allowed them to behave in whatever selfish, petulant way they wished simply because they looked as if they were in charge.

Isobel chewed on her bottom lip. Eventually, he would become this man, selfish or petulant or worse.

Carefully, she said, "What if I don't have five useful things to reveal?"

"I believe," he said, flipping the coin again, "you *do* have five useful things. You wouldn't have agreed to this meeting if you didn't have anything useful to say."

Again, Isobel hesitated. Was that why she'd agreed? So far, she'd not identified a reason, save madness.

He was correct, of course; she had plenty to say. She'd made a list of what she would tell him and what she would not. She'd scrawled it out during the anxiety-ridden hour between Hooke's departure and the duke's arrival. Five things would be no effort.

Isobel took a deep breath and settled on the adjacent bench. She folded her hands in her lap. Speaking to the toes of her boots, she said, "Fine. Here are five things.

"If you intend to travel to Iceland, you must embark very soon. It is exceedingly dangerous in winter. Even the Danes do not sail the North Sea between October and April."

She glanced up, hoping this was an acceptable first thing. It was common knowledge among sailors, but it was useful.

Northumberland stared back with a bland, patient half smile. He looked . . . indulgent. He looked as if he was *indulging* this first answer. He flicked the coin into the air.

Isobel gritted her teeth and added, "I sailed to England in early October, and it was harrowing to say the least. The sooner you go and return, the better."

Without waiting for his comment, she forged ahead. "Despite this, the country itself is not a frozen tundra. Only the highlands see snowfall and it's not much colder than Scotland. Even so, do not underestimate its remoteness, and provision accordingly. And by provision, I would suggest bringing anything you may require, including food, in your kit. There is no guarantee of sustenance once you venture beyond the port cities, and even in port, storehouses and merchants may be low on supplies or refuse to trade with foreigners."

Northumberland nodded slowly. He didn't dismiss this advice but he was hardly writing any of it down.

Fine, she thought. *Flick your coin and pay me no mind.*

"A third thing," she recited, "is that Icelandic 'society' is comprised of ruling families who operate lowland farms. They control the country in an uneasy alliance with politicians in Denmark. If you wish for something to happen in Iceland, you'll want the backing of at least a few of these families. Iceland is like England in this. The landed families are in charge."

Another nod, almost as if he was a professor and she was his pupil. Annoyance began to burn the back of her shoulders, and she was compelled, suddenly, to tell him something he would absolutely *not* know. Something that would wipe the indulgent expression from his face.

"Ah . . . you mentioned *pirates*?" she ventured. This had been the very last item on her list, a detail she'd not intended to mention.

"There is only one pirate band with which *I'm* familiar," she mused casually, "and they conceal their ships in the ice caves of Vatnajökull, a glacier field to the *east.* So if your plan is to sail to Reykjavík and take them by surprise, you'll be on the wrong side of the island."

She said it calmly, the way she'd said the North Sea was stormy in winter. But she raised her eyebrows when she'd finished—*There, I've said it*—and cocked her head. *What have you to say to this?*

The duke had gone still and now blinked rapidly, a man with a bug in his eye. The coin fell to the ground.

That's more like it, she thought.

Then she remembered it was not her purpose to astound or impress the duke; she'd come to be forgettable and disposable.

"How many things was that?" she asked lightly.

"Four," he said.

"Right. Well, the only other thing I can think of is a sort of attitudinal quality you may encounter among the people there. They can be distrustful of outsiders. I'm not sure what manner of diplomacy you plan to employ, but they do not enjoy 'collaboration' with foreigners, even allies who come in peace. So, prepare yourself for incalcitrant locals at best, hostility at worst."

And that was it. Five things.

Isobel took a deep breath. She patted both knees with her hands, a gesture of *My work here is done*. She tightened her gloves.

"That is five," he stated.

"Yes, that's five."

By design, she'd gone soft on the fifth thing. Really, what more was there to say? Telling him about Iceland's naturally heated pools, the lava flows, or the aurora borealis was a waste of time. These could be gleaned from any geography book and ultimately made no difference to pirate rescue or diplomacy. He didn't need to know the magical parts of Iceland. She was not selling him a holiday. She'd only met him to reveal a few things and make him go away.

"And now my questions," he said.

"Which I may answer or may not answer."

"Right," he said, "but that I hope you *will* answer."

He leaned forward, elbows on his knees—the pose of a man conspiring with a trusted confidant.

We are not conspiring nor confidants, she reminded in her head.

"The pirates . . ." Northumberland said, refocusing her attention. "Are you saying that you *know* these pirates?"

"Ah . . ." said Isobel, immediately recognizing her mistake. Too much—she'd said too much. "I beg your pardon?"

"I've made no secret of my purpose, Miss Tinker. From the beginning, I've said that I've been charged with rescuing Englishmen from *pirates*—my own cousin is among their group. And now you're suggesting that you actually *know* them?"

Her very first, entirely unhelpful thought was, *Well, of course I know them*.

In her previous life, Isobel Tinker had been interesting. She had not planned the journeys of other girls; she'd forged a journey all her own. It had been so very long since she had shocked anyone, and it felt . . . it felt—

Well, it made no difference how it felt. Now, more than ever, she was meant to be boring and expected.

She asked, "Is that your first question?"

"No, no, no . . ." he was shaking his head, ". . . only a fool would ask a yes-or-no question. Allow me to rephrase." He cleared his throat. "Tell me everything you know about the pirates. And how you know it. Including how they are connected to the ruling families you mentioned. And how I might use the connection to my advantage." He patted around on his greatcoat, and pulled out a small notebook and graphite pencil. He flipped open the book and tapped the point of the pencil against a blank page. He looked to her expectantly.

Isobel stared at the pencil, her heart pounding. She'd

been careless. She'd been selfish and vain—trying to impress him. Of course he would home in on the pirates.

"Miss Tinker?" he prompted. "If you please?"

"That's five questions in one," she said. "You're making a general inquiry about a broad range of topics, which is nothing like we agreed."

"I'm amending what we agreed, Miss Tinker."

"Why am I not surprised?"

"I thought you'd be telling me things like which inns to avoid—"

"There are no inns in Iceland," she mumbled.

"—or to wear a woolly hat."

"Your existing hat will be sufficient."

"Stop," he said, holding up his hands in surrender. "Please. Miss Tinker. You may not know this, but I *could* cultivate and cajole you into telling me. I could finesse the answers from you. I respect you and your cleverness. Not to mention, there's no time. So . . ." He stood up and patted his greatcoat again, producing a bulging leather pouch. "Instead, to speed the process along, I am willing to *pay you*. Fifty pounds. A sum that would do most anybody good. Especially you."

Isobel gaped at him.

"May we dispense with the scorekeeping about the number of questions and get down to these pirates? In exchange for this lovely bundle of money?"

Isobel stared at the pouch. Her heart began to boom in her ears as if it was knocking to escape.

"You would *pay* me?" she asked breathlessly.

He rolled from the bench and ambled to the birdbath. "Forgive me for thinking that a tidy sum would be useful in your current situation."

"Now I know why you were lurking about. You were

listening to my private conversations, searching for some weakness to exploit."

"To be perfectly clear, in no way do you appear 'weak,' Miss Tinker."

"That's because I am not weak," she shot back. "I am . . . backed against a wall."

"You won't take the money?"

"I've no choice but to take the bloody money." She threw up her hands. She took a deep breath. "I regret that it's come to this. I regret *needing* money. I regret being sacked from my job. I regret the painful personal circumstances that keep me from being more useful to you."

It was all true. So many regrets. She detested regret. For years, she'd outpaced it. It was always there, but if she worked hard enough and said and did enough of the correct things, it did not hound her. But now?

Now she did not feel hounded so much as . . . tempted.

She began shaking her head. In a firm but wistful voice, she said, "I was so very contented just twelve hours ago. I had a pleasant job, doing work at which I excelled, with a snug flat above the shop. And without a single thought of *Iceland*." She enunciated the word in the way one might say, *purgatory*.

The duke sniggered. "Ah. A sentiment I understand. I had a life I loved, traveling the world, working for the Foreign Office. I've served in India. In the palace courts of Europe. Spain during the war."

Before she could stop herself, she asked, "You loved the war?"

He was staring into the birdbath, seemingly lost in thought. He looked up but did not answer.

"Forgive me," she said quickly, "I presume too much. I did not mean to inqui—"

"Well, not the death and devastation of war obviously. But the action? Absolutely. The urgency, yes. The *struggle* suited me. I cannot abide idleness . . . sitting behind a desk . . . *waiting*. I haven't the patience for it. I lack patience in general."

"I can see that," she said. "In the twelve hours since I made your acquaintance, I've scaled fences, thrashed about in the bushes, and tramped through alleyways. You've occasioned yourself in a position to 'overhear' not one but two conversations with my employer. If I was a poetic sort of girl, I would characterize our interactions as 'breathless.' "

"No fault in breathlessness, Miss Tinker."

She felt herself smile. "I am *not* poetic. Just to be clear."

This conversation has run away with itself, she thought.

I'm very close to earning fifty pounds, she thought.

She thought and thought, but her brain wanted only to hear more of his story.

"What happened?" she asked quietly, raptly.

"I beg your pardon?"

"To put an end to this work that you loved?"

He didn't answer immediately, and she rushed to add, "Forgive me, I do not mean to—"

"Well, my father died," he said flatly. "After that, not five years on, my oldest brother died."

He paused, staring up at the stars.

Isobel felt her eyes grow large. She'd not expected an answer so devastating or personal.

"Oh y-yes," she stammered. "The whole country has heard of the tragedies in your family. I was so sorry for the terrible . . . sort of, one-two punch of it all. The grief must have been . . . relentless."

"It is not ideal. It's very . . . sedentary—grief. In other words, *not* for me. The only mental state for which I have *less* tolerance than idleness is grief. Much as I tried, I couldn't loll around Middlesex, stewing in it. I was already a foreign agent when my father died, and I threw myself into my work with even greater fervor. America. The British West Indies. Spain again.

"And then . . ." he took a deep breath, ". . . my last brother died. And suddenly there were no more Beckett brothers in line before me. *I* was duke. And all of that grief, and the yawning fields of Middlesex, and a lifetime of idleness, was thrust upon me. I would be a foreign agent no more. I would be none other than a festering, immovable, sheep-counting duke."

"Oh," she said—because she must say something. His easy manner had slipped; there was an edge to his voice. He looked for a moment as if he might wrest the birdbath from its platform and heave it into the brush. "I'm . . . I'm so very sorry, Your Grace."

He let out a bitter laugh. "That is the very great irony, isn't it? Who can be sorry for a duke? It is a rare and precious privilege, is it not? The wealth, the power, the . . ."

"Sheep?" she provided.

Another laugh, less bitter but very sad. "Yes, the great many sheep. Life is not a contest obviously, Miss Tinker, but given your circumstance with odious Mr. Hooke versus *my* circumstances as the Duke of Northumberland, you have it far worse. Your lot is more hopeless—everyone would agree."

"Thank you?" She fought another smile. It couldn't be helped.

"Your lot is so bad," he continued, "I'm trading on your desperation to extract this Iceland information from your unwilling lips."

"Is that what you're doing?" Why was she smiling? *Stop smiling, Isobel. Have you learned nothing at all?*

"Forgive me," he said. "It was not my intention to add to your frustration."

"Yes, I have been puzzling through exactly what your intention might be."

With exaggerated enunciation, he added, "Woe is me, the wealthy duke with the palatial estate and all the . . . the . . ."

"Sheep," she provided. "I believe we have identified sheep among your many assets."

"Right," he said on a sad exhale. "I'm sorry. It's not a joke, I know. None of this resembles a joke."

"Well, don't look to me to trivialize your struggle. In my experience, we are all too quick to dismiss or diminish the pain of others. Whether you are 'trading on my desperation' or simply being sympathetic, I *do* believe that you understand my plight. Life can be rather pleasant. Also, it can be . . . less so. Significantly. For all of us.

"Given the choice," she continued, "I'd rather not have my unpleasantness used as leverage against me, but perhaps that is not a choice."

"That remains to be seen," the duke said speculatively. He gave the pouch of coins in his hand a little toss, rattling the money inside. "Will you take the fifty pounds?"

Chapter Five

On hindsight, Jason could not say why he'd revealed the details of his grief and his work and his . . . sheep.

Informants were often more forthcoming if he gave a little of his own self to the proceedings, but that wasn't what had happened.

He wasn't manipulating her; he was talking to her. He'd *wanted* to tell her. She would not contradict him or smother him. He'd guessed this, and it had been true.

He was intuitive—it was what made him an excellent spy—but what was the value of intuition if he'd rambled on about himself and learned nothing about Iceland?

Who was the excellent spy now? Isobel Tinker knew far more about him than he knew about her.

And she hadn't even agreed to the bribe.

He cleared his throat and gave the pouch of money another rattle. "Your clerk told me you mean to *buy* the travel shop from Hooke. Is this true?"

"Ha." She let out a humorless laugh. "That's unlikely now that I'm meant to *marry him* or get out. Anyway, fifty pounds would not be enough. But it will allow me the freedom to take some time exploring what I will do next."

Jason nodded, watching her. *Who are you?* he wondered. *What of your pain has been dismissed or diminished?*

She caught him staring and said lightly, "Stay away from me, Your Grace."

"I'm standing ten feet from you," he said. "I'm looking at the birdbath."

She'd said it like she was warding off a piece of rich chocolate cake. Or a third glass of wine. A warning to herself.

"No. You're telling me your life. You're . . . *looking* at me."

"Have you noticed that you reply 'no' to everything I ask, whether you mean it or not?"

"If you knew my history with men like yourself, you would understand that 'no' *is* always the correct answer."

" 'Men like myself'?" he asked.

"Never you mind," she said. "Let us talk about pirates. A safer topic."

She leaned back on her hands and looked up. She studied the night sky as if it might help form the words.

She was so very pretty, he thought—small and purposeful and luminous.

Let's not, he wanted to say. *Let us return to the topic of "men like you . . ."*

But of course he mustn't. He'd come for the pirates. Which was fine.

He would be keenly interested in anything she had to say, so long as she was talking to him, and looking the way she looked.

"Right, so the pirates in Iceland . . ." she began.

The litany of details that followed—names of specific pirates and their ships, the location of glacial ice caves, Icelandic allies—came out in a long, steady stream.

Jason had thought he would listen, soak it all in, understand her atmospheric, cultural insights—but no. It was too much to soak. She spouted detailed facts and directions, so he scrambled for his notebook.

The details came out in low, contemplative tones, the voice of someone giving careful instructions on how to get from here to there. Jason scribbled until the graphite was a nub.

"They're not 'Nordic,' as you first mentioned," she was saying. "They hail from all over. France. Portugal. Ireland, even. The leader is actually a Frenchman."

She went on. "For whatever reason, they cease their pillaging and plundering elsewhere during summers and retreat to Iceland. The glacier caves conceal their ships and allow them to train and make repairs. They are usually idle in the summers, only raiding foreign vessels to replenish provisions and stave off boredom."

She made expressive gestures as she spoke, her tight green gloves slicing and spinning the air in the shape of her story.

"They are tolerated by the locals, but only because one of the farming families, the Skallagrímurs, harbors them."

He repeated the family name phonetically. "Will you spell it?"

She chuckled and rattled off the spelling. "I believe that's correct. A niece in the family married one of the pirate leaders. This union afforded an alliance which serves both sides."

He asked her to explain what could be mutually beneficial among pirates and Icelandic farmers. Her answer, just as the others, was well considered, full of detail, and made perfect sense. She was like a book he'd plucked at random from a shelf. He could have learned anything or nothing at all; instead, she was a trove of information.

"The pirates police the coasts to keep the farms' common laborers from fishing," Isobel was saying.

"Prevent them from fishing?" asked Jason. "It's an island."

"Quite so," she said, "but if the commoners could make their livings as fishermen, they would not be available or willing to work the fields. So the pirates suppress any upstart fishermen. And the farmers keep the Danish Navy off the pirates. It has been my observation that, no matter where you go, the people in charge will invoke any means necessary to *remain* in charge."

"Hmm," Jason mused. He left his bench and settled beside her. He took more notes.

He would confirm this—about the pirates and this Skallagrímur family. He would confirm all of it. He'd also have to confirm *her* identity and history. She was his favorite type of informant, but too much was at stake for her to *guess* at these details. If she would not tell him how she'd acquired this expertise, he'd poke around until he learned it himself. The uncle who pulled so many strings to get her home, perhaps.

He looked up. "So, if the job of the pirates is to control local fishing, why capture English merchants and hold them hostage? They are hardly local fishermen."

Isobel shrugged. "This, I cannot say. Ransom money? Have they made any demands?"

"They have actually," said Jason. "But it's not a lot. It wouldn't be enough, to say, retire from pirating and buy a house in the fjords."

Isobel chuckled. "Perhaps your cousin and his friends did not offend the pirates, but the pirates' sponsors, the Skallagrímurs?"

"Just to be clear, my cousin has simply gone along. He's not clever enough to succeed as a smuggler. He was duped into joining this ill-advised endeavor. Poor Reggie, this is not the first time."

"So it's not the members of your family you resent, simply the title? Or is it the sheep?"

"I beg your pardon?" he said, looking up from his notes.

Isobel looked startled. "Forgive me, of course we weren't speaking of—"

"No, I am happy to discuss my family," he amended. "And my sheep, the dodgy little bastards."

"It was intrusive of me to—"

"I am fond of my family. I've three sisters and a mother who are very dear to me. Various aunts and uncles. Cousins, naturally. Reggie is the son of my *mother's* brother—so the nonducal side, but we were brought up in close relation with the maternal branch of the family. I spent summers at the seaside in Lincolnshire.

"Reggie is one of those men who means well but does not . . . er, think things through. My father and two brothers lost patience for him years ago, but I've a history of rescuing him from scrapes. A soft spot, you might say."

"This is the first time you've rescued him from pirate captivity, I assume?" she asked.

"Indeed. If I wasn't so fond of him, I'd alert the Royal Navy and let them sort it out. But he is a gentle soul . . . well-meaning . . . I cannot allow him to be the source of an international incident. Not to mention whatever misery he's enduring at the hands of the pirates. Their correspondence with my uncle is threatening but I don't think they are cutting off body parts and feeding them to sharks. Yet."

"That sounds accurate," Isobel said, thinking for a moment. "Honestly, the pirates could have simply been bored. They are, after all, pirates. It's a dying art, and someone must uphold the traditions."

Jason snorted and tapped the notebook against his knee. He was just about to ask her about the size and speed of the pirates' ship when they heard footsteps on the path in front of them.

Jason went still and held up a hand. *"Shhh."*

Isobel curled her shoulders and pulled up the hood of her cloak.

Jason listened again. The footsteps grew closer. He leaned behind her on the bench, trying to see through the vegetation. Clouds obscured the moon, draping the path in shadows. He eased lower still. The clouds slid eastward and—

"It's the night watchman," he whispered.

"Oh God. That will be Matthews." Her voice was tremulous, barely audible. "I *cannot* be seen. Matthews is a neighborhood friend. He goes out of his way to be generous and thoughtful. I cannot—*He mustn't see me.* My respectability depends on me not being discovered in dark parks with strange men."

She shrank deeper into her cloak and slid to the darkest end of the bench.

The footsteps grew closer. The watchman whistled a tune and then stopped. Jason heard the strike of a match. The smell of burning tobacco filled the air.

The footsteps and whistling resumed.

Isobel spoke just below a whisper. "I must hide, or run, or . . . *hide*. I cannot—"

"No, no, no," Jason breathed slowly. *"Do not move.* Movement will only draw his eye."

From outside the alcove, a nervous voice called out, "Who's there?"

Jason swore in his head. Isobel made a barely audible sound of distress, a heart-wrenching half whine, half hiss.

Another curse. Jason whispered to her, "Would you allow me to pretend to kiss you?"

Isobel Tinker stared at him from deep within her hood.

"It's an old trick," he whispered, "but it can work if you keep your face averted." He held his breath, waiting for her answer. He hadn't lied; it was an old trick, reliable too. It also happened to be his most fervent wish at the moment.

Still, she could say no. She could slap him. She could call for the watchman and claim abduction. He put his odds at fifty-fifty.

Do it, she mouthed. *Hurry. Do it, do it, do it.*

Right, Jason thought. He bit the notebook and pencil in his mouth to free his hand and reached for her.

In one, cloak-fluttering movement, he scooped up Isobel Tinker and plunked her into his lap. She settled on his thighs in a puff of green skirts and emerald cloak. She weighed almost nothing. She stared over the notebook into his face, her blue eyes huge.

He removed the notebook from his mouth and whispered, "Sorry." He settled his hands on her waist.

"I say, who's there?" the night watchman called again.

Isobel's eyes bored into his.

Jason mouthed, *We needn't* really—

She kissed him.

One moment she was staring at him as if he'd grown horns, the next her mouth was on his.

It was not the faux effort he'd meant to offer. It was her head tilted just so, her mouth fitting perfectly against his, partly open; it was her tongue swiping once, twice, against his bottom lip. And just like that, he was plunged into a pool of sensation. The smell of her enveloped him, warm and herbal; the feel of her slight body, teetering on his thighs; her soft lips, firm and insistent.

Jason's consciousness departed the leafy square and he floated somewhere above them. Music swelled in his head and lights popped behind his eyes.

There were kisses, he thought vaguely, and then there was *this*.

Isobel Tinker, he realized, knew how to kiss. And she kissed exceptionally well. There was no shyness, no coquettishness, no ploy for him to draw her out. She fastened her lips to his and feasted.

He had the random thought that Drummond Hooke would be completely out of his depth with this woman. Jason himself, kissing her as if his life depended upon it, strove to keep up. It was exhilarating and sensual and all-consuming. It was quite possibly the best kiss of his life, and he'd enjoyed some rather exceptional kisses.

Only by some miracle did he remember the bloody night watchman. Blinking his eyes, he squinted into the distance. The watchman stood at the mouth of the alcove, lifting a creaking lantern.

Jason closed her in his arms, scooping her closer. He slid a hand up her spine to cup the back of her head. With the slightest pressure, not breaking the kiss, he tucked her face against his cheek. She allowed it, sliding her knees on either side of him, fitting herself astride.

She gripped his biceps as if she might be ripped from his arms.

His body responded, a reaction that would be impossible to miss, and Jason swore in his head and pulled his face away, sucking in air.

To the watchman he called, "Give us a minute?" His voice was gruff. He coughed. Isobel tensed, veritably vibrating beneath his touch. He held her tight against him.

"Square closes at sunset, sir," ventured the watchman. He took a step closer. Isobel burrowed deeper.

"Right, right, sunset," Jason said, imbuing his voice with posh authority. "I'll—My friend and I'll move on. Sorry to be a nuisance. Just a bit of fun . . . summer moon, et cetera."

The watchman took another step and Jason had the momentary fear that he would not be put off. Jason raised his chin, allowing the lantern to illuminate his face. The watchman would not know him—they'd not be so lucky in that—but he would recognize the expensive coat and boots; he'd see the cut of Jason's hair, his aristocratic nose, the lazy expression. Everything about him said, *I do as I please*.

"Very good, sir," the watchman finally said, falling back. "See that you do. The neighbors don't take kindly to cavorting in the park after-hours."

"Good for them," said Jason on a cough. "We'll need a moment to, ah, set ourselves to rights. If you'll indulge us."

"Yes, sir," said the watchman, but he seemed disinclined to go. Jason wondered how long Isobel could remain motionless on his lap. Could she breathe? Had he crushed her? She was lodged so very tightly against his erection that Jason's own mobility would be in question.

"Here's something for the disturbance," Jason said, releasing Isobel long enough to fish a coin from his pocket. He tossed it to the watchman with a good-natured flip. As the watchman struggled to catch the coin, Jason ducked his head against Isobel's neck and breathed deeply. A silent dismissal.

Jason intended to hold that pose, but Isobel shivered. The pulse in her throat raced beneath his lips. She squirmed on top of him, a slow, small, grinding motion. She squeezed her fingers on his biceps.

And just like that, Jason forgot about the watchman and the lantern and even bloody Iceland and he found her mouth again. One more kiss, a final peck, to make it look rea—

Isobel pounced. Her lips opened immediately; her tongue flicked against his bottom lip. He slanted his head and answered. Their tongues met, and he was levitated into another hallelujah moment.

She canted her head to the right, following the ebb of the kiss. Jason redirected, curling them left, keeping her face averted.

He glanced up, checking the clearing, the path, the bushes. The watchman was gone.

Gone, he thought, but he couldn't say the words. He might never speak again. He might only—

Isobel Tinker kissed him like a drowning woman in search of breath, and he returned the kiss as if he wanted to save her life. While she feasted with her lips, her hands roamed his body. Gloved fingers dug deep, moving from his shoulders, down his chest, beneath the lapels of his greatcoat. His only thought was, *Oh God, yes, that, that, that.*

His mind homed to the sensation of her small hands, boldly kneading his pectorals, walking down his ribs, twining beneath his arms. She locked him to her in a desperate embrace. Her thighs squeezed his flanks, squirming her urgently closer.

Jason palmed her hips and lifted her, ever so slightly, resettling her closer still. She moaned against his mouth.

He wondered how long it would take the watchman to make another circuit. Thinking was difficult. Remaining upright was difficult. Kissing her was the easiest thing he'd ever done.

How could he end this kiss? Would it be ungentlemanly to pull away? Or was it ungentlemanly to carry on?

The faint sound of whistling on the opposite side of the park pierced the haze. The watchman doing as requested, giving them time.

"Miss Tinker," Jason panted softly, pulling back. He rested his forehead against her temple. "Isobel."

She ducked her head, breathing hard. She nodded. She knew.

For a long, charged moment, they sat on the bench, bodies throbbing, hearts racing. They sucked air in small pants.

Jason tried to listen for the watchman's tune, but he heard only her. She swallowed hard. Her gown rustled and her hood fell back. He saw her face in the moonlight, flushed skin and bright eyes. She would not look at him.

"Here," he said, reaching for her waist, "let me steady you. Can you stand?"

She nodded and slid from his lap. She turned away, pulling from his fingers.

"Keep to the shadows," he whispered, adjusting his coat and pushing from the bench. He was painfully aroused.

She shuffled to the darkest corner of the alcove, facing

the bushes. Jason recovered his hat and stood in the path to block her from view. She patted and smoothed and tucked. She was silent except for her breathing.

If she'd been a green girl, if the kiss had taken her by surprise and shocked her, he would have said something, taken care to assure her.

If she'd been appalled and offended, he would've apologized.

But she'd been neither, and he didn't know what the hell to do.

"I—ah," he began, peeking through the dense bush for the location of the watchman.

"No discussion is necessary," she said briskly. Her tone was enigmatic.

"Right," he said, plunking his hat on his head.

"How will I get home without being seen?" she asked.

"Do you know the watchman's route?"

She was silent, thinking. Finally, she said, "When I see him, he's usually walking up Lumley Street from Oxford."

"Then we'll take the same route and be careful to stay well ahead of him. Here in the park, we'll pick our way through the vegetation and keep under the cover of trees."

"Yes. Good," she said. "I will follow you." But she'd already identified the thickest, leafiest way, and was drifting in that direction.

Jason cleared his throat. "Miss Tinker?"

"Please," she said. "Don't say anything. Please."

"I—"

"I cannot bear to examine it. I cannot."

"Right."

He stepped around her, inching into a thicket of flowering bushes. He tried again. "Thank you for everything you've divulged tonight. About the pirates."

He held out his hand and she took it. He pulled her along. He whispered, "I might require another conversation, to follow up—"

"Do not approach me again," she said with finality. "Please. If you have any respect for me—which I would understand how you might not—but if you have any *gratitude* for the information I've given you, *do not* seek me out again."

"My respect for you is—"

"Do not. Your Grace. Please." Her voice cracked.

Was she crying? He glanced back. Her face was buried in the hood and their path took them through a tunnel of darkness. He saw nothing but the outline of her small body.

He squeezed her hand, an unplanned, instinctive gesture, and said nothing more.

She held more tightly but remained silent, allowing him to pull her along.

Chapter Six

"I don't understand," Samantha said to Isobel two days later. "Why cultivate new clients if we're being forced to *leave* Everland Travel?"

The two women were assembling a folio with pamphlets and maps for a morning meeting with a dowager countess.

Isobel, employing equal parts *don't-think-about-it* and *pretend-it-won't-happen*, was carrying out her duties at Everland Travel as if she was not on the brink of expulsion. It had been two days, and she hadn't yet been sacked.

Yes, Drummond Hooke held the ax of termination over her head, and yes, she'd allowed a very wild, very overwhelming fragment of her old self to streak through her current life, but otherwise, *nothing had changed*. Yet.

"Life goes on," Isobel told Samantha now, mimicking the sage wisdom of someone who was not wild or overwhelmed. "We do not have the luxury of burning bridges. What if we find work in another travel agency? If this is a possibility, we'll want well-served clients to migrate with us."

"But this woman is not even a client." Samantha gestured to the crisp folio of itineraries and watercolor images of Italy.

"Yes, but she will be," said Isobel, tucking the folio into her satchel. Isobel excelled at winning new clients, especially old women.

This particular old woman, a dowager countess called Lady Harriet Braselton, had sent a card by messenger to request a private audience. The dowager had passed the spring and summer nursing a fractured ankle and wished to celebrate her restored health with an Italian holiday. She had questions about destinations and restricted mobility. She would be accompanied by her goddaughter and travel with a small staff. Her wish list was long and expensive, a talisman of Isobel's most lucrative type of client.

"Things should be slow while I'm out," Isobel told Samantha, tucking the folio in a satchel. "Sir Jamison must deliver payment today or his wife's holiday will be canceled with no refunds on the money already paid. And there are the Austria bookings to post . . ."

"I'll do it," sighed Samantha, slumping behind the counter, "but I won't understand *why* I'm doing it."

"Until Mr. Hooke evicts us, it is business as usual," Isobel repeated for the hundredth time. "There is always the chance he'll forget his misguided proposal and allow us to carry on."

"He won't," called Samantha as Isobel hurried out the door.

Samantha was correct, of course. He would not forget. After Isobel's rejection of him, Drummond Hooke announced he would remain in London for the foreseeable future. He did not mention their row or his proposal. He dropped in and out of the office instead, interjecting his disruptive presence into the business of the day and lavishing Isobel with what she assumed were meant to be the trappings of courtship. He bore droopy flowers, soft chocolates, and invitations to dine. Worst of all, he made awkward attempts at playful affection, pats and nudges and bumps and grazes that made her jump.

As long as Hooke kept quiet on the topic of marriage versus termination, Isobel would too. She accepted the flowers as an office-wide gift; she offered the chocolates to boys in the street. She refused all invitations and skittered away from his bony fingers. Until he actually sacked her, she would *abide* him. They would ooze along: Hooke believing that he was somehow winning her favor and Isobel planning for the day he would give up and send her packing.

Which he would do. He was not accustomed to being told no, especially by someone he believed to be beneath him. Entitled men did not expend effort on *lesser* women for long.

Until that time, she would not sabotage her work of the last five years just because he couldn't see beyond the end of his prick, and that meant cultivating new clients like Lady Braselton.

Her meeting with the dowager was set for a tearoom in Hammersmith, and she hailed a hackney cab for the journey west. Isobel routinely met in the homes of her clients to go over holiday itineraries or to introduce a travel porter to the family. First interviews, however, were sometimes convened in public establishments such as tearooms or the dining rooms of coaching inns. It was a very good sign, Isobel thought, when a lady requested an introduction in a public place instead of the security of her own parlor. It demonstrated an intrepidness and a versatility that would serve her well on her holiday. And also the dowager's estate was too deep in Middlesex for Isobel to travel in a day. Hammersmith was mid-distance for them both. Best of all, the remote meeting meant several blessed hours out of the office and away from Mr. Hooke.

Worst of all? The journey meant time to ruminate over her newest, most ruinous distraction.

The Duke of Northumberland.

And the kiss.

And why it happened.

And what it meant.

Although how foolish to speculate on what it meant. She *knew* what it meant.

To him, it meant nothing—one of a million kisses.

To Isobel, it meant that she'd not actually become the staid and respectable lady she'd worked so very hard to become. She'd merely been acting the part these last seven years.

Isobel Tinker was as wild and provocative and hopeless as she'd been the day she left Iceland.

The cab lurched into the crush of vehicles in Oxford Street. Shops and offices blurred outside her window and she replayed the Grosvenor Square encounter in her mind. Perhaps her favorite moment was him scooping her up: his strong arms lifting her as if she'd weighed nothing. His body had been so very large where hers was small, so hard where hers was soft.

And his fervor, of course. He kissed with an urgency that matched her own. She'd kissed him passionately, and he'd not backed down.

She'd reviewed every second of the kiss countless

times and could not find fault with any of it—save her own brazen indulgence. But that went without saying. The kiss had been near perfect.

Now the cab trundled past Hyde Park. Isobel studied the fine ladies in open carriages, enjoying the summer sun from beneath frothy parasols. Men in top hats were mounted on docile horses, trotting beside the ladies or cantering between the vehicles.

Isobel had promenaded in parks, once upon a time—not in London, of course, but in the grand parks of Paris and the piazzas of Rome. She had taken care with her dresses and carefully chosen her seats in open carriages. She had laughed and schemed and bade the driver to circle back with the hope of catching someone's eye.

No longer, she thought. *I'm all grown up now,* and *I work. Real, actual work.*

With luck, I will continue to work.

Her work this week, however, had been diluted with the entirely useless and futile task of *snooping.*

She'd searched old newspapers for articles about the Duke of Northumberland.

She'd located a copy of *Debrett's Peerage* and looked up his family.

In a particularly low moment, she'd hired a cab and rode past his opulent London townhome.

She was a foolish, foolish girl who'd clearly had learned nothing at all.

But Northumberland had simply been so—

Well, *adorable* was not the correct word.

Puppies were adorable. Five-year-old boys in tiny, grown-man suits were adorable. There was nothing fluffy or tiny about the duke. He was an adult male, older than her by more than five years. He projected an attitude of certainty about himself and the world and the future. He filtered through the dark London streets with confident stealth, an operator. It was clear why men had followed him in battle—she followed him without question and she prided herself on questioning everything done by any man.

His interview of her had been so intuitive and skilled it felt more like a very important conversation than an interrogation. He'd asked all the correct questions and she'd sung like a little yellow bird. How could she not, when subjected to his easy charm?

He portrayed himself like the friendly older brother of a beloved classmate, his trustworthiness guaranteed by association. The longer they spoke, the more she felt herself trust. But he was no one's brother, no one that she ever knew, and she had absolutely no reason to trust him.

One striking problem was that he was so very handsome. No matter how he sat or leaned or stalked, no matter how the moonlight struck him, Isobel gobbled up the sight. He was tall enough to see over the shrubs and so broad shouldered he blocked the moon. His hair was sandy brown-blond, mussed but not unkempt. His eyes held a sweetness but also . . . heat. He was dressed finely but without stiff formality. His attractiveness was so very obvious and known and enjoyed, it felt dangerous. She knew about dangerous levels of attractiveness; she'd learned this the hard way. And yet—

And yet she almost clipped the picture of his face from the newspaper. Like a schoolgirl.

She permitted herself all of this silliness only because she *knew*.

Girls who worked in travel shops served no purpose for a duke except as, well, as travel agents. On the very, very rare occasions, perhaps they served as informants.

She also knew that girls whose mothers were actresses could potentially serve a wholly different purpose for dukes—and she'd very nearly performed this service on the park bench—but Northumberland was a gentleman and he would not seek her out for another go. He would not gossip. She would never see him again.

She *knew*.

Safe in this knowledge, she allowed herself freedom from regret. Oh, she was mortified and shocked at her behavior, but she did not regret the kiss so much as worry over her lingering response to it. Her fixation. Her daydreams—good Lord, her actual dreams.

What bothered her the most was coming to terms with her longing. She'd wanted the charming duke—yes, but what she really wanted was *more*. More of him, and more of life in general.

Being staid and respectable was a challenge, and she might be terrible at it or she might eventually manage it. What she would not manage was the *want*.

Dark gardens with handsome men were exhilarating. She'd forgotten how much. And she longed for it.

She'd been deceiving herself all along.

The cab continued west, picking up speed as the London traffic thinned to the occasional wagon and men on horseback. The stacked houses and shops of town gave way to tidy cottages or clusters of outlying shops. Isobel checked her timepiece. It was not far to Hammersmith, but she mustn't make the dowager wait. Nor should she turn up distracted and flushed by memories of the duke.

She thumbed through her folios, seeing very little, until the cab reached Queen Street in Hammersmith. The driver located the tearoom, a charming stone shop with petunia-burst window boxes and a cheerful awning. Isobel paid the fare and then some, imploring him to return for her in two hours. She smoothed her dress and straightened her hat. She screwed a smile onto her face and hurried inside.

The dowager was easily identified in the dim interior, the only fabulously dressed middle-aged woman. She was flanked by a lady's maid snoozing at the table behind her and a footman hovering nearby. She presided over a window table laid heavily with a full tea.

"Lady Harriet Braselton?" Isobel asked, bobbing a shallow curtsy.

"Yes, indeed," enthused the dowager, "and you are Miss Tinker?"

"The very one," said Isobel, bobbing again and reaching out her hand.

Lady Harriet gushed her gratitude for the remote meeting, complimented Isobel's green dress, and thankfully forwent all the usual comments about her youth and gender. She invited Isobel to sit and began to pour tea, maintaining a steady stream of pleasant chatter. Isobel liked her immediately.

After they'd praised the tearoom (the dowager's family owned the entire block, she said), the distance from London (Isobel would surely be home in time for supper), and the condition of her ladyship's ankle (only a concern when it rained), Isobel pulled the watercolor prints from her satchel and began to spin a tale of Italian adventure, casting Lady Harriet as the protagonist.

The spry, open-minded dowager was transfixed, poring over the watercolors, making breathless sounds of excitement and clapping her hands in delight. In only a half hour's time, Isobel had sold the woman on a six-week holiday from Rome to Venice, invoking every luxury. She was just jotting down the woman's details, preferred dates of travel, and scheduling their next meeting when Lady Harriett dropped her teacup in the saucer with a clatter.

"Oh, but I'd nearly forgotten," exclaimed the lady. "It was my excitement over the journey. But I do have a second purpose here today. He's the very reason I sought you out. My dear nephew. He knew of my desire to travel and wrote to me at Meadowlane to insist I contact you straightaway. But you must speak to him—my nephew, Jason . . . Ah, yes, here he is . . ."

Isobel's hand froze over the parchment.

She'd been only half listening, but her ears went red at the mention of the name "Jason."

She knew of only one Jason.

Of course she did not think of him as "Jason." Her many misguided speculations and remembrances styled him simply as "Northumberland," but she knew his given name. She knew most things about him, considering the wasted hours she spent poring over all available accounts.

Isobel blinked at the notes, seeing only a blur. She bit down on the end of her pen. Finally, she looked up, trying to school her face into passive curiosity.

"I beg your pardon, my lady?"

"My *nephew* urged me to seek you out. My own son would force me to holiday in Scotland every summer and be done with it. Such a tyrant, my son. The world is so very small to him, and he's so protective. But my *nephew* respects my adventurer's spirit—ah, but here he is. Jason, darling!"

Isobel watched in disbelief as the dowager beamed at an unseen figure behind her, beckoning him with the happy twirl of a bracelet-tinkling wrist. The dowager's footman straightened to attention and the drowsing lady's maid scrambled to her feet.

Not him, Isobel chanted in her head. *Not him. Not him. It is not Jason Beckett, the Duke of Northumberland.*

It is Jason Anybody Else, someone I've never met or kissed with wild abandon.

"Hello, my lady," rumbled a friendly male voice from behind her—*an achingly familiar* voice. Unmistakable. The voice she heard in her dreams.

Isobel slowly closed her eyes. She counted the racing beats of her heart. She drew a shaky breath.

When I open my eyes, she thought, *this will not be—*

"Oh, but Miss Tinker is everything you promised," sang the dowager. "Ah, just look at her, so very deep in thought. Planning my journey already."

Isobel was given no choice but to open her eyes. "Forgive me, my lady," she said, locking eyes with the dowager.

She would not look at him. She would not look at him. She *would not look.*

"I was trying to recall—"

"How do you do, Miss Tinker?" said Nephew Jason, now a large, looming blur in Isobel's periphery. He was solid and opaque and unmoving. She could feel the warmth of his body. She could smell him.

With very great effort, Isobel tore her eyes from the dowager's and glanced up at him. "How do you do?" she rasped, a reflex.

It was him, of course, and her reaction to the sight of him was like the crack of a rifle, loud and reverberating. A shattering of the calm. His beautiful face was relaxed and curious and a little amused. His masculine body towered above the dainty tea service. Isobel felt shot—

not taking the bullet, but propelled from the barrel of the gun.

Him.

"I trust you're taking good care of my aunt," he said. "You'll not find a traveler more eager to see the world, I daresay. This journey has been many years in the making."

"So true," bemoaned the dowager, reaching again for Isobel's watercolor illustrations. "You know me too well, darling, and that is why you are my favorite nephew."

"Indeed," Jason agreed. He was staring at Isobel's face. Isobel knew she should look away—she should attend the dowager, she should take a sip of tea, she should look anywhere else—but she gaped up at the duke as if she'd never before seen a human male.

He went on, not looking away. "Would you mind, my lady, if I spoke to Miss Tinker alone for just a moment? You'll remember I said her office sometimes arranges travel for my work."

"Such dangerous derring-do," tsked the dowager, waving them away. "Of course my son will have no qualms about a holiday planned by the same office that looks after your important missions, darling . . ."

"Leave the earl to me," assured the duke lightly, stepping behind Isobel's chair and pulling it from the table. Isobel was given no choice but to rise. "I'll make certain that you get your Roman holiday." He gestured to the staff.

To Isobel he said, "Can I impose on you to join me outside, Miss Tinker? There is something of grave importance I should like to discuss."

Chapter Seven

"Y ou're cross," Jason guessed, holding open the door of the Turnip and Tea.

In truth, Isobel Tinker looked so much more than cross. She looked outraged, or perhaps simply *en*raged, but the open door gave her no choice but to step into the street.

Midday sunlight painted Hammersmith in eye-squinting brightness, and she walked only so far as a window box. She stopped next to a cascade of flowers and shaded her eyes. The high street was thinly trafficked at the moment; only a boy on a pony clomped past.

She glared at the boy and his mount. She checked a watch in her pocket. She studied the petunias in the window box. She would not look at him. Meanwhile, Jason saw only her. He'd spent the last hour watching her charm his aunt from across the dim tearoom and he'd passed the week anticipating this moment.

She'd worn a dress of apple green with a tidy straw hat several shades paler. Her gloves were a faint apricot color, and she'd pinned a small silk poppy to her lapel.

He'd told himself that she would be plainer than he remembered, less sparkling. He'd told himself that the unexpectedness of Isobel Tinker had painted his memories of her far better than she actually had been.

He'd been wrong. There was nothing less about her. She was exactly as compact and bright as he remembered.

He looked his fill, taking time to reseat his hat and propping against the windowsill. In his mind, he played a game he called "Things Not Done by an Effective Foreign Agent."

For example, an effective foreign agent did not feel guilty about using his aunt to trick an informant into meeting in Hammersmith.

An effective foreign agent was not distracted or entranced by said informant, no matter how fetching she looked in her snug green dress.

An effective foreign agent did not waver from the goal of recruiting the informant for urgent missions, no matter how she resisted.

And finally, an effective foreign agent did not use the rescue of hapless cousins as a means to become close—in mind or body—to the informant.

He must not touch her again, no matter how much his hands itched, in this very moment, to run a finger down the slim line of her arm. As a rule, he did not touch women uninvited—in his experience, no one of any gender welcomed random groping by another person—but his impulses seemed to be hung up on a continuous loop. *Stay. Lean. Touch.*

Jason did not touch her. He gave his head a shake and cleared his throat. He realized that if he stood *just* so, he could block the sunshine from her face with his shoulder. He propped a gloved hand on the building and leaned beside her. If he could not touch her, he would shield her.

"So," he ventured, "you're surprised to see me?"

This elicited a look. Finally. Blue eyes stared at him as if he'd just invited her to step off a high cliff.

"You thought our business was finished?" Another guess.

Guessing her mood seemed more prudent than asking her how she really felt. Validate her anger without inviting a vivid account.

When he'd left her that night in Grosvenor Square, she'd dismissed him with a three-sentence entreaty:

Do not approach me again. Please. If you have any respect for me . . .

At the time, she hadn't seemed cross so much as hurried and emphatic and distressed. He'd agreed because he'd wanted to put her at ease. And also, she'd darted up the steps and disappeared inside before he could speak.

And now here he was, seeking her out again, just as he'd promised not to do. He'd also spoken of her to others. Not many others, but a few. His chat with her uncle, Sir Jeffrey Starling, would be among the more difficult interviews to reveal.

But authenticating her information was allowed—nay, necessary. Everything he did was necessary for the recovery of Reggie and the avoidance of an international incident with the Danes.

He was in the right. He'd never had to remind himself of this, and the mental exercise was growing tiresome.

He tried one more time. "You enjoyed meeting my aunt?" he ventured. This she could not deny.

At last, she opened her mouth. She sucked in a little breath. Jason stared at the small, pink perfection of her lips and was immediately distracted. He'd revisited their kiss as often as he'd revisited every other fact and figure from the night in Grosvenor Square. He'd devoted his week to confirming and researching and building on the details. The kiss should have been irrelevant to all of it; instead, it felt like a beginning.

Finally, she spoke. "Is the dowager's holiday part of the ruse?" Her voice was soft and a little weary.

"What? No, of course not. There is no ruse, Isobel—"

"I prefer 'Miss Tinker,' if you please," she said lowly, glancing about them.

"*Forgive me, Miss Tinker.*" He exhaled and started again, whispering, "My aunt has dreamt of a sojourn to Italy for an age. It was my pleasure to introduce you. Her patronage will keep you busy for the better part of a year."

She stared at him like he was trying to sell her a house with no door.

"I merely meant to join two purposes," he explained. "My aunt was in need of a travel agent, and I needed, urgently, to speak with you. I was mindful of not bursting in on your office again, and a simple request for another meeting seemed . . . ambitious."

"There will be no future meetings," she stated.

"Which is why I cultivated this errand. To bring us all together."

"You and I have already *been* together," she bit out in a whisper. She paused and a pink blush bloomed on the cream of her cheeks. He watched it spread down her throat and across her collarbone. Jason's memories engaged, replaying the warm pleasure of their kiss.

Miss Tinker cleared her throat. She repeated, "I've provided all the information that I am able. I bade you, as a gentleman—"

"Yes, yes," he cut in. "I'm a gentleman and you've

bade me to the devil. But at the moment, I'm here on earth and working on behalf of the common good. Look, Miss Tinker, the information you provided in Grosvenor Square was, to put it mildly, a treasure trove. I was able to confirm, corroborate, or build upon nearly every nugget. When I first sought you out, my only intent was to gain a general sense of the Icelandic geographic and cultural landscape. Instead, you handed me the key players in my cousin's capture and quite possibly their purpose. It's been a very *fruitful* week, to say the least. I cannot say when I've had a more helpful informant." He paused, waiting for some reaction. Flattery never hurt, and in this case, it was also true.

"I'm happy to hear it," she said, not at all flattered. "But now you'll *repay* my usefulness by—"

"*I need more,*" Jason said, emphasizing every word. He'd not lured her to Hammersmith to beat around the bush.

"More what?"

"I need you to join me on my voyage to Iceland to recover my cousin and the other captured Englishmen."

There was a long, airless pause. From somewhere nearby, a chirping bird began a cheerful trill. The birdsong, so normal and abiding, served only to mock the highly irregular and improbable thing he was asking her to do.

"No," she said, a statement more than a denial.

Jason celebrated inside his head but kept his face very calm. He doubled down.

"You couldn't know this about me, Miss Tinker, but I'm known in my work for seeking unconventional solutions from unlikely sources."

"No," she said. Again, the word was floated more than tossed down.

"Protocol and procedure?" he went on. "These have always been afterthoughts. As a strategist, my plans are known as 'unorthodox.' "

"No," she repeated.

"And then the success we all enjoy is as far-reaching as it was inevitable. A great surprise to everyone but my closest allies."

"No, no, no."

"Which is why," he rushed to finish, "*you* may be surprised at the very outrageousness of this plan."

"Surprise is only one of several very strong reactions to this plan, Your Grace."

"It could work," he said. "It *will* work. It is brilliant and resourceful and kismet."

"*Absolutely* not. Out of the question." She spun on her heel and stomped up the street in the direction of London.

Jason swore and went after her. "Hear me out," he said, catching her in two strides.

"Go away, Your Grace," she said. She would not look at him. "Go away, go away, go away."

He pressed on. "You would serve as a guide, a translator—a sort of cultural attaché. Based on what I confirmed this week, you know exactly how to get *me in* and *my cousin out* as quickly and as quietly as possible."

She kept walking and he swore again. He was literally chasing her down the street.

He tried again. "Will you hear *why* I need you? Or what I'm prepared to offer in exchange?"

"No."

Now *he* was cross. "You *will*," he informed her. "Because lives are at stake and the government of England could benefit from your usefulness. It is decent and honorable to—"

"Do not say it," she cut him off. She came to a stop before an empty storefront and whirled around.

"Do not suggest I lack decency or honor when I know the War Office or the Home Office or Whitehall could provision you with unlimited resources if you require them. I am merely one woman, alone. I'm fighting to keep my livelihood. I deplore Iceland for reasons too personal to share. And I also suffer from wretched seasickness; as such, I've sworn off ocean voyages. So do not expect me to politely ask how I might help. Don't tell me that *I* am your only hope—*and* I have no wish to go—because I don't believe you."

"Fair points, one and all," he said, which was certainly true. "But I've an answer."

"Yes, and the answer is, 'How right you are, Miss Tinker. I'll leave off plaguing you.' "

He laughed. "Actually—no." *But how adorable you are,* he thought.

He could hardly say that. He cleared his throat.

"Look," he began again, "if I'm being completely honest, my efforts on this mission are not entirely under the, er, *jurisdiction* of the Foreign Office. That is, it's not an *official* undertaking. I won't be operating under . . . sanctioned authority."

"What does that mean?" She sounded skeptical.

"I'm sufficiently high in rank—or I was before I retired—but even I'm subject to a chain of command. When I explained the pirate capture and the attempted illegal trade to my commanding officer, he was . . . not convinced. I told him these men from Lincolnshire could die and England could face a diplomatic quarrel with Denmark, but he wouldn't budge.

"He didn't block me from going so much as reminded me that I'm meant to be retired." Here Jason made a grimace. "That I'm . . . *no longer in play*."

"Stop," she pleaded. "Not an appeal for sympathy. On top of everything else."

He laughed, a bitter, ragged sound. "I don't want your sympathy, Isobel; what I want is to be a foreign agent. That's been taken from me. Fine. So be it. I *also* want to recover my cousin. This is in reach. If handled with care and delicacy and the resources at hand."

She narrowed her eyes. "You plan to strike out on your own?"

He let out a disgusted harrumph. "Was I forbidden to embark on the mission? No, I was not *forbidden*. Do they know I intend to give it a go? Yes, they do. But will I be working on behalf of the British government *when I enact the recovery*? Not . . . entirely.

"Of course, if things go badly . . . if the pirates begin to kill the merchants or Denmark learns of their attempt to smuggle with Iceland . . . the Foreign Office *would* be invoked. They'd send reinforcements, official diplomacy would commence. My goal, with the consent—although not the support—of my former employer is to keep ahead of that.

"*My goal*," he finished, "is in and out, and no one knows. *My method* is to recruit outsiders—which means you—and make as little fuss as possible. The Foreign Office is overburdened with larger concerns. I'm . . . I'm managing this on my own."

By the time Jason had said all of it, he was sweating.

He snatched off his hat and ran a finger through his hair. He raised his eyebrows.

Miss Tinker studied his face, saying neither yes nor no. Also, she did not say, *How brave and noble you are*, or *How very full of rubbish you have been*.

But she did begin to slowly shake her head.

"What?" he asked.

"You." Her head was still shaking. "It's as if your very person has been carefully assembled from all the cast-off parts of my former . . . former . . . *poor* judgment."

Now it was his turn to ask. "What?"

"It's a test, clearly," she said, speaking to herself. "A challenge to all I've accomplished."

Again, "What?"

And then he did the thing that he'd wanted to do since he'd watched her descend from the cab. He reached out and touched her. A gentle but firm gloved hand encircling the bare skin of her arm. She'd left her shawl on her chair, and the sleeves of her summer dress did not reach her gloves. Her arm was firm and warm and strumming with energy.

She looked first at his hand on her arm and then up at him. "I do not think we should touch."

He explained, "I'm making a very important point."

"You're *touching* my arm."

"Will you hear what I have to say?" he asked, dropping his hand. "There's more."

She didn't answer. Instead, she took off her hat, jerking at the ribbons like she was fashioning a hasty noose. The pins came next. When the hat was unfettered, she pulled it from her head and fanned herself with it.

Jason paused, giving her time.

They stood before an iron fence that separated the

walkway from the empty shop. He leaned against the corner post. He crossed his arms over his chest and propped a boot on the bottom rung. He studied her, now free of the tidy straw hat. She'd styled her hair in another large poof of a yellow bun, high on the top of her head. Upswept tendrils broke ranks and feathered her neck.

"Do not *gaze* at me," she remarked.

"Oh right," he said, looking away. "No given names. No touching. No gazing. But may I—?"

"Fine," she exclaimed. "Out with it. *Tell me the rest*. All the exciting, noble, unsanctioned bits. Why not?"

Jason nodded and dug for a coin in his pocket. He flipped it, and hopefulness made the same flip in his chest. Her resistance seemed to have more to do with an internal battle and very little to do with him. He remained calm. He kept his body lax and his voice even. He explained how he'd verified the information she'd given him, how he'd come to realize that *she* would be his ideal translator and guide.

Finally, he said, "I haven't yet decided how I will approach the mission. I could negotiate with the pirates for the life of my cousin and his comrades. I could simply pay the ransom. Or I could steal away the lot of them under the cover of darkness. However I do it, I must be quick, efficient, and leave no diplomatic trace. I could devote another month to planning and research and anticipating all the things that could go wrong. *Or* I can simply enlist *you* as my translator and guide—and leave next week."

He snatched the coin from the air. "*That* is why I need you."

"What if I've already said everything there is to know about—"

"I spoke to your uncle, Miss Tinker," he said. "I know about your time in Iceland."

She went still, her hat frozen midarc. If possible, her blue eyes grew wider. She looked as if he'd held up a stolen broach.

"Isobel?" he said carefully.

"My uncle will not have told you everything," she said finally. "Please be aware."

"No," Jason said, "I don't suppose he did."

"I don't want to know actually," she said, but she sounded anguished. She replaced the hat on her head, jabbing the pins and tying the ribbons.

"Your uncle said," Jason recited calmly, "that your youth was spent traveling Europe in service to your mother's career."

"Ah yes," she said, "my mother."

"It goes without saying, I suppose, that I learned she was the actress—"

"*Renowned* actress," Isobel amended. "Of international acclaim."

It was the first time he'd heard her boast of anything but her own competence as a travel agent. She was proud of her unconventional mother. As well she should be. Good for her.

"Quite so," he agreed. "Georgiana Tinker. I, myself, am a fan. I had the good fortune to catch her Lady Macbeth in Copenhagen. It was '09, I believe. Transformative."

She would not look at him. She closed her eyes. He was treated again to her profile. Full swoop of lashes, pert nose, plush lips, defiant chin.

He went on. "Your uncle described your girlhood and youth as unorthodox, but he passed no judgment."

"No," she said, "he would not. He is a decent man."

"He said that by the time you reached Iceland, you'd outgrown it all."

She laughed, a sharp, jagged sound. It left a cut on Jason's heart.

"We talked about the number of months you were in Iceland," he recalled. "The estate on which you lived. On the topic of your return to England—'outgrown' was all he said."

Sir Jeffrey Starling's lack of elaboration meant there was far more to the story, but Jason didn't require the full story. He did want to *know,* but it wasn't necessary for this mission.

"I sought out your uncle only to verify your time in Iceland. You are an unlikely source of intelligence, Miss Tinker, but you offered so very much of it. It was too valuable not to confirm."

She seemed not to hear. She turned to face the fence, gripping it with both hands. She looked ready to rip out an iron slat and stab him with it.

"All this for a 'mission' that you now say is more like a personal errand," she said.

"It is not uncommon," he said, "for officers of rank to . . . act of their own volition for the common good. In the field."

"But you are not in the field. You are in Hammersmith."

"I am in the world," he gritted out, "and I am a capable agent, and when I see injustice, I am obliged to set it to rights. I'm not staked behind a bloody desk in Middlesex—at least not yet."

This came out with more rancor than he intended. It had pained him even to travel to Hammersmith today. The placid, agrarian tediousness of every part of

Middlesex caused him to twitch and pace and scan the green horizon for a hidden door *out*.

Soon, he'd be back here to stay.

Soon, there would be no way out, and he'd twitch and pace and run mad with the stifling sameness of it.

But not today.

Today, he'd come for her and—lovely surprise—it hadn't been as bad as he'd expected. She was resistant to reason and stubborn to a fault but she kept things interesting.

Now she watched him with open curiosity. He pressed the advantage.

"Will you indulge me a moment more? Let me make my offer? Learn what you'll receive in return?"

"Oh yes. Another fifty pounds." She stared at the empty storefront behind the gate.

"No, in fact. Not money. Something far more useful, I hope."

"What is more useful than money?" A bitter laugh.

"*Property*," he said.

Slowly, ever so slowly, she turned her head.

He kept his voice light. "It's not in London, I'm afraid, but here. In Hammersmith. Not prohibitively far, as your journey in the hackney hopefully demonstrated. It's another reason I wished you to meet with Aunt Harriet at her beloved Turnip and Tea. My London buildings do not really lend themselves to travel agencies—those are flats and warehouses mostly. But the Northumberland dukedom owns most of Hammersmith, or so I'm told, and that includes this high street."

He went on. "You could choose this very building, for example." He nodded to the storefront before them.

"If it doesn't suit, there are others scattered throughout town."

He watched her. She tore her gaze away and looked at the empty building as if she had not noticed it before.

Jason gave her time to study it.

"If you will help me, Miss Tinker," he said softly, "if you will travel to Iceland and assist me in recovering my cousin without incident, I will set you up in your own office, and you may have a travel agency on your very own terms. You may employ Samantha and whomever else you like. You may lure away all of your devoted clients, my aunt among them, and be free of Mr. Drummond Hooke. *You may do as you please.*"

He swung the creaky gate wide and stepped through it. He could feel her watching him as he mounted the steps. His heartbeat began to pound.

This was, of course, the thing he'd wanted to say from the moment she'd appeared in front of the tearoom.

He'd wanted to give her a building, even if she wouldn't help him.

Surely this was one benefit of being duke? Bestowing his copious properties on whomever he chose.

He reached for the doorknob. It was locked, of course, but he'd had his brother's steward—*his* steward, he reminded himself miserably—furnish him with keys to all the buildings up and down Queen Street. He unlocked the door and pushed it open.

"What say you?" he asked, gesturing to the dim interior. Anticipation welled like a shaken bottle of champagne. She was on the cusp. Her expression had gone from frustration to disbelief to—dare he say?—*hope*. He bit back a smile, watching as she looked over the building with wild, searching eyes.

"You would simply give me a building?" she confirmed.

She clutched the fence plats as if she might bend them into hooks.

"Well, the leasehold, if that's amenable. Choose a building with a storefront on the ground floor and a flat above for your dwelling. Or use both floors for your work and take a cottage around the corner. You'd have to say good-bye to city life, I'm afraid. And your clients will be forced to leave London to call on you. But perhaps you can convince them their journey to the Continent begins in Hammersmith."

"But why?" she rasped.

"I've told you. I need your help." *I want you, I want you, I want you*, he thought, and he realized this was his purest reason why.

"But it cannot mean so very much as all this. It cannot." She released the fence and took two tentative steps inside the gate.

"What is the value of a favorite cousin?" he mused philosophically. "His life in peril?"

"You would have found another way," she said.

"What is the value of keeping England out of a dispute with Denmark?" he speculated.

"But a whole *building*?"

"What is the value of my finally settling in as duke?" This question held less drama and more obligation. A question just as much for himself. "The sooner I return, the sooner I can install myself in Syon Hall. Do my duty. No more 'derring-do' as my aunt terms it."

The words were painful to say, and he wondered how he'd stumbled upon an informant for whom the price of cooperation was his own painful admissions.

Luckily (and oddly, now that he considered it), he didn't seem to mind the admissions. He found himself wanting to admit to the world if she was willing to listen.

He finished with, "I do not want the dukedom, but I've put it off long enough. My mother and sisters need me. The estate and tenants need me. I cannot devote another year to, er, saving the world. Or even to saving Reggie."

She stared at him. She began, "I—"

She stopped.

She appeared to run out of excuses.

She started again, "I promised myself I would never go back." She spoke to herself more than him.

And now it was his turn to resist, to be stalwart and not give in to her appeal for mercy.

"The building is yours," he said, the most he could give her under the circumstances. "Plus local tradesmen for whatever modifications you might require to set up shop."

She took three quick breaths. She shoved away from the fence. She closed her eyes and squeezed her hands at her sides—she was the figure of someone wringing consent from their very soul. She exhaled and opened her eyes. She blinked.

Jason said nothing, waiting and watching.

"Fine," she called. Her voice held a new steeliness. She clipped up the steps and sailed through the door. Her green skirts swished against his boot as she went.

"You win," she called from the darkness within. "Show me every building. If one of them is suitable, I'll do it. I'll make the trade."

Chapter Eight

Five days later, Isobel stood on the planks of the West India Company docks, staring up at a towering brigantine crawling with activity. Sailors scaled masts, swabbed decks, and maneuvered rigging while dockworkers heaved provisions up gangplanks.

The mild August weather had turned wet and windy just in time for her to embark on her first sea voyage in seven years. An omen, perhaps; her stomach would pitch into misery as soon as they made open water.

For the moment, she stood on solid ground; beside her, Samantha wrestled with an umbrella.

"You packed the fan with the sharp spines?" Samantha confirmed. "The one that leaves a mark if you . . ." She made a slapping motion.

"Yes," confirmed Isobel.

"And the cloak that keeps out the water?"

"Yes."

"And what about the—?"

"You've kitted me out with everything I could possibly need, Samantha. Please do not worry."

"I only wish I could join you," Samantha said wistfully, staring up at the tall masts, now disappearing into a foggy mist.

"I know, but we've discussed it . . ."

She let the sentence trail off, glancing at her friend. Abandoning Samantha alone in London was one of a hundred reasons to resent this journey.

And yet . . .

And yet a strange bubble of excitement had begun to swell in the pit of Isobel's stomach. Seasickness would drown it out soon enough, but at the moment, she could not deny her anticipation.

When she tried to regret or dread the journey, she was met with an exhilarating swell of eagerness instead. It had been so very long since she'd felt anything beyond the steady, stable balance of a life rebuilt. And stable and steady were very nice indeed. But oh, to look out and feel swooshing, bouncy anticipation. Was it wrong to crave an event that was unknown? Where anything could happen?

"So . . ." Samantha was saying, showing herself to be a very good sport indeed. "Ten days to sail to Iceland, a handful of days to work with the duke on his *secret mission*, whatever it is . . ." she raised an eyebrow, ". . . and ten days to sail home."

"Yes. Gone the month of September—no more."

"And your mother knows," confirmed Samantha.

"My mother knows."

Isobel took a leave of absence every September to visit her mother in Cornwall. The holidays Isobel sold at Everland Travel were planned with a six-month lead time, and no one traveled in the bitter cold of winter. This allowed the month of September to be devoted to family and housekeeping and interviewing new chaperones, porters, and stewards.

But not this year. This year, September meant the Iceland "mission." Meanwhile, Samantha would stay back at Everland Travel, carefully evading Drummond

Hooke and quietly transcribing five years of Isobel's work.

When Isobel returned, she would call on each client personally and explain the launch of her new agency. They could transfer their patronage to the new shop or remain with Drummond Hooke.

"You'll make certain Hooke won't learn I've left the country," Isobel confirmed, perhaps Samantha's most important task while she was away.

"Do not think of it again," Samantha assured. "He will not know unless he travels to Cornwall and calls on your mother. And God help him if he does that."

Isobel nodded and squeezed her arm. Yes, God help him.

It had been Samantha's idea to give Drummond Hooke no clue about their future. Isobel had constructed a complicated excuse and a threatening but vague hint of "significant changes to come." Samantha ripped up the note, insisting that their only obligation was a reminder that Isobel took leave most of September.

"You shouldn't call to the new building in Hammersmith during the workday," said Isobel. "Go after you close the Lumley Street shop. If Hooke calls and you are gone?" She made a face. "Or you could visit Hammersmith on Sundays; your father will be appalled."

"My father adores you and everything you do, as you know," said Samantha. "I intend to pop in on the construction at odd times actually. Keep the workmen on their toes."

After Isobel had finally consented, the duke had sealed her cooperation by giving her a tour of all potential buildings. He'd been clever and charming—if alarmingly clueless about the buildings in his possession—and she'd chosen a spacious redbrick building on the corner of Queen Street, with a large front window and a flat upstairs.

Northumberland had then charged lawyers to transfer ownership of the new building. They had descended in a flurry of parchment and Latin addendums and moved everything along at a breakneck pace. An architect sent his card the very next day. Isobel met him in the afternoon to discuss her hopes for renovating the property.

Tradesmen came next: carpenters, draftsmen, masons, plumbers, woodworkers. When she returned from Iceland, the office and flat should be ready.

"It's a moment in time," Isobel told Samantha now. They locked arms beneath the umbrella, shrinking from the rain. "There are very big things in store for us. If *I* can manage Iceland. And *you* can manage Hooke. If Hammersmith evolves. If our customers will follow us. If, if, if . . ."

"Indeed," agreed Samantha. "I do hate it that you have to *manage* Iceland to achieve it. You don't even want to go."

Oh, I want to go, Isobel thought.

She said the words out loud, testing them. "I want to go."

"*You want to go*," repeated Samantha slowly.

Isobel paused, listening to the steady chant inside her head, her own voice repeating it again and again: *Go. Go. Go.*

"Yes. I want to go."

After Isobel had finally agreed to the building, the duke had claimed pressing business in London and gone. He'd galloped off, leaving Isobel, heart pounding, cheeks flushed, standing beside the Turnip and Tea, pretending not to memorize his retreating form.

When he was out of sight, when she could no longer feel the warm, firm press of his hand on the small of her back, or smell the woodsy scent of him, she had drifted inside the tearoom and dropped into an empty booth. Even before a fresh pot of tea arrived, she'd taken out her parchment and pen and scrawled out a letter to her mother.

One benefit of having an actress for a mother was never having to pretend to be So Very Good. Georgiana Tinker was bored to tears by Very Goodness.

Instead, Isobel's mother functioned as a listener, an encourager, and an absolver. For as long as she could remember, Isobel's mother had helped her reckon with the whipsawed realities of life.

Dearest Georgiana,

Brace yourself, Mummy, I've been compelled to put off my September visit. I'm sorry. I can anticipate your maddened state of perishing despair. I'm disappointed too. But pause five minutes and take in the reason.

I've been approached by a duke—the Duke of Northumberland (look him up in the papers if you are not familiar)—to assist with rescue efforts on behalf of a lot of stranded English merchants.

Actually, the duke refers to the undertaking as a "mission," I believe.

We are to assist the stranded countrymen and smooth any ruffled feathers with locals.

The effort should take a little less than a month and will occur mostly in Iceland (yes, you read that correctly).

The duke, who has served years in the Foreign Office, is a decorated officer of some merit. He applied to Uncle Jeffrey and learned—among God knows what else—

that I speak the language and have some knowledge of the culture. Add to this my position as a wholly anonymous Nobody from Nowhere, and apparently I am a dream addition to the duke's mission.

I was very resistant, said no a hundred times, and was very difficult to convince. In the end, I was won over by a very fat bribe. (Although some measure of coercion and even seduction did figure into the arrangement. He is very handsome and charming, etc., etc. In fact, the duke embodies so many of your favorite qualities. I include this tidbit just for you; pray do not fantasize beyond this observation and <u>do not gossip about it</u>. We are to be professional colleagues.)

But I digress. The bribe he offered is a small office and flat in Hammersmith, which, as you may know, is a smart village just west of London. The duke owns (for all practical purposes) the high street, and he allowed me to take my pick of unoccupied properties. The gift of the building means that Samantha and I may abandon Everland Travel and Drummond Hooke forever. I may set up my own agency and run the business exactly as I see fit. I can provide for myself, and you, and pay Samantha a decent wage.

I cannot guess which part of this note will give you more joy, but I trust you'll not begrudge my missed visit. I'll have you to Hammersmith instead, conveyed by private coach, and you may see the shop and my new flat for yourself.

I'll remember every moment of my adventure and recount it in colorful detail when we are together again. And I'll bring back a handful of Norse crystals for your windowsill.

In the meantime, my letters will become sparse as I rush to set sail. Samantha will be available for anything

you may need—do not hesitate to send for her if necessary. I've written separate letters to Mrs. Bean; your
staff knows I am unreachable for a time. Carry on as
usual; do not think of me except in anticipation of the
stories with which I'll return.

One final thing: the fearlessness required to do this
comes only from you, my dear. Please be aware.

What did you always say? "Be memorable, not respectable"?

This adage has rung false to me for so long, as well
you know. But here I am, giving it another go. I cling
to the hope that there is value in a journey that terrifies me.

What else did you always say? "If a cart blocks the
road, and you cannot go around it, or over it, or beneath
it, climb into the driver's seat and take it for a ride."

Witness me taking up the reins, God help us.

Alright. Enough of that. Please wear your gloves
and wide-brimmed hat in the sun—*and no more stray
dogs*. Mummy, please. Mrs. Bean writes me weekly and
she is at her wit's end.

All my love,
Bell

Isobel and her mother got on best in small doses, but
their correspondence had always been lively, honest,
and thorough. Isobel had begun traveling alone at age
fifteen—traversing Europe with a merry band of youths,
the children of other actors in her mother's company.
Even in those early days, she wrote her mother daily,
extolling all she'd seen and done, spilling out feelings
she would struggle to confide in person, accounting for
her wild, unfettered life.

When that freedom caught up with her, when she was heartbroken and alone, she wrote to her mother still. Even while Isobel's aunt and uncle did the difficult work of recovering her and nursing her back to solvency, the correspondence with her mother had been another sort of recovery.

If her mother could not give prudent advice—which, God help her, she absolutely could not—at least she was a loving, adoring sounding board.

Now, watching a docker haul her trunk up the gangplank, she told Samantha again, "I want to go." Her voice had risen. It was a proclamation.

"Useful—that," said Samantha. "Because that's exactly what you're doing."

The docker tipped the trunk at an angle, endeavoring to fit it over the lip of the plank. Samantha gasped and shouted at the man. "No, no, no. Not like that. Stop, *stop.*"

The younger woman huffed in exasperation and stomped up the gangplank, demonstrating a more careful way.

Isobel was smiling to herself, watching the exchange, when she heard a male voice behind her.

"I didn't know if you would actually come," he said, "until I saw you with my own eyes."

The rumble of his voice set off a shimmer in Isobel's stomach. She gripped the umbrella tightly. She closed her eyes and then opened them. She turned.

The Duke of Northumberland, dressed for sailing in a long coat and wide-brimmed hat, stood behind her, staring up at the brigantine.

And now she could add "gentleman at sea" to all the inciting ways the duke could look. As if the cravat and trousers or the black buckskins and greatcoat had not been enough. She would not stare. A mantra, perhaps, for this journey.

No staring at the handsome duke. No banter with the handsome duke. Nothing to do with the handsome duke but translate Icelandic and give advice and *not* become affected.

Isobel had devoted seven years to rising above the emotional fray of affectation by handsome men. Prudence and restraint had earned her that lofty perch, and she clung to it. It had not come natural to her, but it felt very safe and very stable. She would not concede it now.

The journey to Iceland would not be a return to reckless behavior.

No matter how lovely and compelling the duke was.

Even if she survived Iceland itself, she would not survive another broken heart. Not from him.

"I trust you have everything you need for the journey?" the duke asked. "I sent a note offering to provision you with whatever you may require."

"Yes, you were very kind, thank you," she said.

"When you didn't respond, I assumed you could manage on your own. Or that you weren't coming."

"Two things you should understand about me, Your Grace," Isobel told him. "First, I *can* manage on my own. Second, if I say I'll do something, I will do it. Trust will not be an issue with me."

"Dare I anticipate what will be an issue?"

Take your pick, Isobel thought. *Impatience. Panic. Seasickness.*

Resisting you.

"There will be no issues," she said. "I will be the model . . ." The word for her precise role in the mission escaped her.

"Attaché?" the duke suggested. "Adviser?"

"Translator?" she countered.

"Well, it's more than that obviously," he said, thinking. "But I'd not bother with a title if I were you. None of the men I recruited for this mission have formal roles beyond helping to recover these merchants and slinking away without anyone being the wiser. I've embarked on missions with looser order and protocols, but I'm not sure when. I apologize in advance. This brig, in particular, is rather crude." He stared up at the boat.

"I am widely traveled, Your Grace, in every manner of vessel. The accommodations do not alarm me."

"Lucky thing," he sighed. "The *Feather* is fast and safe, with a trusted captain I've known for years. He was bound for America but agreed to divert long enough to ferry us to Stokkseyri and back."

She glanced at him, an eyebrow raised. "Stokkseyri?" she asked. "Not Reykjavík?"

Northumberland shook his head. "You were correct about the ice caves and making landfall farther east. You were correct about everything."

Well, thought Isobel, that was gratifying. She was rarely considered an expert, even among her clients. Until she proved otherwise, fathers and uncles and brothers assumed *some man* had planned her travel itineraries.

"Regardless," the duke went on, "we're not sailing 'round the Isle of Wight on a pleasure cruise. It will take nearly a fortnight to make Iceland. There will be precious few amenities for a lady."

Isobel blinked. She wasn't accustomed to being referred to as a lady. Was he teasing? She raised the umbrella.

No. He wasn't. He wasn't even looking at her. With a

cringing expression, he watched a crew member lean over the side and issue a prodigious stream of spit into the Thames.

"You're certain you won't have a maid to attend you?" he said, wincing. "I can provide one if you—"

"I haven't employed a maid in years, Your Grace. It cannot be overstated: I can manage on my own. You'd do well to think less of my comfort and more of my inconsistent skill as a translator and my potential enemies among the locals."

Northumberland raised an eyebrow. "Enemies?"

"In Stokkseyri? Possibly—yes." He might as well know.

"Pity we've not met before this very hour, or I could have learned more about your rapport with the locals."

"Pity," she repeated. "But please remember, I am not *collaborating* with you; I am *cooperating*. I'll only do what is strictly necessary to gain my new shop."

"One marvels at the distinction."

"You did not stipulate meeting before now, so . . ." She hunkered beneath the umbrella like a turtle retracting into her shell.

Isobel had hired her own lawyer to review the duke's legal papers and to assure her new situation in Hammersmith. If her cooperation amounted to work-in-trade, she would know exactly what work was expected.

The duke had sent requests, asking to meet with her, to hear her opinion on provisions and course and strategy, but no such meetings had been stipulated, and she had refused.

"I've been very busy, you see," she said, speaking from within the umbrella. "It is no small thing to leave the country while planning a secret defection from your place of business. In five days."

"Well, you've promised me an appraisal once we're on board. Enemies and allies, sympathetic bystanders, double-crossers, safe and unsafe havens, known traps, dead ends." He leaned to peek at her beneath the cover of the umbrella.

Rain was sluicing off his hat and the yoke of his coat, but he didn't seem to care. He looked so very rugged and impervious and handsome.

"I'll see what I can do," she said, tipping the umbrella to shield herself. "I suffer from seasickness and will succumb within an hour of losing sight of land. I warned you of this. The first few days will be spent confined to my cabin. After that, I may creep to the deck at sunset to take fresh air. We can talk then, but more than that I cannot promise."

"You're always ill at sea?" he asked.

"Every time."

"How can I help?"

"I've already provided meal instructions to the steward. Just leave me be, if you will. I can manage. As I've said."

"Right," he said, his voice growing fainter. He was walking away. "You can manage."

Chapter Nine

*W*aiting for someone, Your Grace?"

Former mercenary Declan Shaw stood on the deck of the *Feather* smoking with the duke. Shaw watched the pale sun arc into the black waters of the North Sea, while Jason stared at a closed hatch on the brig's foredeck.

"What?" Jason asked.

"I said," repeated Shaw, "are you waiting for—?"

"Waiting for you to finish that sodding cheroot," said Jason testily. "You're like a calf on a teat. If I'd only known I could pay you in tobacco."

The duke had assembled a small crew of trusted comrades in arms, retired soldiers, and off-duty agents to travel to Iceland as tactical support. Leading the crew was his old friend Declan Shaw.

Shaw was a retired mercenary who now lived in Somerset with his new wife and infant son. Before his unexpected foray into family life, Shaw had been a cunning warrior, the type of man for whom fighting pirates would be all in a day's work. Jason could think of no one more qualified for this mission, and he'd paid Shaw triple to convince him to leave his young family, even for a month.

"My wife detests smoking," Shaw said, exhaling

a ribbon of smoke. "I am happy to oblige her. You? I couldn't care less. I can't remember the last time I enjoyed a cheroot." He took another puff.

Jason checked the deck hatch again. "Precious few cheroots in prison, I presume," the duke said.

"Precious few visitors *to this deck*," Shaw replied.

Jason shot him a look but said nothing.

Declan Shaw had served time in Newgate Prison after being wrongly accused of kidnapping. Jason had been on assignment in India at the time, and his friend had been spared prison by the woman who was now his wife.

"Pity too," rhapsodized the mercenary. "You. Alone at sunset. The icy waves, the frigid wind, the crusty film of algae and fish guts. So romantic."

"Spare me your fantasies," Jason said, lighting his own cheroot.

"Not my fantasy, mate. You're the man who's ferrying a female translator to bloody *Iceland* so she can have a go at *pirates*. Or so says the gossip. Interesting choice, if it's true."

"Interesting, *why*?" Jason bit out.

"That depends," said Shaw, tossing the butt of his cheroot into the sea. "If the female translator is a sweaty, sour-faced woman who you intend to roll around Iceland in an ox cart. *Or* if she's young and beguiling and will see Iceland riding on your lap."

Jason was just about to tell Shaw to bugger off when the hatch behind them creaked open and a blond head popped out.

Jason's cheroot froze halfway to his mouth. He stared at the face he hadn't seen in three days.

Shaw snickered. "Well, there's our answer, isn't it? Pleasant chat, North."

"Sod off, Shaw." Jason pitched his cheroot overboard. "Miss Tinker?" Jason called, carefully approaching the opened hatch. "Are you—?"

"Do not, if you please," said Isobel Tinker. Her voice was weak. She would not look at him. Her gloved hands grasped the top rung of the ladder with a death grip, and she laid her forehead on her wrist. "I need a moment."

"Should I—?" Jason was at a loss for what to offer. The skin of her face was dull and grayish. She'd plaited her hair against her head in two short, spiky braids. Her body was smothered by a bulky teal cloak.

"A moment," she repeated, turning her head sideways. She sucked in a gulp of air.

"Let me hand you up," he suggested, looking around, cursing the crudeness of the brigantine. "Here, take my hand."

"I will not." She clung to the ladder.

"Perhaps the deck is not—"

"Resist the temptation to see some solution here, Your Grace. I need only fresh air." She lifted her head. "And dry land."

"Do you mean to . . ." he searched for the correct phrase, ". . . crawl out? Entirely unaided?"

"When I require assistance, you will know it. Otherwise . . ." and now she clamped her mouth shut and closed her eyes, presumably fighting a wave of discomfort, ". . . keep back."

Jason employed considerable self-constraint and watched her ascend slowly, shakily, to the deck. She had nearly hatched herself and was reaching a trembling hand for a railing when he said, "Oh for God's sake," and lifted her.

He swept one hand around her waist and another on

her outstretched arm and pulled her up. She reached for the railing that bordered the passage, and he draped her there, like a sheet on a line.

He stepped back.

"Thank you," she said, speaking to the deck.

He made a dismissive sound. "Miss Tinker, but this cannot be—"

She held up a hand, silencing him.

Jason complied. He'd been unprepared for how miserable she would be. The woolen cape concealed an Isobel-shaped body that, already diminutive, appeared to be shrinking. Her head was uncovered, and the wind plucked at her braids, whipping blond tendrils across her cheeks. She looked wretched.

"You look wretched," he said.

"I am wretched."

"I'm so sorry you're afflicted by ocean travel in this way," he said. "If I'd known—"

"If you'd known," she said, raising her head, "you would have bribed me, just the same. And I would have consented, also the same. You want . . ." a tired pause, ". . . whatever it is you want, and I want the new building."

With no warning, they were lashed with a cold wind, an icy spray of seawater pricking their skin. She raised her face into the gale and blinked, opening her eyes. She stood straighter.

"It's less than a fortnight. I will survive." She made a limp, dismissive motion.

"Are you always this stoic?"

"I am, in fact," she said. "Lucky you."

"I supposed I recognized this from the first. I would never have recruited you if you'd seemed . . . fragile."

"Lucky *me*," she mumbled, and he laughed.

But now she was on the move, her sights apparently set on the stern railing. Holding her hands out for balance, moving slowly, she began to shuffle around masts and coiled rigging to the quarter deck.

"Oy!" Jason said, and darted after her. He captured her arm, tucking it beneath his own. She did not pull away. The boat rocked and she nudged inward, allowing him to steady her. She was noticeably slighter than she'd been the last time he'd touched her. Her body beneath the cloak felt less substantial than heavy wool itself. He found her hand, small and limp, and clasped it. Again, she did not pull away.

"Are you able to take food?" he asked. "And water? Broth?"

"I've no wish to discuss food," she said. "Or my condition. Trust that I am miserable but it can be borne. I've done it many times."

"Right," he said. "Stoic silence." He guided her to the railing.

He'd wanted to ask her about what to expect when they made landfall, but obviously she was in no condition to discuss strategy.

"I wish to talk about my uncle," she said. "Sir Jeffrey Starling."

Jason glanced at her once, looked away, and then again. But perhaps her condition did not preclude *all* talk.

Another cold gust whipped across the deck, spraying them with icy water. Isobel gasped and Jason stepped up, meaning to shield her with his body.

"No." She leaned around him, eyes closed, straining to feel the fresh air on her face. "I need it."

Jason stood down, watching as she turned her face to the wind, eyes closed, relief loosening the tension in her expression.

He was still staring when she opened her eyes. She blinked, surprised by his attention.

"I'd put my uncle out of my mind," she said, turning away. "Distracted by the whirlwind of preparations. But now, on this brig, in the very rare moments when I have not been indisposed, my mind has returned again and again to my aunt and uncle."

Jason nodded. It had been a small subterfuge to approach her uncle, just like it had been a small subterfuge to invoke his aunt to entice her to Hammersmith. She would naturally be resentful of both.

"What would you like to know?" he asked.

"How long did you speak to him?"

"Oh . . . an hour? I called on him at home, so there was tea. The conversation came to more than Iceland. We're in the acquaintance of many of the same people."

"Of course you are," she said, shrugging deeper into her cloak. She did not seem angry or betrayed, more like . . . resigned.

"When we spoke of you," he said, "Sir Jeffrey's priority was discretion on your behalf. He was careful to answer only direct questions. He was effusive in praise. He referred to you as a beloved niece. He said you were like a sister to his daughters."

She smiled at this, her first nonmiserable look. She stared into the white foam of the churning waves.

After a long moment, she said, "My aunt and uncle took me in when I was at a very low and desperate point in my life. We were barely acquainted; I'd not lived in England for nearly a decade, and I'd hardly known them before. But when I wrote to them, my uncle did not hesitate. He arranged my passage and they welcomed me into their home. They nurtured me in every possible way—love certainly. But they also outfitted me with a new wardrobe. They saw that I enjoyed watercolors and built a studio in their attic. When they holidayed at the seaside, they included me. I was part of the family in every way. I lived with them for . . . for years. They questioned nothing about my past. They were so very kind."

Now she leaned back, holding the railing with both hands, arms straight. She stared at the spot where the sky unrolled behind the sea.

Jason was transfixed. Of all the things he needed to learn from her—about the pirates and the locals and the Icelandic terrain—*this* was what he'd actually longed for. Her life. She spoke calmly but her voice was steeped in gravity. She was warming to the topic. Familiar impatience crept up the backs of his arms, tickling his shoulders and neck. His fingers twitched.

And then? he wanted to prompt.

Tell me. Tell me who you truly are.

But of course she should not be rushed. He took a coin from his pocket and rubbed the ridged insignia between his fingers. After two beats, he flipped it in the air.

Casually, he asked, "Sir Jeffrey is . . . your mother's brother?"

She chuckled and shook her head. "Sir Jeffrey is no blood relation to me at all. I am his wife's niece. My aunt Bonnie. *She* was my father's sister."

"But Bonnie Starling is sister to the late Earl of Cranford," said Jason.

She turned her head and raised an eyebrow, an expression of *And so she is.*

"Your father was the Earl of Cranford?" Jason nearly shouted. "But your mother—"

And now he trailed off. He gave the coin another flip. *Ah. So that's it.*

Isobel turned away, staring again at the sunset.

Jason's brain churned like the waves. So Isobel Tinker's mother, renowned stage actress Georgiana Tinker, had had an affair with the Earl of Cranford. Isobel was the earl's illegitimate daughter.

Jason hadn't asked about Isobel's parentage because it hadn't seemed relevant. Her mother was an actress— this he knew. Isobel provided for her own living. She'd mentioned no brothers or guardian. The specifics of a father hadn't come up.

"But were you acquainted with your father, the earl?" Jason asked. "Before he died?"

"I was," she said simply. "When I was young. We saw him quite a lot until . . . well, until we didn't. My mother and he had a falling-out. Not long after, she and I left England. She packed up the two of us and we sailed for France."

"During wartime?" Jason asked the question, but his brain was hung up on the fact that she was the daughter of one of the wealthiest and most revered aristocrats in England. And she toiled away in a Mayfair travel shop.

Isobel was shaking her head. "It was '99? So the war had not begun, but we remained in Europe, even after the fighting started. Officers and parliaments need a night out, don't they? My mother lent her considerable talents to stages all over Europe. She was highly sought after and never wanted for work. It was . . . it was an irregular youth, to say the least, but it prepared me for the work I do at Everland Travel."

"You never had a desire to perform?" he asked. He

didn't see Isobel as an actress; she was too sensible. It took too much effort to get her talking.

"Acting is my mother's calling," she said. "Before I went to live with my aunt and uncle, I'd given very little thought to my future whatsoever. Even when I was a guest of the Starlings—even when I *knew* I couldn't remain with them forever—I'd not thought of my future. I was too occupied recovering from my past. Lack of planning is yet another reckless oversight of my youth."

Why not plan to marry? Jason's first thought. But then he remembered Drummond Hooke and his doomsday proposal. Who was she meant to marry? Her speech and manners were impeccable, and she was educated and well traveled. No common man—say, the butcher's son or a sailor or miner—would suit her. Meanwhile a gentleman would . . .

He glanced at her, and her expression said, *And now we can all acknowledge that I am a bastard daughter of an earl.*

Jason frowned, indignant and frustrated on her behalf, but also frustrated with himself. It was thoughtless of him to compel her to spell it out.

"What?" she asked.

"Planning for one's future," he mused, the first, most innocuous thing that popped into his brain. "I, myself, have not managed this for shite."

She narrowed her eyes. "One does not simply wake up and find himself working for the Foreign Office, Your Grace."

"One does," he countered. "Or rather, I did. For better or for worse. And then I became duke almost the same way. Although more relatives had to die for the second bit."

Jason picked up his hat and reseated it over his eyes.

He hadn't wanted to talk about himself, and especially not the bloody dukedom, but he could have embarrassed her by raising the topic of her parentage. He'd say anything to salvage the conversation.

"You're waiting for me to ask?" she said.

"Hmm?" He flipped the coin again.

"How does one awaken in the Foreign Service?" she prompted.

"Oh, that." He caught the coin and said, "It's a boring story, really."

"Do I detect a deep aversion to the notion of *boredom,* Northumberland?"

"Ah, I do not manage well with idleness," he remarked, "if that's what you mean."

"And that is why you dread being duke?"

"That is why I dread being *idle.* Which is the very embodiment of being duke. So yes, that is why. Well, that is one reason."

The words came out more bitterly than he intended. Surely now they were even. He'd spelled out her dubious parentage in ungentlemanly detail, and she'd identified his gnawing impatience. Now they could move on.

"Tell me how you were recruited," she said.

Or perhaps they would not move on.

He tossed the coin again and let out a sigh. He glanced at her. She was so pretty, even wind-whipped and seasick and huddled in a cloak. It was her eyes. Curious, alight with intelligence. They were the opposite of idle, and he need only glance at her to feel the opposite of bored.

"Fine," he sighed. "It was Spain. The Royal Army. I was captain at the time. My company was part of a regiment facing down French troops near Salamanca.

We were in a stalemate because the French had positioned themselves around a working orphanage, and my colonel refused to engage with children in jeopardy."

"I'm glad to hear it," she proclaimed, instantly enthralled. Jason felt a surge of gratification at her rapt attention but tried to ignore it. He'd been a soldier and spy too long to bask in the admiration of a pretty girl.

"We were correct to stand down obviously," he said. "But after three days and nights of crouching in a sodden field, I was losing my mind."

"The idleness," Isobel surmised.

Jason shrugged. "I took it upon myself to, er, approach the French colonel and ask him to kindly distance himself from the children so we could have a proper fight or move on. I made this request without asking my own command. Oh and I recruited nuns from a nearby church as sort of . . . humanitarian shields to wade into the enemy camp with me."

She laughed. "I can only imagine the nuns' resistance to a handsome officer enlisting them to protect orphans."

"The holy sisters? Very cooperative. Every soldier should enjoy such courageous comrades in arms. The nuns and I snuck into the camp at dawn. It wasn't an infiltration so much as a very stealthy and unexpected social call."

"No one endeavored to shoot you? You weren't taken captive?"

"I've a way with people," Jason commented, flicking his coin.

"I've seen your way," she said.

You've seen nothing yet, he thought, but he said, "I began talking, an aide translated, the sisters joined in, chanting prayers. We overwhelmed the man, honestly. He'd not yet had coffee."

"But what did you propose?"

Jason took off his hat, scratched his head, and then reseated it. "We suggested it was 'unsporting' to employ orphans as a strategic cover, and surely this was not what Napoleon intended. We proposed the nuns be allowed to evacuate the children."

"And he agreed," guessed Isobel.

Jason shrugged. "The conversation never progressed so far. I'd positioned my company at the farthest corner of what would have been the field of battle and instructed them to ever so slightly *antagonize* any French soldiers within earshot. A skirmish ensued, confusion and panic began to seize the camp. The officers became suspicious, and the colonel's attention was divided. He ordered me taken prisoner but I'd manage to, er, vanish—"

"Of course you did."

"The nuns sprang into action, wielding their crosses aloft and ferrying the children to safety."

"You left the nuns to evacuate the children on their own?"

"Well, perhaps *vanish* is too strong of a word for what I'd done." He flipped the coin again, very high, so high they both tipped their heads to watch it rise and fall.

"The next bit," he ventured, "is almost too boring to relate." Another coin flip.

"Oh yes, heroics are ever so boring. But can you tell me how this led to the Foreign Office?"

"When the dust settled—we won the ensuing battle by the way—I was approached by our colonel, and then our general, and then Whitehall came calling." Another flip. "And there you have it. I began the day as a captain and awakened . . . oh, about a month later . . . as a foreign agent."

"There is more to it," she guessed.

"Perhaps a bit. The point is, I joined the army because life in Middlesex was tedious—maddening, really—and because the military is a natural path for the third son of a duke. I gave it no more thought than that. I joined the Foreign Service because someone asked me; also with very little thought. And someone asked me because they felt my rashness could be harnessed for the greater good."

She laughed again and he allowed himself to bask in the glow of it. He'd hardly been gunning for a laugh, but when had he ever discouraged the delight of a pretty girl? He'd been in the business of delighting girls for longer than he'd been in the business of rash behavior.

"And that, Miss Tinker, is how the leopard got his spots," he concluded, snatching the coin from the air. "Perhaps we both fly by the seat of our pants. Or we have done. At one time or the other."

Her laughter died down and her expression turned speculative. "Perhaps," she said. "I . . . I actually fell into working as a travel agent after I'd given up on flying. It was during my time at the Starlings'."

"Is that so?" Jason's heart thudded heavily. It was one thing to impress her, but *this* was what he really wanted to hear. He flipped his coin and waited.

She nodded. "But it was not overnight. Or even in a month."

Jason nodded and said nothing. He would wait—he could wait. Admittedly, Isobel Tinker made waiting less painful. With Isobel Tinker, it was exciting even to *wait.*

"The Starlings," she explained, "have four very charming but very demanding daughters—my cousins."

"Oh yes, I saw two or three of them when I called."

She nodded and smiled wistfully. "They are dear girls. And they were a balm to me when I came to live with them. It would be impossible to overstate how rattled and . . . and miserable I was when I joined their household. Most respectable families would have worried about my influence on young, impressionable girls, but Sir Jeffrey and Aunt Bonnie did not restrict my relationship with any of them. To the girls I was exotic, and grown up, and I'm sure I had a vague sort of . . . 'fallenness' to them. But my aunt seated me among them at dinner every night."

Fallenness? What the devil did that mean? Nothing pleasant obviously. Also, nothing consistent with what Jason knew of her. The Isobel Tinker he knew seemed regimented and resilient, not fallen.

She went on. "When I'd lived in the Starlings' London townhome for half a year, their oldest daughter, Jane, was invited to accompany an elderly aunt on a holiday to Paris. Jane was . . . oh, sixteen at the time? Barely out in society. Her parents would not allow her to go, but Jane refused to accept their decision. She begged and begged. For weeks, it was all we heard, unrelenting.

"Finally, simply to validate her, I asked Jane to show me the details of this forbidden holiday so I could, perhaps, explain why her parents—who were generally rather progressive and open-minded—wouldn't agree. I'd spent several summers in Paris and had traveled through France many times.

"Well, her parents had been correct to disallow it. I was appalled when I read the proposed itinerary. The hotels were located in dodgy parts of the city; the schedule and tours were illogical. The porter who was meant to look after them and their belongings had no references or experience. Someone's brother-in-law would collect them in a wagon in La Havre and deposit them at a coaching inn outside Paris. It would have been a debacle. When I began to explain all the reasons why, Jane begged me to suggest how I might restyle the holiday in such a way that her parents would allow it.

"At first, I said no. I was so incredibly indebted to my aunt and uncle I could not undermine their attempts to keep Jane at home. But the girl was relentless, and finally I drew up a brief Paris itinerary—how I would see the city if I was a young woman in France for the first time, a journey I had actually taken when I was about her age. I'd kept my journals and old letters and used them as references. With little effort, I outlined hotels where she might safely lodge, museums and cathedrals that they might see *if* they were in the company of a knowledgeable, trusted porter, and the modes of transport they might hire. It was meant only to be an aspirational, 'in theory' sort of plan.

"But when I showed it to Jane, she whisked it away—first to the elderly aunt and then to her parents, begging them to reconsider the journey. She said they would travel exactly as I had described it. By some very great miracle, Uncle Jeffrey said . . . 'Probably.'

"And that was the very first holiday ever commissioned," she finished. She took a deep breath of cold sea air.

"So you sorted it all and squired the girl around Paris?" Jason asked.

Isobel shook her head violently. "Oh no. I'd vowed not to leave England again, and I meant it. You—well, the promise of your building—has been my only motivation to leave England in seven years.

"I spent weeks researching," she explained, "writing letters, making reservations, calling around London to old friends from the Continent. I planned every mile of the holiday from the moment the family carriage dropped them in Portsmouth until it collected them at the same spot a month later. I talked an old friend into traveling with them. We styled her as a 'travel porter'—a sort of guide and chaperone, which is an amenity all of my holidays include to this day. They followed my itinerary, employed the travel porter's savviness and ability to improvise, and used the old aunt's money. *I* remained in London. In fact, I think I passed the entire month in my bedroom, pacing back and forth, praying for their safe return."

Jason was transfixed. "And did they?"

Isobel smiled at the horizon. "They did, thank God. And they had the time of their lives. Jane could speak of nothing else. For weeks. Soon her sisters and friends wanted their own Paris holidays. After that, they wanted to see Rome. Hamburg. My life as a travel agent was born. Eventually, demand grew beyond what I could sustain. I was working from a tiny desk in my bedroom at the Starlings'. My uncle connected me with the Hookes and their Everland Travel shop—this was when Mr. and Mrs. Hooke were still alive. I was hired on and given this lovely purpose in life. And a way to support myself. By then, I was ready. Mostly healed and eager to be on my own. Since then, I've launched old women, young women, friends, sisters, generations of females, on adventures throughout Europe."

"Remarkable," he whispered, and he meant it. "But

you've no wish to travel yourself?" He flicked the coin into the air and caught it.

Isobel was silent for a moment, staring at the damp leather of her gloves. Finally, she shook her head. It was hardly a proclamation, but she appeared very earnest. She looked as if she wanted very much for it to be true. She looked as if she *needed* it to be true.

She said, "I've traveled. Now I want only to stay back. To be safe. To . . ." she shook her head, ". . . keep out of trouble."

"Does this mission qualify as trouble in your view, Miss Tinker?" he asked, his voice just above the sound of the waves.

She laughed without humor. "Of course it is trouble. Pirates. Smugglers. Dashing foreign agents."

"But we are doing good work, you and I. Noble and honorable work. Someone has to sort out this situation before lives are lost or—"

"Yes, yes," she cut in, "before England is at war with Iceland." She cocked her head and gave him a look. "Highly unlikely, don't you think?"

He opened his mouth to challenge her, but she forged ahead. "Look, it may be good work, but it's hardly 'honorable' for an unmarried woman to travel alone with a—with you."

She looked away. Jason longed to catch her chin and turn her face back.

"You would not have asked," she swallowed, "a *respectable* lady to drop everything and serve as your translator on this journey."

"Not translator," he said softly. "Attaché. And I don't see it as dishonorable. Not in the slightest."

"Come now. Sailing away with you would ruin my

reputation, if I had a reputation to ruin." She looked up at him. "But I don't, do I? And we both know it."

"I've given no thought to your reputation, Miss Tinker," he said. The words were out before he'd examined them for the truth.

Had he thought of it?

"My parents were never married," she stated. "I spent my youth mostly unsupervised, flouncing around Europe with other unsupervised girls and truly laddish boys. The result of this was exactly what one might expect, and I survived only by the skin of my teeth. And because of my uncle and aunt.

"Which," she finished, "brings me back to the reason I asked about Sir Jeffrey. Their compassion may well have saved my life, and I promised myself to repay their kindness by being the most well-behaved, respectable niece in Britain. To be a source of pride and goodwill and no disgrace."

"Your uncle is so proud," Jason said. "It's very clear."

"My uncle would not consider sailing to Iceland in your company to tangle with pirates to be a source of pride, Your Grace. And neither do I."

"Ah . . ." he said.

"I'll not lie about it to them, of course," she said. "Obviously they will learn of the new building and my relocation to Hammersmith. But I would rather . . . mention it in hindsight. Months from now. If and when we all return unscathed."

Now she turned her back to the ocean and flopped against the railing. She looked to him. "My point is, I absolutely must return from all of this business entirely *unscathed*."

She paused. Jason realized it was his turn to speak.

"Don't give it a second thought," he said, flicking his coin.

She laughed.

"No, really," he went on. "I've convened the very best in hired muscle, and I, myself, am very handy in a fight. You needn't worr—"

"I do not mean *physically imperiled*, Northumberland. I can take care of myself when it comes to pirates."

"So you mean . . ."

"I *mean*," she said, "I've a job and a reputation and a surrogate family. They all depend on how I conduct myself. And with whom. In Mayfair, my conduct was easy to maintain. On a brig, cutting across the North Sea with you, the challenge is greater. My aunt and uncle will be well aware of this. *Any person* who understands the notion of 'unchaperoned travel' will be aware of this. *That* is what I mean by unscathed."

"Do you feel . . . unsafe, Miss Tinker?" Jason asked, tossing the coin. It was a stupid question, but he meant to buy himself time. Of course he'd not thought of this.

"It makes no difference whether I feel safe, as you well know," she said. "What care have people for my safety when they can speculate about my purity instead. My clients value my *respectability*. My character and choices must be above reproach. My aunt and uncle want me safe, of course, but they also want a life for me with no closed doors. *I* want this life."

Jason was nodding his head. "I understand how maidenly virtue works. I simply hadn't focused on it."

"No, you wouldn't have. No one expects a bachelor duke to be virtuous."

"Well, I don't expect *you* to be virtuous." The truth, he realized.

She laughed. "No, you wouldn't expect that either."

No, no, no, he thought. "What I mean is—"

"You don't have to explain. You would never have approached my cousin Jane for this mission, even though Jane is intrepid and eager for adventure. And why? Because she is the daughter of an MP and the granddaughter of an earl. She's unmarried and she lives at home with her parents. This 'mission' would be unheard of for her, as well it should be.

"But me?" she went on. "A girl in a shop? With 'a file' in the Foreign Office and no known father? You didn't hesitate; in fact, you hounded me—"

"I didn't hound—"

"You *lured* me to Hammersmith under false pretenses and then bribed me with property."

"Also there was no lure—"

"Make no mistake," she cut in again. "I don't say this to accuse you. I know which way the wind blows for girls like me. This is merely a reminder. There are many ways to be 'scathed.' And just because I am an actress's daughter who *works* for a living, I shouldn't be—"

"Stop," exclaimed Jason.

". . . shouldn't be—"

He pulled off his hat and pressed it against her face, obscuring her from the forehead to chin.

"*Pause*," he said. "Please."

Isobel, her face now covered by his hat, raised a gloved hand and pressed the hat halfway down with two gloved fingers. Her blue eyes peeked out over the brim.

"A small benefit of being duke is the privilege of finishing a sentence," he said. "On rare occasion. Or so I've been told."

He pulled the hat away and she interjected with, "What I meant to say—"

He extended the hat again, covering her lips. Again, only her eyes were revealed. Unless he was mistaken, they twinkled with amusement.

"Miss Tinker," he began. "I do not see you as the daughter of an actress or a girl in a shop. I see you as a resource. From the beginning, your noted qualities were independence, intelligence, and a sort of . . . oh, let's just call it 'lack of fuss.' "

If he also saw pretty, exciting, and incendiary, he elected not to mention these. Yet.

He continued. "Call me selfish, but your reputation or impressionable sensibilities, whatever they may be, did not figure in. If *Cousin Jane Starling* had a history in Iceland, spoke the language, and had knowledge of the miscreants who now hold my cousin hostage, I would have recruited her instead—and it would not have mattered about her father or grandfather. Any of my superiors will readily attest that I've never had patience for what is 'appropriate.' It is one of the many qualities that made me an effective spy and will, no doubt, make me a terrible duke.

"As for your respectability, I *offered* to provide a companion or maid—I urged you to include your girl, Samantha Smee, for this journey. You refused. Fine, I don't care, one fewer person with whom to bother. But please don't accuse me of targeting you because you somehow view yourself as . . . as *an easy mark*. If you must know, all women are easy marks for me, and I don't distinguish. I would never split hairs over how pure they may or may not be. But also, I'm no predator. Make no mistake. *Women* come to *me*."

Now she laughed, as he'd hoped she would.

He shot her a grin and shoved his hat back on his head. "Release yourself," he finished, "from worry about being 'scathed'—not by our proximity or this mission. If anything inappropriate happens, it will be by *your* hand."

He leaned his hip against the rail. "But thank you for reviewing the reasons you are to be held suspect in this area. One can only hope there is more dubious behavior to discover. I'm beginning to feel it is *my* virtue we should be worried about. Not yours."

She was shaking her head. "You're ridiculous."

He *was* a little ridiculous, but Jason wouldn't be accused of preying on her or her alleged murky reputation. What care had he for anyone's reputation? None.

"No one bothers with the virtue of a handsome bachelor duke," she informed him. "You're *expected* to be indiscreet—which is why I raised the topic in the first place."

"Handsome, am I?" he asked. "Seems to be the second time you've mentioned this. Perhaps the seduction has already begun. Compliments are a known enticement. I can feel myself softening to you already."

She let out a frustrated gasp. "If I intended to *entice* you, Your Grace, the last thing you would feel was *soft*."

Jason laughed, a loud, delighted bark into the wind. Isobel smiled too. He saw her moment of triumph before her face tightened with indignation.

"But we've already kissed," she said. She exhaled in defeat. "You kissed me."

He crossed his arms over his chest. "Did I?"

"You know this." Her pale cheeks were turning red.

"Yes, I suppose I did. But it was done in service to this delicate reputation of yours. To evade the night watchman. If I'd been recruiting your cousin Jane, I would have kissed her too."

Isobel seemed to think about this, a frown tugging at the corners of her mouth. Perhaps she didn't fancy him kissing her cousin Jane Starling.

Not that it mattered. Jason saw only her. In his mind's eye. In his memory. In his dreams. Now. He hadn't lied when he said he wasn't a predator. But that did not mean he did not *want*.

He watched Isobel shake her head in the manner of someone dislodging a bad thought. The motion loosened her cloak, and the heavy wool fell open. Her neck and collarbone were bare. She tapped two gloved fingers at the base of her throat.

Jason tried not to look, failed miserably, and watched her fingertips. What did she wear beneath the cloak? How much weight had she lost to seasickness?

He felt sweat on the back of his neck. The late-summer air was just above freezing and it was colder still in the wind, and he was sweating. Jason didn't *sweat* because of women—not on the deck of a freezing brig or anywhere else for that matter.

He was just about to tell her again not to worry, but a wave rocked the brig, tipping the vessel nearly forty-five degrees. Rigging clanged and swung, wood creaked. With no warning, Jason and Isobel were pitched sideways. He lashed out his right arm to catch the railing just as Isobel lost her footing. He caught her at the waist with his left hand and dragged her against him.

"Careful," he shouted over the sound of crashing waves. "I have you. Hold on."

She froze against him for a long, sideways moment. The brig rode the swell of a wave. Jason held to the railing with one hand and to Isobel with the other. At the highest point, the angle of the deck was nearly put to rights. The ship seemed to hover in the mist. Then it dropped, slamming downward with bone-cracking force.

Isobel let out a little moan, breathing against his chest. Jason cinched his arm around her and she burrowed deeper, wrapping her arms around him and nosing inside the open flap of his coat.

"I have you," he repeated into her hair, straining to hold on to the rail.

She made a nodding motion against his chest and mumbled something indistinguishable.

"What?" he shouted.

She plied her head off of his chest and peeked up. "My cabin," she said, her voice cracking. "I need my cabin."

"Yes, of course," he said. "I'll take you. Will you allow me?"

She nodded again and ducked her head against him, pressing so tightly he almost lost his footing. He shifted, finding a more secure hold, and began the careful, unsteady journey from quarter deck to forecastle hatch.

Isobel tripped along with him, shifting a little with every step, making their progress easier. She fitted her tiny body more securely to the hollows and dips of his. With every step, she burrowed closer.

It occurred to him that dragging her across the slippery deck of a bobbing ship felt like the most correct, natural thing in the world. A small, bright spark flashed in his chest, the flick of flint against stone. A beckoning. He put one boot in front of the other, following the spark.

Chapter Ten

Isobel told herself that her sunset rendezvous with the duke had been a known—nay, a *planned* encounter. She'd pursued the conversation to be perfectly clear. The duke's intentions must be honorable. Her intentions must be prudent and with an eye toward her future. They spoke to be reminded that no respectable person would approve of their circumstances.

If, in that encounter, she'd revealed *too much*; if she'd (God help her) clung to his muscled body with too much enthusiasm—well.

Not every planned thing went off perfectly.

She'd not failed at making her point.

And rough seas could not be helped.

As to her unknown wish to share the details of her life with him?

It all just sort of spilled out, didn't it?

And so now he knew.

Rather than punish herself, Isobel embraced mindless seasickness instead. For the next day and night, she lay on the cool floor of her cabin, riding the waves of nausea and the heavy hand of skewed balance.

When, finally, she felt well enough to drag herself again on deck, she vowed to do better. If the duke was there—and perhaps he would not be—she would exchange pleasantries and one or two facts about Iceland, but *nothing more*.

"She lives," called a familiar voice when she finally made it down the corridor and up the ladder that led to the deck.

The sound of his voice sent a twinkling shimmer through her, like a chime that had been softly tapped with a mallet.

She frowned. She'd spent the last thirty-two hours barely able to rise from the floorboards and now she *shimmered*?

Isobel ignored it and concentrated on climbing steadily from the hatch, finding her balance, and putting her face to the wind. The great, roaring whoosh, even before she felt the gust, was a relief. When the cold slap hit her with salt and sea spray, she sucked in her first restorative breath.

"I tried several times to look in on you," Northumberland called behind her. "I listened outside your door. All I heard were a few muffled thumps. The steward assured me that he'd seen signs of life, so I left you to it. You're . . . better, I hope?"

"I am the same," she said, squinting to adjust her eyes to the light. The sun was setting, but the sky at dusk was brighter than her candlelit cabin. It was a balm to see natural light and breathe fresh air.

The railing at the stern was yards from the hatch, but she reached it without assistance. The smooth wood was cool and solid. She clasped it with both hands, breathing hard from exertion.

"If you're trying to make me feel guilty," he said, coming up beside her, "it's working."

"No effort is required to make you feel guilty," she said. "You *are* guilty."

"Ah yes, that's right. Guilty of—?"

"Dragging an afflicted woman across a roiling ocean to . . . entertain your itch for adventure."

The duke thought about this and nodded slightly to the open sea. "Another reference to this mission as *less than essential*? Come now, Miss Tinker, be honest, what do you really think?"

"I think I've fallen into ownership of a beautiful brick building, all my own, with an adorable flat above it and an opportunity to exponentially improve my life. Beyond that, it doesn't really matter, does it?"

"What of my cousin and the other men from Lincolnshire? You care so little about them?"

"I've no doubt that your cousin and his friends are rather uncomfortable at the moment. How lucky for the both of you that this rescue delivers them *and* postpones your ascension to duke."

"You think this mission is a diversion for me," he accused.

"I think perhaps becoming a duke will be no diversion at all—for you."

Northumberland chuckled and shook his head, but he did not argue. They turned their faces to the wind, watching the sky turn from pale blue to indigo, with streaks of apricot and cream. It was a breathtaking canvas.

"Good God, what a view," he said, exhaling.

Isobel squinted into the mist. It was undeniably beautiful, and the heavens would only become more vivid and otherworldly the farther north they sailed. The strange colors and mystic light would take his breath away.

Isobel could acknowledge the beauty but it flooded her with painful memories instead of awe. Seven years ago, the strange, spectral sky had made her homesick and she hadn't even had a home to pine for—not really.

Suddenly, her eyes were wet with tears. Isobel sniffed, blinking them away, praying the duke would not see. She fidgeted, fingering the braids in her hair. She'd endeavored to wash and braid it before it was fully dry, and now the plaits stuck to her head like a cap. When she'd caught her reflection in the small mirror in her cabin, she'd barely recognized herself. Gaunt face, dull hair, grayish pallor. Had she really presumed the duke would . . . would . . . desire her? First seasickness and now crying?

"Is the air not . . . helping tonight, Miss Tinker?" he asked gently.

"I'm alright," she said, clearing her throat, swiping a hand beneath her eyes.

"I'm so very sorry that you're ill. I wish I'd comprehended how uncomfortable you would be. No matter what you say, I could have made some precautions."

"There is no precaution," she said, "save dry land. There's never been anything for it. Have you never suffered from seasickness?"

He shook his head. "I cannot say that I have."

"Oh, well, you wouldn't understand. But what about panic from a confined, airless place?"

"No. Not that I recall."

"Are you bothered by the cold?"

"No."

"What about heat?"

"No."

"Do you suffer from allergic reactions? To nuts, perhaps? Or goose-down bedding?"

"No."

"Does saltwater sting your eyes? Do you suffer night terrors in your sleep? Are you uneasy at great heights?"

"No, no, and I actually enjoy great heights."

"Right. You are invincible obviously."

He did not argue, and she laughed. "Is that possible, Your Grace?"

"Well. I have a strong aversion to becoming duke. Does this count? You have so kindly pointed this out."

"Oh right—*that*. And what is the source of this aversion, do you think?"

He looked out at the horizon and frowned. "I don't want to talk about the bloody dukedom."

Isobel found herself disappointed by this answer. She'd wanted to know. She was also a little surprised. In her experience, men of rank needed to be reminded of their greatness at regular intervals, even if only by their own boasting. Northumberland wanted to ignore the dukedom rather than crow about it.

"Do you not enjoy Middlesex?" she pressed.

He shrugged. "Middlesex is adequate. For a time."

"For how *long* do you find Middlesex 'adequate,' I wonder."

"Twelve hours?" he speculated. "Eighteen?"

"That long?"

"It's not the location of Middlesex, it's—" He shook his head and looked away.

Isobel was frustrated. "It's—?" she prompted.

He shook his head again.

A polite woman would not press, she thought. Moreover, a woman who had no real interest or attachment to this man would not press.

A self-preserving woman *would not press*.

"It's your family, then?" she pressed.

Now he gave his head a violent shake. "Not that," he insisted darkly. "Never that. I love my family. My mother and three sisters are the finest a man could hope for. I do not deserve them. And the tenants are decent, hardworking people. They—" He dug in his pocket for a coin. Instead of flipping it, he held it out, studying it from a distance. Speaking to the coin, he said bitterly, "They also deserve better than the likes of me."

"I don't understand," she proclaimed. She'd asked too much to feign polite disinterest now.

"That makes two of us, Miss Tinker," he said. He palmed the coin and leaned against the railing. "I don't understand why but I dread it. And I despise myself for it. But there is no dark secret here. No hidden pain. No great sin. I am simply suffocated by the sedentary life of a country nobleman. Walking around in the footsteps of my father and brothers causes my skin to crawl and my heart to race. I feel caged behind the desk in the duke's library. I lapse into a numb sort of trance when I ride the property. I am bored by the ledgers, apathetic about the farmland, and fall asleep when subjected to the neighbors. There are too many servants, too many portraits of dead relatives, too much sitting about, and too many doors that lead to empty rooms."

He turned back to the water. "If you believe these reactions to be spoiled and indulgent and petulant you would be precisely, exactly correct. My pitiful attitude is almost worse than the numbness and boredom and suffocation. Almost."

"Oh," said Isobel, "I see." Although she was not certain she did see. His pain and bitterness were real; he was clearly tortured by his future, but—

He took a deep breath and exhaled it slowly, a man

facing a terrible reckoning. "Perhaps it's the thought of remaining there forever," he said. "And ever."

"You needn't remain at Syon Hall if it doesn't suit you," she offered. "The city is awash with noblemen who prefer their London residences."

The duke shook his head. "My father traveled to London for parliamentary business—no farther. My brothers traveled even less. The estate, when run properly, is demanding. The dukes of Northumberland have prided themselves on being present for the land and the tenants. It is the responsible way to manage the great bounty into which we were born. A good and worthy duke knows every family in his purview and every mile of his land. Doubtless, my father knew every bloody sheep. There is also a great foundry on the property. The mechanics of this and the safety must be monitored constantly. The whole lot is like a watched cauldron that must be kept forever at a low simmer. Never to boil over, never to go cold. Are you aware of the patience and care required to maintain a constant, relentless *simmer*, Miss Tinker?"

"No," she said, her traitorous heart bending toward him.

"It is as unending as it is tedious. When I resign myself to it, likely I will never leave Middlesex again."

A thought occurred to Isobel. Perhaps she'd seen this before, and wouldn't that be ironic. Was she being taken in by a second man who preferred skittering around the world to settling down? Before she could stop herself, she said, "You're afraid to grow up."

"On the contrary," he said flatly, "the work I've done for the Foreign Office has hardly been child's play. Representing the Crown in foreign courts, keeping and trading national secrets, saving British lives—it was not the work of a boy. And I was good at it. In contrast, I'll be rubbish at calculating the price of wool or the date of the last frost. And I'll die if I'm forced to sit behind a desk."

"You will not *die*," she said, a reflex, and she could tell by his bitter expression that it was the wrong thing to say. She scrambled to add, "You will have a family—a duchess and children to sustain you and give you purpose."

Another bitter look. Isobel puzzled over this. She could understand not wanting a provincial life of a country squire, but Northumberland did not seem like a loner or even a rakehell. It was not a stretch to envision him with a wife and children. She looked closer, watching his expression—and then it occurred to her.

"They've a wife picked out for you already," she guessed. She felt a sharp jab, like a knife digging into her side. "Your mother and sisters have already chosen someone."

It doesn't matter, she told herself. *It doesn't matter, it doesn't matter, and you knew this. You've known this all along.*

He shook his head. "A wife is a priority to my mother, but she knows I do not respond well to being 'managed.' "

Isobel was swamped with relief. There was no reason for it; she had no right to care. Even so. *Relief.* She took hold of the railing to steady herself.

"I didn't mean to distress you," she said. "It's none of my business and clearly you take your responsibility very seriously. Forgive me for prying."

"I am not distressed by you," he said.

She *had* distressed him, and she regretted how far

she'd pushed. She scrambled to turn the conversation around. "Will you . . . tell me something you relish about being a spy?" she asked.

He looked up. "What do you want to know?"

"Tell me . . . about your favorite mission."

"Favorite?"

"Why not? I've made you say what you don't wish. Regale me with a tale of glory."

"I've never thought of my work in these terms. My favorite jam, however, is raspberry. Undoubtedly."

"So very clever," she tsked. "You know what I mean. I'd be shocked if you did not, in fact, have a favorite."

"Favorite . . ." he mused, looking at the sky. She followed his gaze, watching bright stars wink to life in a cloudless sky. He flipped his coin in the air and caught it. "Do you mean most successful? Most impactful? Most fun?"

"How about the one that is the most opposite of what your life will be like as a duke."

"Ah. Yes. Well, that would probably be the time I escaped from a Spanish dungeon."

"No," she marveled.

"Yes." He flipped the coin and caught it.

"And how did you manage this?"

"Timing, I suppose. Observation. Some convincing French, an academic pursuit that I resented until the moment the words came out of my mouth."

"That is the most insufficient answer I've ever heard," she said. "Unacceptable and you know it. After you've spent weeks pumping me for every detail of my entire life."

"I'm not sure 'pumping you' is an accurate description of what I've done, although . . ." He raised an eyebrow.

Isobel swallowed. "Tell me what happened. I am a sick woman."

"If I tell you, can we talk about this mission?"

"Yes. But I was always going to tell you what I can."

"Doling it out when we need it, are you? I can respect that."

"Has anyone ever suggested that you are too—"

"Handsome? Cunning? Strong?"

"I was going to say 'cavalier.'" There was laughter in her voice. It was becoming more and more difficult to hide it.

"If that is what you think, perhaps a different story would better represent how very rigid and exacting I am."

"No, no—Spanish dungeon," she insisted. "Out with it."

"Alright, escape from the dungeon. So, this would be Spain. Again."

He glanced at her and she nodded.

"It was 1811," he added. "You would have been a child."

"I would have been one and twenty," she corrected. Before she could stop herself, she asked, "And how old were you?"

"Well, older than one and twenty obviously."

"Obviously."

"Probably—seven and twenty? I was already working for the Foreign Office by this time. I'd been reassigned to Spain to spy on a wealthy merchant who was believed to be secretly provisioning French troops with food and weapons.

"In my role as foreign agent, my duty was to the mission. I wasn't in the Peninsula to be a solider. But I'd followed a lead to Ciudad Rodrigo and was quartering with British troops because one of the officers was a friend from school. When a skirmish broke out—the conflict that would come to be known as the Battle of Albuera—I was . . . at the right place at the right time."

"Meaning you joined the fray?"

"Ah, that is one way to put it. The end result was, I was ultimately captured as a prisoner of war and locked in a seventeenth-century dungeon with about fifty other British troops."

"No," she whispered, captivated. She turned to face him, leaning an elbow on the railing.

He nodded. "Putrid, crumbling Spanish dungeons are a rung above dying on the battlefield, but only barely. The torch smoke alone nearly killed us. There was no water or food. Even the vermin were sick, and the catacombs were crawling with rats. None of us would survive captivity if we did not escape."

"And you . . ." she guessed, "trained the rats to steal the keys to your cell?"

"No. I lay in wait for the lone, sleepy guard to look in on us in the middle of the night. Then I knocked him unconscious with a rock."

"Of course you did. And then you stole the keys?"

He shook his head. "No, the man was not in possession of the keys. There was only one set, and these remained well above dungeon level. So we undressed the guard through the bars of the cell. I then put on his uniform, and we dragged him to the farthest corner."

"But he was still on the outside of your cell?"

"Everything was done through the cell bars. I told each prisoner to remove a nonregimental article of clothing—something dirty and forgettable, like a sock—and we arranged them over him in a heap. When we had obscured his body and I was wearing his uniform, we lay in wait.

"Eventually they sent a second guard to determine what had become of the first. I was ready, and before his eyes adjusted to the gloom, I *pretended* to be the first guard, now captured by the prisoners. I shouted for help, claiming I'd been overpowered and locked in the cell with the British soldiers. I ranted in hysterical French; I shrank away from the raucous mob of prisoners in the cell, all of whom clambered to tear me limb from limb. In panicked diatribe, I ordered the second guard to fetch the keys and release me at once."

"But how could this work?" she laughed. "Did the second guard not recognize you? Did it not occur to him that locked prisoners have no way to pull a guard inside their cell?"

He shook his head. "The guard staff were a hastily convened mix of Italians and Frenchmen. I'd been careful to obscure my face and pretended to fight off fellow prisoners as I ranted. And all those years of detested French lessons served me remarkably well. It's amazing what you can pull off with a faux prison riot percolating behind you. The second guard didn't consider the implausibility of it. He allowed the shock and fear to carry him away. He rushed to get the keys and returned with reinforcements, but we were ready. There were more than fifty of us, and the moment they unlocked the door to recover me, we overpowered them.

"Our motivation to escape was greater than their will to fight us to the death. We dispatched them, but we did it very *quietly*. This allowed us to creep up, to surround and subdue other guards along the way.

"When, finally, we reached the outside, I led the men to a cache of provisions that I'd discovered in pursuit of the merchant traitor. We ate and drank and stole as much as we could, and then we set fire to the rest."

"Oh lovely," she said, smiling at him. "An escape and sabotage. All in one night."

"It was a rather efficient use of our time, considering we started the evening as prisoners. They were brave lads." He paused for a moment, smiling a small, sad smile. "They carried out my plan to the letter. The ruse was one half prison uprising, the other half stealth. And we lived to tell the tale. There's a man on this mission, Declan Shaw, who was with me that night. Intuitive fighter, deuced good friend."

He shook his head, turning again to the sea. The fading light had transformed the ocean from blue-gray to black.

Isobel studied his profile. Before tonight, he'd not indulged in philosophical musings, and he never stared into the distance. Staring and distances were endeavors *too still* for Jason Beckett, Duke of Northumberland— too still by half.

And he was usually very direct. Isobel valued directness, but the quiet musing allowed her to consider him in a new light. The pile of shimmers in the pit of her stomach popped and fluttered.

"I'm not certain I can give farming or forging steel its due," he said. "I'm not sure I can be serious about anything if there is not some life-or-death stake to it."

"You can," Isobel heard herself say. She should not care about his future. He was one of the richest, most fortified men in England. *She should not care.*

He made a dismissive sound.

"Look at me," she said, her words out before she'd considered them. "I never thought I would find myself sailing from England, not ever. Now I'm embarking on a journey that makes me ill, returning to a country that harbors the most heartbreaking memories, and facing off with pirates. But here I am, *doing it*, out of necessity.

"You *can do* things that you cannot imagine," she said. "And if you don't like it, you can . . . determine a new way to manage it. You will have choices, Your Grace, when you are duke. Management of the farms and the foundry can be hired out. People will *work for you* if you wish to delegate."

He was shaking his head. "This was never the way of my father or brothers. There are expectations. My mother has been through so much—to lose a husband and two sons? I cannot be derelict, or absent, or manage the estate halfway. And I cannot lead prisoner-of-war uprisings in Middlesex. For everything, there is a season, I suppose." His voice was grim and tired and resigned.

"Do not reject it before you've even begun," Isobel said lowly, reaching out. She wanted to spread her hand on his chest but she redirected to his arm. A friendly pat. A squeeze. Her fingers held on.

"Rejecting it is not a choice. And I refuse to complain. I am fortunate."

"It's obvious that you feel so very fortunate indeed."

She patted him again. A double pat. *Pat pat.*

The arm beneath his coat was as hard as the railing, and it had a lovely little swell where the wool stretched over the muscle.

She gave it another pat. A very short little rub. Back and forth, a gesture of comfort.

Once more, back and forth.

Touching his arm was totally acceptable, she thought.

She touched it like she might touch a very good book, as if she'd just read the last page, and gently closed the cover, and now she was . . . patting it. In fact—

She bit off her glove and returned her hand, rubbing the rough wool of his sleeve.

A squeeze. *Such a good . . .*

Man.

Not a book, she lectured herself, *a man.*

He's a man. And I don't care about his tortured view of retirement. And I will stop touching him. And I do not want him to touch me.

"Say something that will make me stop touching you," she whispered.

"I, ah—?" He stared at her hand on his sleeve and then at her.

She couldn't look at him. She also couldn't seem to release him.

"You want me to *make you* stop touching me?"

"Yes," she lied.

"Are you mad?"

Her fingers moved down his arm to graze his wrist. There was a gap between the glove and his bare hand, and she slid her fingertip so that it nudged his skin. She wouldn't look at his face.

He turned his wrist, pulse up, and gave a little jerk. The motion notched her index finger *inside* his glove, along with two other fingers.

And now they shared the same glove.

"No man would make you *stop* touching him, least of all me," he rasped.

Isobel was awash in shimmers. She slid deeper into his glove, so deep the tight leather refused to give. Next she peeled the offending accessory from his hand. The duke wiggled his fingers, helping. When his hand was bare, she interlaced their fingers and squeezed.

"I don't feel sorry for you," she whispered, finally meeting his eye.

"At the moment, neither do I," he said.

"And I cannot be intimate with you."

"You've mentioned this."

"I've had my heart broken before." She held his hand tightly between them.

"Tell me," he whispered. "Tell me who hurt you."

The very odd thing was, even odder than her clasping his hand between them, was that she *wanted* to tell him.

She shook her head wildly. *No.* Tears stung her eyes.

"Why not?" His voice was gentle.

"Because you will be compassionate." This was true, she realized. He would not scoff or deride or hold her at an arm's length. It had been a wretched time, and he would understand. She was already too fond of him. He was too handsome and clever. And the prison escape story and orphanage rescue? So capable and brave. His fear of retiring, the vulnerability.

Isobel Tinker was not made of stone, but perhaps she was made of something like . . . porcelain? Strong but also breakable. And she could not allow herself to become his random, unaccounted lover.

She recited in her head, *Dukes do not marry travel agents and I cannot be his lover.*

"I will *not* be compassionate about it," he assured her.

He was trying to make her smile. She *wanted* to smile and laugh and make light of it all. This particular conversation should not feel so very important. She could not discover another irresistible piece of him every time they spoke. First he was charming and dashing.

Then he was anxious but resigned. Now he was brave and commanding. What next? Did he fly?

She didn't have the stamina to learn another reason to want him. She was too old for the racing heart and the belly shimmers—and for the hope.

Slowly, without any real design, their joined hands fell to hang between them, still joined. It was less like they were arm wrestling, more like they were sweethearts. It was worse.

They stood so very close. The sun had been swallowed by the sea, and the moon slid into position, frosting them in silver light.

"I wasn't trying to charm you, Miss Tinker," he said. "I was illustrating one of the many miserable contrasts between life as a spy and life as a duke."

"Miserable?"

"Perhaps 'miserable' is an exaggeration." His expression was miserable. " 'Dull' may be a better word. When I am duke, there is a good chance that I will drop into the ducal bed at Syon Hall and never awaken."

Isobel had a flash vision of Northumberland's "ducal bed" and felt a ping of desire.

"Life is what you make of it," she whispered, staring up at him. "Has no one said this to you?"

"Not really. You know what has been said? I've heard different variations of the same thing: your father is dead, and then your brother August, also dead; and now your brother James, dead too. The job that killed the three of them now rests on your unwilling shoulders. So pack it in and *get home*."

"They said this to you. You were summoned?"

He shrugged. "Not in as many words, but—"

"If there was no summons, then perhaps it is not what was expected, not to the very letter. Perhaps you may reinvent the dukedom in a way that allows you freedom to—"

"There is no reinvention, Miss Tinker. There is only five hundred acres, eighty-three families, a foundry, four ancient structures in various states of modernization, a mother and three sisters, and countless sheep. The lot of them cannot mind themselves."

She opened her mouth to contradict him and then closed it. He knew his responsibilities obviously. Anything she offered was only conjecture.

She studied his profile: his shoulders, large and powerful beneath his coat; his broad chest, exactly at the level of her gaze. His body seemed impossible to defeat; he was muscled and nimble and effortless. Why, then, did she want to reassure him? To lay her cheek against his heartbeat? Why did she clasp his hand as if the next strong gust might blow him away?

She wanted to kiss him.

No, that was inaccurate, the desire to kiss him had been an ever-present hum in the back of her mind since Grosvenor Square. Now her mind's eye *envisioned* the kiss. She saw herself step forward, go up on her toes, and tip her face up. She saw him manage the rest.

One of the many lovely things about the Duke of Northumberland was that he would manage the rest.

"I want to kiss you," he said suddenly.

Isobel's eyes snapped to his. Had he read her mind?

He went on. "You've said that we will not, and for good reason, but I cannot *not* say it."

"If there is a pretty girl in the vicinity," she guessed, "of course you must kiss her."

"No. If I initiate a kiss, I guarantee that it's *not* because she's convenient."

Why is it? Isobel thought, her breath held.

"It's because," he whispered, reading her mind again, "I've the feeling that I'm flying, and I don't want to do it alone. Are we flying, Isobel?"

"Northumberland," she said breathlessly.

"Please call me North," he whispered. "My friends call me North."

"Are we friends?"

"We are not enemies. You are not my family nor my commanding officer nor anyone I'm trying to impress."

I'm so impressed by you, she thought. She looked into his amber eyes and saw patience and longing and sweetness reflected back. He cocked an eyebrow.

He said, "Or you could simply call me Jason. My given name."

Jason. The shimmer inside her chest made a swooping revolution. She cleared her throat. " 'North' will be sufficient, thank you very much." She repeated it. "North. Like the star."

"More like you've bitten off the first mouthful of the title and spat out the rest."

She giggled and he laughed with her.

"North," she sighed, feeling the shimmers flick on and off.

And then, before she allowed herself to think, she pushed up on her toes and kissed him. Just a quick peck, her cold lips against the warmth of his mouth. A confirmation. She was flying too.

North made a noise, half surprise, half delight, and scooped her up. His hands went around her waist and she was against him. His mouth moved possessively, kissing her like he'd stolen her. She relaxed in his arms, allowing the kiss to launch them higher and higher.

The peck melted into a real kiss, and she wound an arm around his neck and sunk a hand in his hair.

She could barely breathe, and standing upright was out of the question. He leaned against the railing of the ship and held her.

For a minute, or an hour, or a year, they were lost in the roiling sensation of that kiss. The boat rocked and swayed, and their pressed bodies rocked and swayed together. The wind whipped around them and they clung, warm and secure and *flying*.

"Isobel," he whispered gruffly, pulling away to breathe. "It doesn't have to be—"

"Don't say it," she begged, panting for breath.

"You don't know what I'm going—"

"There's too much at stake," she insisted. "My new life—your responsibilities to the dukedom. We cannot be reckless."

He kissed her again, hard and demanding. "The best things in life are reckless," he moaned against her ear. "It is flight."

He went to kiss her again, his hand moving from her waist to palm her bottom. He pressed her against his erection and her body pulsed with sensation.

Her eyes watered, her breath caught. She bit her lip and pulled away.

Breathing hard, she said, "I am not flying. I am drowning."

"Wait, Isobel, no—" He reached for her.

She hopped out of reach and backed away. "Thank you for taking the air with me, Your Grace—er, North. In the future, we will speak only of pirates. And ice caves. And Icelandic farmers and their alliances. And nothing more."

He opened his mouth again, but she held out a hand

with her index finger raised, the universal gesture of *Do not say it*.

He closed his mouth. He stooped to retrieve his discarded glove. He did not take his eyes from her face.

Isobel fled, running from the conversation, and the sunset, and him.

Chapter Eleven

This open door is an invitation, is it not?" asked mercenary Declan Shaw, standing in the passageway outside the Duke of Northumberland's cabin.

" 'Invitation' is a stretch," said the duke, not looking up. He'd been staring at the same page of a Scandinavian atlas for twenty minutes, seeing nothing. "Invitation for what?"

"We've not seen you for two days, Your Grace," said Shaw, stepping inside. "The men want to know what to expect when we make landfall."

"What to expect . . ." repeated Jason slowly, drawing out the words.

"Not me, mind you," said Shaw. "My philosophy, as you'll remember, is 'Surprise me.' Especially when it comes to pirates."

Jason laughed. Declan Shaw was a known planner. Jason tossed the atlas aside.

"Tell the men," the duke said, "to expect very little ice—the country's name is misleading—and lichen apparently. Cod at every meal? This is what I've been told."

"Hilarious," said Shaw. "So tell them you haven't the slightest notion?"

Jason leaned back and closed his eyes, propping his

boots on the desk. "These men were chosen for their ability to improvise. Why the hand-wringing? We are three days out."

"We are a day and a half out," corrected Shaw. "And clearly you really *don't* know. North, this cannot—"

He was cut off by a sudden knocking. Shaw blocked the door, but the force of the knock and the speed of the *rap-rap-rap* could mean only one thing. Jason sat up and slid his feet on the floor.

"Excuse me, Your Grace." Isobel Tinker stood in the corridor behind Declan Shaw.

Jason pushed to his feet. She was dressed in a smart, moss-colored suit, her hair swept neatly into her signature bun. She stood straight and steady, clutching paperwork to her chest.

"I'll call back," said Shaw. "If you'll excuse—"

"You will *stay*, if you please, sir," said Isobel, extending her small, gloved hand. "Miss Isobel Tinker," she said, introducing herself. "I'm—well, I've been given the title of 'cultural attaché' on this mission. Or so I'm told."

Shaw had no choice but to take her hand. He affected a confused half bow, shooting Jason a glance that said, *Surely you're joking.*

Jason nodded back. *Introduce yourself.*

"Declan Shaw," said Shaw. "Leader of His Grace's, ah—"

"Hired thugs?" provided Isobel.

"Yes," confirmed Shaw.

"Very good," said Isobel. "Then of course you should remain. I've come to share my knowledge of the port in Stokkseyri. I've had previous experience dealing with the locals, so I'll tell you what I can. This may be helpful as you plan your recovery mission."

"*Plan?*" said Shaw, coughing.

Jason shot him a look and said, "Please come in, Miss Tinker. How heartened I am to see you. Are you . . . well?"

Jason plunked a chair beside his desk and Isobel, skirts swishing, settled in. Pushing away detritus with the blunt end of a pencil, she cleared a spot for her notebook on his strewn desk. Jason watched her, unable to conceal a smile. He realized he was staring, looked away, and then turned back. He felt as if someone had opened the door of a very dark cell to the bright light of day.

She'd come. Dressed, alert, potentially healthy. And she appeared ready to work.

He'd not seen her since the kiss and he'd replayed it in his mind a hundred times. She'd left of her own accord, but it felt like she'd been snatched away by demons from her past.

And yet now, here she was.

"I wasn't certain," he began, "when we might benefit from your wealth of experience." He kept his tone light and teasing, but he wanted to snatch up her hand and feel her pulse, test the strength of her grip. She was visibly thinner but no less robust. Her color was good, her eyes bright.

"Nonsense," she was saying, spreading her paperwork on his desk. "What purpose would I serve as a cultural attaché if not to share my experience?"

Declan Shaw coughed.

Jason shot Shaw a warning look and swiveled to Isobel. "Would you speak more freely if Mr. Shaw were not he—"

"No, I would not," she said. "Shaw remains. If he goes, so do I."

"Mr. Shaw, it is," amended Jason, narrowing his eyes at his friend. He cocked his thumb toward the small stool.

"Now," began Isobel, fanning out watercolor renderings and unfolding a map. "The port at Stokkseyri is here, and we will, no doubt, approach from the southwest . . ."

She went on from there, talking about currents and the number of harbor warehouses.

Jason tried to listen. He leaned forward in his chair, he nodded, he mimicked the pose of rapt attention. And in fact, he was paying very close attention, but not to her words—not yet. He was taking her in. The pink had returned to her lips. She spoke animatedly, her hands expressive. Tight, smooth wool sheathed her body, curve by curve, in a snug jacket.

"What do you think, Your Grace?" she was asking, pointing to a watercolor painting of a wide river cutting through a barren plateau.

"Ah," said Jason, scrambling.

"I think you've the right idea, miss," provided Shaw. He gave Jason a look that said, *Pathetic.*

Jason had spent the last four nights prowling the passageway outside her cabin. He'd interrogated her tight-lipped steward, a man who'd developed a fierce and protective loyalty to her. He'd berated the men in the berth belowdecks for banging the floorboards. He'd sent her notes.

Despite this, there had been no reliable sign that she was well. Or willing to cooperate. Or that she did not hate him.

He'd missed sleep and meals worrying about her. For a time, he'd forgotten about poor Reggie or the cursed dukedom waiting for him in Middlesex. He'd wallowed in something like "regret," a sentiment in which he rarely indulged, especially not for kissing a pretty girl who absolutely needed to be kissed.

"And *that*," she was saying, sketching a wide circle around a blue area on her map, "amounts to all I know about the harbor in Stokkseyri. Which admittedly is not a lot. The comings and goings of ships simply was not a focus when I was there. I spent a great deal more time inland."

"Very thorough," praised Jason. He needed to say *something*.

Isobel stared at him, unimpressed.

"But do you have some plan for what you intend to say when you reach the docks?" she asked. "To the locals? Who is meant to be your contact or resource in Iceland?"

Jason blinked, glancing at Declan Shaw.

Shaw piled on. "Yes, Your Grace. Tell us of your contact or resource in Iceland?"

"Ah," Jason began, unaccustomed to accounting for his plans, or rather lack thereof. "I have the letter sent to my uncle, asking for ransom money in exchange for the safe return of my cousin." He riffled through papers on his desk. "I believe it says something about asking for a man in a certain street in Reykjavík called *Hans* . . . Something or other. It was cruder than most ransom letters I've seen, almost comically cloak-and-daggerish, but it made it clear the pirates want money.

"Of course we've not sailed to Reykjavík," Jason conceded. "Honestly, I'd hoped to circumvent any formal meeting with pirates and steal away with the captives without relinquishing a single farthing. The ransom was difficult for my uncle but not impossible. The money sent by the families of the other merchants, however, will bankrupt them. And it's not as if they could scratch together *gold* on such short notice. They've sent bank notes. Not a pirate's preferred form of currency, one would assume."

"Alright," conceded Isobel slowly. "So you hope to evade the ransom and outwit the pirates. How?"

"Well," Jason ventured cautiously, "by using whatever lovely intelligence you share with us."

She narrowed her eyes. "Me? *Me?* Is that all? You know no one in Iceland and will have no local support?"

Jason drummed two fingers on the desktop, allowing this (apparently) unsettling bit of (also apparently) bad news to sink in.

Shaking her head, Isobel began scribbling a note on a piece of parchment. Jason tried to read it but saw that it was in a different language. He felt a little like an insubordinate pupil who had just been taken to task by a very irritated, very pretty teacher. Unbidden, he felt a pulse of desire.

Isobel continued. "But what will you claim when you sail this not-small brigantine into the very tiny harbor of Stokkseyri and drop anchor? The locals will be curious. You must have some narrative about who you are and why you've come. If the pirates have a man in Reykjavík, you can be certain that Stokkseyri is thick with their spies and allies. It's far closer to the glacier caves."

"Honestly, I hadn't planned to offer any excuses at all. When I discern the way the wind blows, so to speak, I'll either steal away with my cousin and his colleagues in the middle of the night. Or I might simply demand that they are returned. I didn't set out on this mission with twenty . . ." He looked at Shaw. "How did she describe you?"

" 'Hired thugs,' Your Grace," provided Shaw.

"Ah yes, I didn't embark with twenty hired thugs to be marched around by pirates or protocol."

Isobel shook her head and made more notes. "That will never do. You underestimate Doucette."

"Doucette?" asked Shaw.

"The pirate band that make Iceland their summer home is led by a Frenchman called Phillipe Doucette," said Isobel.

"Fine," said Jason, "we'll say we're scientific researchers, come to study the volcanoes or the . . . moss."

Isobel narrowed her eyes and glanced appraisingly back and forth between Jason and Declan Shaw. "You look nothing like scientists, neither of you—and I've seen the others. You look like woodsmen. And before you take a shine to that idea, let me remind you that Iceland is almost entirely devoid of trees."

"Perhaps we'll say we lost our way at sea . . ." considered Jason.

"So you mean to portray yourselves as idiots?" Isobel surmised.

Shaw chuckled.

Jason said, "Why don't we simply suggest that there is some mechanical issue with the brigantine, and that we've sought safe harbor to repair it?"

Isobel thought for a moment. "That should work, so long as the captain can name some legitimate issue with the ship, something about which the locals can reliably gossip. You'll want to order up repairs from the village. Everyone will be curious. Visitors are a rare and precious commodity in Stokkseyri."

"But should we drop anchor out of view and endeavor to slip into the port unnoticed?" asked Shaw.

"Not if your plan is no plan at all. Even if you knew the location of the captives and meant to steal in and out in a night, complete anonymity would be a challenge. Anything out of the ordinary will be noticed. This part of the island is flat and treeless; there is literally nowhere to hide. You *will be* seen, that is my opinion. It sounds reasonable to claim damage to the ship, but you must also be able to say where you were going and how you came to limp into Stokkseyri."

"Fine," said Jason. "I'll say I'm writing a book of travel essays, and we were bound for Greenland. How's that?"

"That should . . . suffice." She was clearly not impressed.

"If we devise this elaborate fiction and chat up the locals, then I can rely on town gossip to inform what's become of my cousin."

Isobel looked at him, tapping her pencil against the back of her hand. "Are you asking me or telling me, Your Grace?"

"Ah . . ." Jason hedged. She was so very stern and irritated and . . . alive. He felt another lick of desire.

She went on. "Am I to believe that you've no plan at all, Your Grace? Nothing?"

Jason suppressed a smile. She was so very difficult to impress. He should not value this, but he did. Impressing her became the most important thing on his list of Important Things. After recovering poor Reggie, of course.

He cleared his throat. "The manner in which I've always conducted my work, Miss Tinker, tends to be a more gradual, friendly kind of . . . *amble*. I turn up,

I make friends—lucky for me, I'm a likable sort of fellow—and I observe. I scout for weakness and oversight. Unless I'm meant to infiltrate known enemy territory, I prefer a relaxed perusal of the field of play. I take it all in. I seek alliances. You'll recall this tactic from the first time I encountered you."

This elicited a satisfying crimson blush from Isobel.

Behind her, Declan Shaw closed his eyes and looked away, biting back a smile.

Jason cleared his throat. "To you, this sounds like 'not planning.' To me, the plan is, be nimble. Be efficient. We'll not be locked into some overstudied, overprovisioned choreography. Not before we've even clapped eyes on the place."

Isobel took up a fresh piece of parchment and made more indecipherable notations. Speaking to the sheet, she said, "Nimble it may be, but a 'gradual amble' takes time. By very definition, it's slow and extended and, honestly, wasteful. Returning to England may be something you dread and wish to postpone, but for me it's a priority. This is a sentiment I can only guess is *shared* by your cousin."

"Fine," he said, "here's the plan. Hardly my style—I prefer to make friends rather than enemies—but my *plan* will be to locate one of the pirates, isolate him— 'abduct him,' if you will—and interrogate him. Assuming I can get reliable information from this method, we'll know more within hours."

"And just where do you plan to locate a pirate?" she asked.

"The pub."

Isobel harrumphed. "How simple you make it seem."

"I've never been to a port in the world that does not boast at least one establishment where men congregate to drink and gamble. Furthermore, never once has such a place been devoid of pirates. Trust me."

"Alright," she said cautiously, "if you manage to turn up a stray pirate, I will pay a call to my old friends. The Vagns."

"Go on," Jason said, taking up a piece of paper and pen. Now they were making progress. Old friends were far more useful than captured pirates.

"They are a family I knew during my time in Iceland," she said unsteadily, "who have a warehouse in the small dockyard at Stokkseyri. Assuming their warm regard for me has endured, this should give us somewhere to begin. I'll ask them about the news since I've gone, especially anything about missing Englishmen. At least one of the brothers should be in the warehouse office. A visit from me will be odd and unexpected, but I will have your story about the brigantine repairs and we'll invent some addendum about why I happen to be on it."

"So now you will have an alias," Jason said.

Isobel looked at him like he suggested they all leap off the deck and fly to Iceland.

"Of course I will have a story. A single woman, traveling alone, cannot turn up with no justification. I can hardly say you bribed me with a building to translate your pirate attack."

Jason glanced at Shaw, who was slowly shaking his head.

She went on. "As an English lord—in fact, simply because you are a man—you may step off a boat anywhere in the world with no excuses or explanation. You don't even have to be cordial."

"I am always cordial."

"A single woman cannot turn up on foreign shores or even on the doorstep of an old friend without a litany of reasons why her presence is proper and approved and sanctioned and allowed. You *know* this, Your Grace; you would be a terrible spy if you did not."

He opened his mouth to reply but she cut him off. "Perhaps what is at issue here is not that a *lady* requires a backstory, but whether *I* am a lady."

"Stop," he said, sitting up. "Call me a terrible spy if you like, but please do not make assumptions on whether I view you as . . . *ladylike.* Any oversight about our fabricated biographies can be chalked up to my personal brand of spy craft or to sheer laziness. But it's nothing more than that, I assure you. Contrary to what you think, I don't pass my days speculating about whether you—or anyone—is *a lady.*"

She was silenced by this and shifted in her seat. She glanced at her notes.

"Look, Isobel, of course you must have a backstory," Jason said, softening. "What would you like?"

"Well," she began, calm again, "if you pose as a writer, I can be your translator—let us keep close to the truth—and perhaps also I am painting illustrations to match your text? I am never without my watercolors, and I was known to paint even seven years ago. Beyond that, I should be cast as your, oh . . . niece?"

Jason made a choking sound. "Surely you are too old to be my niece."

She raised an eyebrow. "Or perhaps you are too young to be my uncle. In any event, I must be a relative."

Behind them, Declan Shaw asked, "May I be allowed to leav—"

"Yes," barked Jason in the same moment Isobel said, "*No.*"

"I've got it," said Jason. "I'll pose as your bodyguard. Shaw here has had a lovely run with this gambit."

"Don't be ridiculous," she said.

Jason ventured, "Perhaps we should pretend to be married."

Isobel waved a hand. "That's overdone, believe me. And it presents all sorts of logistical problems with how we met and why we suit and forced proximity."

"Sounds worth the effort to me," mused Jason, thinking of touching her whenever he liked, sharing a room with her.

"It's not," she said. "We will be cousins."

"Cousins," he repeated, eyeing her. There was nothing cousinly about his regard for Isobel Tinker. He wasn't certain he could manage the theater of it.

Declan Shaw was rising from his stool. "Honestly, these details are—"

"Stay," Isobel sang out in the same moment Jason muttered, "*Go.*"

Shaw slumped on his stool.

"And which local family is this?" Jason asked. "For whom are we now posing as cousins?"

"The patriarch's name is Sveinn Vagn," said Isobel. "The boys are Stefen, Gisle, and Sveinn the Younger."

Jason scribbled his own notes, taking great liberties with the unfamiliar spelling. "What else should I know about them?"

Isobel shrugged. "They're one of the ruling farm families in Iceland. Their estate is inland, but they warehouse their wool near the port for export to Denmark. They have a long-standing feud with the family that is allied to the pirates."

Jason looked up. "Oh yes, you mentioned the pirate

allies. Another bit of luck if they don't get on. Perhaps your friends will be motivated to help us."

"Perhaps, but I would not count on it. The Vagns do not fight with the other family, more like complain about them. And please be warned, they *may well* complain about me. I cannot say how they will receive me. Even if they are pleasant—which is by no means a guarantee—they may be disinclined to gush about local gossip. I've been away for seven years, and I was here under very strange circumstances. They may look back on my time in Iceland and feel a bit . . . deceived." She blinked twice and looked down at her notes.

Jason watched her, staring at the bun on the top of her head. Moments ticked by.

Would she offer . . . nothing more? he thought. These people accounted for their only connection in Iceland. Surely there was more to the story. Jason bit his lip in frustration. He tapped the pen against the desktop.

After a moment, he said, "And you knew this family how, Miss Tinker?"

He'd meant to be casual but the words came out hard. Why would she speculate about the reception of a lot of Icelanders? Anyone should be happy to see her—it shouldn't matter what happened seven years ago or if she was his cousin or translator or Anne Boleyn.

Who were these people and what had they done to her? He'd wanted to know this from the start. Even her uncle, Sir Jeffrey, had been evasive about it.

She was taken in by a respectable family who treated her as a guest, was all the older man said.

"Isobel?" he prompted, but she wouldn't answer.

She shook her head at the parchment.

The room went very quiet. Shaw shifted on his tiny stool and the wood creaked. A clock ticked on a shelf.

Jason dropped his pen and the motion of the ship caused it to roll across the desk. The three of them watched its progress in loaded silence.

Finally, Isobel raised her head. "I knew them as . . . friends," she said. "Why must you know more than this? You will not even tell us your plan."

"I thought we established there is no plan," said Jason. "And it's useful to know about these people because . . . perhaps I should accompany you to this warehouse. Perhaps several of us should be with you. Perhaps our alias can be more effectively portrayed if I know more. Most of all, I cannot authenticate anything we learn from these brothers if I don't have a sense of who they are."

"They are Icelandic farmers," she insisted.

"Fine, but are they thoughtful? What might cause them to be biased or unreliable? I want to know what we're sailing into," he said.

"Now?"

"Sooner rather than later."

"It doesn't matter," she insisted. "It's not relevant."

"You've just said we must devise alibis and backstories and pretend to repair a fully functional brigantine, just to survive local gossip. Your history with these people may matter a great deal. It is very relevant, I'd say."

"No," she disagreed, albeit weakly. She was shaking her head miserably. Jason's heart began to throb.

"Look," he said, "I may be casual and appear carefree, but the key to my success has always been information. The more I know about everybody, the more I can either help or hinder whatever happens. It is, at its heart, the essence of being a spy. *Knowing.*"

Without warning, Isobel shoved from her chair.

Jason and Declan Shaw scrambled to stand.

"I need air," she said.

"It's raining," Jason said.

"I don't care."

Without another word, she turned and quit the room.

Jason grimaced at Declan Shaw, took up two coats, and followed.

Chapter Twelve

*H*ow foolish she'd been to believe she would never tell him.

She was always going to tell him.

And not even because he truly needed to know.

She could make up a lie that served the mission and protected her privacy, but no.

She would tell him because she *wanted* to.

If the duke followed her to the misty haze of this rain-drenched deck, she would tell him.

Isobel moved blindly in the fog, navigating crates and coils of rope, making her way to the railing. She was invigorated by the gusty chill. Her nerves were stretched taut, strained like the rigging; the threat of this conversation was wind to the sails. The raindrops were cold when they kissed her cheeks, but turned hot on her flushed skin. The fog seemed to swallow her up, and she was grateful. She wanted to be swallowed. Perhaps saying it all would be easier from behind a screen of mist.

Almost no one knew what had happened in Iceland. With whom could she share such a great burden? Casual friends or relations would judge her, and those who loved her would feel undue pain on her behalf.

She had told her mother, which, then and now, felt correct. She drew comfort from her mother. And a small part of her *blamed* Georgiana Tinker for all that happened.

But Samantha? The Starling daughters? She had not elaborated. Why introduce the heartbreak to them?

Northumberland's heart will not break, she thought.

No, not "Northumberland," she reminded herself. He wished for her to call him "North."

North was big enough and strong enough and, perhaps most importantly, unrelated to her future (enough) to survive this story. He could absorb the terribleness of it without breaking stride.

She wanted to try. It had been such a great relief to tell her mother. Perhaps every time she said the words, she could believe in her survival a little bit more.

"Isobel?" North called from somewhere behind her.

Shimmers dripped down her insides. He had followed.

"I'm here," she called back, speaking to the fog. "Starboard."

He materialized out of the vapor—first a man-sized shadow, then a silhouette, then all of him. Brown eyes and broad shoulders and large hands. His black overcoat swirled about him and his hat was pulled low against the rain.

He held out a navy greatcoat to drape across her shoulders. The coat settled around her in a *whoosh*, immersing her in the musky, outdoorsy smell of him. Isobel closed her eyes and breathed in.

When she looked up, he was hovering beside her. He looked alternately at the low, seeping sky and her dripping hair. He frowned.

"Will you not come back inside?" he asked. "The rain is not likely to let up. And you can sit."

"No." She shook her head. Drops of rain flung from her hair, piercing the fog. "I'm too restless to sit. And I've no wish to look you in the eye while I . . . say the words. I am impervious to the rain."

"My God, Isobel," he whispered, "what is it?"

"I think you should call me Miss Tin—"

"I will not call you Miss Tinker, so please stop asking. If you can reveal this very great secret history to me, so tragic that you cannot even look me in the eye, I will call you Isobel."

"The irony is," she sighed, "my secret, tragic history is not half as harrowing as what you have doubtless seen on a field of battle or in godforsaken parts of the world. But it was devastating for me. I am still recovering. It is difficult for me to relate."

North stared a long moment. He looked like a man who'd opened a door he wasn't certain he wanted to walk through. Finally, he nodded. He leaned a hip into the railing beside her and crossed his arms over his chest.

Isobel tried to hold his gaze and failed. She looked out at the fog. It swirled in great, white drifts over the sea. She squeezed the railing and pinned her shoulders back; she soothed her throat with a gulp of cold, damp air.

There should be no preamble, she thought. The preamble had been every evasion since they'd met.

"Very well," she began. "I've said my mother was an actress."

"Georgiana Tinker," provided North.

"Right. When your mother is an actress, your playmates are the children of other actors and people in the theater. We—that is to say myself and these other children—grew up in myriad backstage wings, dressing rooms, and theater-district boardinghouses. Even before we left England, this had been my experience, although we had a proper flat in London.

"In Europe, we traveled constantly, lodging mostly in boardinghouses and hotels. The children of the other players, and of the costumers, and of the musicians and dancers—they were like brothers and sisters to me.

"We were tight-knit . . . more than a little wild, largely untended, surrounded by music and dancing. We bore witness to the romantic entanglements of our parents. We slept when we fell over in exhaustion—which was rarely—ate whatever we liked, dressed how we pleased.

"Actors change cities when a show wraps, as do members of the crew, and every production convened a different set of creative luminaries. I might see one family for the length of one production, and then not again for a year. The next time I would see them, we would be in another city or another country."

"I've never considered," said North, "the childhood of someone raised in the shadow of the stage. Fascinating. But you are clearly . . . educated. Did your mother arrange for tutors?"

"My mother did not," Isobel said. "She taught me to read and do sums. Beyond that, she subscribed to the theory of 'life is your schoolroom.' I was a curious girl, a voracious reader. I was a repeat visitor to every museum in every city. I prowled ancient churches; I picked up languages quickly."

"You've been classically educated in the most unclassical of ways," he observed. "Extraordinary."

Isobel gave a half nod, keeping her head down. "When I reached the age of fourteen or so, my friends and I began to travel on our own, independent of our parents or their commitments to the stage."

"A girl of fourteen traveling alone?" marveled North.

"I know it sounds shocking, and it was, but it happened so gradually. My mother would close a show in Rome and pack up for Salzburg to undertake a new role. I wouldn't want to leave Italy, or I would have a holiday planned with another actor's family on the coast. I would remain in Rome and join her in a fortnight, traveling with someone's older sister or a maid.

"*Or* she would take a role in a city I hated, such as St. Petersburg, and I would beg to travel with a group of other youths to Budapest, at first only for a fortnight."

"And she allowed it," observed North.

Isobel took a deep breath. "It was not as if she did not *care*," she ventured, even though Isobel had wondered, at times, about her mother's ability to see beyond her own goals and preferences. "It was more like she did not have the patience to argue. I understood this about her and became an expert at simply wearing her down. If I wished to go ahead, or stay behind, or ramble, I need only try her patience. And I *always* wished to go or stay behind or ramble."

"As much as you now like to stay put?" he asked.

"Exactly the same amount," she said.

"But did you have . . . resources?" he asked gently.

"Oh, we traveled in lavish style. My mother was highly sought-after and well compensated. Until my father died, he actually sent money as well. Mama would have nothing to do with his contributions, and she gave all of that money to me. I was too foolish to save it, and my wardrobe was a work of art. I employed a Paris-trained maid; I dined in the best restaurants and drank the best wine. Mama and I hired a beautiful carriage and driver as soon as we arrived in any city. It was," she said, "either the perfect combination of money and freedom, or the most dangerous combination of these. I suppose it depends on how you view it."

"Perfect," said North wistfully.

Dangerous, Isobel countered in her head. "This from the man who is running from a dukedom."

"Perhaps I should endeavor to be adopted by a traveling actor," he said.

Isobel chuckled and touched her hair. Her bun was soaked and dripping rainwater down her neck. She'd begun to shiver. The cold felt less exhilarating now, more punishing.

North removed his hat and plopped it on her head. It wabbled on her saturated bun, far too large, and she was swamped again with the smell of him.

Without warning, tears shot to her eyes. Her throat clamped down. For a long moment, she struggled for composure. She tipped her head so he could not see her beneath the brim of the hat.

How far she'd come in seven years, she thought. She had a home—a new home, if she survived this mission—a schedule where days were day and nights were night and she earned a living wage doing work that she enjoyed. A friend in Samantha. A family in the Starlings and her mother.

If her encounters with the Duke of Northumberland felt like a regression—a very wonderful, deceptively harmless regression—well, this story would put an end to all of that. He could mumble, "Extraordinary" and "Fascinating," and be perfectly lovely about it but the reality of her indiscretions meant there would be a wedge between them now.

Before, the wedge was small and vague. Now it would be as tall and sharp as the spire of a church. Now she would cease her silly, middle-of-the-night fantasies about him. And the future. And her.

She flashed him a resigned smile and forced herself to continue. "By the time I was fifteen, I'd become part of a cluster of youths—all the grown children of theater people—who traveled Europe on a sort of . . . whim. That is, we would convene for opening night of our parents' productions, and then we would set out. Gone was the suggestion that I might join my mother in a week or so. I traveled with these friends for months at a time, embarking on some adventure."

"Like the sort of adventure where you explored the streets of Paris?" guessed North.

She chuckled. "Like climbing a mountain in Switzerland. Like swimming in the Aegean Sea in Greece. Like learning how they train bull fighters in Spain."

"But . . ." began North, now struggling to comprehend, "how did you not run out of money? Your mother could be the most successful actress in history and not support the life you describe. And how did a lot of untended youths gain access to—forgive me—decent establishments? What of your safety? Europe was at war. Was there no adult to mind you?"

"Excellent questions," Isobel conceded. Defensiveness had begun to creep in, although she had no idea why. This time in her life felt without defense. She'd been dangerously reckless; many nights, she'd been downright stupid. She'd been out of control.

She glanced at North. He watched her expectantly,

his expression not so much judgmental as concerned. She turned back to the sea.

She reminded herself that she did not have to tell him every detail. She didn't have to do anything but traipse through the tundra of Iceland and translate the language and return home to claim her lovely new building.

"How did we not run out of money?" she repeated, determined, in fact, to tell him every detail. "Our lodging and food came mostly as the guests of people we met along the way. Some nights we dined lavishly in the chalets of local bourgeoisie; others we ate bread and cheese and drank wine from the bottle. Some nights we slept in canopied beds inside a castle; others we made camp on the side of the road. We traveled very light; we were prepared for whatever the journey might bring.

"What can I say but . . ." She sighed. "We were young and beautiful and resourceful. We were from different countries and we spoke various languages, but all of us were interesting and attractive and could, if necessary, demonstrate lovely manners. We could also pick pockets and fight. All of us had traveled since we were children. We were shrewd and savvy, daring and unafraid. We invented new identities based on our needs in any given city. One town saw us as brothers and sisters in a missionary family; in the next we styled ourselves as obscure Baltic royalty."

She took a deep breath, thinking back. How clearly she could see each of their faces, some fondly, others she barely tolerated. Even then, it mattered less that she enjoyed the group, more that she'd been included in it, that she could keep up, that she was fearless enough.

She shook her head, clearing it. "What else did you ask? How were we safe? We were not safe. More than once we fell in with unsavory characters and escaped only by our luck and our wits.

"Have I, you might wonder, done serious injury to a man who climbed on top of me in the middle of the night? Yes, I have done, more than once.

"Have I leapt from a speeding carriage? Also more than once.

"Have I been picked up by the local magistrate only to talk my way out of jail? Yes."

She snatched off her hat, gave it a shake, scattering rainwater. She glanced at him, reseating the hat.

He was staring at her as if she was a shiny curiosity found in the attic. He looked as if he wanted to hold her up to the light and examine her from every angle.

"And you thought you were the only one to escape from prison," she teased.

"I had not thought," he said. "Obviously. But what did your mother know of this? Was she not . . . concerned?"

"Wait, allow me to finish the last bit." She held up a finger. "You ask if there was no one minding us. Ultimately, no. However, there was a leader to our merry band. It was a boy—older, but hardly an adult—called Peter Boyd."

"Peter Boyd?" he repeated. "He was English?"

"Yes, from Manchester of all places. He was the oldest among us, about nineteen at the time. His family was the wealthiest of the theater crowd; his father produced many of my mother's productions. He was . . ." she paused, staring into the fog, trying to find words to describe Peter Boyd, ". . . Peter was a dangerous combination of handsomeness, confidence, cleverness, charm, boldness, and . . . an inability to stay still."

"Is that all?" asked North, laughing a little.

"No, in fact," she admitted, "but you get the idea.

Think of the most charming, most enticing person you know, give him the face of an angel, and then allow him to take your breath away on a daily basis. That was Peter Boyd. We followed him blindly and he led us on the journey of our lives.

"If Peter wanted to break inside the Vatican in Rome," she listed, "we did it. If he wished to herd goats in the Alps, we did it. If he wanted to harvest pearls, or dance with a royal princess, or learn to hold his breath for four minutes—we found a way to do it."

"You belonged to him," North guessed solemnly. "You were lovers."

Isobel watched him, trying to read criticism or disappointment in his tone. His expression was enigmatic. He appeared only attentive.

Isobel shrugged. "Peter Boyd had one very favorite among our group, and I was not her. He loved Ana-Clara, a Portuguese girl, the daughter of a renowned set designer. She was tall and serene and darkly beautiful where I was small and pale and . . . *not* serene. I was an amusement to him and a resource. I spoke more languages than any of the other Lost Boys."

"The Lost Boys?"

"That is the name Peter gave us, the Lost Boys."

"But you are not a boy."

"It didn't matter. When the group first began these far-reaching rambles, they counted only boys among their number. Then he began to invite AnaClara and me and another few girls. The name had already been established."

"But did you ever . . . challenge this Peter Boyd? His choices or his whims?"

"At the time?" she mused, thinking back. "I did not.

You asked if he was my lover—he was not, er, always. But I did love him. Every girl did. I've never known a single female of any age that did not fall a little in love with Peter Boyd. It pains me to say it, but I would have followed him anywhere. I did follow him anywhere. I followed him to Iceland."

She clasped the railing of the brig and dropped back, allowing her weight to hang at an angle. "So now you know."

"On the contrary," he said gruffly, "I feel as if I have only scratched the surface."

"Are you shocked?" she asked, standing straight again.

"Yes, a little," he said. "If I'm being honest. But not the kind of shocked that is also appalled. More like the kind of shocked that means I'm in awe of the life you've led."

She laughed, a bitter, humorless sound.

"You don't believe me?" he asked.

"I think 'awe' is a bit of a stretch."

"You forget the one thing I cannot tolerate," he said.

She thought for a moment. "Becoming duke?"

"Being *bored*," he said.

She was going to clap back with some retort, to disprove what he'd claimed, but she came up short. Her girlhood had been anything but boring. She glanced at him. He watched her now with rapt attention. From the beginning, he'd always looked at her as if he was afraid he'd miss something if he looked away. The shimmers in her belly swirled to life.

"But why did this person bring you to Iceland?" he prompted.

"Peter wanted to see the volcanoes and experience the thermal pools and the strange northern lights in the sky," she said. "We arrived in early spring and stayed through the summer. He made friends with this family I hope to visit, the Vagns."

"This family simply . . . welcomed you into their home?"

She shrugged. "He had an aunt who was married to one of their relations. That was all it took with him—some small connection, real or imagined. He met people, and they wanted to be a part of his world. He told them some lie about his father being a wealthy investor who was scouting scenic locations around the world to build hotels."

"And they believed him?"

"People believed whatever Peter Boyd told them," she said sadly. "I believed him, even though I'd seen him lie to at least one person every day of our lives."

"Believed him about what?"

"Well—" she said, and then her voice broke. She stopped, blinked, and raised her fingertips to her mouth.

"Isobel," he said softly.

She dropped her hand. The first tear fell and she wiped it away. "Each of us was hurt by the pace at which we burned through life, or by Peter Boyd, or by both. It was only a matter of time. Before it was my turn."

"Your turn for . . . ?"

"My turn to catch fire, I suppose?" Another tear rolled down her cheek, and she swiped it away.

"What did this man do to you?" His voice was harder now. He sounded upset. "Isobel?"

She studied his face. Was he angry with her?

No, she didn't think so.

Was it Peter that he resented? No one ever resented Peter Boyd.

She continued carefully, watching him. "Well, Peter's favorite, AnaClara, did not enjoy Iceland. It was too cold, the sky was too white, and she did not get on with the Vagns, our hosts. And so she left. After just a month. Sometimes she did this—she left us. She was the only one brave enough to walk away without the fear of not being invited back in. Naturally, that is why Peter loved her the most. She was not held entirely in his thrall.

"And when she left, Peter finally, at long last, after two years of traveling together, turned his attention . . . on me."

"Oh," said North, his voice filled with dread.

"I'd waited so long to have him, only him, just for myself," she said through a lump. "And for a time, I was the chosen one. Also for a time, it was everything I thought it would be. He was charming and affectionate and attentive. I worked doubly hard to please him. Like most revered leaders, he was conveniently helpless. I served as everything from his valet, oiling his boots, to his minstrel, singing him to sleep. I set about learning the Icelandic language at an eye-burning pace."

"And you were in love," said North quietly.

"I was so in love." The tears fell freely now.

"Do you love him still?" asked North, his voice less than a whisper.

She shook her head. "No. I have no regard for him. Hate is too strong a feeling for what I have for him. When I think of him, I feel nothing but an empty road, going to nowhere."

"But you are crying," he said.

She swiped at the tears, smearing them with the rain-drops on her face. "I cry for the girl I was. The stupid choices, the stupid hope, for how I believed I was a part of this wonderful, special thing, when I was really all alone."

"What happened?" A whisper.

"What do you think happened? By July, AnaClara had returned, saying she missed us, that life was dull with her parents. She began a campaign to lure us to the French seaside."

"And you . . . quarreled?" North asked.

"With whom? AnaClara? No. She and I rarely spoke, and now we had even less to say than before. Peter and I? Also no. I became an *observer*. I held my breath, and waited, and watched to see who he would choose." She laughed a bitter laugh. "To think I actually thought it might be me. He'd seemed so contented in Iceland. The volcanoes captivated him. He'd made the acquaintance of these pirates who captured your cousin—this is how I know of them—and he spent days playing high-seas adventurer in the water off the coast of Reykjavík. He longed to see the phenomenon of the lights in the sky in late September."

She laughed again. "If I required the scenic highlights of the country to sway him in my favor, I *knew* the answer."

"How did he settle it?" North asked.

"He came to me the evening that AnaClara returned—he cornered me alone—and said something like, 'I've moved your case from my bedchamber to the room with the other girls. We would not want to confuse or distress AnaClara now that she's finally returned to us.'"

"*No*," North said, exhaling, drawing out the word like a hiss. He reached out and grabbed Isobel at the biceps, holding her at arm's length.

She allowed this, sagging a little, soaking in the strength of his large hands through the bulk of the coat.

"There is more," she said, her voice as quiet as the fog.

He shook his head, ducking a little to see her face beneath the brim of the hat.

"I was with child by then."

The silence that followed this was as wide and as lonely as the sea.

"Oh, Isobel," North finally whispered.

She nodded. Her ability to form words had gone. It was always like this when she talked about the pregnancy.

She sucked in a breath, trying to work loose the knot in her throat.

She said, "I hadn't yet told Peter about . . . my condition. I was terrified to tell him."

North made a groaning noise and closed his eyes. Isobel searched his features for disgust but his face was creased only with pain.

Yes, Isobel wanted to say. *Yes! It was unbearably painful. That is why I have not wanted to return to Iceland. That is why I cannot trust you or any charming, handsome man. That is why I cannot trust myself when I am near you. I want too much from the wrong men.*

While she studied him, his eyes opened. She forced herself to hold his gaze. She wanted to say all of this too, but she'd already said so much. And none of this was North's fault.

He said, "What happened, Isobel?"

"Well," she said, "my mother was halfway across Europe doing a long run of *Tartuffe,* her favorite play."

She simply let the words spill out, flowing like her tears.

"The other Lost Boys—the girls, perhaps—might seem like natural confidantes, but they were all waiting hopefully for their chance to have a go at Peter. They idolized AnaClara. I was alone."

She dragged in a deep breath, but what she really wanted to do was scream. To scream for the lonely, terrified girl she had been.

She finished with, "Before Peter reunited with Ana-Clara, I was going to tell him. But then she returned and he threw me over. When it was clear I was an after-thought to him, second best, then I sort of . . . stopped. In all things that pertained to him. I stopped watching, stopped scheming, stopped hoping. I simply . . . *was*.

"I held myself very still for the first time in as long as I could remember. I thought of me and me alone— well, and the baby. I considered my situation. When I fully grasped what had happened, when I allowed myself to conceive everyone's role in it—mine, Peter's, AnaClara's, my mother's, even these Icelandic people in whose home we were living—I experienced a sort of . . . awakening.

"Peter's selfishness had finally pierced the fog of my hero worship. Something like . . . good sense, and inde-pendence, and self-preservation began, ever so slowly, to stack up, brick by brick, inside me. I had the strength to choose my own interests ahead of the group's. I had the strength to see beyond Peter, to not look at him at all actually. I could determine some way to survive for myself and for this new life. Alone. I had to . . . *grow up*."

"But where is—?"

"I lost the baby," Isobel said quickly.

There was no way to say it except to force the words out. They cut her every time she said them. She was cut in two to say it.

"*Isobel,*" he breathed. His hands went gentle on her arms but he did not let her go.

She nodded, responding to the softness in his voice. Tears streamed down her cheeks.

"I'd already written to my uncle by then. The letter honestly and frankly described my situation so that the Starlings could decide what manner of help, if any, they were willing to lend. They had a houseful of impressionable daughters. My uncle was running for parliament. And I was alone and unmarried and expecting a child. Sir Jeffrey, God bless him, arranged for me to sail to London as soon as a ship could reach Iceland. By the time that ship made landfall in Reykjavík, I'd lost the baby. I was only about eight weeks along. My body simply . . ."

She couldn't finish.

"Were your friends with you when . . . ?" he asked softly.

She shook her head. "I was alone. The Lost Boys had gone, but this family, the Vagns, had allowed me to stay behind. I told them I wanted to continue to learn the language and implored them to host me for a while longer. They sensed some distress, I believe, and allowed it. They never knew about the pregnancy."

She stopped talking then and wept in earnest. Her face crumpled; her throat cinched painfully tight. Despite her sobs, she heard North make a mournful noise—a sort of moaned oath—and the next thing she knew, he was pulling her against him. She felt hard chest and warm arms, but her brain was consumed with the old pain and guilty relief of that night. She cried until she was wrung out, until there were no tears left to cry. He held her and she lacked the energy to move away; she didn't want to move away. Her breath came in slow, raspy gasps. She sounded like a dying thing. Without thinking, her hands found the lapels of his coat and she squeezed, holding on.

She should say something, she thought. This was her terrible history and she'd revealed it of her own volition; no one expected such vivid detail, least of all her.

She looked up to his face.

He looked down, his brown eyes gentle and also . . . bright. Wet. With tears. He cried too.

The realization hit Isobel like a roiling wave from the North Sea. When the force subsided, the shimmers in her belly, as resilient and reliable as the tide, bubbled up.

She was doomed.

She took a deep, shuddered breath. "There," she whispered. "So now you know. *That* is why I was in Iceland and *that* is why I did not wish to come back. And that is how I am in the acquaintance of the Vagns, God love them."

"I was wrong to compel you," he confessed. The look on his face was pure misery.

"I would never have agreed without the offer of the building—you did not compel me, you made it worth my while. *The building is worth it*," she assured him. "The building will change my life. And, ultimately, this return to Iceland will have no impact on me, except perhaps to allow me some . . . reckoning."

"Does 'reckoning' with pain really ever make a difference?" he asked, his voice a scoff.

"I think, perhaps, it does. On the very rare occasions that I have related this story, I have felt better. Perhaps I feel better already."

"You do?"

"No," she said, laughing sadly, "but I can see where I might."

"You are too generous." His words were angry. "I have wronged you on behalf of . . . of *Reggie*." He made a face. "It's exactly the sort of thing he, and only he, would cause me to do."

"It's your cousin's fault, is it?" She released the handfuls of his coat and laid her palms flat against his chest. She could just feel his heartbeat through her gloves.

"Of course not. Even when it *is* Reggie's fault, it is never really his fault. I did this, and cannot think of what I've done to deserve anything but resentment from you. But I am grateful. And I understand your . . . trepidation."

"If I'd told you from the beginning, I feel sure you would have left me alone. And perhaps that is why I did not tell you. I didn't want to be left alone—not yet—by you."

His face took on a sharper expression. He ran a hand through his hair, slicking it back and sluicing rainwater onto the yoke of his coat.

"Do not," she said. "We're both 'adults of the world,' so I needn't feign obviousness or pretend there is not a considerable . . . attraction between us. But as an adult, I can make responsible choices. And I will. I chose to assist you on this mission but also to do nothing else with you. So flatter yourself if you must, but don't indulge in delusions of grandeur." She forced herself to drop her hands and shrugged out of his hold. It was the adult thing to do.

She added, "And do not feel guilty about dragging me to Iceland. I am many things, but a coward is not one of them."

"No," he said softly, "I would say that you are not."

They stood a moment longer, staring at each other through the mist, rain soaking every garment, the brigantine gently rocking beneath their feet.

"So, what do we do now?" she asked softly. Her brain hadn't allowed her to think beyond telling him.

"I suppose we plan for how to quickly and peacefully extract my cousin and his lot."

"I may put on dry clothes first," she said, shrugging out of his coat.

He watched her peel the wet garment from her shoulders. If she'd asked him to accompany her to her cabin to assist with the dry clothes, he would have done it. If she'd asked him to take her to his cabin, to see her dry and comfortable and *comforted*, he would have done it.

Her pulse leapt at the thought, and desire began to beat back the cold.

She would not, of course. And he would not. And his expression, although hungry and proprietary, was also assessing. He was looking at her with new eyes. He looked at her like a stranger who'd just revealed that they hailed from the same hometown. They'd hit upon this sort of shorthanded intimacy. A new kinship. They knew some of the same people and places. They understood the culture of this shared thing.

Did he consider her *less* for having traveled and cavorted and leapt from carriages? For having loved and lost so much? Or more like him? Or both?

Again, she dared not ask.

"Meet again in an hour?" she asked quietly, extending his wet coat.

"Alright," he said. "An hour."

"Do us both a favor?" she said, turning away. "Bring your friend. I learned too late in life the value of a chaperone."

Chapter Thirteen

Dear Mama,

Hello. I hope this finds you well. I have a precious few minutes to dash this off and hurl it in the general direction of Cornwall. Forgive the obvious haste and the disorganized thoughts. How long has it been since I've written you in a manner "on the run"? Not long enough—and yet here I am.

The most relevant news first: I've reached Iceland safely and in good humor. We sailed from the Thames Estuary at Margate up across the North Sea. We enjoyed fair weather and made excellent time.

We've dropped anchor in the waters outside the small port city very familiar to me, not far from the home of the Vagn family.

As expected, the voyage made me very ill, although the practice of frequent walks on the deck and lots of fresh air gave me some relief. The moment the barrier islands were in view, I was vastly improved.

The Duke of Northumberland has been very generous—both in allowances for my discomfort and also in terms of my contribution to this mission. I am the only woman among twenty men at least. You *would love it; the evenings want only a piano and a buxom soprano. But the men are cordial to me and I feel very safe. I've been left to my own company mostly (at my request) and any anxiety I have felt has been due to my own missteps or wrong-mindedness. Obviously my life in Mayfair felt very safe and unchallenged (bland and boring, if I'm being honest) while this endeavor is the opposite. This has called for some adjustments, but I've discovered a well of versatility that I thought had long since run dry.*

Once in Iceland, the duke relied upon me to navigate our reconnaissance within the port city.

I've sought out the Vagn family and enacted a small reunion to learn local gossip.

I was uncertain of how the family would receive me but they were warm and welcoming and appeared delighted.

In the interest of brevity I will not detail our reunion, but allow me to skip to the bit that you'll want to hear. According to the younger Vagns, I've not been the only Lost Boy to venture back to Iceland. <u>Peter</u> has been back, and more than once. I know you keep in touch with his father so perhaps this will not surprise you, but I was wholly unprepared for the news. It was never Peter's nature to revisit an area, especially somewhere as remote as Iceland. I'm not afraid of Peter Boyd, but I have no wish to encounter him. I am grown now, a new woman; I am . . . beyond. How loath I would be to circle back.

The Vagns said that Peter, although not in Iceland at the moment, has returned often to take the healing thermal waters, nose around the volcanoes, and— most compelling of all for our mission—engage in some revelry with the very blaggards who committed the crimes we have come to undo. The world is very small indeed.

So, onward. I will close this letter now and race to deliver it. Another vessel in port is sailing this very night for England. I've paid a steward to post it as soon as they make landfall. If we are very lucky, this will reach you within days of my own return to England.

If you don't receive this, there is no great loss. You will see me again soon enough. It has felt restorative to write these words, even if they sink to the bottom of the sea.

One thing I might add: seeing Iceland again has not been as terrible as I once thought. In truth, it feels little more than vaguely familiar or like the scene of a small, personal triumph from long ago.

There are places that we thrive and places that we merely survive, and perhaps they are both important.

I do not regret this journey, even without gaining the new building from the duke.

But now, on to recovering these Englishmen and returning home. I pray that you are well and behaving yourself. I look so forward to seeing your beautiful smile very soon.

Love,
Bell

Chapter Fourteen

$\mathcal{T}$he Duke of Northumberland lay on his back on a table in the kitchen galley. At the end of the table, bound loosely but effectively, sat one Donatello Beddloe, pirate and outlaw, snarling in some combination of Italian and Welsh.

Jason had just asked him a question in broken Italian and was waiting for an answer. To entertain himself while he waited, Jason extended his right arm above his chest and balanced an orange on his pointer finger. He'd almost managed it when—

"What in God's name are you doing?" a familiar voice called from the galley door.

The orange toppled and rolled away. Jason swung upright.

"North?" asked Isobel Tinker, her gaze swinging back and forth between the pirate and him.

"What am I doing?" he repeated. "What are you doing?"

"I came for my traveling case," she said. "Mr. Shaw rowed me from shore. The Vagns invited me to take a room in the living quarters above their warehouse while we are in port. But . . . is this a *pirate*?"

She was examining Mr. Beddloe from the distance of the door.

Jason shot the man a warning look and stepped into the passageway. Isobel scuttled back. He'd stripped from his coat and waistcoat and wore only his shirt, open at the throat, sleeves pushed to his forearms, and buckskins. She openly eyed his bare arms and chest; she'd have to be blind not to notice.

He raised a muscled arm over his head and propped it on the doorjamb. "It is, in fact, a pirate," he said.

"But I cannot believe you actually managed to locate *a pirate*," she whispered, craning around him to study Mr. Beddloe.

"Wasn't that the plan?" he asked. "Pirate interrogation?"

"Well, yes—I never dreamed you'd run one to ground so quickly. It was meant to take days. I thought you might—"

She paused and craned around him, trying to see through the crack in the door.

Jason reached behind him and closed the door.

She exhaled in frustration and shot him an exasperated look. He cocked a brow. The stale air of the passageway stirred. A bright energy sparked whenever they were alone. It hummed between them.

"I would like to observe the interrogation," she said.

"*Isobel*," he began.

"It's so terrible, is it?"

"I can certainly think of better ways to pass an afternoon. Roughing up unsuspecting criminals to pick through his profanity for truth is not my favorite activity."

"Is it working?" she asked.

"I would not trust him to lead me to a chest of buried treasure, but he has revealed one or two truths, given sufficient motivation."

"Good Lord, you're not beating him, I hope?"

Jason bit back a smile. His reputation at the Foreign Office had been built on strategy and intrigue, not brawn. He lowered his arm and leaned against the door with his arms over his chest. Perhaps he wouldn't correct her.

"Would you like to know what I've learned?" he asked.

"Yes. If I cannot observe."

Jason swallowed another smile. It felt so very good to collaborate with her. Her mind was quick and inventive and she showed uncommon courage. He'd loved almost every second of his career, but he was discovering how much more fun it was to play out the last act with a skilled accomplice.

He told her Beddloe confirmed what they'd suspected. An international band of pirates had abducted seven Englishmen here in the port village of Stokkseyri. They now held the Englishmen as captives.

Pirate captain Phillipe Doucette had sent the ransom letter to Jason's uncle. Doucette would hold the captives until he had some answer to that letter—or until he grew weary of keeping the captives alive. His spies were awaiting some answer in Reykjavík.

"At least that is what I think he's told me," Jason added. "Our chat has been complicated by his outrage and my inability to speak Welsh or Italian, his two languages of choice. He speaks a small amount of English and I speak a bit of Italian. Our relationship is . . . evolving."

"A Welsh-Italian pirate," she marveled.

Jason nodded. "But what of your reunion with this family, the Vagns?"

A success, she told him. She'd been warmly welcomed and learned that her friends *had* encountered the Lincolnshire merchants before they disappeared. The Vagns even considered joining their offer of smuggled goods—but then, with no warning, the Englishmen had disappeared.

"One day they were in Stokkseyri," she told him, "and the next they were gone."

"Taken by the pirates," provided Jason.

"The Vagns had the same suspicion."

"But did they venture a guess as to *why* they absconded with the hapless Englishmen?" Jason asked.

Isobel nodded. "The Vagns believe another family, the Skallagrímurs, were angry because the Englishmen had not approached them, and them alone, about the smuggling. The Skallagrímurs are allied to the pirates. They used that alliance to have the Englishmen removed from the island."

"Useful resource—pirates. If someone doesn't get their way."

Jason's brain was ticking through all they'd learned. He'd require far more details to mount any sort of a rescue, and the interrogation with Beddloe was progressing painfully slow.

He glanced at Isobel.

"The answer is yes," she said.

He'd never meant to put her in the path of living, breathing pirates. When it came time for the actual recovery, only himself and the men he'd hired were meant to approach Doucette. But they were bounding over the discovery and thundering toward the rescue. To be fully effective and efficient, he *could* use her help.

And she knew it.

"Isobel," he began cautiously.

"Stop playing nanny," she said, already moving around him and reaching for the door.

"Wait," he warned, blocking her way. She collided with him. An Isobel-shaped imprint sizzled on his chest. "You don't know what I was going to ask."

"Yes, I speak Italian, and yes, I will translate."

"I worry I'm taking advantage of you by asking this."

"You're not. I am not afraid of pirates." She reached around him again.

Again he blocked her.

"I beg your pardon," she said, a challenge. She tipped her face up.

He put his hand on her waist. She was too close not to touch. The motion was familiar, grounding. He'd not touched her since the rainy night on the deck. It felt so very natural. The unnatural thing would have been *not* touching her.

He lowered his voice. "Dealing with this man is not essential. I can manage if you don't want the bother. This is hardly what we discussed."

"'Tis no bother, I assure you," she said. "And the ship has long sailed on my doing only 'things we discussed.'"

Her tone was convincing, boastful almost, and he gave her a little jostle, pulling her close enough to fall against his chest. She stopped the motion with a palm to his pectoral.

"I've missed you," he whispered. Three words, already too much. He should have left it. Any sane, reasonable, respectful man would have left it.

She didn't break his gaze.

He added, "I want whatever you will give me."

Perhaps he'd not thought about what he wanted in as

many words, but it was true. He wanted whatever she would give him.

"I will translate, Your Grace," she whispered. "Please do not ask for more."

"I'm perishing," he whispered, surprised at his own poetry. It was not untrue.

"You're not getting exactly what you want," she corrected. "It is not the same thing as perishing. Believe me."

A loud bang from the other side of the door shattered the moment, and Jason released her. He reached for the door and she drew a shaky breath and patted the bun on top of her head.

"He's not happy about this . . . interview," he told her, trying to refocus. "But he's bound to a chair. And I will be beside you. You are safe. Do not be alarmed."

"Very little alarms me," she said. "Although I do wonder who will protect me from you."

"I'm sorry," he said. It felt like the correct thing to say. He did not want to irritate her. He did not even want to wear her down. He couldn't say what, exactly, he wanted beyond simply . . . *her.*

"Yes, we're all very sorry," she said. "Open the door."

Inside, they discovered that Mr. Beddloe had overturned a stack of orange crates with his boot. Splintered wood lay in heaps and oranges rolled to the far reaches of the galley.

Upon seeing them, Beddloe let fly a long string of invectives in Italian.

"Mr. Beddloe," announced Jason, "I see you've been busy. If you want an orange, all you need do is ask. This is my associate, Miss Isobel Tinker. How lucky for you that she's come along; now we may come to terms in earnest. She speaks fluent Italian."

Jason glanced at Isobel to confirm this and she rolled her eyes. To Beddloe, she rattled off some version of his introduction in slickly accented Italian.

"See? Better already," said Jason. "Now, with a lady in our midst, it's never been more important that you put forth your most gentlemanly behavior. She will translate, but she will not tolerate rudeness or disrespect. I will tolerate even less."

Isobel translated with far less flourish—four or five words—and crossed to the snarling pirate, studying him. In more rapid Italian, she made some sort of invective followed by a handful of questions.

Beddloe answered with another round of surly profanity. Isobel made a face, shook her head in exasperation, and took a step back.

Jason moved around her and dropped down on one knee. "I'll say this only once more, Beddloe. You will address the lady with respect."

He reached behind the chair and gave the ropes a firm yank, tightening the binding at his wrists. The pirate snarled and exclaimed something in Italian.

Jason returned to Isobel's side. "I hate interrogations," he mumbled.

"He's saying," translated Isobel, "that he wants his money now." She looked at Jason. "What money?"

Jason shrugged.

"He's saying," she said, "that you are *paying him* for any information he may reveal."

She looked back and forth between Jason and the bound pirate. "So you haven't beaten him?"

"*Beaten* may be a relative sort of term for what I've done. Perhaps a little? Although I allowed Shaw to do most of the work. Pirates must be convinced to leave perfectly warm taverns and perfectly potent rum to be rowed offshore and tied up for questioning."

Before she could respond, the pirate let forth another stream of angry Italian.

"What is he saying?" Jason asked.

Isobel looked back to the pirate, asked two questions in Italian, and listened to the spittle-punctuated reply.

To Jason, she said, "He says your cousin and his friends are surrounded by heavily armed guards on a barrier island off the southeast coast of Iceland. The island is a mile from the glacier caves, very remote, and difficult to navigate. Icebergs abound. He says rescuing them is out of the question, so make no attempt. He says the ransom demanded by his boss is the only way you'll see the Englishmen safely returned."

Jason let out a noise of frustration. Jokingly, he asked, "Should we ask him if Doucette accepts bank notes?"

Before she could answer, the pirate spoke again. His tone had changed, although still heavily laced with contempt. Beddloe sounded as if he had made some realization.

Isobel looked at the pirate. When she answered him, her Italian was slow enough for Jason to follow.

"*Perhaps I am,*" she told the pirate. "*So?*"

Now the pirate was off again, exclaiming in rapid-fire Italian. Jason was lost, but Isobel listened, stepping closer to look the man in the eye. Twice she held up a gloved hand and asked for clarification.

When their conversation was over, she turned to Jason. "This man has recognized me."

"A former patron to Everland Travel, is he?" Jason teased.

"Very clever. No, a former, er, *friend* of Peter Boyd's.

Peter has been back to Iceland—the Vagns said this too. As late as last year."

"Alright—so?" Of all the things Jason did not care to discuss, at the top of the list was Peter Bloody Boyd.

"Peter returned to ramble about the volcanoes and soak in the thermal pools. But the Vagns said he also spent time with the pirates, which Mr. Beddloe has just confirmed. He's asking me where Peter can be found."

The pirate and Isobel exchanged a few more lines in Italian.

"Apparently," she reported, "Peter's last visit to Iceland resulted in a deteriorated rapport between Peter and the pirate band. Not only did Peter beat Phillipe Doucette at cards, which cost the pirates a large sum of money, but also Peter *stole* something from them. Doucette is outraged."

"Stole? Stole what?" Jason didn't care, not really, but she seemed to think it was important. Jealousy singed, just beneath his skin. They didn't have time for this.

Isobel spoke again to the pirate. Looking back to Jason, she said, "He stole a watch—a diamond-encrusted golden watch that was precious to Doucette. Of this, I have no doubt. Peter collected timepieces. If he encountered an example of a rare or precious pocket watch, he would beg, barter, or steal to have it."

"Alright," said Jason slowly. "And this means . . . ?"

Isobel turned back to Beddloe and fired off more questions.

"He says the pirates captured your cousin and his colleagues because their Icelandic allies ordered it, but the pirates *retained* the Englishmen and sent the ransom because Doucette has a significant grudge against anyone who is English. Because Peter is English. He is very focused on recovering his watch."

"Poor Reggie," sighed Jason, "always stumbling into someone else's quarrel."

Isobel wasn't listening; she spoke again to the pirate— or rather, the pirate was speaking to her, his dander renewed, his voice loud and angry.

"Careful," Jason warned. *"Watch your tone*, Beddloe."

Isobel paused, staring at Jason.

"Tell him," urged Jason. "Tell him he must be cordial or he may swim back to his barrier island, dodging icebergs as he goes."

"North," she said softly.

Jason paused at the sound of his name. He looked to her.

"North," she repeated.

It wasn't like her to speak to him with such personal emphasis. His heart contracted. He crossed to her. "What? What is it?"

She put a hand on his arm. "Do you realize what this means?"

"Ah?" he began, staring at her hand. "What *what* means? I told you I barely speak Italian."

"Peter's return. The angry pirates. The stolen diamond watch."

Jason sighed. "Look, Isobel, I'd hoped not to say this, but I actually couldn't care less about Peter Boyd. I would venture to say that my sole interest in him is calling the blaggard out—if ever I have the fortune of stumbling upon him. Stolen watches? Cheating at cards? I don't ca—"

"Listen to me," she said, squeezing his forearm. "I raise it because the pirates' anger at Peter may predispose them to a *trade* with us."

"What does that mean?"

"It means, they may hand over your cousin and his colleagues without having to pay the ransom. They might do it in exchange for—" She paused, allowing her words to hover in the air like a net. Jason had the acute feeling he was about to be caught up.

"In exchange for," he prompted, his stomach tightening in dread.

"Trade your cousin in exchange for someone with a connection to Peter Boyd. Trade *for me*. I am Peter's known associate. His former lover. They will want me."

"What?" The word came out like a rasp. Jason wondered for a moment if she had reverted to Italian. He didn't understand.

"What Mr. Beddloe is telling me," she explained, her voice a whisper, "is that his boss, the pirate captain Phillipe Doucette, has been nearly driven mad by Peter Boyd. Peter shamed him and deceived him and robbed him of this rare and precious timepiece. Doucette would be thrilled to acquire one of Peter's known associates as a way to entrap him. This means, you could actually *trade me* for your cousin."

"Forgive me," said Jason, "I don't mean to be difficult, but I'm struggling to understand what you mean by a *trade*."

Isobel glanced at the pirate and then marched from the room, gesturing for Jason to follow.

He trailed her like he was stepping off a cliff.

"Look," she said, whirling on him in the passageway. "I've never seen this pirate before in my life. I knew Doucette very little. I knew his Icelandic wife—also a little. But this person?" She pointed in the direction of the bound pirate. "I don't know him. I barely distinguished one pirate from the next when I was here. And yet clearly he *knows me*. From this, let us assume that *all* the pirates will remember me."

He wanted to tell her that she was unforgettable. He wanted to tell her that he, himself, would never forget her. That one of the reasons he would never forget her was that he meant to *never trade her to pirates*.

"They will believe I've remained one of Peter's Lost Boys," Isobel was saying, starting to pace. "If they are searching for Peter and this missing diamond watch, they would take me in a heartbeat. To use me as bait. For Peter."

"What?" The more she explained it, the worse it became.

"Stop saying 'what'!" she ordered, shoving at his chest with her palms. "I know you understand what I'm proposing."

"I do *not* understand what you are proposing. I would never hand a woman over to pirates, especially not *you*. My God, Isobel, what do you take me for? What good is gaining my cousin if I have lost you? To pirates, for God's sake!"

He watched her blue eyes expand as she contemplated what this statement revealed. Jason seemed to have stopped caring what he revealed; she might as well know.

"Please stop," she said, a scold, although there was a new sort of lilt to her voice. "Of course I will not be *lost*. You think I cannot evade Phillipe Doucette? You insult me."

"But you didn't even want to come here!" he said. "Not even to translate. And now you're offering yourself up to pirates?!"

"I'm here now," she said, "and I will do whatever is necessary to finish the job and return home. Did you hear what Beddloe said about a recovery mission on this glacier-strewn barrier island? Impossible, he said."

"Do not underestimate me or my men," he said.

"I'm not saying it cannot be done, but I know it will take time. And resources. It will extend our stay in Iceland. Let us not forget that winter draws ever nearer. Autumn is here. The longer we remain, the more arduous our journey home."

"Fine," he said, "I'll pay the ransom."

"The ransom money is in bank notes," she countered. "You said so yourself. You don't have gold."

"Where would the desperate families of Lincolnshire acquire *gold*?" he said, making excuses that didn't matter. "They could barely scrape together credit from the bank."

"Trust me when I say that bank notes will be poorly received by pirates. They will reject them and wish to renegotiate. I cannot dicker around Iceland, changing over bank notes with pirates! I must return home as soon as possible. I've a new life to begin. Samantha needs me. My mother needs me."

"But, Isobel," he said lowly, breathlessly, trying to level with her, *"pirates*?"

"I mean to escape almost immediately," she explained, the words slow and deliberate, as if she was denouncing imaginary monsters for a child. "It would take almost no effort. The trouble with escapes, as we both know, is managing *a group*, shepherding a *group*, into the clear. Think of your Spanish dungeon story. You had fifty men to secret from the cell. Imagine if it had been only you. How much easier?

"Now imagine," she continued, "you are a small woman, widely underestimated—*if* you're noticed at all. Yet with all the necessary skills."

"I will not imagine it," he vowed, "if the escapee *is you*."

"You may even aid and abet me," she assured. "With me on the bargaining table, you can manage the terms. Set the transfer somewhere close and safe. Then *you* may facilitate the rescue, if it heartens you. How much easier to rescue me alone, on dry land, than seven Englishmen in varying degrees of wretchedness from a barrier island surrounded by ice?"

Jason could not speak.

"I promise," she said, "you will scarcely have left the bargaining table with the merchants before I'll have escaped. We'll establish a rendezvous point. I will meet you."

"I thought I was rescuing you." He was grasping at straws.

She wasn't listening. "Did you not hear me describe the life I led before Mayfair? I have not always been a girl in a travel shop. I can do this."

"Please," Jason said, holding up a hand. His mind spun.

"Please—what?" she demanded.

"Fine," he said, "allow me to ask you this. I'm not entertaining your idea, it's merely a question. Sheer curiosity. *Why*, exactly, would I claim to be in possession of you? Miss Isobel Tinker, former 'Lost Boy,' up for trade to pirates? Why?"

"You would say that I am your prisoner," she informed him. "Of course."

"Of course!" Jason blurted. He walked to the galley door and—*bam!*—gave it a shove. Beddloe could be heard behind the door, shouting in Italian.

He turned back to her, trying to think of some reply

other than, *Absolutely not*. And yet his brain was consumed by those two words.

"You could say," she rhapsodized, "that you heard
I had a bounty on my head and you captured me in
order to gain back your cousin. Or you could say you
stumbled upon me as a vagabond, picked up in a foreign port. The pirates would buy any number of stories,
considering what they knew of the Lost Boys. It would
be no surprise to see me washed up and in your possession. We would play it up. Put me in chains, prod me
with a stick, that sort of thing. With the correct props
and costumes, the pirates would see what they wanted
to see."

"*Absolutely* not," Jason declared, falling back on what
he really wanted to say.

"But why not?" She threw her hands in the air.

"*Because,*" he said, "I do not relinquish women to
known criminals. Because I do not trade human life
for . . . for anything—"

"I've said it would *not be a real trade*."

"Also because," he pressed, "I did not recruit you for
playacting. I recruited you to translate, serve as our
guide, and . . . and because I . . . I value you." It was a
weak word—*value*—for how he felt about her, but that
was a conversation for another day.

He glanced at her. She'd sucked in a breath to counter
him but now closed her mouth.

He added, "You're mad if you think I would ever turn
you over to pirates."

He thought she would say something—he *waited* for
her to say something—but she was silent. She blinked
up at him, her blue eyes wide with a mix of confusion
and disbelief.

"Isobel," he said, a plea.

She would not answer. Her expression evolved into an impatient sort of, *Yes—and?*

She crossed her arms over her chest.

She *tapped* her tiny, booted foot.

"You told me you wanted to be treated like a lady," he said. "You wanted to be treated with the same regard I might pay your cousin—who, by the way, I would also not *trade to pirates.*"

"And *you told me*," she countered, "that you've infiltrated enemy camps to extract orphans. You told me that you've staged jail breaks from Spanish prisons, pretending to be a captured guard. From the start, you've insisted that improvisation is your style, that you pull plans together based on the unlikely resources at hand. Which is precisely what I'm endeavoring to do. And yet you refuse? I'm sorry, Your Grace, but I'm beginning to think your wartime tales are a wild exaggeration."

He laughed. He actually laughed. "If you think you can bait me by wounding my pride, Isobel, you don't know me at all."

"Perhaps I know you or perhaps I don't. But one thing is certain: you *don't know me* if you don't trust me to manage this." Her eyes flashed.

Jason stared back, his heart pounding. He did trust her. But he also—

He could not risk her safety.

He could not risk losing her.

"If ever you *wanted* to know me," she added, fresh challenge in her voice, "you would allow this. So that I might demonstrate."

Jason leaned his head to the side and narrowed his eyes. "Trading you to pirates is the key to your true self, is it?" he asked. "If I won't go along, you'll keep me forever at arm's length?"

"That's not what I meant," she said defensively, and Jason cocked an eyebrow.

"Look," she went on. "We *will* do this. We'll do it because it's quick and clean and efficient and cheap. And when we're finished, I'll return to England in time to book spring holidays in my new shop. And I will celebrate my mother's birthday. And prevent Drummond Hooke from poaching all of my clients."

The image of her . . . behind a desk . . . planning holidays for rich women . . . toiling in her old life . . . took shape in his mind, and Jason felt a wave of something like panic.

"I cannot return to port now," she proclaimed. She took up her case and began backing away. "Going forward, I must look like your prisoner. I'll send a note to the Vagns asking them to not discuss my visit today with anyone."

"You're not commanding this mission, Isobel," he said, but the words came out like a test. He sounded nothing like a duke or a spy.

He sounded like a man who could not tell her no.

"I want to go home," she reminded in a singsongy voice. She was still backing away. "This is a bit of luck, North—a wonderful bit of luck. Do not squander it out of some misplaced sense of caution. Unless this is about your avoidance of the dukedom."

"It's not," he called, and he meant it. It was about her.

It is about you, he wanted to call, but she'd turned and was striding down the passageway.

"Make Mr. Beddloe comfortable but don't release him," she said over her shoulder. "If he reports what he's seen and heard to his comrades, the plan will never work."

The plan, thought Jason, his stomach filling with dread.

Isobel made the corner at the end of the passageway and was gone.

Chapter Fifteen

One day later, Isobel stood in her cabin, examining tidy stacks of green garments on her bed. This would never do. The soft wool, the fine muslin, the silk and lace detailing of her wardrobe—these were the clothes of an elegant Mayfair shopkeeper, not . . . pirate bait.

She'd evolved in so many ways by returning to London, including the way she dressed. She adored the color green and had made it her signature hue. Fashion and finely made clothes had always been a passion, and her London wardrobe had been designed to impress her female clients and make her feel tasteful and confident.

When she'd been one of Peter's Lost Boys, she'd dressed to appear careless, natural, and wild, relying on a versatile collection of well-made staples: men's linen shirts; brocade skirts; a silk shawl that could be worn as a sash, cloak, turban, or ten other ways. The result had been provocative—but not because it was revealing (although it was often revealing)—but rather, because it seemed *unconsidered*. She cared so very much but worked very hard to look as if dressing had been an afterthought.

None of that mattered now, except that she would work very hard to make herself, now seven years older, appear as carefree as she once had.

Starting with this very morning, when she would have to leave the brig and go out. Stokkseyri was hardly known for its shops, but there would be a meager mercantile and a storehouse selling provisions for fishermen and sailors. She had other needs too. One did not submit oneself to pirate capture without a ready supply of decoys, distractions, and defenses. How proud Samantha would be.

Isobel sent a note to the duke, requesting a trip to shore. Now that the plan was to trade her life for the Englishmen, she must always appear to be Northumberland's captive.

"This feels risky," North told her an hour later. She balanced on the bench seat of the swaying tender while sailors lowered it to the water with a splash. Mr. Shaw sat at the helm, ready to row them to shore. North sprawled on the opposite bench.

"If Mr. Beddloe can be believed," she told him, "there are no pirates or pirate spies in Stokkseyri. He was only in town himself because of a woman."

"His first mistake," grumbled Jason, and Mr. Shaw snickered.

"Calling to shops in Reykjavík would be a risk," she predicted. "But a quick trip to these shops will not disrupt our plan. Although you should pretend to sort of . . . lord over me, just in case."

He laughed at this, amused, she assumed, by the notion that she could be *lorded over*. Isobel smiled a little herself. In fact, he did not lord over her. He was not happy about trading her to the pirates, but he was doing it. He'd consented.

She'd worried so much about fighting her attraction to some man—any man, especially him—but had the real triumph been her newfound ability to speak her mind? To fight for her notion of the best plan?

The thought of telling Peter Boyd what to do, or how, or when, had been absurd. Everything about him pointed to complete acquiescence. He alone played the tune to which they all danced.

It was not the same with North. Yes, he'd compelled her to come on this mission, but he'd earned her cooperation with something very valuable.

And trading with the pirates had been her idea. In this, they were equal collaborators. He'd resisted heartily, but in the end, he'd taken her seriously and done things her way.

"What do you need in the village?" he asked, staring at the craggy rocks of the shore and rough-hewn wharf.

"Clothes actually," she said. "Doucette will expect to see the Isobel Tinker he remembers, not a travel agent from Mayfair."

"You expect to find a dressmaker in Stokkseyri?"

"I don't need a dress," she said. "I need to cobble together some semblance of a costume." She took a deep breath. "And I require a few other . . . staples."

"Dare I ask?"

"Better, perhaps, if you do not."

The tender slid to the pier, sloshing unsteadily as North handed her onto the slick planks. She turned her back to the warehouses and pulled up the hood on her cloak, shielding her face within its velvety folds. Her peripheral vision was blocked, but she could feel Jason hovering beside her, large and uneasy. Even on the rowboat, the tight set of his shoulders and his glower conveyed deep objection. He wasn't happy, a circumstance she did not relish, but at least it would play well with the locals.

"Has your messenger reached Doucette's man in Reykjavík, do you think?" Isobel asked, keeping her head bowed, her posture submissive. They walked briskly to Stokkseyri's lone shopping street.

"By dawn, I hope." A weary sigh. "The die has been cast."

"I suppose we can rely on Mr. Beddloe's claims about the best site to set the swap."

"The entire plan is built on supposition," said North flatly. "Where to meet, who will come, if they will want you, what they'll do with you when I *trade you*."

He was unhappy. This was no secret. Even so, he'd made a handful of declarations to her. Not promises. Not poetry. Overtures. And she'd made no response.

No, that wasn't true. Inside her mind and her heart, hidden where no one could see, her response had been the most wonderful sort of unfurling. She'd heard everything he'd said, from the smallest half sentence to the declaration that he "valued" her too much to trade. The words had been a warm sun to a thawing soil. Her heart had sprung up, growing from a hard seed, buried deep, into a life that wanted to flourish.

On the *inside*.

On the inside, she'd grown and flourished.

On the outside, she must appear dormant and stony.

Dukes, no matter how much they "valued" girls like Isobel Tinker, did not love them and respect them—not as their wives or the mothers of their children.

They did not acknowledge them in public places, or pass Christmas morning in their company, or introduce them to family and friends.

They did not marry them.

Isobel had seen this, and she was certain she would not survive being anything less.

"Here we are," North sighed, rounding the corner on a muddy street lined intermittently with clapboard buildings and crude stone structures. "Let us make haste. Shaw and I have plans to ride to the proposed meeting site to scout the terrain."

"I'll come too."

"Nosing around this fishing village is one thing," he said, "but it's too risky for my bargaining chip to scout a meeting site alongside me. You must hole up on the brig like a good little captive. Unless . . ." he glanced at her, ". . . you're having second thoughts."

"No second thoughts."

"I felt like it was too much to hope. Enjoy your last breaths of freedom until this is over." He looked up and down the street. "What first? The milliner or the stationer?"

"Very clever," she said. "If I recall, there is a fish stall whose proprietor will, for the right price, part with one of his very handy little gutting knives, which is the perfect—"

"You're buying knives?" he gritted out, stepping in front of her. "I've escorted you on a shopping trip to buy *knives*?"

"Shhh," she warned. "Remember you are my captor. If you must know, I left my favorite dagger at home."

"You have a favorite dagger?"

"Lower your voice and keep calm or people will take notice."

"Oh, and a young woman buying a dagger will come off as unremarkable?"

She was just about to tell him that a fish-goring knife would not be considered an odd purchase for anyone in rural Iceland, but her eye was caught by an unfamiliar shop across the wide street. She paused. Took a step closer. The shop was crowded in between two existing structures, the blacksmith's and a wainwright. Seven years ago, there had been nothing there but an open space.

The new shop was housed in a wooden building with a cheerful awning, a wide front window, and a walk-way littered with what appeared to be merchandise spilling from an overrun inventory.

Above the door, a rustic sign hung crookedly, the red lettering surprisingly bold despite the obvious age.

"Godfrey's Treasure Trove," read the sign. A sub-heading beneath said, "Fripperies, Oddities, Baubles, and Relics."

Isobel squinted at the shop, surprised to encounter plain English signage in a remote Icelandic fishing vil-lage. All of the other businesses were labeled in Icelan-dic, if their owners bothered to advertise at all.

The items scattered beneath the shop window in-cluded a dress form, a yellow velvet chair, a basket of sculptural driftwood, and colorful wooden crates balanced in a stack.

With North trudging behind her, Isobel crossed the street to have a closer look. Inside the glass, translu-cent stones hung on silk threads, catching the pale sun. Crystals glistened from within goblets that lined the windowsill.

Isobel stepped back and read the sign again.

"This is an English establishment, I believe," she said.

"Perhaps they will be fresh out of daggers," said North, "and you can pick up a heavy Saxon bludgeon instead."

She spun on him. "Stop. You would not send me into the pirates' lair unarmed, so do not suggest otherwise.

You know me well enough by now: I'm neither delicate nor clumsy. You've made it clear that you do not like the plan, but you agreed to it, so let us not pretend I should face pirates unprotected. This cannot be the first time you've provisioned your team for some subterfuge, it cannot."

The duke exhaled deeply and turned his head to the side. His aristocratic jaw was granite, but he appeared to be grinding his teeth. He was so handsome it took her breath away. She wanted to fall against him and thank him for being afraid for her. She couldn't remember when anyone had worried that she might be out of her depth. She wanted to shake him and tell him *not* to worry, that Phillipe Doucette scared her not in the least.

But she must not thank him or shake him or touch him in any manner.

She must simply go through the motions of rescuing his cousin and slogging her way back to England.

"I'm going inside," she said. "If you remain in the street, please endeavor to look beastly and vigilant. Actually, your current expression will do nicely."

North swore under his breath and snatched off his hat. He ran an irritated hand through his hair. "Can you not comprehend how difficult this is for me?" he gritted out. "Will you make no allowance for how wrong it feels? Everything about it?"

He looked so miserable then, like a man inside a cage watching her stride about beyond the bars, jangling the key.

Isobel sighed and reached for his hand, tugging him into the shop.

"Pretend you're dragging me," she ordered, although it was plainly clear who dragged whom.

North followed. It occurred to her he'd always followed her. Since they'd met. He'd adhered to her. Another tendril of life unfurled inside her.

"Good afternoon!" sang a voice from inside the dim shop. "Godfrey's Treasures, at your service, sir, madam. I am Mr. Godfrey; do let me know how I might assist you."

"Hello," Isobel said cautiously. "You are English, are you not, sir?"

She looked about, noting shelves of books with English titles, at a moth-eaten Beefeater's uniform hanging from a hook, a bust of Shakespeare surrounded by faded silk roses.

The shelves held talismans from other cultures too. A glorious Mayan headdress, a Venetian mask, Swiss clocks ticking on a wall.

The shop was veritably bursting with merchandise. Sagging shelves, overflowing trunks, bins filled with everything from shoes to crockery. The smell of strong tea and something sweet—raspberry tarts?—wafted in the air.

Mr. Godfrey was a tall, soft man, with round shoulders and a large belly. He was dressed in the striped waistcoat and arm garters of a shopkeep. He stood behind a wide counter as if they were all in Bond Street.

"I am English, in fact," he confirmed. "Although I pride myself in stocking novelties from around the world."

"How did you come to set up shop in . . . Iceland?" asked North, appearing, at long last, to notice the sheer oddness of the place.

"Oh, I move about, sir," assured Mr. Godfrey. "This shop has served customers in twelve countries and two island territories. Diversity wants travel, I've found, and so does Mr. Godfrey." He chuckled. "I've had a lovely run in Iceland. Been here about six months, I'd say. I may move on before winter, or I may not. One never knows where one will wind up, do they?"

"No," muttered Isobel, nosing around the shelves, "one does not."

Mr. Godfrey was certainly unexpected, but he seemed harmless and very useful. She could provision for every contingency from among these offerings. She lowered the hood of her cloak to take a closer look.

"But how do you transport your inventory?" North asked. A fur rug of some indeterminable animal brushed his foot and he jabbed at it with his boot.

"Oh, this way and that," said Mr. Godfrey. "Carriage. Coach. Cart. Camel. Caravan. Canoe—"

"Right," said North, cutting him off. He leaned to Isobel and whispered, "The less we know about this place, the better. Hurry, can you?"

Isobel nodded and crossed to a display of leather goods. Her eyes lit immediately on a worn kid scabbard protruding from beneath droopy foliage of a spidery plant. She reached for it, nudging the leaves to the side to reveal a knife handle made of antler, its finger demarcations worn smooth. Isobel picked it up, tested its weight, and slid the dagger free.

She let out a little gasp. Perfection. The blade was short and wide, her favorite dimension, and keenly sharp. She'd always preferred a fat, stunted blade to long and thin.

Scooping a basket from the floor, she tossed the dagger inside.

Next, she found a length of heavy fabric, striped red and black—probably a former curtain—and stuffed it into the basket.

She came upon a tangle of belts and shook free a wide strip of floppy leather and added it to her pile.

Next, she chose a length of rope, two golden necklaces with paste stones, black boots with pointed toes and high heels in exactly her size, an eel-skin pouch on a string thin enough to secret beneath her clothes, a voluminous linen shirt with long sleeves, a felt vest likely designed for a fourteen-year-old boy, and a clutch of feathers, secured at the quill with a wire. She snatched up one item after another, dropping them into her basket.

As North chatted with Mr. Godfrey about the heat in India and the snow in Bavaria, she grabbed a few more items, then she made a final circuit of the cluttered shop and joined North at the counter.

"Ah, I see you've found one or two things to delight you," exclaimed Mr. Godfrey, peering inside her basket.

"Indeed," said Isobel. "What a boon your shop has been. I hadn't hoped to find so many treasures in one place. In fact, I had not hoped to find so many treasures in all of Iceland."

"We aim to please, miss," he said unpacking her basket. "But have you found everything you require? I have a few more items in the back, and I am happy to order custom items from my headquarters in London."

"You have a London headquarters?" repeated North, a strange look on his face.

"Actually," replied Isobel, "I noticed the old apothecary's case of vials and bottles. There, in the corner? Although the vials appear to be long since empty of any potions."

"Oh yes," said Godfrey. "The original owner, I believe, made the poor choice to consume all of his own inventory. After he recovered, he traded the case for a set of juggler's pins and a harpsichord. Likely a better path for the man."

Isobel flashed an impatient smile. "But I was wondering if you have, among your inventory, any medicinal herbs or tinctures? Especially anything that a lady might use . . . sort of . . . in—well, as a defense? That is, in *self*-defense? Fast-acting sleeping drafts or something that might induce sickness but not, er, death?"

Beside her, she heard North make a miserable sort of moaning sound.

Mr. Godfrey hummed contemplatively. "Hmm. In fact, I might have just the thing you're looking for. I traded for something like this in a market at Wandsworth."

He disappeared behind a curtain that concealed the rear of the shop.

Isobel glanced at North.

"Poison," North stated. "You're asking for *poison*?"

Isobel shrugged. "It's more of a drug, I'd say. It was my weapon of choice, once upon a time. It is nonviolent but incapacitates someone just long enough for me to . . . do whatever I may need to do."

"I should wait outside," North said, glancing around, but Mr. Godfrey bustled back to the counter bearing a small leather pouch.

"Are you familiar with the effects of ground apple seeds, miss?" the man asked.

"Oh, cyanide, yes," Isobel mused. "But is that dried apple seed?"

"In fact, it is. I've been told when ground into a fine dust, apple seeds can make a strong man very sick, but not kill him. In small doses."

"I need only a small dose," Isobel assured him, reaching for the pouch.

She could feel North watching her as she tugged open the tie and tapped the seeds into her gloved palm. "But might you have a book I can reference to get the dosing correct?" she asked.

"Let me see . . ." said Mr. Godfrey, disappearing behind the curtain again.

"I'm beginning to think I would be safer if I traded *myself* to the pirates," said North.

She chuckled. "I'm more than you bargained for. I know. I tried to warn you."

"I'll not underestimate your warnings in the future. Nor will I accept any refreshment you may offer."

I would never hurt you, she thought, funneling the seeds back into the pouch. *If only you could promise the same.*

Mr. Godfrey returned with a dusty leather-bound book. "I'm afraid I have a reference book, but it's written in Dutch."

"Not a problem," said Isobel. "I'll take it all. These items, the apple seeds—and the book. How much, if you please?"

"Oh," tsked Mr. Godfrey, "but did you not read the sign, miss?" He pointed to a faded wooden sign. "Godfrey's Treasure Trove does not operate on a system of *monetary* exchange. I only deal in *merchandise for trade.*"

"I beg your pardon?"

"Currency is not accepted here," he proclaimed. "You must trade something in your possession for these items."

"Currency not accepted," challenged North, his voice hard.

Isobel waved him off—they didn't have time to argue. "Very well," she said. "What sort of trade? How many of our own items will compensate for all of *this*?" She gestured to her not insignificant pile of purchases.

"That depends," mumbled Mr. Godfrey speculatively. "What do you have?"

North was growing indignant. "Now wait a bloody min—"

"How about this?" Isobel cut in, reaching inside the collar of her gown to pull up a small compass on a gold chain.

"*Ah*," said Mr. Godfrey, his eyes lighting up. He held out meaty hands, fingers spread eagerly as Isobel un-looped it from her neck. "*What have we here?*"

"Isobel, wait—" ordered North, but she ignored him.

"The pendant of this necklace is a golden compass," she said. "The needle actually spins; it functions like a real compass. You may take the chain too, if it is enough for these items."

"*A compass necklace*," marveled Mr. Godfrey, holding it up to the light.

While Isobel waited and North drummed his fingers in irritation, the shopkeep examined the necklace under a magnifying glass and smoothed his fingers over the compass face.

"Oh, it's engraved," cooed Mr. Godfrey.

"It is," confirmed Isobel.

" 'Second star to the right,' " read Mr. Godfrey, squinting at the back of the compass. "EoC."

"Yes," said Isobel. She was well aware of the inscription. She waited for some reaction inside her chest, some cry of regret or clawing hesitation, but she felt nothing. The inscription might as well have read, "Made in Birmingham." She was glad to see it go and what better place to part with it than Iceland?

"But was this a gift, Isobel?" North asked lowly. "Who is EoC?"

Isobel shook her head. "It doesn't matter. If Mr. Godfrey will accept the trade, we can be on our way. We've lingered in the village too long."

"Look," said North, turning to Mr. Godfrey, "I've a sword on my ship, Spanish steel, gold and silver on the hilt, if you must have—"

"Swords are of far less interest," dismissed Godfrey. "Jewelry with some function—like this compass—is rare, and this piece is also beautiful. A true 'treasure' for my 'trove.' I'll gladly accept this in trade; in fact, I am in your debt. Will you not take something else from the shop?"

Isobel exhaled in relief. "Thank you. I require nothing more, but if you will remain quiet on the topic of this visit, I would be grateful. No man and woman called today, nothing was traded, you *did not see us*."

"Never you fear," assured Mr. Godfrey. "All of my clients are entirely confidential."

"Excellent," she said.

While North glared at Mr. Godfrey, shaking his head and making wordless noises of discontent, Isobel loaded his arms with her purchases and wound her way out of the shop and into the street.

The sun had burned through the white haze of morning, and wet rooftops and slick pathways sparkled.

"Isobel," North said lowly, coming up beside her, "the initials on the necklace were *EoC*. That can only mean *Earl of Cranford*. Have you traded a piece of jewelry given to you by your father?"

"I did, in fact," she said, "and good riddance." She pulled up her hood.

If she expected him to protest or scold her for making

the trade, he did not. He stood silently beside her, frowning at the possessions in his arms.

Isobel said, "These clothes will need to be . . . roughed up a bit. There is a canyon just outside of the village. A shallow river runs through it."

She looked right and left. The street was deserted except for milling dogs and a handful of sailors from their own ship. No one would notice them slipping away.

"If I dunk them now and beat them against a rock," she mused, "they should be dry by tomorrow. I'll need to look worse for the wear."

North nodded and said, "God only knows what you've been through, Isobel, and *you* look no worse for the wear. Beautiful and unscathed, that is how you look. I'd wager you'll remain so, no matter how many times you dunk yourself in the river."

It was an odd compliment, part acknowledgment of her past, part nod to her courage. Also, he said she was pretty. The shimmers inside her belly tumbled.

She set out in the direction of the trail. "I intend to dunk the clothes, not myself."

Chapter Sixteen

Isobel led him to the end of the street, and then another, and then civilization seemed to drop off and the wilderness opened up to a vast plain of rough green, cut here and there by jagged rock. In the far distance, thick mountains loomed like the shoulders of giants.

The sky was a color of blue Jason had never seen. The air smelled loamy and verdant, undercut by an acrid wind. When the grass swayed, it made a light hissing noise. He no longer heard the sea.

A trail wound through the tall grass, and Isobel set out, her heavy cloak bending the blades as it dragged behind her.

"I would have paid for these provisions," he called, following. His boots made a crunching noise on the black silt of the trail, and he looked around, making certain they were alone. "I'd never hold you responsible for supplies."

"The man didn't accept money," she called back.

"There is a sum he would've accepted, I assure you, given the correct placement of the decimal."

"Why challenge him? It's part of the character of the shop."

"Yes, and that character just robbed you of a necklace that might've had sentimental value. Likely it held some tangible value. It looked to be real gold."

"The compass had no value to me," she said.

"You *wanted* to be rid of it, is that it?"

"Yes," she said, "I wanted to be rid of it."

"What did it mean?" he prodded. "The inscription?"

"It meant nothing," she said. "Meaningless poetic drivel."

Jason exhaled in frustration. She didn't want to tell him. Fine. It was his nature to be curious about people—it made him an excellent spy—but it wasn't his nature to pry family secrets from women who didn't want to explain. Or at least this hadn't been his nature before he'd met her.

Not that it mattered; she was impervious to prying. She did as she pleased obviously.

They trudged on another five yards. Jason paused, shrugging from his coat and fashioning it into a crude sack to carry her myriad purchases.

But was it prying, he thought, to sense pain or injustice and to want to know?

Was it prying to strive for greater understanding of her?

Isobel Tinker was like a very bright, very warm thing that he—

That he *wanted*.

There were no other words. He wanted every part.

Alarmingly, and perhaps for the first time ever, he had no idea how to attract or sustain her. Learning her history seemed as useful as anything else. If he meant to travel to the moon, he would need a map.

He glanced around him, acknowledging the beauty of the landscape. Iceland was spectacular, he'd give it that. Untamed and dramatic. They'd progressed through a field of tall grass, but the vegetation had given way to rocks. Lichen edged out the grass, glazing every stone with green.

"What did it say?" he asked, trying again. "The inscription on the compass?" If she could not tell *him*, perhaps she could tell the landscape. The vast wildness would swallow it up.

"I don't remember," she said.

"You do remember."

"What could it matter?" she sighed.

"If it didn't matter, you would say it freely."

"Fine," she said, stopping to lean against a craggy outcropping. They were climbing steadily higher. Pillars of rock had formed a stone forest around them.

She caught her breath. "It said, 'Second star to the right.' And before you ask, I'll tell you what it meant. The earl meant, 'Seek direction in your own imagination. Or in your dreams. Or your heart.' As I said, useless babbling."

She shoved off and climbed on. Over her shoulder, she said, "What he meant was, 'You are not important enough for me to make an effort . . . you'll have no one to guide you or to protect you . . . unfortunately your mother is bollocks at anything approaching guidance . . . so good luck sorting out life's challenges, large and small.' "

She turned to face him, walking backward. "*That's* what the engraver should have stamped on the compass."

"Perhaps there wasn't room?" he joked.

She laughed. His heart tapped against his chest. *He* could protect her. *He* wanted to protect her. She turned back to the trail.

They came to a dropping-off place where the ground

formed a low cliff over a wide ravine. At the bottom, some ten yards beneath, a shallow river snaked right and left, the water obscured by a rising mist.

"How do we descend?" he asked.

"The rocks form steps just . . . here."

She led him around an outcropping of stone and then to a natural ramp.

The canyon was enchanting, an open-air cathedral. Rock statues loomed, jagged and gnarled, veiled by vapor from the stream.

When they reached the water, Isobel removed her heavy cloak and rolled up her sleeves. She bade him unfurl her purchases on a high rock, and she collected the striped fabric, the linen, and the vest from inside his coat. Kneeling beside the water, she lowered the pieces into the river, weighing them down with stones. The water was shallow, no deeper than her hand, and they were easily pinned. Water rushed over and under, soaking the fibers until they fluttered against the riverbed.

Next she located a paddle-shaped rock and scooped up a slug of sediment. Bending over the striped fabric, she scraped the mud here and there, streaking it with black.

Jason sat down on a nearby rock, relishing the view of her bending over the steamy water, skirts hiked over an elbow, deft hands ministering to the clothes. She'd worn lavender today, a departure. He couldn't remember her in anything but some shade of green. The pale purple fabric seemed to glow in contrast to the landscape. Here and there, small purple flowers dotted the riverbank, their blossoms almost the same color as her dress. The combination of purple against green grass was as beautiful on Isobel as it was on the flower. The mist from the water set her creamy skin glowing; blond hair dropped from her bun in damp tendrils and curled against her neck.

The urge to go to her, to take her by the waist and pull her to him, to kiss her, to *really* kiss her, was almost too much to bear. He bit off his gloves and dug his hands into the serrated rock. He forced his brain to return to their conversation. More than he wanted to hold her, he wanted to *know* her.

"Would it have been better to have no relationship whatsoever with the earl," he asked, "than to know him only a little?"

She sat back on her haunches on a smooth flat stone. She extended her palm, hand up, like a footman with a tray. The gesture of *Who knows?*

Jason waited, allowing the question to float between them. He unbuttoned the top two buttons of his waistcoat. The air was cool but there was no shade from the sun. He unbuttoned two more.

After a moment, she told him, "You should feel the water."

He paused, the waistcoat halfway down his arms. He looked to her.

She had begun to remove her boots. "You've traveled all this way," she said. "You might as well experience the heated waters."

Jason shucked the waistcoat with due speed and pulled at his boots. He hiked his buckskins to his knees, and picked his way to her.

She was sitting with her knees drawn up, her discarded boots and a pile of her stockings beside her. Small feet poked from beneath her skirt. She wiggled her toes.

"Sit here and put your feet in," she instructed, not

looking at him. "Careful, it's rather hot. Hotter than you expect."

She extended her feet and held them over the rushing surface of the clear water. He watched her dip her toes in the stream and stir them in a small circle. He'd stopped breathing or he was panting, he didn't know. He didn't care.

"If you move about," she said, "you'll hit upon a streak of cold to temper the very hot. The cold is runoff from the mountain snow. The hot is water heated by the volcanoes. You'll want to find the place where they mingle." When, finally, she sank her feet in, she let out a little sigh.

Jason swallowed hard and tried to tamp down his body's response. Every newly revealed part of her— trim ankles and shapely legs, delicate toes and high arches—was beautiful. His heart thudded. His loins tightened.

"Go on," she said, glancing up. She was smiling, but she must have seen the look of longing on his face, because her smile faded. She blinked slowly, sensually, once, twice.

Jason forced himself to move, dropping beside her on the rock and extending his feet. The heat was so hot at first touch, it registered as cold. He jerked back, and she laughed. "I warned you," she said.

He stood up—it seemed like the manly thing to do—and waded into the boiling water, his hands on his hips. She laughed, and he looked back, winking at her.

"It's glorious," he said. Goose bumps rose on his skin. The water, when he found the right spot, was deliciously warm.

"You're glorious," she whispered, and he missed a step. He went very, very still. He turned.

"Isobel?" he asked softly.

She stared back through a veil of mist. Her bun had slid to her neck; damp ringlets framed her face. Her throat was wet. Her cheeks were pink. Her blue eyes had narrowed to lazy slits.

Jason's body felt languid and heavy but his need for her was very hard and utterly relentless.

"What could it possibly matter?" she asked softly. He studied the dewy beauty of her face.

"S'bell?" he asked, wading to her.

He came to a stop before her, looking down. She stared at the swirling water. After a long, charged moment, she reached out and placed a small, flat hand on his leg, just above the knee. Pleasure radiated from the imprint of her hand. Every cell in his body strained to her.

Spreading her fingers, she kneaded his quadricep. Slowly, almost dreamily, she slid the hand higher.

Jason let out a hiss.

"We are alone," she remarked softly to his leg.

She extended the other hand and clasped it around the back of his knee. He staggered a little. His body was as hard as the riverbed.

"Why aren't you terrible?" she asked, looking up.

"Well," he began. His voice cracked and he cleared his throat. "I am prepared to trade a young woman to pirates. Does this count for nothing?"

"I want you to kiss me," she whispered. "I cannot bear it if you do not."

It was what he'd been waiting for. In an instant, he dropped to one knee in the water. She grabbed his shirtsleeves in handfuls.

"Say it again," he clipped, "so that I am certain."

"I want it." Her voice was barely above a whisper. Her blue eyes, as bright as the sky, bored into him.

Still, he hesitated. This was not what she'd said before. Before, she'd said the opposite.

"I can barely remember the reasons it would be so very wrong," she said. "My survival depends on my ability to resist touching you or any man, and yet—"

"Ah, must we invoke '*any* man'?"

She laughed and ducked her head.

His heart slammed against his chest. His mouth watered. Rocks dug into his knee and searing water soaked his buckskins and he didn't care. His body registered only his raging desire to kiss her.

"You've been the perfect gentleman," she whispered, leaning in.

"Have I?"

"You're clever and agreeable, so handsome. You listen and understand and pretend to care—"

"I do care," he said, staring at her mouth. A scoundrel's favorite lie, but it was true.

"I'm just a woman," she sighed. "I can only resist so much. You know my terrible history and all the reasons for it. And you know my narrow future and all the reasons this can happen only once."

"This?" he asked.

He was going about this all wrong, and he knew it. His oh-so-proficient powers of seduction had been swept away; only a windy cavern remained.

"Unless you don't care to . . ." she ventured, squeezing her eyes shut. She seemed to waffle.

Jason's reflexes took over.

"I care to," he assured her, leaning closer. He flattened one hand on the rock beside her hip and cupped the back of her head with the other. She opened her eyes and gave a little whimper. She wrapped an arm around his neck.

He descended in the next breath, locking his mouth on hers.

He was instantly submerged, like every other time. The first contact with her lips sucked him under. He was swept from the river, and the wilderness, and the island, and the Atlantic Ocean. He existed only to taste her, to breathe her.

They could have been anywhere in the world; he lived inside the kiss.

After a torrent of lips and tongue and breath, he collapsed on the rock beside her, panting. He reached for her, pulling her into his lap.

"I'm sorry you had to tell me you needed this."

"I prefer it," she assured him, breathless. She hiked her knee and straddled him, tugging her skirts to her hips.

He gathered her by the bottom, molding her to him, and dug his heels into the riverbed, leveraging them.

"I typically pay closer attention to the bit when the kissing comes in," he said.

"I like to manage things." She dropped her mouth on his.

"I can live with that," he said, his last words before he could no longer speak.

HE COULDN'T SHATTER her heart, she thought, if her heart was held together by spackling and patches. It would not break so much as . . . distort?

And also they would do this only once—well, once *more.*

And "this" would be so very fast and fleeting. Just enough to tide them over.

And anyway, how could she feel more heartsick than she already did?

The only true Worse Thing, she reasoned, would be *not* having this. Not having some small part of him, here and now, teetering on the top of the world, alone together.

Her justifications didn't really matter. Every thought was dissolving; he was so very good at kissing, the best she'd ever known. She didn't want to miss a lick or a nip or a swipe or a—

He sucked in her bottom lip, and she flicked her tongue against him. He pressed her against his erection, and she pressed back, reveling in the explosion of sensation.

He was taller and broader than any man she'd known, and the logistics were delicious. If she wanted to kiss his eyelids, or press her ear to his mouth, or scrape her throat across the roughness of his whiskers, she had to *climb* him.

He helped her, kneading large hands up the backs of her thighs, cupping her bottom, lifting her.

They did not speak.

They kissed as if they would never again experience human touch.

They kissed as if he were a duke and she was a Lost Boy and they'd fallen in love, but neither had the good sense to stay away.

Good sense had no part of their embrace, the very best kind.

When he fell back on the rock, she followed him down, pausing only to claw at his shirt, popping buttons until she reached bare skin. He dug his hands into her hair, flicking pins into the rocks. Her hair fell down around them like sunshine.

"So long," he said between kisses, panting against her cheek. "I had no idea."

"Unfashionably long," she said. "My mother has made me swear never to cut it."

"Beautiful."

"*You* are beautiful," she said, rising up to gaze at his chest. She spread her hands on his pectorals, fanning her fingers over the muscle. He shouldn't be so hard and strong—he was a duke, after all; he should be soft and fragile. But he was also a spy, and although he claimed to waft about, tricking people into revealing secrets, she saw how he moved, how he stood. He was a man of action, and his body was a testament to his work. She dropped her mouth to the warm skin of his clavicle and kissed her way to his nipple.

He let out a groan and clasped her waist with both hands, squeezing, and then slid his hands up her rib cage. When he reached the hollow beneath her arm, she trembled, feeling the tickle. His fingers danced there a delicious moment before sliding around to cup her breasts.

Isobel sucked in a breath and rocked against him. He found the neckline of her dress and tucked two fingertips beneath the ribbon, sweeping downward. She rocked again and returned to his mouth.

"I want you," he said. "I want all of you."

She shook her head to deny him but did not break the kiss.

"You want this too," he said. "Your eagerness has set me on fire. I've never wanted anyone more."

"Kiss me," she said, and she gave him a sensual, feather-soft kiss. "And feel me." She found his hands and intertwined their fingers. "Enjoy this moment because I cannot risk more. I cannot risk—" She couldn't finish. She shook her head.

"But what of—"

She kissed him, hoping for silence. Why would he squander one moment of this stolen . . . stolen *heaven* to discuss what they mustn't do or what would not happen?

"I will not misuse you, Isobel," he said, pulling back.

When she tried to kiss him again, he untangled their hands and flipped them. One moment she was leaning over him, the next he cupped her head and braced her back and rolled left. He settled her gently on the stone, protecting her spine with his hand. Now he hovered above her, staring down.

Her hair spilled across the rock. Her feet hung in the warm, rushing water. He settled on her and the hard weight was a delirious pleasure. She surged up, making a whimpering sound.

He dipped his head. "I will not misuse you," he repeated, speaking next to her ear.

She closed her eyes to stop the tears. "You misuse me now by talking instead of kissing."

"I cannot fully enjoy this for wanting more."

She opened her eyes. "You can't?"

"Well . . ." he kissed her again, ". . . I can enjoy it, but I'm terrified of making a wrong move. You are . . . uncharted."

"Oh, I'm charted," she teased, pulling him to her lips.

"The risk of hurting you is very high, Isobel, and I won't do it. You must tell me what is possible."

"I'm better equipped to tell you what is *impossible*."

"What does that mean?"

His frustration was mounting; she could hear it in his

voice. Instead of caressing her, he held her at the waist. His grip was tight and possessive. She loved it; who had ever held her like this? He held her as if she might, at any moment, be ripped away.

But possession was never meant to be part of this encounter.

"Kiss me again," she said, "one more time, and I will tell you what is impossible."

He moved his hands to her face, cupping it. He teased soft circles at her temples with his thumbs. "Why don't I kiss you again, and then *I'll* tell *you*?"

She snaked her arms around his neck, pulling him down.

North resisted—his expression was bent on challenging her—but she licked her lips. His eyes were drawn to her mouth, and he dipped down, kissing her once, twice, and then lowering himself, muscle by muscle against her.

She could feel him holding himself off, trying to protect her smallness from his great size, but she hiked up her leg, hooking her knee on his hip, pulling him down. She wanted to feel all of him; she wanted his weight to pin her to this rock, to fossilize their embrace.

Their last kiss was hot enough to imprint on stone, a kiss for the ages. It would be forever preserved in her memory. Kissing him was like any of life's ultimate pleasures; it gave and gave and gave while, at the same time, it was completely without effort.

In the end, he was the one who pulled away. He gave her a final kiss, ground his body against hers, and made a growling noise. He rolled up. He turned his back to her, standing in the water.

Isobel lay on the rock, breathing hard, feeling cool

air move over her heated skin. She closed her eyes. She tried to remember every buzz and shimmer before it faded away. The unrequited desire—all the things they hadn't done—felt almost like pain. He would feel the same. He'd been frustrated before, but now? Now frustration would give way to bitterness, and bitterness would make him resent her. He was too kind for that, so he would pity her instead. Poor Isobel and her pitiful history that had landed them both in misery.

Or perhaps he wouldn't.

He'd not taxed her with any of the typically male, typically selfish reactions. She'd made near constant refusals to him, and he'd shown only compassion. It was the reason she now found herself on this rock, her body humming.

But even if he was never bitter or resentful or piteous, he would not marry her. This, she knew. And she was no man's mistress; this she also knew.

If, by some miracle, she ever had a child, the baby would be legitimate and claimed and *known*. It would not bumble through life with vague advice on the back of a compass.

Isobel sat up and straightened her dress. She quickly braided her hair and tied it in a knot on top of her head. She glanced at North. He was staring at the mountains in the distance.

"Will you walk with me?" she asked. "We can wade to the place the river bends; there is a waterfall. It is worth seeing. After that, we can walk back. The time will allow some of the water to drain from these clothes."

She began fishing the fabric and linen from the water, wringing them out, and draping them on the stone in the sun.

"Is that what you want?" he said, turning. His look was earnest; there was no bitterness or resentment. He was so handsome it bent her heart.

"Yes," she said, flattening the boy's vest against the rock. "It is what I want." It was one of the many, many things that she wanted, but likely the only thing she would get.

She added one more thing. "And to talk."

Chapter Seventeen

*J*ason struggled to comprehend something as complex as *words*.

Also in question: walking and breathing.

As a rule, he drifted through life with a casual manner and a carefree sort of easiness, but underneath it all, he prided himself on self-control. The casualness and the carefree prevailed because, at the end of the day, *he was in control.*

Today had felt like the ultimate test. Today, he clung to the splintering timber of self-control like a raft at sea. He was veritably drowning in desire. She was, without question, the most sensual woman he'd ever known. He wanted to swallow her whole.

"So, my father. The earl . . ." she was saying, walking beside him through the shallow river, the rushing water flashing hot and cold.

He forced himself to focus.

"The earl," he repeated. He cleared his throat and rolled his shoulders.

"His lack of guidance or protection wasn't his greatest fault," she said, "not really. I can be a . . . challenge to guide."

"I've noticed this about you," he said.

He concentrated on the searing water rushing in

gusts over his feet and ankles, willing the fog of lust in his brain to clear.

"To explain it, I must go further back than the compass. Honestly, I don't even remember when he gave the bauble to me. He was a constant presence in our lives for years, and he brought frequent gifts."

"When you were a child?"

"From infancy, really. Until I was about ten years of age. He did not live with us obviously, but he visited us often. Once a month? More when parliament was in session."

"Oh yes, he was an outspoken member of the Lords." Jason's voice took on the flat, resigned tone.

Isobel glanced at him. "You did not agree with his politics?"

"I am indifferent to his politics." Jason was shaking his head. "Forgive me, I'm spinning the conversation around to myself. Rude, I know. It's only that your comment made me think of my own seat in the House of Lords. Another expectation of the dukedom."

"It does not interest you?"

"Parliament is more interesting to me than farming, I suppose," he sighed, "but to do it properly, one is expected to research taxation and write opinions and loll about in smoky clubs, convincing other researchers and writers that your view is superior. It's so . . ."

"Established?" she guessed.

"Sedentary," he said on a breath. "Established, certainly. It's simply that I thrive on *doing* things, not . . . considering them."

"Was school a great chore for you?"

"You have no idea."

"If only you'd had my education," she said.

"Indeed. I hope you do not regret that part of your

history. You were very fortunate, in my view. I did more damage to Oxford, I believe, than the school did good for me."

She chuckled. "I don't regret my cobbled education. But I would've also enjoyed traditional school, I think— or at least the traditional schooling afforded to girls. I meet girls in the travel shop almost weekly. Some of them know so very little of life beyond England. Others are knowledgeable but have been taught to be afraid of the outside world. These sorts of restrictions were never part of my experience."

"I could tell this about you from the start," he said. "I couldn't put my finger on it, but I can see now it was a lack of fear and an open mind."

"So transparently fierce, was I?" she asked.

"So exciting," he corrected. "To me. But I digress. Will you finish your story?"

She made a noise that was half sigh, half moan. "Far less exciting—that."

"I would hear it," he said. "If you are willing."

"Right." She took a deep breath and squared her shoulders. "Cranford. Well. He was a fixture in our lives, and honestly? A jolly, doting father. He was clever and sweet and full of surprises. I adored him—loved him like any girl loves her papa, I assume.

"And my mother? Goodness. His presence brought immediate delight, which is saying quite a lot. She is prone to moodiness and petulance on a good day, but not in his company. She loved him so very much. We both did."

Jason nodded. "My parents enjoyed a love match. As a boy, I took it for granted, but as a man, I can see the foundational benefit of their harmony on my life. And I remember my shock upon witnessing the unhappy marriages of my friends' parents. My mates from school were equally as shocked when they witnessed my father's open affection to my mother."

They came to a giant bolder and worked their way around it, walking their hands along the cold, damp stone.

Jason added, "Their love is one of the many reasons I must return to Syon Hall and look after things properly. My father would be outraged, knowing how I have left his duchess adrift these last eighteen months."

"You will go when we finish here," she assured him.

"Yes," he said bleakly. "I will go."

"I cannot say for certain," Isobel said, "but I assume my father's actual marriage to Lady Cranford was *not* a love match. He was happy when he was with us, but it was more than that. Even as a child, I could see he regarded our flat as a refuge. His secret sanctuary. Of course, I was unaware of what—or from whom— exactly he was taking refuge. Well, until I became aware."

"Isobel," he said sadly. He was already so very sorry for whatever she would tell him.

She shot him a wan smile. "When I would ask my mother why 'Papa' did not stay with us always, why he did not *live* with us, she simply said that he was a very important man, a *nobleman*, and he did the important work of leading the country and advising the king, and all of this kept him terribly busy."

"Advising the king is a stretch," said Jason. He'd been indifferent to the Earl of Cranford before, but his opinion was rapidly sinking.

"When he visited our London flat," she continued, "it was like Christmas morning. The best meal was prepared, Mama and I dressed in our most beautiful clothes, and the house was filled with flowers.

"Some months, he would send for us to join him in Brighton, near his seaside estate—a house that sat empty most of the year. We were never invited *to* this home, mind you, but he arranged for us to have a lovely suite of rooms in a hotel overlooking the sea, and he met us for meals and stayed overnight with my mother."

Jason took her hand. He found he could not *not* touch her. She gathered her skirts in one hand and held to him with the other.

She said, "The only thing more delightful than receiving him in London was meeting him at the seaside.

"One day, when I was nine or ten, he'd sent for us to meet him in Brighton. We'd been there two days and he took us in his carriage to a beautiful café in the high street. He'd promised the chef did delectable lemon ices and peach tarts. Papa—"

She stopped herself, cleared her throat, and began again.

"*The earl* ordered a sampling of everything, the most extravagant tea, including champagne. The summer sun shone on a glistening sea, visitors milled in the street, and the three of us were enjoying the most delightful meal when, out of the blue, the earl caught sight of something out the café window.

"I'll never forget," she went on. "He was scooping up a dollop of cream, and he simply stopped, his spoon halfway to his mouth. His pink face went white; he dropped the spoon and splattered the cream all over his waistcoat. Mama was reaching for a napkin when he leapt up from the table. If my mother had not caught hold of his chair, it would have toppled.

"I remember laughing a little—he had an amusing manner, and his large gestures and wild stories delighted me—and I thought he was putting on a show. When I spun to see what he would do next, he'd turned his back. He was walking away—actually, he was bolting away—from our table.

"I opened my mouth to call him back, but my mother pounced and fastened her hand over my mouth."

"Oh God," Jason whispered under his breath.

"She was strong enough to keep me in my chair, but not to prevent me from craning around. And do you know what had happened?"

Jason did not want to guess.

"A family had entered the café. A fine lady, children, servants. Quality and money and manners emanated from the lot of them like the soft trill of a trumpet. Their movements were restrained but also smooth. I remember thinking they looked as if they rolled into the café on an invisible cart. There were three little boys, and they came to a stop before a glass counter of pastries and puddings. The café had beautiful confections; the display would've delighted any child. But these children simply stood near the glass, not touching or pointing.

"The lady was a substantial presence, tall and upright, with a subtle dress in a forgettable tone and a pursed frown. The servants stood on the periphery, fastidiously balancing armfuls of parasols and pails and toy boats. Beside the woman stood a little girl who looked to be five or six. She wore a white dress and a frown just like her mother's.

"Cranford hurried to the group," she went on. "At first I thought this family had displeased him—the café was small and their sheer number would overwhelm the room. If nothing else, we'd been having the most delightful tea and they all looked miserable.

"But Cranford was not displeased. He was scrambling to exonerate himself from the illusion—nay, the reality—of taking a meal, in public, with his mistress and his bastard daughter."

"Bloody hell, Isobel," Jason exclaimed, his voice echoing off the canyon wall. The lingering heat in his blood began to percolate with a new passion: loathing for the Earl of Cranford.

"The family that entered was his own," Isobel went on, ignoring his outburst. "His *real* family. The woman was the Countess of Cranford. The oldest boy was his heir, the next—now current—earl.

"And the little girl was his daughter. His actual, legitimate daughter. Lady Wendy Bask."

"No," said Jason, as if he could refuse the story. He stopped walking and turned to face her. He caught her other hand and pulled their joined hands to his chest, hiking her skirt.

"I struggled," she said, speaking to their hands, "trying to break free of my mother, but Georgiana kept her hand sealed firmly over my mouth and didn't budge."

Isobel looked up. "Was she restraining me to save my pride, or *her* pride, or *his* neck?" A shrug. "I don't know. She leaned down and whispered in my ear. 'Papa does not belong to us, Bell. He has another family. These people are his family and he belongs to them. We must allow him to go.' "

"Isobel," Jason hissed.

"I didn't understand," she said, "but at the same time, perhaps I did. Maybe I had always known but hadn't reckoned with it. Certainly I was unprepared to face the reality in that moment. This had been *our* time. *Our* holiday. And he was *my* papa."

"This story is unbearable," Jason said. "I can't believe you never pounced on the earl in a dark alley and choked him with the bloody compass."

It was a joke, but she didn't laugh. She stared up at him.

"How did it end?" he asked.

She shook her head. "No, no, it *is* an unbearable story."

"It's not obviously, because you have survived. You have borne it."

"Well, I have not perished. Yet. Is this surviving?"

"Yes. Indeed it is. And anyway, you've done more than 'not perish.' You are thriving, Isobel. You are a businesswoman in your own right. You are clever and beautiful and afraid of nothing apparently. Besides, the Story of Isobel Tinker is not yet finished. And perhaps I know how it ends."

She cocked her head, gazing at him. "You don't."

He gave a shrug. He wasn't sure why he'd said it, but it didn't have to be untrue. The tragedy that had marked Isobel's life would not follow her forever. Not if he had any power over it. He was, after all, a bloody duke.

She stared at him warily and then continued, dropping one hand and walking on.

"The next terrible bit is that we couldn't leave the café. The arrangement of our table, the door, the smallness of the dining room, prevented it. Georgiana could not rely on me to cooperate; I was in the throes of a temper fit, and the sheer commotion and *pardon-me*'s of maneuvering to the door in the cramped space would have caused a scene.

"In hindsight, I'm certain the countess was suspicious

of the earl's proximity to us. My mother is remarkably beautiful, as you may remember. She causes a scene wherever she goes. We were both lavishly dressed. Georgiana Tinker loves a costume.

"Considering this," she sighed, "we were forced to sit, as heaps of uneaten delights congealed on the table before us, and watch as the earl welcomed his family in the same booming voice with which he always greeted us. We watched him indulge them with treats, and then we watched him *dine with them* just steps from us. He regaled them with clever stories and made spirited inquiries about their days since he'd been away.

"His family believed him to be in London, I think. Meanwhile, he'd not known they would sojourn to their seaside home. It was a chance meeting. And it destroyed me for a very long time."

"Of course it did," said Jason. He tipped his head to the sky and closed his eyes.

"Most people," she said, "would think me and my mother should expect nothing more than what happened that day."

"I am not one of those people."

"I know you are not," she said. "I would not have revealed it if I did not think you would somehow . . . understand."

"What is there to understand? Your father abandoned you to maintain harmony with people he prioritized over you. It was a selfish cruelty that neither you nor your mother deserved. Even his 'other family' did not deserve the duplicity. You've been remarkably resilient, Isobel. There are many girls who would not recover from this sort of betrayal."

Isobel nodded, and he was glad he'd said the correct thing. He'd meant it, every word, but bald honesty could cause fresh hurt. He did not want to add to her pain.

"Do you believe *your* father had no by-blows?" she wondered. "No kept mistress on the side?" Her tone was not accusing, simply curious.

"He did not," Jason said. "I'd stake my life on it. He was not necessarily a jolly man, not verbose—nothing like Cranford; he was serious and reflective. But he made no secret of his affection for my mother, or of any of us. And we were—we *are*, those of us who remain—a colorful bunch. My eldest brother vowed early on that he would never marry. My middle brother was an accomplished musician and studied music to the exclusion of almost anything else. I've been consumed by a restless sort of energy from the moment I could crawl. I was bollocks in school and descend into a sort of stupefied madness whenever I'm expected to remain in Middlesex for more than three days. He loved and accepted us all."

"You miss him."

"I do miss him," said Jason. "If not for his memory, I would have foisted the whole bloody dukedom on an eager uncle and washed my hands of everything but my mother and sisters."

"Perhaps grief is easier for you to bear," she said, "than inactivity."

He harrumphed. "Aye. But who would admit to that? 'I'd rather be sad than bored.' "

"You cannot help how you feel."

"One thing is certain," he said. "Your story is a reminder that fathers can create far greater burdens than dying, and certainly greater burdens than saddling the new heir with a dukedom he doesn't want. The misdeed done to you by Cranford is inexcusable."

"It is not a contest," she said sadly.

"No. But do not diminish what you have overcome. Will you tell me the rest?"

She took a deep breath and let it out on a contemplative sigh. "Well, ultimately my mother dragged me into her lap to restrain me; she could not lean across the table forever. Whenever she removed her hand from my mouth, I gasped and sputtered and sobbed. She begged me in my ear to be silent, and I would promise to do it, only to sob, 'Pap—' before she could clamp down her hand again.

"Eventually, the earl's daughter, Wendy, said, 'Father, whatever is the matter with the little girl sitting by the window?' Cranford glanced at me—our eyes actually connected—and he looked away. He said to his daughter, 'Do not look at her, Wendy darling, she may be touched in the head or affected in some way. Allow her mother to tend to her.' "

"My God, Isobel," Jason hissed. "And you heard this?"

"We heard every word," Isobel said. "We heard it all and we witnessed it all. Tears streamed from my eyes, soaking my mother's glove. I could not believe the doting man I'd known as my papa would knowingly reject us.

"When, at last, his family finished their tea—it took nearly an hour—they drifted out. The earl did not look back, not once. Outside the window, I saw him take up Wendy's hand and swing it between them as they walked. They disappeared into the crowd.

"When my mother finally released me, I fell onto the floor in a heap, sobbing. In hindsight, I'm sure I *did* appear affected. I was consumed with jealousy and hatred and a frustrated lack of understanding of how the world worked.

"Meanwhile, my mother was forced to deal with the staff, to apologize for my behavior and for the fact that we actually *could not pay* for the expensive tea ordered by the earl. She'd carried no money—we never required money when the earl was with us. She was forced to beg the owner to allow her to return later to settle up. We ate lean for a month to pay for the champagne."

"But did he ever come back 'round? Did he have nothing to say for his behavior? My God, did he reimburse your mother for the abandoned bill?"

"Mama refused to see him after that, or to take his money. Ultimately he found a way to send money to me, which I spent on silly extravagances—sweets I gave to the street boys, rabbits for sale in the market I released into the park. We left England not long after and began traveling to the playhouses of Europe.

"The great irony is, if it hadn't been for me, I think my mother would have continued the affair. She was not troubled by the fact that the earl was married nor that their relationship was a secret, open or otherwise. She adored him. But the stunt in the café outraged her on my behalf. She loves me, for all of her faults. And the pain of that day interrupted any future relations she would ever have with Cranford." A deep breath. "And good riddance. In hindsight, I cannot believe I kept the compass as long as I did."

They reached the bend in the river. Jason hadn't noticed the rising sound of rushing water. A thick mist rose in the distance. Below it, a shimmering waterfall spilled down.

Isobel led him to the shore, and they picked their way beside the water until they could observe the cascade from a ledge. The tumbling water, swirling wind, and fine spray was quietly beautiful. He'd seen crashing, violent waterfalls in Scotland and Germany, thunderous shows of the power of nature, but this was a slower, gentler scene. The crystal water spilled and bounced.

Isobel pointed out the route of the river beyond the falls and the watermark on the ravine wall where the depth swelled from melted snow in late spring. She scratched green fuzz from a rock and told him that Iceland was home to more than a hundred types of moss and lichen.

Jason listened, trying to absorb the strange, mystic beauty of the place; even so, what he really wanted to know was *her.* How had she recovered from the rejection of that day, and how had she cultivated such a beautiful self-assuredness, despite society's view on fatherless children? The taunts of Drummond Hooke sprang to mind, and Jason was alternately furious and also simply in awe of Isobel's confidence.

Despite the beauty around them, the true marvel that day was Isobel Tinker. She'd been a marvel since the moment they met.

They returned to their possessions by walking along the riverbank, picking their way barefooted over warm, smooth rocks.

"I am sorry, Isobel," he said softly. "For this terrible part of your life. I knew the old earl. He was as you described, jovial and verbose. I had no idea he had . . . another family."

"Make no mistake," she said, laughing, "the man was in possession of only one family. My mother and I were . . . afterthoughts. Amusements. Pretty little things that he admired when it was convenient. We held no lasting value. The value belongs to the *legitimate*. The chosen. The recognized."

She shook her head so violently she had to pause and

catch her balance. "Better to mean nothing to the man than to be an afterthought."

"I would not argue," he said.

"I'll never be an afterthought," she declared softly. "Not ever again."

"Peter Boyd—" began Jason.

"I was not an afterthought to Peter," she corrected. "No more than anyone else. Even AnaClara was second best to Peter's own self-interest. When I was with him, I was included in the group, whether I had a place in his bed or not. The Lost Boys were a family. They were a wild and uneven family. But they were loyal. The reason I trailed him around Europe was, I longed so desperately to be part of a recognized *family*."

"He left you," insisted Jason, "carrying a baby, alone, here." He gestured to the raw landscape around them.

"No," she said. "*I* left *him*. I refused to go on. I could have gone if I'd wanted."

"*Isobel,*" he began, although he had no idea what he wished to say. He wanted to recover her hand. He wanted to haul her against him. He wanted to pick her up and sink again into the warm water.

"She wasn't even pretty," said Isobel, jumping from rock to rock on the shore.

"I beg your pardon?"

"Wendy, the earl's daughter," she said. "My mother made our appearance such a priority when the earl called. Our best clothes. She sent for a special maid to dress our hair. She was a tyrant about pretty manners too. We were always to be cheerful and clever and agreeable. I'd been groomed to do everything to endear myself. But when his real family appeared, I saw the truth. None of it had mattered. Wendy Bask was sour and bland. Her mother, the countess, enjoyed a fraction of the beauty of my radiant mother. I realized then that even beauty, an illusion my mother has pursued her entire life, means nothing compared to *approval*. To being among the *'sanctioned.'*

"For years, I was angry that the circumstances of my birth situated me so far outside the realm of it—of *approval*. I became a Lost Boy because it was a thumb in the eye of who is approved and who is not."

"And here I thought you enjoyed the travel," he joked.

"I do enjoy travel. But travel for a young woman alone is hardly *approved*. That is why my work at Everland Travel feels important. It creates an 'approved' way for women to see things beyond their own gardens. I do not hate women of privilege," she corrected.

She took a deep breath. "I don't hate anyone, honestly. Even the 'approved.'

"Raging at the world is no way to live," she continued. "When I made the happy discovery that working in a travel shop could be acceptable, and that *I* was acceptable enough to pull it off, I knew I'd stumbled upon the very best chance of survival. I have found satisfaction in that."

The hopelessness of that statement made Jason a little ill. And she'd said it to convey hope.

Speaking to the horizon, he said, "That is what I am aiming for in my life as duke. Survival."

She made a noise of acknowledgment. "I suppose you see some great irony here. You have no wish to be duke, and I come off as wanting to be an earl's daughter. But please do not misunderstand. I didn't want to be an *earl's* daughter. I would've been happy to be *anyone's* daughter. Or no one's daughter. I simply did not want to be deceived and then rejected by a . . . by a nonfather."

"I see no irony," Jason said. "Only selfish men who have mistreated you. They had the opportunity to experience the joy of knowing you and loving you— instead, they took advantage. No wonder you've asked me to . . . to stay back. But—"

He glanced at her, determined to address their intimacy in some way.

He said solemnly, "I'm not sorry we were together today. And as I look ahe—"

"Please do not make promises, North—please," she said. "I know better than anyone the realities and responsibilities of a nobleman. You've barely scratched the surface of what your life will be like at Syon Hall."

They'd reached the rock on which she'd stretched her clothes. They were damp but not dripping. She gathered up her purchases and folded them into his coat.

"Not everything will be mandated," he predicted. "I would not survive it if it were so."

"Your wife and heirs will be mandated," she said, "trust me. And I will not be your mistress. I am no one's mistress."

She said it like a vow. It seemed important to say the words, and he did not contradict her. The topic was sensitive, clearly. He could not address some potential future for them in an afternoon, not when pirates and an ocean lay between now and when . . . and when he *did* return to Syon Hall and when he would marry whomever the bloody hell he pleased.

For now, he would allow their time together to marinate. Let her remember the happiness and understanding and passion.

He was glad he'd told her, *I know how your story ends.* He didn't know exactly what it meant, but he knew the ending was happy.

He could wait.

She could not evade him forever. Middlesex was not so very large.

He would wait.

Chapter Eighteen

Osobel was in possession of a very durable pair of buckskins.

Like all of the clothes she'd formerly worn to ride horses and scale walls and tangle with pirates, the buckskins had been originally made for a boy. The britches had traveled home from Europe and lived in the bottom of her trunk at the Starlings'. After that, they had progressed to her flat above Everland Travel. She'd gone to throw them out several times, but something always held her back. When she'd packed for Iceland, she'd tossed them in the trunk as an afterthought.

Now she slid them on and dropped the linen shirt from Godfrey's over her shoulders. Taking up her new dagger, she cut the tail from the shirt, leaving it to hang only so far as her hips.

Her hair, which annoyingly she would leave entirely unbound, tangled in the neck of the shirt and fell over her eyes. It would be in her way, but yellow hair, entirely unbound, was a known distraction to men, and she would need every advantage.

Plucking out several strands, she plated loose braids here and there. She took up the feather ornamentation and pinned it just above her ear. As a Lost Boy, she'd adorned her hair with feathers, beads, ribbon, and fresh or dried flowers. It had felt provocative and wild, but now it seemed a little like dismantling a hat and hanging bits of it in her hair.

Tucking her hair back, she was just about to mold the red-and-black striped fabric around her hips when a knock sounded on her cabin door.

"Isobel? Twenty minutes." It was North. The sound of his voice set off a rain of shimmers inside her chest.

"Are you . . . ?" he went on, speaking through the door. "Having second thoughts?"

She squeezed her eyes shut. She was not having second thoughts. In fact, her determination mounted with every passing minute. The longer she remained in Iceland, the more wrenching it would be to return to her old life. And her old life was the key to her survival. Her old life would not shatter her heart.

She looked at her stockinged feet, the buckskins, and the linen shirt. She was clothed enough to open the door, surely. It wasn't as if she was dressing, more like . . . layering. And she was not back to her old life yet.

"No," she said, pulling open the door, "no second thoughts. Have Shaw and his men gone?"

She stepped away to mold the striped fabric around her waist like a skirt.

"Yes," he said, "I sent them ahead to—"

He stopped talking.

He said, "*No.*"

She looked up. "No, they haven't gone?"

His expression was the most gratifying mix of disbelief and admiration. "No," he corrected, "you cannot be serious about this . . . attire."

More shimmers tumbled in her belly.

"Do not begin," she sighed, forming a skirt from the fabric. Her hands had taken on the tiniest tremble.

"What are the chances that Doucette will not show?" she asked. She took up the leather belt and cinched it tightly around her waist, securing the fabric over the buckskins.

"I hope he does not show," said North, watching her. He checked the passageway and leaned a shoulder on the doorjamb, crossing his arms over his chest.

The night Isobel convinced the duke of her plan, he had dispatched a man to find the pirate liaison in Reykjavík. He delivered an offer from the Duke of Northumberland to pirate captain Phillipe Doucette. The offer was, let's make a trade.

"Isobel Tinker," the offer had read, "so-called Lost Boy and Known Accomplice of the International Grifter Peter Boyd, in exchange for the seven captive Englishmen."

"I'm wondering now why we sent something so dull as a letter. A sketch of you in this ensemble would have been more effective. Any man who saw you dressed like this would be at the bargaining table. Early. With the captives. *And* a pot of gold."

"Doucette will not want me for himself," she assured him.

"The devil he won't."

She sighed and picked through the golden necklaces from her trip to Godfrey's. The first she looped around and around her neck like a choker. She looped the other once, allowing it to hang to her waist.

"I'll set the tone from the first moment," she explained. "Seize the upper hand. It's not always a matter of who will possess whom; what matters is my perceived role in their lives."

"Yes, and your role will begin as currency, but rapidly shift to—"

She said, "Informant," in the same moment he said, "Plaything."

"Stop," she said, taking a seat on the bed and hiking up her makeshift skirt to pull on the black boots. "I am currency to you, because you want your cousin."

"You are not currency to me, damn it." He stepped forward and dropped to his knees, taking over the job of fitting her feet into the boots. With deft, sure movements, she slid one stockinged foot inside and he began to lace. The task was subordinate and intimate, but his movements were terse and jerky.

He said, "Never forget that this was your idea."

"Ouch," she pronounced, frowning at his angry lacing.

He mumbled an apology and cinched the stiff leather with less force.

He took up her other foot, squeezing it. After a long moment, he guided her foot to his mouth and pressed a kiss to her instep.

Isobel closed her eyes and let out a little whimper.

"So small," he mumbled, massaging her foot. He slid it into the other boot. "They could overpower you in an instant. Even I—even *Shaw*—can be overpowered if we are outnumbered by armed men."

"I've dealt with this lot before, please don't forget." She opened her eyes and watched him, staring at the top of his head.

The ordinary head of an ordinary man, she thought. *It is not beautiful or perfect. I am not falling in love with this head or with him.*

The lies she told herself.

He was in fancy dress. Fine overcoat, brocade waistcoat, cravat. Every inch the duke. He was a duke who laced her boots.

Tears filled her eyes and she blinked them back, staring up.

"Men overpower when they feel threatened," she declared to the ceiling. "I am not a threat; I am a means to an end to obtain Peter Boyd. I can be used as bait or . . . I actually hope to convince them that I can *lead them* to Peter. I'm an asset."

When the boots were secured, he sat back on his haunches, gazing at her.

"You are an asset," he repeated blandly.

"Stop worrying," she continued, shoving up and stepping around him. "The plan is to extricate myself by nightfall. There won't be time to menace me. We've a primary plan. We've a *secondary* plan. We have that dashing *third* plan where you kick down the door and rescue me at gunpoint. Please have faith in my ability to do this."

"My lack of faith is not with you," he said, rising. He caught her hand, stopping her. "It's these men. There are reasons to overpower a woman that have nothing to do with feeling threatened, and I think we both know it. We could plan for weeks, and yet, so many things are out of our control."

"Everything is out of control," she said, pulling her hand free. "I haven't the stomach for chaos. I've outgrown it."

"And yet you're willing to undertake this incredibly risky, wholly chaotic 'trade'?"

"If it hastens us along—yes. I will do it." She turned to face him.

"The only reason I've consented is because it feels important to you. I'm doing it for you."

"And I'm doing it for you. How altruistic we both are."

"Is that it?" He raised an eyebrow.

The air between them strummed with energy. He was watching her closely, waiting for her to give some sign. A *yes*, or a *please* or an *I-feel-it-too*.

"Can you excuse me?" she asked, turning away. There was no time for *yes* and no future for *feeling-it-too*.

"Isobel." Not a request, simply a statement of her name.

"Not long now," she said. "Meet on deck in ten minutes?"

She glanced at him, perhaps her greatest act of courage today. His eyes were anguished and searching, but he nodded and quit the room.

With considerable effort, Isobel forced the duke from her mind and settled at her desk. Working quickly, she laid open the small black vest and secured the dagger inside the lapel. She'd devoted several hours last night to sewing by candlelight, engineering a slot to conceal the blade. She preferred to seat a dagger tip *up*, so it could be drawn and ready for defense in one, slick movement.

Next, she took up the apple seeds. Another nighttime hour had been spent in the galley of the brig, grinding the seeds into a fine powder and measuring the dust into a tiny saltcellar. She'd scoured the reference book to be reminded of the procedure. To do lasting harm, it would take ninety apple seeds, but Mr. Godfrey had sold her fewer than twenty. It was enough to cause intestinal distress but nothing more. She hid the vial inside the tiny black pouch and secured it inside her belt.

Lastly, she scrawled out a note to her mother.

"Georgiana," it read.

I'm up to my old tricks. The situation here has demanded a touch of drama and daring. Luckily, I've been able to call up these skills and find them not entirely withered inside me. If you are reading this, something may have gone a little off, and I am sorry.

Please know that I have been fearless to the end and that I love you. There is money to see you through many happy years in Cornwall. Samantha will know what to do.

Yours,
Bell

After she sealed it and tucked it among her things, she cast one look around her tidy cabin and quit the room.

Isobel Tinker was afraid of many things, but pirates were not one of them.

JASON PACED ON the deck, going over and over the ill-advised plan in his head. If it had sounded like a bad idea three nights ago, now it felt like Certain Doom.

He'd spent hours squabbling with Isobel about her safety and even more time poring over maps with Shaw. In the end, he'd given the plan his reluctant blessing.

Their goals were: give the pirates very little time to prepare, hence the three-day window between his proposal of the trade and today.

Give off the impression that he and his party were stiff and untrained. He'd laid the groundwork for this in the language of the proposal. He would further cultivate it at the bargaining table.

Finally, separate the pirates from their ship on dry land.

Jason had designated a remote tavern beside the River Pjorsa as the location for the trade. According to Donatello Beddloe, the tavern was known to the pirates because it was near to the farm of their Icelandic allies. To reach it from their location in the eastern part of the country, the pirates would sail around the southeast tip of the island, drop anchor at the mouth of the river, and row smaller crafts inland. They would have their row-boats but be half a day's paddle from their ship. They would also be exhausted from rowing upstream.

Meanwhile, Jason, Isobel, and their team would be two hours' ride from the village of Stokkseyri.

If Isobel managed to drug the pirates as she proposed, Doucette and his men would be incapacitated long enough for everyone, including a horse-drawn cart containing Reggie and his lot, to return to Stokkseyri and the waiting brigantine. When they convened on the *Feather*, they would sail for home.

As if on cue, Isobel now emerged from belowdecks, her long, loose hair blowing in the wind like a pennant, skirts swishing to reveal the buckskins and tall boots.

He hadn't known what to expect when she vowed to "dress the part" of her old self, but nothing could have prepared him for the effect of her full costume. She looked like a lady-pirate-fairy-enchantress. Other descriptors also sprang to mind, but Jason dared not explore them. He was already struggling. He was in so far over his bloody head.

"You look far too beautiful for this," he muttered, helping her into the tender that would row them to shore.

"You miss the point of a costume," she said.

They settled on opposite seats while two sailors rowed them to shore.

"If you think I've missed a single thing about the way you look, Isobel, you are sorely mistaken."

He'd not missed her logic or cunning either, not from the beginning. Her plan was brilliant. Efficient, light on resources, and low on violence. Best of all, if she could manage the pirates, the chance of success was high.

At some point—likely right now—he would be forced, as a leader, to let go of his reluctance and anxiety and embrace an attitude of "Go." In his mind, he would analytically and tactically win. Missions succeeded when every operative did the correct thing at the correct moment, and then did it again and again. There was zero time or energy for worrying about her. It had been unprofessional and sloppy to remain so reticent for so long. This *was* happening.

Letting out a huff of breath, he took up a silk rope coiled on the bottom of the boat.

"I suppose it's time," he said, holding up a frayed end.

"I suppose it is." She held up her hands, wrists together.

"From the moment we set foot on the dock, the charade will be on."

Isobel leaned in, extending her wrists.

Jason glanced at the shore. "One kiss," he said. Not a question.

North, she mouthed, glancing at the sailors churning the oars.

"For luck," he said. "Or . . . just in case."

She bit her lip.

"To remember me by?" he tried. "Until we meet again. For love's labor's lost. For King and Country? Dong dong dell—"

"Fine," she laughed, touching a gloved hand to her mouth.

He took that hand and tugged her against him. She went, tumbling into his lap. He buried his face in her hair.

"I wouldn't mind seeing this ensemble again," he whispered in her ear, "without the paid mercenaries or the pirates or my cousin."

She laughed again. "These garments will be retired to a watery grave as soon as we are safely under sail."

"You take my breath away," he whispered.

"North," she sighed, sounding fraught, which had never been his intent.

"Forgive me," he said, rising up to kiss her. She threaded her hands around his neck and met his lips. Her hair enveloped him; he breathed in the sweet smell of her, the taste. Sensation washed over him, and he basked in the rhythm of the kiss, at once familiar and thrilling. He held her like she might jump overboard and swim away.

Isobel kissed him but she kept part of herself back. She was tense and reserved.

He growled in frustration. *I love you.* He said the words in his head. He dared not distress her; he dared not distress himself when she pushed the words away. He would wait. He would send his love for her silently into the universe and wait patiently for it to circle back.

In the meantime, he would bind her hands and drag her behind him like a prisoner.

Chapter Nineteen

Doucette came, as Isobel had known he would.

He was standing outside the little tavern, a phalanx of pirates flanking him, a grimace on his bearded face.

Isobel's vision of the scene was obscured. They'd positioned her in the wagon to increase suspense and suggest docility and defeat. She kept her head bowed. When she could steal a glance, she saw that Phillipe Doucette looked much as he had seven years ago. Likewise, his pirate crew seemed largely unchanged. Their clothes were disheveled and mismatched, everything from ratty evening attire, to far-flung military uniforms, to kaftans and turbans. Long hair and beards prevailed, interspersed with a few shaved heads. There were no women, including no sign of Doucette's Icelandic wife. To a man, they looked highly suspicious and anxious to fight.

Isobel took a deep breath, bracing herself. Since the kiss in the rowboat, North had, thankfully, set aside his hesitation and hand-wringing and regarded her with a professional detachment. He would deliver the performance of a lifetime, of this she had no doubt. He would seem overstuffed and out of his depth while Shaw and the other men would appear twitchy and uncertain.

The pirates must be made to feel at ease. Isobel, when she was revealed, must come off as outraged and defiant. She would be flashy and difficult to control, a very exclusive prize they were lucky to have won.

The more appealing Isobel could look, the more the pirates would be ready to offload the captives, who had, no doubt, been a hassle to keep alive and held very little appeal.

After Isobel scouted the ragtag array of pirates, she took in the surroundings. Their pirate informant, Donatello Beddloe, had settled nicely into his role as "adviser." They'd offered him thirty pounds and the promise of a lawyer back in Wales for an unnamed legal battle. After that, he'd sung like a bird. The tavern on the River Pjorsa had been his idea.

North and Declan Shaw had scouted the area and briefed Isobel on what to expect. Casting furtive glances, she saw the tavern, a stone structure half-buried in the sloped side of the riverbank, the rocky area that lined the river, the open plain inland, and, in the misty distance, the lip of the cliffs that dropped off into the sea. It was like most places in Iceland, desolate and untamed.

The pirates numbered eight or nine, but there would be more, she knew.

North's great hope was that the pirates would bring no horses. The river had been strategic for this reason. Pirates always traveled by boat when possible.

At the moment, North was the only mounted rider in their party, not including the four horses that pulled the cart. This allowed him to appear vulnerable and plodding, even while a band of mounted horses had been secretly stabled at a missionary outpost nearby.

The amount of time Isobel must remain with the pirates depended primarily on the condition of the captives. If they appeared well enough to tolerate a bouncing wagon speeding away at a fast clip, she could begin trying to escape very soon, an hour at most.

If, however, the captives were in poor health, if the cart was forced to trundle away without jostling or jolting, Isobel would need to occupy the pirates longer.

Assessing the condition of the captives had actually been her first priority, but so far she'd seen only pirates. She wanted to glance at North, but that would be out of character. Instead, she kept her head bowed and listened.

"Captain Phillipe Doucette," North called, speaking in tight, formal English, the English of aristocrats from a generation ago.

"I am the Duke of Northumberland. I've come to recover my cousin Reginald Pelham and merchants from the town of Grimsby in Lincolnshire, England."

"So you have," said Doucette, his English thickly accented. "Show me the girl."

"You can see her there, bound inside the cart," said North touchily. "And there she will remain until I see my cousin."

"How did you come into possession of this girl?" asked Doucette.

"The same way you came to be in possession of these men. I captured her."

"Where?"

"Greece."

"But why?"

"Why capture a group of merchantmen from Lincolnshire?" North shot back.

"Because I hate the English. Now say your excuse."

"I made a study of what you might value instead of the exorbitant five hundred pound ransom, and discovered that she was an answer. I am a negotiator at heart, you might say. I'm sorry I could not deliver one Mr. Peter Boyd, but I ran out of time."

"Did you see him? Boyd?" blustered Doucette.

When Isobel heard this, she knew they had him. His voice burned with vengeance. His open desire for Peter betrayed any useful strategy or bargaining. He would take her. They were very close.

Swallowing hard, Isobel checked the dagger and the concealed apple seeds with her bound hands. He'd tied her in such a way that she looked constrained but could, in fact, free herself at any moment. That moment had not yet come. Close, but not yet.

"BRING ME THE girl," Jason ordered Declan Shaw. He dismounted from his horse and squared off with the pirate captain.

Phillipe Doucette was like any pirate Jason had ever met, overconfident and undergroomed. He wasn't fond of pirates on a good day. As if navigating oceans and skirting hurricanes wasn't enough, pirates forced honest sailors to dodge cannon fire too. He viewed pirates as petty thieves who stole everything they possessed. Add the abduction of his cousin and their voracious interest in Isobel, and Phillipe Doucette ranked very low on Jason's list of people he tolerated.

But now he must pretend not to care—not about piracy or about Isobel. He must pretend to have eyes only for Reggie.

"Show me the Englishmen," North said, "or the girl remains in my possession."

"Doucette!" called a female voice from behind him.

North ground his teeth. They'd not rehearsed this bit,

line for line, but he knew Isobel intended something like shock and awe.

"Captain Doucette!" she called again.

The pirate stepped around to see Shaw lifting Isobel from the cart, her hands bound in front of her.

"Get off of me, you oaf!" she yelled at Shaw.

Very slowly, North turned to see. His regard for her was meant to be irritation and disgust. It was the most challenging duplicity of his career.

Shaw dragged Isobel forward by the wrists. She staggered, blond hair tossing, skirts fanning out. When they reached Jason, he twisted his expression into extreme distaste and fastened his hand around her arm. He held her out from his body, as if her nearness offended him. She raised herself up to her full five-foot-two-inch height.

In rapid-fire French, the accent so thick Jason struggled to follow, she cried out, "I can give you Peter, Doucette. I know where he is. And when he discovers that this *Coward Aristocrat . . .*" she sneered and pointed at Jason, ". . . has bound me like chattel and traded me like a mare, Peter will come for me. You know he will. I'll help you. I'll do anything if you'll get me away from these ham-handed Englishmen!"

Doucette's hard eyes had gone wide, taking in the sight of her. He stepped up and took Isobel by the chin to examine her face. She glared at him, her eyes flashing, and Jason held his breath. She was safer when Jason appeared not to care.

"*Never mind the ravings of the girl,*" North warned, pulling Isobel from the pirate's hold. "She's not yours until I have the Englishmen."

Doucette glared at North, examined Isobel again, and then shouted something in a language that was neither French nor English. A pirate jerked open the tavern door and seven men in chains were prodded into the sunlight, staggering, squinting, holding on to each other for support.

Jason almost forgot his panic for Isobel. The men looked wretched, beaten and starving. He searched the bruised, haggard faces for his cousin.

How many times had he retrieved Reggie from gaming hells, brothels, and gentlemen's clubs of dubious repute? Reggie was frequently drunk or recovering from a fight or both, and he always needed money. This was so much worse.

It was Reggie who spotted him first.

"Jason?" called a stooped man with matted hair. "Jason Beckett? Your Grace?"

Jason followed the sound and finally distinguished Reggie from the other haggard men. His cousin endeavored to wave but the chains prevented it. He tried to make himself taller but appeared too feeble to stand upright. His yellowish pallor and hollow-eyed expression were corpse-like. He was brittle-thin, unwashed, with a bloody nose and open sores on his face and neck.

Panic spiked through Jason like a lance. He'd gotten Reggie, or rather he'd gotten some half-alive version of Reggie, only to deliver Isobel to the men responsible for *this*?

She must have sensed his hesitation, because she pulled her arm from his grasp and skittered from him.

Shaw stepped up, but she pointed a finger and said, "Stay back, all of you, or I swear I will fight you to the death." She looked wild and beautiful and deadly serious.

Shaw took a step back.

"Quiet," Jason said flippantly, dismissing her.

To the pirate Jason said, "These men have been starved and beaten, Doucette. Is there no honor among thieves?"

Doucette shrugged. "They are weak. Too soft for our way of life. But they are alive."

"Barely." To Shaw he said, "Help them into the cart."

"Give me the girl," said Doucette.

The next words were the most difficult Jason would ever say. "Take her. She will walk to you as the English-men walk to my men."

Jason nodded to Declan Shaw and the large man gave her a shove. Isobel affected a perfect stumble, righted herself, and then walked, head high, to the pirate captain.

A pirate unlocked the long chain confining the merchants and they trudged in the direction of the cart.

"Jason, you've come!" Reggie rasped, his voice a prayer. "You've come, you've come. Thank God. I said that you would come. But who is the woman?"

Reggie disentangled from the group to watch Phillipe Doucette snatch Isobel's arm and jerk her to his side.

"No, Jason, you mustn't allow this," Reggie called weakly. "A woman has no place among these barbarians. It's no good, Jason—"

"Reggie, shut *up*," ground out Jason.

"But she'll be—"

"I said shut it, Reggie," growled Jason.

Shaw stepped up to push Reggie back to the group. His grumbling continued and he craned around to catch sight of Isobel. The wagon was small but sturdy and the other merchants had begun to comprehend what was happening. They heard the King's English, saw English faces, and hustled into the wagon, dragging Reggie along with them.

"Our business is done," proclaimed Jason, turning to remount his horse. "Take her."

"Yes, go," spat Doucette. "Hopefully these men will spread the word to other ambitious exporters. Keep out of Iceland. All smuggling will be managed by the Skallagrímur family and Phillipe Doucette."

"The devil take the lot of you," grumbled Jason. He swung into the saddle and gave a nod to Shaw. The wagon began a slow turn in the direction of Stokkseyri. Shaw's team took up positions flanking it, marching in formation.

Reggie was talking—Reggie was always talking—calling to him, explaining to his fellow merchants that his cousin was a duke and a foreign agent. "I can't believe he's traded that girl to rescue us," he marveled.

Jason ignored him, watching the assembled pirates and the little tavern on the horizon. His last glance was to Isobel. She glared back with believable contempt. They'd planned for this last moment. If he touched his hat, it meant she could begin trying to escape almost immediately. If he made no gesture, she should hold off for as long as possible—at least an hour—so the wagonload of injured Englishmen could make more progress.

The merchants in the cart looked as if they'd been collectively kicked in the teeth, but Jason didn't care. He wouldn't leave her in the hands of these criminals for a second longer than necessary. He would be back for her as soon as the wagon was out of sight and the pirates were distracted.

He glanced at her, touched his hand to his hat, and then kicked the horse into a spin and cantered away.

Chapter Twenty

*N*orth idled in the distance, his impatient horse stamping and throwing its mane, while the wagon with his cousin trundled ahead. When the procession of men and cart made fifty yards, the duke spun the animal and cantered ahead. He did not look back.

Isobel watched him disappear onto the horizon, savoring the sight of him, and buying time. Three main thoughts jostled around in her head.

First, the pirates were not, in fact, the same as they had been. They were harder, leaner, more desperate. It appeared as if they'd not only starved the English merchants, but beaten them as well.

Second, she would need to win over Doucette. If he was an ally, they all became allies.

Third, the Duke of Northumberland had faith in her abilities. He would not have left her if he did not.

She was determined to prove him correct.

If Doucette had allowed it, she would have watched North until he was a tiny speck on the horizon, but the pirate captain was already dragging her around the side of the tavern.

"To the boats!" he bellowed.

The boats? Isobel felt a jolt of panic. She looked around.

The pirate crew was lurching to comply. Doucette's face was set with a sort of greedy determination; he looked as if he intended to sail to Peter Boyd's unknown location this very night. But they couldn't go now, not before they'd taken refreshment at the tavern. They were meant to be exhausted from rowing upriver. And thirsty. Very thirsty.

Isobel dug in her heels. "Stop, Captain, if you please!" she demanded in French. "I need food and drink."

She employed her most upper-class French accent and used tenses consistent with an order. The pirate paused a fraction of a second.

Isobel swallowed and doubled down. "The English duke has starved me, *and* beaten me, *and* humiliated me. He and his men were crude and brutish. I've never been so grateful for your recovery of me."

"There is food on the ship," he said, moving again, dragging her along.

"I will not make the ship if I do not eat. I'll faint. I'll faint and have to be carried. I am strong but I require food, just like anyone." She pulled against his hold, straining her entire body toward the tavern door.

Doucette hovered between the river and the building, his expression torn. This was the moment of truth. He'd agreed to release the Englishmen because he gained *her* instead. Extraneous, irritating captives for one highly prized ally. She was trying to shift his view, make him believe he'd *rescued* her.

"The tavern will have *rúgbrauð*," she insisted. "And butter. Oh God, my kingdom for a dab of butter!"

The bread she'd named, a traditional Icelandic dark rye, was meant to prick Doucette's nostalgia and remind him that, for a time, Isobel had been a local.

His grip loosened, and she dragged him to the door of the tavern like a child. With every step, she expected to be snapped back. Her heart raced.

When they reached the tavern door, Isobel fell against the wall, making a show of breathing in and out. The pirates gathered around, watching her with uncertainty.

Just you wait, she thought, putting on a show. Silently, she counted the men, sizing up who would be a challenge and who could be ignored.

"Only one drink," Doucette hissed to her in French. "While you drink, you tell me what you know about Peter Boyd."

"And about Filip Skallagrímur," Isobel added. She'd come prepared with local gossip about the Icelandic family allied to the pirates. She would need every lie and ruse and all the flattery she could muster. It wouldn't be enough for *her* to eat and drink. Doucette must drink. They all must drink as much and as long as possible.

"What about Skallagrímur?" sputtered Doucette, bending his pepper-red face to hers.

"Idle prattle, perhaps," she said. "But I'll tell you what I've heard. *But sustenance first? Please!*"

Doucette relented and dragged her inside, his pirate crew crowding in behind him. The tavern was dark and rustic: a dirt floor, stone walls, a few tables, and a counter. There was only one way in and out. The bar was tended by an old man in a woolly hat. There was not, in fact, bread and butter, only the local ale. Without asking for permission, Isobel switched to Icelandic and ordered a round for every pirate.

As one woman working alone, Isobel knew that motion and sound would provide distraction, her most reliable tool. Step one, never stop talking. From the moment the pirates stepped inside the dark, smoky confines of the tavern, Isobel chattered. Switching easily between French and Icelandic and other languages in between, she complained in colorful detail about being captured by the duke. She invented a reason for being in Greece and extolled the virtues of the Greek islands as potential territory for enterprising pirates. She asked how much money Peter Boyd had won in their card games and revealed that he was a prodigious cheat.

Meanwhile she scooted chairs across the dirt floor, stirring up dust. She kicked the bar with her boot. She swished her skirt and flipped her hair and petted the dogs sleeping by the fire.

The pirates watched her as if they'd not seen a woman in a year, a circumstance that could have well been accurate.

"Sit!" Doucette finally bellowed, ordering her away from the hearth. Isobel complied, but not before she kicked a log from the tinderbox to the base of the hearth. If it caught flame, she would have another distraction. Every move was calculated to benefit the next five minutes of survival. By her count, she'd been within pirate company for fifteen minutes. She had forty-five minutes to go at least.

When she sat, she asked to have her wrists unbound so that she could drink. Doucette reached for his knife, but she turned away and offered her wrists to a nearby pirate. While the man worked at the binding, she spoke to him in various languages. He answered her finally—he was German—and she chatted with him to distract from the fact that she'd been bound with copious rope but *no actual knot*. The German pirate was so beguiled by the end, she held out her hand for the loose rope as if it had been hers all along. He returned it to her and she tucked it smoothly in her belt.

"Tell me about AnaClara," Isobel said, whirling back to Doucette.

"What? Who is AnaClara?" sneered Doucette.

Isobel spun a half-true tale about the beautiful girl with whom she "shared" Peter Boyd, the one who lured him away from Iceland and, in fact, from Isobel. With exaggerated jealousy, she painted a convincing picture of how she came to be separated from Peter and the Lost Boys.

While she talked, she fidgeted with her hair and vest. She claimed the fire was too warm, the afternoon too cold, the tavern too dark. The last thing she did before she ceased fluttering braids and feathers and skirts was tug the black pouch from inside the shirt to hang by her hip.

Doucette was frowning into his tankard. "Boyd was surrounded by all the beautiful ones," he grumbled, "just like always."

"But not me," Isobel exclaimed with bitterness, throwing up her hands. As she did it, she purposefully knocked over her own tankard, sending the metal cup clattering to the ground and soaking the pirate with pungent ale.

Doucette lurched back, cursing and trying to flick drink from his coat. Isobel seized the chance. Working quickly and stealthily, she recovered the cup and tapped a good portion of the apple-seed dust into the pirate's drink.

When the dust was back in her pouch, she affected an elaborate apology and took up two rags from the bar. She used one to dab Doucette's coat and the other she tossed very near the fire.

Doucette shoved away her ministrations, angry about the spill. She fell back and made her way to the bar, stooping to pick up empty tankards on the way. She plunked them down and told the barman in hurried Icelandic to refill all of them.

"Another round?" she called, pretending to be a little drunk.

"We must make the ship by sundown," Doucette called out, slurping his own drink.

"I've never been so grateful," Isobel shouted, raising an empty tankard, "to sail away from this godforsaken island . . ."

The pirates shouted their agreement.

In that moment, the alcohol-soaked rag she'd dropped by the fire sparked and caught flame, shooting flames into the air and startling the dogs. The dogs yowled and scuttled away and two pirates leapt up to contain the fire.

It was the ten seconds she'd been waiting for. Moving quickly, she tapped the remaining apple-seed dust into the tankards waiting on the bar.

When she turned around, hands filled with tankards like a Bavarian barmaid, the pirates were just reclaiming their seats. She beamed and sang a little song, distributing the drugged tankards to mystified pirates.

In her head, she thought, *I've done it.*
I've actually done it.
They need only drink, and I need only wait.

The next half hour passed in flashes of distorted time.

She fabricated the location of Peter Boyd by recounting one of her Spanish holiday itineraries, stop by stop. The words came out quickly and she gestured like a demented uncle making finger shadows for children.

Tankards hit tabletops with a heavy *clunk*.

Pirates belched and slurped.

Someone sang a little sea chantey in Italian.

She spoke about Peter and his prized collection of stolen timepieces.

She described how Peter would, without a doubt, *come for her*. Doucette need only dangle her like bait, she said. The pirate captain listened but said nothing. Time seemed to stop.

She was just about to begin with local gossip when an old pirate across the room stood up, made a gagging sound, and then collapsed on the floor.

"Oh dear," said Isobel, leaping up.

She put her hand on the hilt of the dagger. Her speeding heart raced so fast she couldn't distinguish the beats.

One minute later, another pirate made gurgling sounds and staggered to the slop bucket in the corner.

A minute after that, another slumped against his table. Another doubled over.

Isobel spun around to check Doucette, and he was leaning back in his chair, his head facing the ceiling, eyes closed and mouth open.

That was her cue. She slid the dagger from inside her vest and backed herself against the bar. Whispering a warning to the barkeep, she inched a wide circle around the room, keeping her back to the wall. She kept the knife drawn but at her side. All around her, the room became a morass of collapsing, gasping pirates.

Five steps from the door, she bolted, charging past an unaffected pirate. Isobel saw him in time to fake left but darted right.

His reflexes were good, and he caught her by the arm. Isobel tried to break free but his hold was punishing.

He reached for her neck with his other hand. Lashing out, Isobel transferred the dagger to her free hand and buried the blade in his bicep. He shouted in pain and released her. She scampered away, but a second pirate stepped up to block the door.

"No, you don't," he said in English accented with an Irish lilt.

"Move," she demanded.

He swiped for her with a meaty hand, and she leapt, barely evading him. He kept coming and she scrambled back. She tripped over the body of a pirate and fell.

The pirate on the ground was ill, but not too ill to reach for her ankle. She kicked him with the heel of her boot and he rolled in pain.

Meanwhile, the Irish pirate was still coming, his eyes locked on her dagger. He was large and seemingly unaffected by the poison; it would take no effort for him to overpower her. She had time to scramble to her feet or throw the dagger but not to do both.

Without hesitation, Isobel flung the dagger in the direction of his shoulder. The blade sliced through the air and caught him at the top of the arm. He roared in pain, struggling to pull out the knife. Isobel leapt up and darted to the door, overturning chairs and scattering tankards as she went.

When she reached the door, she flung it open without stopping to see who was in pursuit. The sky outside was a gray-lavender. Dusk fell, bringing with it a foggy sort of vapor. She darted into the mist and slammed the door behind her. Shoving her shoulder against the door, she unlooped the rope at her belt and bound the door handle to an iron torch claw on the wall. It was a feeble obstacle, but it would buy her time.

She was giving the rope a final tug when she felt the door shudder with the weight of a pirate on the other side. Isobel yanked the knot once more and bolted.

The plan had been to follow the river in the direction of the sea. It would be the route the pirates would take back to their ship, and the very last direction they would expect a fleeing woman to run. She ran low, darting from bolder to bolder, keeping fifty yards from the water in case they managed to gain their boats.

For five minutes, she ran full out, falling twice, recovering, running again. The air was cold and acrid, and she drank it in. She loosened the vest and then stripped it off. The belt and fabric skirt came next. Only the buckskin, the linen shirt, and her boots remained.

Her lungs had just begun to protest when she saw him—North, thundering over the next rise on his horse, pulling a spirited mare on a lead behind him. Isobel said a silent prayer and stepped away from the rock to wave a hand.

North galloped up, yanking on his rein. Isobel glanced at him in the dim light, a look of triumph and relief and love, and then held up her hands to the dancing mare. North tightened the lead and she got close enough to put a foot in the stirrup. She calmed the horse with a caress to her neck and soothing words. When North dropped the lead, the animal spun, but Isobel was already vaulting into the saddle.

"There's no time," was all she said.

She dug the heel of her boot into the flank of the horse and the animal sprang into a gallop.

North did the same and they sprinted into the cold, indigo Icelandic night.

Chapter Twenty-One

ason and Isobel rode neck and neck, following a bright moon along the circuitous route he'd planned. The lowlands of the country offered two landscapes: open grass with no cover, or craggy rock outcroppings, impossible to navigate on a running horse. Jason led them through both, pushing the horses but making them difficult to track. When they reached the second spate of rocks, they reined in, allowing the animals to pick their way through a shallow canyon of slick basalt columns.

When the labored breathing of the horses subsided, Jason spoke. "Are you hurt?"

"No." She sounded breathless, exhilarated.

"Did they touch you?" he asked. He hadn't quite reached exhilaration. He was exhausted from fear.

"They took my dagger," she said.

"They *did* touch you."

She shook her head. "I flung it into a man's shoulder and never recovered it."

"You flung it—"

He reined around, kneeing his stallion to her. He searched her face with desperate eyes, looking for blood.

She beamed at him, tall and glorious in the moonlight. Her breath came in winded puffs; her cheeks were flushed, her hair wild. Her smile was the smile of a champion.

"Isobel," he said, a whisper.

He was just about to reach for her—he would die if he didn't touch her—when a gentle streak of light pulsed the dark sky. Then another, and another. A vibrant glowing curtain of light.

Jason reeled his horse around. The pirates, he thought. They'd concealed horses and now pursued them bearing bright torches.

Except the brightness was nothing like torchlight; it was too white. The horizon was obscured with distant volcanoes, barely visible in the dark. Now they stood out in inky relief against wave after wave of heavenly light.

"North," Isobel breathed, turning her face to the sky.

"What's happening?"

"The *Norðurljós*," Isobel said, using the Icelandic term. "The northern lights. It's a natural phenomenon of cascading spectral light. Look up. Effervescence will . . . will ignite the heavens." She sounded reverent.

"Ignite the heavens," he repeated, suspicious. He squinted at the light spilling downward to the earth.

"You've heard of this, surely," she said. "It's like a show of lights painted across the dome of the sky. Green, blue, pink, orange. It is breathtaking, a once-in-a-lifetime sight."

She reined the mare around. "You must see it."

The white light on the horizon seeped up and over the rounded cap of the night. The colorless glow gave way to a peachy hue; the peach faded to a rose pink. It was color and light at once, like a flame. But where fire was thin and jumpy, this was milky thick and low. It draped in uneven bands across every part of the sky.

Isobel dismounted and tethered the mare.

"We cannot stop," he said, watching a ribbon of green seep through the pink.

"We can," she countered. "Most of the pirates are in the throes of intestinal distress. The others could not possibly follow this far on foot, even if they knew which direction we fled, which they do not.

"We did it, North," she said, turning to him. She stood beside his horse and touched his leg. Her beautiful face was lit by a veil of pink and orange light.

Without another thought, he dismounted, sliding in between Isobel and the stallion.

"Look," she cooed, pointing to a puff of aquamarine. He blinked up, following her finger. The sky was a color he'd only seen on the scales of a fish, translucent and opaque at the same time.

"Magical," she said, smiling.

"You're magical," he said, and he scooped her into his arms.

He desired her—he never stopped desiring her—but in that moment, he wanted nothing more than to confirm that she was with him, safe and unharmed. His hands moved searchingly: waist, ribs, shoulders, throat. He felt her back, her bottom—so perfectly available in the snug buckskins—the sides of her thighs. She was perfect, and whole, and strumming with life. He buried his face in her hair and breathed in, memorizing the smell of her.

He dragged his face across her neck and cheek, scraping her with his emerging beard. He felt her shiver, felt her turn her face to catch his jaw with her lips. Lust and longing roared to the surface; he was immediately hard, and he bit down on the inside of his mouth. She'd said no, she couldn't risk—

She kissed him.

She grabbed his face with both hands and pulled him to her.

In the same moment, she leapt up, jumping into his arms. He made a wordless sound of pleasure and relief, barely managing to catch her bottom with both hands.

She wrapped her legs around his hips and hooked her boots around his back. She feasted on his mouth. They were, at once, a staggering tangle of lips and tongue, hands and breath. He widened his stance, kneading her bottom, kissing her like he was suffocating and she was air.

He opened his eyes in wild, quick blinks, catching snatches of her hair, her cheek, and the mystical, heavenly light.

"Jason," she panted, and he growled at the sound of his given name. Finally.

"S'bell," he panted back.

"Make love to me."

He groaned. She would tear him apart.

"*Please*. Jason."

"Isobel," he said again, devouring her with a kiss.

"Why should we not?" she breathed, speaking to herself, or to him, or to the lights in the sky.

"Please don't make me think," he said.

He forced himself to raise his head and look around. While she kissed his neck, he scanned the canyon for a smooth rock or a tuft of moss . . . grass . . . anywhere to drop to one knee. She weighed nothing, but desire sapped the strength in his legs. He needed to be down, she needed to be beneath him; he needed something hard and unmoving to leverage his granite erection—

"There," she panted, pointing to a murky hollow cloaked in steam.

"Where?"

"It's a pool," she said. "See the steam? It's a heated pool. Like the river, but deeper. We can bathe. Float. Swim."

"Now we're swimming?" he managed.

She squirmed from his grasp and slid down his body. Catching his hand, she led him to the mystical haze hovering over the pool of fizzing water.

"This country is enchanted," he mumbled, staring into the rising steam.

She bit off a glove and went down on one knee, testing the water. "Ahhh," she moaned. "Heavenly." She bit off another glove. "And the air is freezing. I'm cold, Jason—aren't you cold?" She began tugging at the laces of her boots.

"No," he said. He was incinerating.

By the strange green light above, he watched her remove her boots and stockings and then—in perhaps the most sensual act he'd ever witnessed—peel the buckskins from her legs. Next, she shucked the linen shirt. Within moments, she stood before him in only a thin shift and loose drawers. He stood gaping, his brain struggling to absorb her sensual beauty. She winked at him—winked!—and then dropped to sit at the edge of the pool. She sank her feet into the dark water with a sigh. Steam rose around her. She took up her hair and tied it in a loose knot on the top of her head. Her shift dissolved into damp translucence.

Jason had never been more aroused in his life.

"Remember when you first came to Everland Travel," she asked, "and you wanted passage to Iceland?"

Remember? There was no remember, he thought, there was only now. He began jerking open the buttons of his waistcoat.

She continued. "I suggested that I did not enjoy Iceland? It wasn't the country—obviously. It was my own reckoning here that scared me. Speaking strictly as a travel agent, I can tell you that Iceland does three things like no other place on earth: mystical landscapes, northern lights, and heated pools." She kicked her feet in the water.

"I'll never see anything but you . . ." he rasped, "sitting there . . . like that . . . ever again." He shrugged from his coat and ripped off his waistcoat. His shirt, boots, and buckskins came next, tangled in a heap on the canyon floor.

There was no time for heated pools, of course. In the back of his mind, he knew this. The crew of the *Feather* would set sail as soon as Isobel and he convened with the captive merchants in Stokkseyri.

Tactically, it was a disaster to strip naked and *swim* in the middle of the night, with pirates in pursuit.

Jason didn't care. He cared only for her.

When he'd stripped to his drawers, he dropped beside her on the lip of the pool, sinking his feet in the warm, fizzing water. Isobel reached for him at once, taking him by the shoulders, climbing into his lap. He gathered her up with a groan, kissing her deeply with his tongue, with his soul.

"In, in, in," she urged, pulling him from the lip of the pool into the steaming water. Jason sank down, his aroused body now buzzing with gooseflesh from the effervescent water. He hiked her legs around him, carrying her, and waded in. The pool was shallow, but he moved slowly. He was losing his mind. He could step off into an abyss and he would not care. She kissed like his wildest fantasy; the thin lawn of her shift and drawers floated away from her skin. She was soft, and slick, and writhing in his arms. Above them, the heavens bloomed color.

When his knee bumped a smooth rock he pivoted, sinking to his shoulders to sit. His hands slid over her slick body of their own accord, palming her pert breasts, tracing the curve of her hip. She dug her fingers into his hair, massaging his scalp, delving down his back.

"You're remarkably formed," she whispered. "So strong."

He kissed her hard and mimicked the motion with his hips, pulsing his erection against her. She moaned and arched her neck, pressing up.

"Please don't make me beg," she whispered. She reached her hand between them.

"Isobel," he pleaded between kisses, "this is not what we discussed."

"We discussed the real world," she mumbled. "This is not real. This is a fantasy."

"I assure you, this is very real," he rasped, grinding his very real erection into her hand.

"We are alone in a cauldron," she said. "The sky is on fire. We've bested *pirates* . . ."

She kissed her way from his mouth to his sideburn; she traced the whirl of his ear with her tongue. She whispered, *"Not real."*

Jason growled and gathered her closer, but he plucked her hand away. He pumped his erection against her center, and they both moaned. He interlocked one hand with hers and brought up the other to cup the back of her head.

"I've fallen in love with you," he said.

She smiled at him. "But don't you see? That's the beauty of this moment. You don't have to profess love to me. You don't have to do anything but—"

"There is virtually nothing I do because I *have to*, Isobel," he told her. "I do and say what I want; I always have."

"Except for the dukedom," she said.

He frowned.

She continued, speaking almost nose-to-nose. "You will assume all the responsibilities of a duke because you *have* to do it."

"I didn't mea—"

"And if you do it correctly, as you've told me you are determined to do, the real-world Duke of Northumberland will not have the freedom to profess love to the real-world Isobel Tinker."

"I *will*," he told her, kissing her hard.

She shook her head, and he saw tears had begun to roll down her cheeks.

"You will not," she told him softly. "Loving a woman like me is not a part of being a proper duke. Not the type of love that I want. Legitimate love. Family love. *Give-me-your-name* love."

"We will marry," he declared. He kissed her again, and she was silent for a beat.

He'd not planned to say this, not yet—but why not? Love was not enough for her. Fine. He knew the reasons, love alone *shouldn't* be enough. It wasn't. She deserved it all.

"You deserve my name," he told her. "You deserve to

be duchess, God help you. Why you'd want this bit, I have no idea, but if you'll do it . . ."

Isobel shoved herself back with a splash and began to tread water two feet away. She was shaking her head. The tears were falling faster now.

"Why are you crying?" he asked. He shoved from the rock and swam to her, collecting her. He kissed her ear, her jaw, her eye. "Isobel, I love you. Is this—? *Why* does this distress you?"

ISOBEL HELD ON to his shoulders with a death grip.

Please don't go, she thought.

Please don't take the words away.

Please comprehend how afraid I am.

Please don't go.

"I'm sorry," she said, speaking to the wet skin of his neck.

"Sorry?" he demanded. "But what does that mean? There is no sorrow here. There is only joy and love and, if we're quick and can manage some form of it, possibly sex."

She laughed through her tears but shook her head.

"You do not feel the same," he guessed.

Another laugh. She loved him so much she ached with it. She could heat this pool and illuminate the sky with how much she loved him.

"I do love you," she whispered.

It deserved to be said. If nothing else.

A love this strong could not be denied or kept secret. She could say the words.

He gave her another shake. "Then what is it?"

In a burst of frustrated energy, she pushed away again. She swam to the rocks at the side of the pool. She stared up at the green swirls in the sky.

"What you've just . . . said—what you've proposed—will be so very difficult and complicated when we are back in England," she said, speaking to the horizon. "It's easily proclaimed here, but it will not be simple there."

"I don't care about *simple*," he said.

"You don't have to care about anything at all," she said. "*You* are a duke. Your world is assured and provided. I, on the other hand, am a girl in a shop. I am responsible for my mother. I feel responsible for Samantha. She lives with her father but she finds purpose in the shop, and honestly, they use the small salary I pay her. I am responsible for my own very tenuous future. My aunt and uncle love me in good faith, and I would die before I disgraced them. I don't merely *care* about 'simple,' I fight for it. I strive for simple, and straightforward, and the expected. Anything more feels like the first step to chaos and heartbreak."

She heard splashing. He swam up behind her. She could feel him floating, an inch from her back.

She swallowed hard and continued. "For me to accept your declaration of love? To trust it? To guard my heart? This is a colossal leap of faith that threatens everything that has sustained me since returning to England. And it terrifies me. I want to believe it—*I'm crying* because I want to believe it so much. But, Jason?"

"Yes?"

She shook her head, unable to finish.

He pressed himself against her back, caging her on either side with his arms. He kissed her neck, setting off an upward stream of fizzy shimmers inside her.

"Can you not admit," she whispered, closing her eyes, "that the excitement of this mission, the spectacle of this sky, the remoteness of this country, of our very wet, very tingly proximity in this pool . . . all of this worked together to make your declarations seem probable? Of course you professed love amid all of this."

"I will not admit that," he said simply, kissing her jaw. "I've lived my life on the road, Isobel. I've experienced wild, remote, beautiful things in every corner of the planet. For me, *real life* is remote—it's seeing different things, it's spent in the field, on a mission. This is—"

"But that will all change at Syon Hall," she insisted, spinning around.

He scooped her up. She met his next kiss but then pulled back. "You cannot fathom the pressures and expectations of being duke, Jason—truly, you cannot. You've guessed enough to put it off, you've dodged and dreaded it, but I fear the reality will be far worse. Learning you are not permitted to marry a girl like me will be only the beginning of your new life."

"I will do what I want when it comes to who I marry, damn it," he said. "I am the bloody duke, after all."

"Did your brothers?" she challenged.

"My brothers did not marry. My oldest brother, August, did not care for women and my middle brother, James, was too overwhelmed with the duties thrust upon him when he inherited." He made a bitter sound. "Until August died, James's only vision of the future had been his violin. And then suddenly he was duke, and there was no time for women. He fell ill within three years and was then too sick to consider them. Poor James," he sighed. "God love him."

"And this proves my point," she said. "Two men who would have pursued their own bliss if the dukedom hadn't disallowed it. Your older brother could have presented himself to the world as a confirmed bachelor, with no illusion of eventually marrying. Your next brother could have filled his short life with music instead of . . . estate management. You will discover the same—"

"Make no mistake, sweetheart," Jason cut in. "August told us all very early on that another Beckett male would be responsible for begetting the heir; he would never marry. And James could have courted any number of potential duchesses, but he didn't. I actually learned how *not* to do it from him.

"But I assure you," he finished, "there is no officer of protocol at Syon Hall. Has my mother made my eventual marriage a priority? Yes. But she knows better than to coerce me or manage who I choose. She wants me to be happy. We've had so much tragedy, so many funerals. She understands what truly matters."

For this, Isobel had no answer. She stared at his wet hair and face, just inches from her own.

He reached up to trace a finger around her mouth. "You make me happy," he said. "You make me more than simply 'happy.' You . . . you give me the will to go on."

"I'm the balm that allows you to tolerate the dukedom," she guessed, being deliberately obtuse. "If you were doing as you liked, still working as a foreign agent, you would have never settled for me."

"If I was still working for the Foreign Office," he said softly, pulling her face to his, "I would marry you, then I would recruit you, and we would travel the world, preventing wars and routing slavers and fighting pirates."

Again, Isobel's eyes filled with tears, and she collapsed against him. With slick hands, she felt her way around his chest, savoring each muscle. She wanted to be as close as possible; she wanted to dig to his heart and swipe it, to hold it, to protect it.

"Is that a yes?" he asked, speaking into her hair.

A trail of shimmers revolved in her stomach. She floated in the hot pool and in the green heavens and in love with him. A tiny sliver of hope could just be made out on the horizon of her life. She allowed herself to reach out and jab at it, testing its durability and staying power.

"What was the question?" she asked, speaking to his chest.

He laughed, tickling her ribs with provocative fingers. "Do you love me?" he stated.

She paused in the act of kissing his nipple. She nodded.

He tickled her again, his fingers playful and sensual at the same time. His erection bobbed at the junction of her legs, a delicious, throbbing hardness.

"Will you marry me," he went on, "and become the Duchess of Northumberland?"

She paused again. The shimmers had crystalized into tiny, sharp pinpoints of hope. She was so very torn. The shimmers of hope could swirl again or slice her to ribbons.

He could slice her to ribbons.

Jason went still, waiting for an answer.

When she said nothing, he swore, disentangled himself, and splashed away.

She stared after him, suddenly cold despite the fizzing heat. She treaded water, watching him. His handsome face was shrouded in steam and backlit by green swirls in the sky.

"Answer me," he demanded.

He grabbed her ankle beneath the water and pulled her to him. She let out a whimper and allowed herself to glide. When she floated against him, she wrapped her legs about his haunches and looped her arms around his neck. He ground against her and she sighed in pleasure.

"An answer, if you please," he growled in her ear.

"*Yes,*" she finally said breathlessly. "Yes, I will do it. *If* you do not change your mind. *If* your family will allow it. *If* society will allow it and it will not decrease your influence or the stature of the dukedom. I will do it."

She finished on a sob, and he kissed her, swallowing up the sound.

Isobel's conscious mind floated away, and she allowed herself to simply sink into the kiss and into him. Sensations built, throbbing between them, and when she could no longer bear the pressure, she reached between them and grabbed his erection.

He jerked and caught her hand, holding her there, moaning into her mouth.

She stroked him but was impatient. She began to shimmy from her wet drawers.

"Not this way," he whispered against her ear. "We cannot remain here all night. I want to do it properly."

"But . . . but . . ." she insisted, kissing him, "there are so many ways to properly do it. Quickly can be properly."

He chuckled and shook his head. "I'll not get you with child until you are my wife, S'bell. You deserve this much."

She made a noise of frustration, she kicked her feet, but in her head and in her heart, she fell a little more in love.

"So how do you want it instead," he growled, kissing her. He was tall enough to touch the bottom of the pool, and he walked to the side, carrying her.

"I beg your pardon?" she managed.

"You will see stars before we leave here, Isobel, even

if I don't." He moved his own hand to her center, and she gasped at the contact.

"I see more than stars," she panted, blinking at the hanging green light in the sky.

"No," he teased, tracing kisses down her throat, and then lower, to her breasts. "Not that way. Close your eyes."

Isobel complied, and the duke feasted on her body with hands and mouth, sending her to a place that she'd never been. When she reached climax, she was consumed by the shimmers that had teased her from the first day he came to her. She was a woman-shaped pile of shimmering love and light, floating against him. She opened her eyes and saw every shade of green and blue and indigo glittering above her. She saw her future in a hazy glow of warm, soft light. She wanted to turn away, to not risk burning her eyes, but she allowed herself to take it all in, to bask, to absorb it.

When, finally, her sense returned, she realized she was kissing him—he was such a good kisser—and she reached into the water for his body, but he gently pulled her hand away.

"There's no time," he said. "The wagon will have made it to the brig by now. You and I cannot be long after. The pirates may not find us here, but they can row downriver to their ship and pursue us in the harbor. We must put as much distance between ourselves and Iceland as possible."

He gave her a final kiss and then shoved from the pool, water sluicing down his glorious body.

Isobel nodded dumbly, reaching up. He pulled, sliding her from the pool to balance beside him.

She glanced down. His drawers were strained by his hard, demanding length. She put one hand on his chest and reached for him with the other. "Jason . . ." she began.

He made a hissing noise and doubled over, grabbing her hand at the wrist.

"I'm endeavoring to do the correct thing here, Isobel," he rasped. "Do not make it impossible. You will owe me, and I will expect a great many things from that debt, but let us not dash this mission in the eleventh hour."

She slid her hand away, and he gave a full-body shudder. He swore and cleared his throat.

He turned away. "Get dressed?" he suggested, shucking his wet drawers and wrestling into his dry clothes. Isobel did the same, shivering now without the hot water.

"It's cold," she said.

"Take my coat." He dropped his greatcoat over her shirt and buckskins.

"What will your friend Declan Shaw and the captives think when I return wearing your coat?" she asked. "Oh, and how is your cousin? The merchants looked wretched."

"Reggie? He's fine. Hungry and defeated, but he will survive. There are other captives in far worse condition. The pirates were brutal. It nearly killed me to leave you with them."

"You should have seen me," she sighed, rubbing the flank of her horse. "I was a spinning top. Once I danced them into the tavern, I was home free."

Jason shook his head and smiled, a wordless show of admiration. He vaulted into the saddle and Isobel smiled too, admiring his muscled grace.

Mounting the mare, she followed Jason up an embankment out of the canyon, shrugging into the warm, musk-smelling confines of his coat.

"Jason?" she called.

"S'bell," he answered. Her stomach flipped.

"I . . . I have a request."

"I've already said there isn't time, love."

She bit back a smile. "I would like you to keep our . . . our—"

She couldn't say it.

"Are the words you seek *wild, passionate love*?" he asked.

"I was going to say *betrothal*." She reined her horse beside him. In her mind, she repeated the sentence.

"But is that what actually happened?" she asked. "Are we betrothed?" Her heart pounded.

"What happened was the most illicit, wettest betrothal of all time," he said. "With the greatest lack of jewelry or paperwork. I apologize, but I am not sorry. I'll correct the jewelry and the filings when we reach London. But yes, if you can abide it, that was the Jason Beckett version of a betrothal."

Isobel felt herself nod. Hearing the words again made her breathless. She looked at the blue-green lights hanging in the sky. The aurora borealis looked dull compared to their love and their impending marriage. *That* was the supernatural phenomenon. *That* was the miracle.

"Right," she said, kicking her horse into a cantor. "My request, then, is that we . . . we not discuss it with anyone? Not yet?"

"What?" He kneed his horse forward.

"It's just—when we see your cousin, or when we make landfall in London. If we could simply . . . keep it . . . kind of like a secret? For a time?"

"Why?" he ground out. His anger was clear.

"Well, because I want you to settle into your role as duke without . . . without having to explain your relationship with *me*. Without having to accommodate me and show me about and introduce me. Without the burden of a fiancée."

"You believe that when I am immersed in the so-called real world I will reconsider my offer. You believe," he clipped, "that I'll discover what a poor fit you may be, and keeping it secret allows me to disentangle?"

It was exactly what she believed, but she had no wish to quarrel with him. The night had been too perfect.

"The transition from spy to duke," she explained, "will involve stewards, and advisers, and weeks of reading and property tours. You will be inundated with family. Your life will be turned upside down for a time. Please indulge me in this: go home. Get settled. Make some accounting for your reticence all these months. And then, if everything goes smoothly, we will announce it."

He exhaled. He was frustrated, unhappy.

"No matter how reasonable your family," she said, "they will be alarmed by the presence of a—of me. If we sweep in from foreign shores after this wild adventure— after having worked so very closely together—I'll not only seem like the most unexpected bride of the decade, I'll look calculating and . . . and seductress-y as well. It will look like I enchanted you while we sailed about the Atlantic Ocean, rescuing cousins."

"But that is what you've done," he teased.

"In *contrast*," she pressed, "if we allow some time to pass, if I have time to settle in as well and establish my new travel agency, I'll have a better idea how I'll operate it while also serving as your duchess—"

"Syon Hall is just miles from Hammersmith," he cut in.

She cleared her throat. "If I settle in, and you settle in, and time passes, *then* you may introduce me to your family. They'll meet me simply as a translator who advised you on this mission. There'll be no need to mention that I'm the girl who introduced you to . . . to—"

"Bathing in a heated pool?"

"Yes," she breathed.

"But when will I know that you're ready?" he asked. *"When* can I introduce you?"

Isobel shrugged. "It's impossible to put a date on it, isn't it? Until we are home and we see what life will be like for us both?"

"Impossible," he repeated bitterly. "Is it really 'impossible'?"

"You will know when you're ready," she said.

He swore and kicked his horse into a gallop.

"Or perhaps," he called, his voice hard, *"I* will wait for *you* to come. And *you'll* be the one to know when *you're* ready."

Before she could answer, he darted ahead, leading the way across the grassy plain.

Chapter Twenty-Two

Dearest Georgiana,

I'm home, Mama. I am home. I'm sending this letter by private messenger from London so you will know straightaway.

The mission was a success; you'll not believe all we managed. I'll share every detail when I see you. Unfortunately, the return sailing was dreadful. Autumn weather caught up with us and storms from the north made for relentless rocking and plunging, dipping and bobbing. I was sick for ten days, unrelenting. When finally we reached London, I staggered off the brigantine in search of fresh bread and ginger tea and chocolate.

But this is not what you really want to know, is it?

Before you expire from curiosity, I'll tell you that the duke and I did . . . grow close on the voyage, but our farewell was largely without ceremony. The duke's family was at the dock to greet him when we reached London. An important component of the mission had been to recover an abducted cousin, and Northumberland sent word to this man's parents when our ship entered the Thames at Margate. The note was meant to put an anxious aunt and uncle at ease, but the result was a family reunion at the East India Company docks.

His desperate mother and sisters, aunts, uncles, and cousins created quite a raucous welcoming party, but they served as a useful distraction to my green-gilled quest for solid ground.

So there you go.

I have other news.

Your Norse crystals are in my possession.

I am so anxious to see you.

To that end, please begin to think about what you will pack for a visit. When I come for you, I'll have no time to indulge this process. We will leave the same day I arrive, please be aware.

I should be relocated to Hammersmith by the time this reaches you. My work in the new shop will be exhausting and very pressing because we're endeavoring to outplace any retribution from Drummond Hooke. That said, the joy of my own agency will not be as sweet without you there to share it.

All my love,
Bell

Chapter Twenty-Three

Four weeks later

"*M*other?" whispered Isobel. "I'm afraid you'll have to take yourself and your watering can outside to the garden. If you please?"

"What?" asked Georgiana Tinker innocently, looking up from a potted geranium.

"You're distracting my clients," Isobel sighed, nodding to the baron currently ignoring Samantha as she tried to explain lodging choices in Malta.

"But I'm merely tending to the—"

"You know very well what you're doing," said Isobel, "and we need the baron's undivided attention."

Despite being nearly fifty years old, not to mention retired, Georgiana Tinker took center stage wherever she went. The lobby of Isobel's new travel shop was no exception, and Georgiana could sense male attention without even looking up from her reading. Her vocabulary of guiles and wiles ranged from melodious humming, to requests for the loan of handkerchiefs, to exaggerated fanning with a folded broadsheet.

And when she wasn't distracting fathers and husbands, Georgiana was asserting her opinion of foreign cities. Most well-traveled people agreed that Venice smelled like a sewer in August, but to make a go of the new shop, Isobel needed *all of* the families to book *all of* the cities. Even Venice, even in August.

"You're unsettling the baroness," said Isobel, thrusting the watering can in her direction. "Out. Go. Take your hat."

Two weeks had perhaps been too long for her mother's Hammersmith visit, but she was sending her home on Monday. They need only survive three more days.

"Do forgive me," said Isobel to the baron, relieving Samantha. "Now where were we?"

Baron Peyton had come to finalize his wife's itinerary for a late-spring holiday to the island of Malta. The baroness and their two daughters had accompanied him, and the ladies mooned over watercolors of the island while the baron settled the bill.

The baron and baroness were among the first wave of former clients—two dozen in all—who had transferred their patronage to her new shop, Tinker's Travel. Now a second wave had begun, families who had originally remained with Everland Travel but experienced terrible service or abject confusion since Isobel's departure.

"I always knew you were the brains of the operation," the baron had said. "I'd wager Drummond Hooke cannot find the island of Malta on a map."

Isobel had thanked the baron for entrusting his wife's journey to Tinker's Travel and sealed the deal by introducing her own watercolor renderings of the island. She said nothing about the shop on Lumley Street except that it might take some months for Mr. Hooke to set things to rights.

The truth was, Isobel had no idea how Drummond

Hooke would carry on without her. She'd had no time to travel to Shropshire to inform him of her resignation in person and had written a letter instead.

"Just to be perfectly clear," she had written, "it was your proposal that drove me to this, Mr. Hooke. When my job became contingent on marriage to you, I was left with no other choice. Please consider this letter to be notice of my immediate resignation."

Had it been unfair to give him so little notice? To not walk him through how he might carry on without her? Perhaps. His parents had been lovely to her; was there some debt she could pay to them through their terrible son?

But she'd endeavored to explain the business to him years ago, and he'd shown no interest. It had been like teaching a squirrel to count. Since then, he'd been a constant source of condescension and a fledgling letch.

In response to her letter, Hooke had scrawled out an angry note that seethed with legal doom and slander. She had expected this, but the language and threats had unnerved her. She had new locks installed on the doors and, through an old Lost Boys connection, hired a man from London to serve as her "groundskeeper." This man tended her new building and garden with casual lack of interest but kept a keen eye out for Drummond Hooke and would render the man quietly ineffective if he dared turn up to cause a stir.

Ultimately, Hooke hadn't shown his face in Hammersmith. And no subsequent letter followed. Old neighbors on Lumley Street told Isobel that Hooke had reported to his shop with a scrum of office-y looking gentlemen in tow. They had clattered around the shop at odd hours, but there had been very little client traffic.

Now Hooke had not been seen for days and an ever-decreasing number of office clerks wafted in and out.

Isobel had gradually allowed worry over Drummond Hooke to ebb away. Partly because she was so very busy those first weeks, and partly because she thought she was about to become . . . well, a duchess. And what threat could Drummond Hooke be when this happened?

When.

If.

Only in her dreams.

What a fool she'd been.

The duke, in fact, had not come.

Not for the first week, or the second, or the third.

Now she'd been back in England for a month. Every day, another puff of hope rose from her chest, stripping off a layer of her heart.

The misery was worse than the seasickness. It was worse than anxiety over the new shop or the fear of Hooke's retribution. It was far worse than anything she'd ever felt for Peter Boyd.

Her only consolation was that she had been correct about the imposed silence. They'd absolutely done the right thing by keeping their . . . their "betrothal" (had it been an actual betrothal, all things considered?) a secret.

He'd needed the unencumbered time to do whatever a reluctant new duke did to assume the title. His absence meant, in hindsight, that the gaps in their station were too great to allow for what had seemed possible in Iceland.

It was cold, bitter comfort to acknowledge it, and a hundred times she wished she'd put herself and her heart first when his family met the brigantine on the docks.

What if she'd lingered? What if she'd attached herself to the duke's side and forced him to introduce her? What if she'd walked up, bold as brass, and introduced herself?

Instead, she'd touched Jason's arm, given him a wink, and slipped away, allowing him to greet his family and step into his new life without the surprise introduction of a heretofore unknown woman from the ship. At the time, she'd been unchaperoned, pale and wan from seasickness, and unable to properly wash her hair for a fortnight. It hadn't been the time to meet his family, nor had it been what they'd agreed. And so she'd gone, and he'd been swallowed up by his family, and checking in with the Foreign Office, and . . .

And his new life as the Duke of Northumberland.

They hadn't even said a proper good-bye. She'd been so very ill on the return voyage, far worse than when they'd embarked. And the ship was crawling with the recovered merchants, including Jason's very demanding cousin.

The Englishmen had shared a collective fascination with "the girl traded to the pirates." Jason minimized the ordeal by describing her as a colleague whom he'd easily recovered within moments of their cart rolling away.

It was always going to be a bizarre story, but Jason assured Isobel that the injuries and trauma of the merchants would overshadow their memory of her in ropes being thrust into the possession of the pirates. Isobel did her part by staying out of sight, and, in particular, she was careful never to be seen in the company of the duke.

Jason looked in on her often, but she always sent him away. If they were ultimately meant to be together, the last thing she needed was his cousin reporting to relatives that they'd fraternized on the ship.

Not that any of that mattered now, as clearly they were *not* meant to be together.

The worst part was, she missed him. Terribly, achingly, unrelentingly.

With every swing of her shop door, she looked up, hoping he'd come for her. Every night, she peered out her bedroom window into the dark street, hoping to see a shadowy figure flicking a gold coin.

The hard work of setting up the new shop had been her only saving grace. Every night she read and wrote correspondence until the early-morning hours.

She'd begun to include Samantha in more of everything she did, hoping she might one day require the younger woman to take on a larger role because Isobel would be duchess.

But even while she worked herself into exhaustion, she was hounded by a chiding voice inside her head.

You knew.

You knew.

Why in God's name would you expect anything different? Isobel Tinker, a duchess?

The chosen wife of Jason Beckett, the most handsome, clever, strongest, kindest—

He's a man, she would then say.

Just a man. Like any other man.

And I am a fool.

Of course he's not coming.

He was never coming.

But at night, when she lay in bed and replayed their time together, she felt the wind on the deck of the brig, the kiss at the river; she remembered his dread of the pirates, his passion in the heated pool. It seemed so real.

And yet.

And yet she awakened every morning alone. She was no one's duchess; she was nothing to anyone but a friend to Samantha, a travel agent to her clients, and a vexing confusion to her mother.

In truth, she'd invited Georgiana to Hammersmith in part because she'd wanted her mother to bear witness to the moment the duke would come.

How her mother would have been impressed and thrilled by the duke. How happy she would be that Isobel had fallen in love.

Isobel had intended to tell Georgiana everything. In person. No more letters. But then one day turned into the next, and the next, and when no duke appeared, Isobel glossed over that part of the Iceland story. She'd said they'd shared a heated moment on the deck of the brig, but nothing more. She dismissed and deflected every question about him.

Now she would send Georgiana home, and Isobel would be alone in the new building. She would begin to accept that aloneness and the long, terrible reckoning of her shattered heart.

"What of gratuities?" the baron was now asking Isobel, shaking her from another pointless spiral of sadness.

"I beg your pardon?"

"Will the baroness be responsible for tipping staff everywhere she goes?"

Isobel was assuring him that gratuities would be handled by the travel porter when Lady Peyton and her daughters drifted from the watercolors to join the baron at Isobel's desk.

"Have you begun shopping for your holiday, Lady Peyton?" Isobel asked the baroness.

"Oh yes, and luckily I have my daughters to advise

me. I understand it will be rather hot, and I am so very partial to wool. The girls tell me this will never do."

"I would listen to your daughters, my lady. I wore exclusively cotton, crisp and light, when I was in Malta, even into dinners."

She winked at the daughters. "But when may we plan a holiday for you girls? We cannot let the young men have all the fun with their grand tours. I've planned several holidays for girls your age. Paris. Rome. Hamburg. A journey like this expands your mind as well as your wardrobe."

The first girl, a round-faced, large-eyed brunette who remined Isobel of an owl, said, "We do not very much care for travel, Miss Tinker."

The other girl, whose hair was secured with a strange, two-pronged hat that could have passed for rabbit ears, agreed. "Homebodies, the both of us, I'm afraid. We've heard the food is very *spicy* outside of England. We are not at all fond of spicy food."

"Oh yes," said Isobel, well aware of a lost cause when she met one. "That can be true."

She turned back to the baron to show him the itemized gratuities in his wife's file, but the two girls continued to speak, gossiping with their mother behind the baron. Isobel ignored them until a single name struck her ears like the clang of a bell.

"You don't mean the Duke of *Northumberland*?" the baroness was asking.

"Oh yes, Mama," said the owlish daughter. "Patrice is friendly with the youngest of his sisters, and she told us the situation is rather grave."

The baron was ticking off service positions, accounting for anyone who might require a tip, but Isobel's brain had departed their invoice. She stared at the point of his pen as it bobbed up and down along the page. Her rib cage grew tight. She held her breath, straining to hear the girl's next words.

"It was all of those years outside of England that did it," the owl went on. "Spicy food is only the beginning; too much travel can take a terrible toll. But you must be very careful, Mama."

"But what did Patrice say had become of the duke?" asked the baroness.

"Oh, he's incapacitated, to be sure. Worse than an invalid. He doesn't get out of bed, and when he does, it's only to lie facedown on the floor. He barely dresses and grooming is entirely out of the question. He sacked the previous duke's valet—he's sacked all of the duke's personal staff. Such rash behavior as can be expected of someone with too much exposure to other countries . . ."

The rabbit-ish sister said, "You cannot devote years to traipsing around the world and expect to remember what's what when you return. You see this all the time among families returning from India. Remember Eleanor Stapleton-Block? That kohl around her eyes? And all the scarves?"

"The duke was hardly traipsing about the world," corrected the baroness. "Northumberland fought in the war and was lauded a hero for his diplomacy and routing of the French. Let us not be disrespectful. Perhaps he's in his cups. He's lost two brothers in the last ten years, the poor man."

The rabbit shook her head. "His sister claims he is *not* drunk, he's 'depressed.' He hates being duke. Can you imagine, finding a dukedom hateful? Apparently he's at a loss for how to manage the estate."

The owlish sister nodded. "The duchess and his sisters waited and waited for his military career to end so he could come home and do his duty, and now this. Patrice says they're at their wit's end."

"Pity," mused the rabbit, "that giant estate and all of the land. But what good is property if he cannot manage it? They say his tenants are on the verge of revolt. The foundry's stopped operation, cold and dark for the first time in centuries. Meanwhile, he sleeps all day and rides his horse all night."

"Pity," repeated the owl.

Isobel had gone stiff and still behind the counter. Her heart thudded in her ears, the sound of thunder, until it stopped beating altogether. It felt like a suspended bomb waiting to go off.

"Miss Tinker," the baron was asking, "are you quite alright?"

Isobel stared at him. He spoke words, English words— words she knew—but she comprehended only the conversation behind him.

"Can you post a copy of this bill to our home in Marylebone? I'll want one for my files and one for my steward."

"Yes," said Isobel. She had no idea what she'd agreed to post to Marylebone. She'd stopped listening.

She stood up, her pen still clutched in her hand. "Will you excuse me?" she said.

"But have we finished?" asked the baron. The owl and the rabbit ceased talking and stared at her.

"For the moment," she said. She dropped the pen. She backed away from her desk.

She'd captivated them now—her odd jerky movements and her blank expression. They watched her to see what she might do next.

Somehow she found the words to say, "Forgive me. I've . . . I find myself suddenly indisposed. If you would be so kind as to call again. I will be in touch. The holiday will be lovely, my lady. The trip of a lifetime."

While the baron and his family stared, Isobel threw open the door to the stairwell and bounded up, already unbuttoning her dress.

Chapter Twenty-Four

O f Isobel knew nothing else, she knew how to pack in extreme haste for an indeterminate journey. She bundled up the very few essentials that she absolutely could not survive without and raided her stash of money so she might buy the rest.

The essentials included clothing for two days, correspondence from the travel shop, and Samantha.

She hadn't worked out how, exactly, she would gain access to Syon Hall, but she knew she could not turn up as a young woman alone.

"I am like a bodyguard," guessed Samantha, sitting beside her in the carriage Isobel hired to drive them the five miles to Syon Hall.

"You are my assistant," corrected Isobel. "You accompany me and assist me. You are always with me in my work as cultural attaché."

"I am your maid," Samantha concluded glumly.

"I have no maid," corrected Isobel. "It's not my goal to portray myself as a fine lady or even as a woman. I'm simply . . . a colleague of the duke's. Which is true. I *was* the duke's cultural attaché. You *are* my assistant. And I do not have a maid."

"Well, you are a woman," said Samantha, "so I'd not press the issue on that. Given a choice."

Isobel had worn a light-green dress that fit her petite figure like a snugly wrapped stocking. She'd concealed the length of her hair with her signature bun. She carried a navy leather satchel to appear businesslike. Her attire had been easy; she'd sold enough holidays to esteemed women to know how to impress.

Her introduction at the door of Syon Hall would be far more complicated and nuanced. Even as the carriage made the last turn, she had no idea what she would say.

"Your mother felt a little left behind, I fear," said Samantha, sounding not at all sorry.

"The only thing to make this situation more fraught would be Georgiana," said Isobel, gazing at the autumnal woodlands outside the carriage window. "She'll manage in Hammersmith alone for a night or two. Or for the afternoon. Or two hours. We could be sent away the moment we arrive, mind you. I've no idea what to expect. Whatever happens, I'm afraid there will be very little for you to say; you are simply there so that I'm not calling on the duke *alone*. I'm sorry. Simply follow my lead. And whatever you do, do not mention weapons or fighting or show any kind of . . . aggressiveness toward them."

"Do not worry, Isobel," assured Samantha, "you can rely on me. And of course the topic of weaponry will not come up, not at the stately home of a duke."

"Thank you," said Isobel, barely listening. What if they turned her away? What if *he* answered the door? What if—?

"Even so," continued Samantha, "you mustn't be so afraid of learning to *defend yourself*, Isobel. If you would but explore the training as I have—"

"Oh my God," said Isobel, turning from the window. She pressed a gloved hand to her mouth.

The view unfolding outside was unlike anything she'd seen in all of her travels. An ancient stone gate marked the end of a long, crushed-gravel drive. Sprawling parkland unfurled, foggy and dotted with red and gold trees, on either side. At the end of the drive stood a Palladian-style manor house so grand it looked like a small city. The yellow stone glowed in the sunlight like a wall of gold.

As the carriage drew closer, the parkland gave way to smoothly manicured estate grounds: rounded hedgerows, sandstone walkways, immaculately weeded flower beds of autumnal vegetation. Swans paddled a slow circle in a fountain.

Syon Hall was nothing short of a palace. Versailles had been no grander.

"Just to the front door, miss?" the driver called.

"Ah—yes, thank you," said Isobel.

To Samantha, she said, "Pay him. When we alight, pay him with the money I gave you and send him on."

"Just as I predicted," sang Samantha, "I am the maid."

"Samantha!" hissed Isobel. "Please cooperate."

"I *am* cooperating," insisted Samantha defensively. "It's simply not *clear* to me *what* we are *doing*."

Isobel turned away from the grandeur outside and blinked at the dusty black interior of the carriage. She sucked in air with short, shallow gasps.

"I'm sorry," breathed Isobel.

She turned to her friend and clutched her hand. "When I was in Iceland with the duke, I fell in love with him—or perhaps I was in love before we left, it doesn't matter—and he claimed to have fallen in love with me. He proposed marriage while we were there, but I bade him return and settle into . . . into—"

She stole another look out the window. "To settle at

this palace before we made the betrothal public. The agreement was, he would send for me afterward. *If he still believed in our*—well, in a future. Together. With me. As you may have noticed, he has not turned up. However, I learned this morning from Baron Peyton's daughters that the duke is rumored to be somehow . . . incapacitated, or consumed with ennui or—or something has gone wrong. I don't know exactly what the problem may be. I . . . I probably shouldn't have come. I had *no call* to come. His family doesn't know me; *he* doesn't want me. But I love him too much to think of him struggling alone." A deep breath. "I love him more than my pride and more than my own self-preservation. And *that* is why we are here. Unmarried women cannot turn up alone on the doorstep of bachelor men. I took advantage of you, I know, by dragging you along, and I'm sorry to use you this way, but I am frantic with worry."

Isobel looked at her with an expression that was half smile, half cringe. "You are too good to me," she finished.

Samantha's eyes grew large, understanding dawning on her face. She craned to study the manor house rising before them, now just yards away.

She turned back to Isobel. "This is a very important errand indeed," she said. "I am happy to help. Do not worry, Isobel. You were right to come. I liked the duke from the beginning, and you know how I feel about tall men."

Isobel let out a breath that was half laugh, half sob. She squeezed her friend's hand, closed her eyes, and braced for the carriage to lurch to a stop. Before he opened the door, she took three quick breaths.

When the driver opened the door, she bounded out, propelled by her desire simply to see the duke. The gravel of the circle drive crunched beneath her boots, a deafening sound. A chirping bird in the distance sounded as if it perched on her shoulder. Every sense was heightened; fear hounded every step.

Isobel mounted the cascade of steps, certain that servants or guards would stop her and demand their business. Clipping up, she waited to be called out. Surely hired carriages couldn't simply drive up to this imposing home and expel strange women to knock on the door.

No one came, and Isobel knocked. Four firm raps on the giant oak planks of a door strong enough to resist a battering ram. The sound barely registered, swallowed by the sheer magnitude of the structure. *Calmness,* Isobel ordered herself. *Hold the satchel rather than squeeze it in a death grip. Breathe as if you are on dry land.*

After an eternity, the giant door swung slowly open. Isobel's heart stopped thudding and ran away inside her chest.

A stout butler, his expression as inscrutable as a sandstone pillar, stared down at them.

"May I help you?"

Isobel swallowed. "How do you do? My name is Miss Isobel Tinker. I am a colleague of His Grace, the duke . . ." she spit out the next bit, ". . . having served as his cultural attaché on his most recent mission. To Iceland. I have business with the duke, if you please."

The butler stared at her, saying nothing. Behind him Isobel could see a flurry of activity. Servants rushing to and fro. Someone pushed a potted fern on a cart. A man with a length of rope chased after a dog.

Oh Lord, Isobel thought, *there is some palace-related crisis. I've come in the exact moment of Bedlam.*

She said, "If this is an inconvenient time, I can—"

"And who else may I say is calling?" intoned the butler. He stared at Samantha.

"Oh," said Isobel, "I am accompanied by my assistant. Miss Samantha Smee."

The butler narrowed his eyes, considering this. He said nothing more and made no move to admit them. Time stretched in excruciating silence. Isobel wondered if, in her extreme anxiety, she'd actually *said* the words rather than simply thinking them. Had she spoken English? Had her request so shocked the man he'd entered a trancelike state?

Isobel was just about to turn and tiptoe down the steps and search for perhaps a servants' entrance when a young woman strode past the door. She paused, squinted out at the steps, and then joined the butler at the door.

"What is it, Norris?" asked the young woman. She was eating a stalk of celery.

The butler leaned in to whisper in her ear.

The girl's eyebrows rose, she cocked her head, and extended the stalk of celery, tapping the air accusingly. "But you're the girl who rescued Reggie! On the boat, with Jason. Thank God! Perhaps you can reason with him—and just in time. Come in, come in. Norris, don't just stand there, fetch Mama!"

Chapter Twenty-Five

$\mathcal{T}$he Dowager Duchess of Northumberland had a gentle face. Grief had hollowed her beauty, age had creased it, but her smile was genuine.

"He's not allowed staff to tidy the library," Lady Northumberland said, leading Isobel down a wide corridor. Servants passed swiftly around them like salmon swimming upstream. "Even I have not been allowed inside. There's no hope for it tonight; the door will have to be locked to hide the mess."

"Tonight?" asked Isobel.

"Oh yes, the ball," said the dowager dismissively. "My daughters insisted. I put it off as long as I could, hoping the duke could get on his feet. But it's been a month. The girls believe some social interaction may help matters."

A ball, thought Isobel. *The palace-related crisis was not a crisis at all, it was a party.*

If the duke was as bad as gossip suggested, a crisis was still highly likely.

Isobel ventured, "It has come to my attention that the duke is . . . at an impasse."

"Yes, well," tsked the dowager, "there's nothing for it, is there? He is who he is. The girls and I have not been able to rouse him. I blame the unresolved deaths of his brothers. He never reckoned with the loss. Here at home, we were forced to carry on, but he was always working, doing his duty for the country, running about—always running. Since he was a boy, the notion of rest or stillness tortured him. And now here we are. There is nowhere else to run. There is quite a bit of stillness, I'm afraid, when one is a duke."

They came to a stop before a closed door.

"Quite," said Isobel. "I . . . I am grateful that you have allowed me to look in on him."

"I've kept his uncles away; they are circling like vultures naturally. But he's spoken so fondly of you. And to have returned poor Reggie to his parents? My brother was overwhelmed with gratitude and relief. But how can I make your visit more pleasant?" She made a scoffing noise. "When you see him, you'll acknowledge the futility of this question. There is nothing pleasant about his current . . . state. We are grasping at straws, I'm afraid. But tea never hurt. Perhaps you can coax him to eat. What do you think?"

Isobel had no idea what to think. Her theory that he was being tortured by an unfeeling family was entirely wrong obviously. The notion that the estate was in penury or ruin had been, if true, very well disguised.

She smiled at the dowager. "Thank you, Your Grace. If you could be so kind as to see my assistant settled somewhere that will not disrupt the household?"

"Do not give it another thought," she said. "I've put the two of you in a suite of rooms on the third floor, dear. I'll send up tea. It is our great hope that you will stay with us a day or so, if you believe there's any good for it."

"Thank you," was all Isobel could say.

"Lovely," said the dowager. "And the ball tonight—of

course you must attend. Reggie and his parents have traveled from Lincolnshire, and they'll wish to thank you. I know we must keep the nasty business of the smuggling and the pirates a secret, but a handful of family members are aware of what happened and how very brave you were."

"Ah," began Isobel.

"Think on it," she urged, reaching for the knob of a giant door.

"Yes, Your Grace," said Isobel, staring at the door as if it opened to the edge of a sharp cliff.

"Very well, I will leave you to it," said the duchess.

She turned the knob and pushed the heavy door open. "Northumberland?" she called.

Silence.

"You've a visitor . . ."

The dowager rolled her eyes and gave her head a shake. "He's in there," she whispered, backing away. "Good luck."

Isobel nodded her thanks and leaned to peer inside the dim interior of the library. For a long moment, she hovered. She listened. She sniffed.

The feeling of *almost* seeing him, of knowing he was just beyond the open door, was burning her up from the outside in. Her skin tingled, her chest felt molten. She wiggled her fingers, trying to release nervous energy.

Oh for God's sake, she thought, pushing the door open. She was anxious, but she was not a coward. She'd come all this way for a reason.

To her great shock, the scene inside the Syon Hall library was almost exactly as the baron's daughters had described.

The duke, dressed only in a linen shirt, buckskins and boots, lay facedown on a vibrant Persian rug. The opulent library was in shambles. A giant desk was awash with papers, open books were scattered on the floor, a globe had been turned on its side. Furniture was strewn with discarded coats and unfurled cravats. Hats had been lined up in a row, brim-up. Balls of wadded-up paper surrounded them as if they'd been thrown. Some wads filled the upturned hats, but most had missed their mark.

While Isobel took it all in, a gust of wind from an open window swept through, launching papers into the air, blowing cravats. A cat leapt inside the window from the garden and picked his way over the inert duke to the desk. Leaping, he made himself at home on the blotter and began grooming, one white paw pointed to the ceiling.

Isobel looked again to the prone duke. Her first instinct was to go to him, to crouch and gently prod and ascertain, but something held her back.

Instead, she crossed her arms over her chest.

"Get up," she said, her voice brisk.

She watched the familiar lines of his broad shoulders for any sign of life.

Nothing.

"Northumberland," she said sharply.

Unless she was mistaken, she discerned the tiniest twitch, a tensing about the bicep.

Her heart skipped like a stone on the surface of a pond. She said it again. "Northumberland. *Get up.*"

He turned his head, keeping his face averted. He had not shaved. His hair was long. He pressed his cheek to the rug.

"You," he said. His voice was level—not loud, not soft, not hoarse. He did not sound ill. He did not sound mad.

"Yes," she continued carefully, leaning a hip against the desk. "It is me. Get up. This library is a disgrace. Your family is beside themselves with worry. Gossip is rampant in London about what has become of you. Get up and tell me *what has happened*."

She waited, holding her breath. Finally, the duke rolled his body from back to front.

And there he was. His glorious body sprawled on the floor, blinking at the ceiling.

He looked . . . not unwell, but certainly not happy. He had a full beard, and he was pale. His clothes and hair were disheveled.

Well, she thought, if nothing else, his handsomeness had endured. It took all of her willpower not to go to him. In her mind's eye, she saw her spreading herself on top of him, taking his face into her hands. She imagined the feel of his mouth.

But she didn't dare.

She shoved off the desk and crossed to the window, closing it with a slam. The cat meowed and slunk from the room.

"You're scaring the animals," he said.

"Why are you on the floor?" she asked. She began to pick up papers, one by one, stacking them in the crook of her arm.

"I'm resting."

"What of your bedroom?"

"My bedroom is where I sleep. *This* is where I rest."

"What of all of these papers?"

"God only knows," he groaned, rolling to sit. He leaned against a towering bookshelf and propped one leg on his knee. "Ledgers, accounts, deeds to property, taxes, taxes, taxes, regulations, correspondence."

He ran his hands down his face like he was rubbing his features away. "I cannot make sense of it. I've tried, and I cannot."

"No," she corrected, "you don't want to."

"*And* I don't want to."

One piece of paper led to the next, and the next, and the next. She moved without thinking, grateful for the task. He had not even said hello.

"It's as bad as you thought?" she asked.

"It is so much worse, Isobel," he said. "*So* much worse."

"You must determine some way to manage it, North, you must."

"North?" he repeated, a challenge.

Isobel missed a step. The familiar rain of shimmers set her insides alight. She glanced at him.

He looked back. Ever so slowly, he cocked an eyebrow. Handsomeness and boyish charm rolled from him in waves. He was attractive and commanding despite being unshaven, despite his . . . his . . .

She looked at the mess around her.

Despite whatever had happened in his life.

She glanced to him again. She couldn't resist. He gazed back, and they locked eyes. Unless she was mistaken, he gave her the smallest quirk of a one-sided smile.

The shimmers exploded again, and Isobel looked away, trying to catch her breath.

"Come to your desk," she said, "and help me sort these papers."

"What will you give me if I do?" he asked.

"What will I give you?" She was confused. Did he *tease* her?

"If I come to the desk . . . if I sort the papers?"

"I'll give you the first very small step toward a functioning dukedom?" she tried.

He laughed and rolled to his feet.

Isobel unearthed a stool from beneath cast-off clothing and dragged it beside the desk. The duke collapsed into the leather wingback and ran a hand through his hair.

"Lovely," she said with forced brightness. The inside-out burning had gone from a sizzle to licking, jumping flames. She was jittery and twitchy. The shimmers inside her chest flew about like his paperwork.

Through sheer force of will, she blocked out his gaze, his smell, *his leg*, which touched her skirts. She bit off her gloves. With trembling fingers, she held up the first piece of paper.

She read the title at the top of the page. " 'Tenant-Lodging Repairs before Winter.' Very good. Now, we shall make stacks. You'll want files for each of these. I'll keep a tally here of divisions we'll need. Make a space, that's it. Down it goes. My God, Northumberland, there's cat hair everywhere. Alright, on to the next."

She picked up the next sheet. She read the title. He mumbled some explanation about what it might mean and she created a new stack.

She took up the next recovered paper, and the next. As interactions went, it was strange, a bit mechanical, but not difficult. It was nothing like she'd imagined, but perhaps it was what he needed.

One small step toward solvency. Progress by force.

Because she loved him. She loved him more than she loved her own need to be with him.

She loved him too much to allow him to fail.

She would set him to rights, help him hire stewards and foremen and overseers, and then she would go.

That was how much she loved him.

AFTER TEN MINUTES, Jason began to wager with himself.

Could he continue in this manner for an hour? For two? How long would he slouch beside her, not a foot away, and not touch her?

How long would she resist touching so that instead she could *organize his files*?

Would she do more than march him around? He'd never minded her bossing, for all that. It was arousing in a way. He was aroused now.

He wet his lips and glanced at her profile. "Isobel?" he said lowly.

"You're right," she said, leaning to drop a paper into one of her many neat stacks, "best file it with the taxes and ask a solicitor to look it over. There may be an exemption."

"Isobel," he repeated his voice a growl.

"No," she said, a senseless answer. She dabbed a pen in the inkwell, refusing to look at him.

He called her name a third time. "Isobel." A whisper.

She paused, her fingers frozen over a stack of papers; she looked to him. Her face was tight. If he wasn't mistaken, she held her breath.

"North?" she asked.

"Yes?"

"Are you . . . ?" She studied him with narrowed, searching eyes.

He scratched his beard. He began slowly shaking his head.

Whatever she meant to accuse, it wasn't—he wasn't. He *hadn't*.

She'd not come to him as she said she would.

The estate was every intolerable thing he thought and more.

He hadn't planned to lure her here by going a little mad.

The air in the library, previously cold from the open window, had grown hot. He was sweating. It took every ounce of self-control not to reach for her.

She tried again. "Are you *teasing* me?" A whisper.

He continued to slowly shake his head. Their eyes remained locked. She looked at him as if she was trying to find a hidden lever, to see beyond a ruse or a lie, like she was trying to see the real him.

It's me, he wanted to say. And then he did say it. "It's me, S'bell," he said.

"You're not overwhelmed," she realized, her voice rising. She dropped the papers in her hand.

"The devil I'm not," he breathed, leaning back. He glared at the library in disgust. He was overwhelmed and miserable and desperate for her. He was also terrified of how he would manage it all for the rest of his life.

"Perhaps, but you aren't . . . *immobilized*." She shoved up from the stool and took a step back from the desk. "You don't need me."

"Isobel," he said loudly, firmly, "I need you more than I need my next breath." He would perish, he thought, if she left now.

"Do not," she ordered coldly, rounding the desk. She held up one angry finger.

He gave in and reached for her, but she darted away.

"Why didn't you come for me?" she demanded. Her voice broke.

"Do not cry," he said. "I cannot bear it."

"Do not sprawl on the floor and pretend you're out of your depth. I was worried for you. I was beside myself with worry."

"I am out of my depth and you should be worried," he said, raising his own voice. He stood up. "Did I exaggerate my distress, creating some incentive for you to come? Perhaps. Do I regret it? No. Not when I *was* actually immobilized. Do not deceive yourself about how miserable I have been. And news of it *did* work. Clearly. You're here. You've finally come."

"Why, in God's name, would you wait for *me* to come to *you*?" she asked. "You know my insecurities. You are rich, and handsome, and dashing, and a bloody *duke*. The burden to come *was on you*."

She pressed her hands to her chest in the most heartbreaking gesture of self-preservation. It killed him to see her so upset, but this was always going to be a difficult conversation.

"S'bell," he began.

"No," she said. "Do not. Does your family know you've been . . . been pretending to be incapacitated?"

"They know what *you* know. That I'm stupefied. Miserable. That I've made no progress on taking the dukedom in hand. It cannot be said enough: I'm not pretending to struggle with the bloody estate!"

"You are," she insisted.

"I deplore this tedious, mind-numbing, body-atrophying drivel. I cannot look at it for more than a quarter hour without hoping I catch yellow fever like my brother and die."

"Do not say that."

"It's true. *That* is how much I hate it. Can I manage it? Probably. Will I be miserable doing it? Always.

"Look, Isobel," he continued. "Is my mother worried? Probably. Are my sisters afraid for my sanity? Probably *not*. Are people in London talking about me and my inabilities and my failings as a duke? Certainly. I don't care.

"That said," he countered, "I've cared very much about when you might come to me. Now, did I think you might hear of my distress and be motivated to come more quickly, to overcome your own insecurities and . . . bloody . . . *look in* on me? Yes. The thought did cross my mind."

"So you . . ." she began, "you encouraged the gossip because you thought I'd hear about it and come here?" Her voice was high and searching. Her expression was creased with confusion.

"No, I did not encourage the gossip. But servants talk and I didn't prevent it. My sisters have guests to the house and I did not care what they saw or what they said. And yes, Isobel, I hoped you'd come for me. It's part of the terrible secrecy you forced me to keep within moments of our betrothal—"

She let out a breathy sob when he said the word.

"Not to mention," he continued, "the *blind sprint* in which you left the brigantine the moment we reached London. Not even a good-bye, Isobel! Not even a moment to say when I might see you next. One moment you were locked in your room, the next you were winding your way through dockworkers and sailors to flee the scene."

"I was very ill on the return trip."

"You were afraid," he said.

"I was—"

"You were afraid to meet my family, or you were afraid that you would *not* meet my family. Either way, you were running scared. I understand why, and I am sorry for the circumstances of your life that cultivated this fear. However, I know you to be a brave woman and I believed you when you said you loved me."

"I do love you," she said softly.

His chest clenched. "Well, God forgive me. Because I know that my struggles here forced you to face your fear to come to me."

He dug a coin from his pocket and flicked it. "Do I misremember," he pleaded, snatching the coin from the air, "that you swore me to secrecy about our betrothal? Did you or did you not flee the brigantine without saying good-bye?"

"Yes. The silence was meant to give you a clear head and no other obligations as you eased into the dukedom."

"It didn't work."

"And yes, I fled—because the ship was met with cheering relatives whose priorities were reclaiming your cousin and welcoming you. It was the wrong time and place for introducing me. I . . . I was green. My skin was actually greenish-grayish-tannish in color at the time."

"I'll admit that Reggie's parents and my mother and sisters complicated the arrival, but never would I have simply . . . left it—left *us*. Not without a plan, a good-bye, nothing. But you sprinted away. I could hardly chase you through the docks while my family watched. Green or not, how would *that* have improved your introduction? What choice did I have but to let you go? You *made me* let you go."

"I do not mean the docks," she said in a small voice. "I meant afterward. You were meant to *come for me*."

"To what end, Isobel?" he asked in frustration. "So you could relive your insecurity again and again with every new relative to whom I introduced you? No. I've wanted you to *want me enough* to put your fear aside and face my family."

"Wanting you was never the problem," she said, louder now.

"What was the problem?" he begged.

"Feeling . . . worthy of you," she shot back.

"Meanwhile," he said, his voice now raised, "I'm the one who cannot do my own filing. Who is unworthy now? *I* wanted *you* to see this. I wanted you to forget your alleged lack of worth and see that we are both simply human!"

"So you admit you lay in wait for me to come here," she demanded.

"I will not admit it. I have not had a moment's clarity, Isobel, until you walked through the door. I understand that you feel . . . uncollected by me—"

"Try 'rejected'—I felt, I *feel*, rejected by you."

"I see now that you feel rejected, and I regret this, but I beg you to consider that I had no intention of upsetting you. There was no grand scheme. I was here, struggling. You were in Hammersmith, waiting. I was waiting too. I waited every day for you to come. Yes, I could have rescued you, Isobel, but you seem to enjoy rescuing yourself."

He spun away and walked to his desk. His heart was pounding; he wanted her so badly he felt physical pain. It wasn't meant to play out this way. When she came. If she came. He made a sound of frustration and ran a hand through his hair. He looked at the stacks of parchment on the desk and wanted to scoop them to the floor in an angry sweep. But then where would he be? Faced with sorting it all again.

He chuckled bitterly to himself. "Although I have no aversion to you rescuing me. Obviously."

Across the room, Isobel was silent. He did not look at her. He did not need to look at her; as always, he *felt* her presence, her flickering energy. He smelled her.

After a tense moment, he asked, "Has Drummond Hooke, your former employer, harassed you in any way?"

"What?" She stared at him as if he might burst into flames.

"The illustrious Mr. Hooke. Has he harassed you in the new shop?"

"Well, he sent a letter the first week. I responded but heard nothing back."

"Good. I hope you don't mind my paying him a visit. Rest assured, he understands now that it's in his best interest to not bother you again."

"I . . . I did not know," she said softly.

Jason nodded, watching his coin spin upward. In his peripheral vision, he saw her drift in his direction. He held his breath.

"But have you," she ventured softly, "told your family about . . . about your offer?"

Jason exhaled. He smiled to himself. If she raised the topic of "his offer," surely she was conceding. She wanted him still. They were nearly there.

He propped his hip on the corner of the desk. "Which offer would that be?"

"You wouldn't make me say it," she said.

"I would make you say it. I made you come for me, didn't I?"

"You've just claimed—" She stopped herself. She narrowed her eyes. "Answer the question."

Her voice was sharp but she'd taken another step in his direction. His muscles twitched to reach her, but he remained calmly, coolly, on the edge of his desk.

"*No*," he answered, enunciating his words flatly, "my mother and sisters do not know that we are *betrothed*. You forbade me from telling anyone, remember? *No one knows.* You'll have to endure that particular revelation in front of everyone—assuming you'll still have me. But see? How much easier will it be now that you've enjoyed this lovely foray into a typical day at Syon Hall? Now that you've met my harmless mother and sisters, all of whom couldn't care less who I marry? They believe you've come to take me in hand. Which you have. In one sense at least. That alone will win you approval."

"You could have managed," she tried, still a little confused. She took another step. Jason licked his lips.

"The hell I could've."

"I thought you weren't coming for me," she whispered, her voice breaking again.

Jason's teasing bravado fell away. He shoved off the desk. He met her where she stood. He dropped to his knees before her.

"I was always coming, S'bell. If you never made it here—and I was praying every day that you would—I *would've come for you.* I love you. I want you to be my duchess, if you will have me."

Isobel's face had gone the most charming shade of pink. Her mouth was half-open. Tears dropped down her cheeks. She had just extended her small, shaking hand when the door behind them made a loud, slow, creaking sound.

Jason closed his eyes.

"Oh lovely!" said his sister Veronica from the doorway, her voice light with genuine pleasure. "You've finally begun sorting the ledgers. *And* the tax bills. Well done—"

Jason swore.

A stray wad of paper lay on the floor beside him and he took it up and pivoted on one knee.

"Out, Ronnie," he sang, pitching the ball of paper at the door. His sister made a yelp and hopped back, slamming the door.

The room fell silent. Jason took a deep breath. He closed his eyes. He turned back to Isobel.

"Sorry," he said, gazing up at her. "Where was I?"

While he watched her, Isobel's tearful, silent sobs made the most inelegant transformation to giggling. She shook her head and pressed her hands to her mouth, unable to stop the happy, excited sound. Her face was lit with delight. She leapt at him and he caught her up.

His mouth found hers in the first moment, kissing her with the passion and possession wrought of four weeks of waiting. Within moments, they were a clawing, pawing tangle of arms and lips, tongue and breath.

They were just about to tip sideways when a knock sounded at the door.

Jason ignored it but Isobel paused.

"Tell them to go away," he mumbled.

In the direction of the door, he shouted, "Whoever you are, go—"

Isobel placed her hand over his mouth and craned up to stare at the door. The knock sounded again. Through the door, his sister Veronica could be heard calling to them.

"Just a note that the tax on the foundry should actually read half of the listed sum because we supply swords to the Royal Marines . . ." Her voice was muffled through the wood.

Isobel looked at him, looked at the door, and then shoved up.

Jason slapped the floor with his hand in frustration.

He heard the door creak again, and then he heard Isobel say, "Hello."

"Sorry to disturb," apologized Ronnie, "but Mama said you were helping Jason sort out the filing?"

"I was endeavoring to do it," Isobel said. "I . . . I don't believe we've met. I am Miss Isobel Tinker."

"Oh yes, I know who you are," said Ronnie cheerfully. "Jason has told us how you saved our cousin from pirates. Well done. But I hope you'll forgive my very obsessive need to make a few suggestions about the filing." Ronnie drifted into the room with the cat.

"But do you have some . . . interest or expertise in the management of the estate, Lady Veronica?" asked Isobel. "Er, may I call you Lady Veronica?"

"Oh, please call me Ronnie," his sister said, brushing past, making her way to the desk. "It's just that I've been managing the correspondence and figuring the ledgers since our brother died, and I could share a few things with Jason—when he's ready."

"Is that right?" said Isobel, sounding inspired. "But do you . . . enjoy the work of managing the estate, Ronnie? That is, does it disrupt or postpone your other pursuits?"

"Oh no," assured Ronnie. "I'm loath to give it over to him, honestly. And not only because he will cock it up almost immediately."

She plopped down in Jason's chair and spilled the cat on the desktop. "I was just beginning to have everything sorted when Jason returned home. He's made quick work of turning everything upside down. Naturally."

She took up where Isobel left off, stacking papers into piles.

Isobel came up behind her, her arms crossed over her

chest, and watched appreciatively as Veronica sifted through his tangle of papers, setting things to rights.

"I think perhaps you've found an answer to your problem, Your Grace," Isobel said. "You have a capable sister right here at Syon Hall who not only wants to do your job, she's already been doing it."

Jason was shaking his head. "I won't allow the dukedom to ruin her life too. She deserves to marry, start a family."

"Actually," said Veronica, not looking up, "I've no aspiration to either of those pursuits. I'd much rather remain in my own beautiful home and play the duke instead. Given the chance."

"Lovely," said Isobel, beaming at him. She was so beautiful his heart ached.

"Ronnie," he said, "why didn't you tell me you could help? Couldn't you see me struggling?"

His sister shrugged. "You seemed so very determined. You were behaving so strangely. I was afraid my interference would make you more hysterical, honestly."

"Quite so," he said, scratching his beard. "Well, the hysteria is over, you'll be happy to know. And I would be forever grateful for any estate business that you wish to manage. I'm rubbish at it, as you've suggested. I've solicited potential stewards to interview. Outsiders who could take things in hand, but it makes far more sense for you to do it. You were always smarter than the three of us boys combined."

She winked at him but said nothing, pointing out some tabulation on an invoice to Isobel.

Jason wondered how he'd gone from kissing his betrothed to watching her do sums with his sister.

"Ronnie?" Jason called. "Is this business of a ball still happening?"

"Yes, of course," said Ronnie.

"When is it?"

"Tonight, Jason. We've said this again and again."

"Right," said Jason. "But has anyone thought to invite Isobel?"

The younger woman finally looked up. She spun in her seat to beam up at Isobel. "But you must come, Miss Tinker. Reggie will be there—and all of us, of course. A small crowd from London. It's meant to be great fun, and how much more fun now that you appear to have fixed whatever was wrong with Jason."

"Yes, Isobel," said Jason sardonically. "You must come. Especially now that you've 'fixed' me."

Isobel blinked up at him, her heart in her eyes. "Alright, Your Grace," she said. "I should be delighted to attend."

Chapter Twenty-Six

Dear Georgiana,

Can I beg a favor, Mummy? I've a gown in my bedroom that I need sent up to Syon Hall. The groom bearing this letter will wait for you to fetch it and return with it. It's the emerald-green silk with moss-colored trim; you'll find it in the back of my second wardrobe. I've only the one gown appropriate for evening, so it won't be difficult to find.

The duke's family is hosting a ball, if you can believe it.

Tonight.

Here at Syon Hall.

In their inveterate generosity, his family has included Samantha and me—and you.

Yes, you read that correctly.

Forgive me for not leading with it, but I did not want my request for the dress to be lost in the excitement. (I must have the dress—so do not forget!) But also you should determine some attire for yourself. I would worry this catches us unprepared except for the three trunks that traveled with us from Cornwall. Show no restraint, Georgiana Tinker. It's a ducal ball.

Northumberland will send a coach for you at six o'clock. Samantha will remain here with me until the ball and borrow a dress from one of his sisters.

There is more to say, but you'll forgive my brevity here. I'm hoping to send off the groom straightaway. Thank you for gathering up my evening gown. I look forward to seeing you tonight at Syon Hall. You will not believe it, Mama, you simply will not believe it.

Much love,
Bell

My Darling Bell,

Here is the dress; I hope it is correct . . .

Please thank the duke for the invitation. A more gracious mother would decline and leave the fun for the younger set, but I am not that mother. I will be ready at six o'clock. Do not fear, I will make us proud.

In case we are not afforded a moment alone at the ball, I would wish you a most unforgettable night, my darling Bell! And remember, caution is <u>not</u> a virtue, it is a fail-safe. It can keep you safe but it can fail you in other ways.

Do not miss the sweetest moments in life because one time, long ago, you took too much sugar.

Your adoring mother,
G.

PS: Perhaps try your hair in some style other than the bun?

Chapter Twenty-Seven

Jason valued society balls about as much as he valued farm inventory, but the event had seemed important to his mother and sisters, and so he'd agreed. Now it seemed predestined. Isobel had come to him, and the ball was an opportunity to make a demonstrative gesture in a very public way.

If his proposal had been too atypical—the two of them alone, together, in a heated pool—he'd declare for her in a crowded ballroom. Far less arousing but hopefully the sort of undeniable gesture that Isobel could accept.

He snatched the small jewel box and the special license from his dresser and paced his bedchamber, flexing his shoulders and tugging his sleeves. He was never comfortable in snug evening clothes. He passed the mirror and did a double take, seeing his father's reflection in his own face. A day ago, he would not have been able to look Gerald Beckett in the eye. But tonight, his father would . . . if not *approve* of Jason, he would at least not fear for the survival of the family. Tonight his father, God rest him, would be able to see some way through.

He made a face at his reflection, a little unnerved by how much he looked like his papa. The beard was gone at least—and good riddance. What a relief to shake off his debilitating malaise and feel like himself again.

He could scarcely believe his two most pressing problems solved themselves in one day. The woman he loved had come to him, and his sister had revealed herself as savior of Syon Hall.

Knock, knock.

Jason looked to the door. "Oy," he called, pulling on his gloves.

"Jason?" His sister Veronica stuck her head in the room.

And here she was, said savior. He heard a chorus of angels every time he saw her face.

"Ronnie, catch," he said, taking up the gold ring bearing the Northumberland crest and flipping it to her.

Veronica yelped but caught the ring just before it thudded against her chest.

She frowned at the man's large pinky ring. "I cannot wear this."

"The devil you cannot," he said.

They'd spent the afternoon talking about the degree to which she'd managed the dukedom since their brother James's death. She revealed that she'd actually been trained in estate management since the earliest age. Their older brother, August, had taught her. By the time James inherited, she was able to manage the estate at his side.

"You're the rightful Duke of Northumberland," Jason had realized, slamming shut a folio of ledgers. He'd spent so much time abroad he hadn't known.

"Only you would say something so irreverent," Veronica had sighed. "Look—James didn't want anyone to know how much I helped him. It made him feel a little inadequate, I think. When he died, Mama forbade me from burdening you with the notion, at least not right away. She believed you were saving the world and shouldn't be bothered."

"How right she was," he'd mused, staring stoically into the distance.

Now Veronica studied their father's ring and ultimately, Jason was gratified to see, tucked it into her pocket. He joined her in the corridor and they walked toward the sound of the musicians tuning up in the ballroom.

"Look, Ronnie," he said, "Isobel has suggested that I speak to the lawyers about how you might inherit more of the estate when I—" He made a throat-slitting gesture against his neck. "It's hardly fair for you to do the work of the duke and have one of my brats steal away with half of Middlesex in the end."

Veronica chuckled. "Isobel is very progressive. It's obvious that she is a businesswoman in her own right. I'm doubtful anything can be done, although I appreciate the gesture. Regardless of what happens 'in the end,' I enjoy being mistress of Syon Hall. The land and foundry, the tenants and property—they are a small but important orbit, *my* orbit, and I'm so very honored to be steward of our place in the larger world."

Jason made a sad whistle. "I feel like the most derelict landowner who ever inherited. You humble me, Ronnie."

"You've served the king and saved countless lives, not the least of all—Reggie's. That said, it was difficult to have you turn up and take it all away. And then you behaved so strangely—lolling about, allowing the work to pile up." They came to the top of the wide, curved stairwell that swept into the grand hall.

"Yes, well, that last bit was partly because of a woman," he said.

Veronica paused on the stairs. "A woman?"

"Indeed. Miss Tinker, in fact. We've been betrothed since Iceland. Didn't I mention it?" He beamed at her.

She made a scoffing noise, hurrying after him down the stairs. "No, you did not mention it. Jason!"

"The whole, sordid business wants only jewelry and a vicar."

"*Jason*," she said again, placing a hand on his sleeve.

He turned to give her a wink. "Could you really not see it?"

"Well," she began, tears forming in her eyes.

"I don't think I betray Isobel by saying that we were . . . rather thrown together on the mission. She preferred to wait until we returned and settled in before we announced it. And then I sort of . . . fell apart, didn't I? And she came for me."

He squinted into the grand hall, searching every head for the familiar yellow bun.

"But she will do beautifully," Veronica said, thinking out loud. "She's clever and confident, and look how smitten you are. Perhaps I *did* see it. I've been so focused on reclaiming my office. Mama said she'd taken you in hand and my only thought was, *Please don't wad up another document and toss it at your hats.*"

"I'm sorry I was torturing you," he said.

"We would have come to terms eventually, you and I." She popped up and kissed him on the cheek. "But no real damage was done in four weeks. And now, a betrothal. This is wonderful news."

They descended two more steps and Veronica paused, catching him by the arm. "Oh no," she said. "You are aware that Susana and Margaret have invited half the debutantes in London tonight, hoping to distract you with a courtship."

Jason shrugged, clipping down the steps. "I'm as good as married, Ronnie." He patted the paperwork in his breast pocket. "Thanks for the warning about the debutantes. Isobel has known enough uncertainty without being thrust in the midst of a bride auction. She should be with the dowager. I'll seek her out."

"Actually, I think 'Bride Auction' was exactly the theme Sue and Meg had in mind . . ." Veronica called, but he was already weaving through the crowd.

THE DUKE'S MOTHER had asked to squire Isobel around the ball as her special guest. Isobel had been hesitant—so much, so soon—but what could she possibly say but, "I would be most honored, Your Grace."

It was true, she *had been* honored. It was one thing to be seen on the arm of the duke, but such open approval from his mother was even more profound. And Lady Northumberland was lovely, a gentle soul who'd been navigating society balls since she was a girl and hosting them for half as long.

She was practical—"Let us stay clear of the torches; I've seen more than one lady catch flame"—and gracious—"Let us greet the dowagers first to make certain they are comfortable." And she introduced Isobel to every guest they passed. Never once did she seem impatient to be rid of Isobel or chagrined that her introductions were so very spare. "And please allow me to introduce you to my friend, Miss Isobel Tinker, our new neighbor in Hammersmith."

What else was there to say? Isobel had no title and no formal connection to the family. "Neighbor" was the truth, as bland as it was, but the dowager said it warmly, as if her favorite niece had moved to town.

Isobel floated beside her, trying to keep track of the names inside her head. The guests smiled politely at her. If their smiles were not wholly genuine, at least they were respectful to the dowager and keenly interested in who Isobel might be. Her seven years of travel service to society families meant that she actually knew some of the guests. They made no mention, but she could see questions on the tips of their tongues: *But are you planning travel for the duchess?* Or worse: *What of the Rome opera tickets we'd hoped for in June?*

No one dared to say more than, "Pleased to meet you, Miss Tinker." "What a beautiful dress, Miss Tinker." "How fortunate you are to enjoy the ball as the guest of the dowager duchess, Miss Tinker."

Isobel smiled and dipped curtsies and returned compliments, and in her head, the same budding thought kept bumping up against the surface of her conscious: *I'm approved.*

This family loves the duke so very much they will validate even me.

"I see you looking for the duke," the duchess whispered, leaning toward Isobel. "He'll be along shortly. Thanks to you, he's actually made some effort toward his comportment and grooming—and just in time. This ball may prove largely unnecessary for its intended purpose, but it never hurts for a man to be seen out in society when the gossips have painted him a lost cause."

Isobel laughed. She was laughing too much; she made a mental note to control the excessive laughing. Without thinking, she asked, "But what was the intended purpose of the ball?"

"Oh, two of my daughters felt a pretty girl from

among London's debutantes might snap Northumberland out of his gloom." She saw a friend across the ballroom and waved.

Isobel nodded, only half-comprehending. She rolled the dowager's words around in her head, unprepared for such honesty.

"Do not fret, my dear," assured the dowager, back in motion, tugging Isobel around hopping dancers. "I couldn't be more delighted in the young woman my son so very clearly wants for his duchess."

"Me?" Isobel heard herself ask.

The dowager chuckled. "Of course you, darling. An adventurer! A true wit! A woman who knows every language—"

"Well, perhaps not every langu—"

"—who saw his suffering and came to him. My daughters are ambitious and will look for any excuse to host a ball, but I told them from the beginning that not just any girl would do. And you're not just any girl, are you?"

"No," said Isobel, the word out before she could think of a more erudite answer.

Tears swam in her eyes and she looked away, blinking. She pressed a green-gloved hand to her throat, hoping her skin was not splotchy.

How had something so difficult become so very easy? Would everything for which she hoped now fall into her lap? Did things like this happen? She floated in a tingly numbness of gratitude and disbelief.

The dowager led them around the dancing to the buffet, waving to friends as she went. A footman passed and the dowager signaled to him, whispering instructions. Isobel bit her lip to keep a wild, beaming grin off her face. She glanced about, taking in the glittering ballroom, illuminated by hundreds of candles and rapidly filling with fancily dressed guests. A page at the doorway announced their names and titles as they arrived. Music soared from a stage at the front. Never in her life had Isobel been to such a beautifully lavish affair, not in her years with the Lost Boys, nor as a part of her aunt and uncle's family. It was like a scene from a fairy tale.

And then she caught sight of the duke, and her heart stopped. He was taller than most guests, his beard gone, his handsome face heart-stopping in the candlelight. He walked beside his sister, Lady Veronica, greeting guests.

Isobel was plunged into a pool of shimmers so deep it stole her breath. Her belly and chest swam in sparkling lights. She loved him so very much. The pretty party trussed up the experience, perhaps, and the lovely family made her hopeful and grateful, but she would have loved him despite all of this—she *had* loved him despite it. And now, it seemed, they would share it. Or at least the bits that suited them.

She was just about to raise her hand to wave to him—a small, elegant, future-duchess arc of her fingers—when the first of two very tenuous events began to unfold.

First: her mother arrived.

Isobel had been waiting for Georgiana when the dowager had taken her under her wing, and that experience had been so overwhelming Isobel had forgotten to watch for Mama.

Now Isobel's eye caught on a flutter of indigo and magenta, far more vibrant than the subtle tones of whispering silk in the ballroom. One glimpse and she knew.

Isobel followed the flutter, her breath held in anticipation and also the smallest measure of wariness, and the colors materialized into the shape and form of renowned actress Georgiana Tinker. Her gown was exponentially fuller and brighter and sprouted more sparkles and clackety, quivery *things* than any other gown in the room. Her blond hair was piled high in the front and hung unfashionably low down her back. Her cheeks had been rouged and her eyes lined with kohl. She was a breathtaking sight in a room that clearly preferred to keep its breath gainfully under control. Heads turned; every eye followed Georgiana as she cut a hurried path across the ballroom.

Isobel had known it would be like this. Her mother relished nothing more than making an entrance, and tonight would be no different. Tonight, in fact, just might be the boldest and most striking entrance she'd ever made.

Isobel glanced to Jason, checking for some reaction. If he'd wanted her to come to him, well—why not arrive with every part of her? Including her radiant actress mother.

But of course this was the bold confidence she'd felt *before* his lovely mother had taken her into her safekeeping and introduced her to all of her friends. It was before the dowager had *approved* her.

And how had Isobel responded? She'd seen Lady Northumberland's approval and raised her by the force of nature that was Georgiana Tinker.

Before Isobel could make some statement that sufficiently prepared the dowager to meet her mother, the second heart-stopping event of the night burst into the room.

"Lady Wendy Bask, daughter to the late Earl of Cranford," announced the page at the doorway to the ballroom. "And the Dowager Countess, Lady Cranford."

Isobel lost all powers of self-possession and spun at the sound of the names.

The sight in the doorway was this: her half sister, Wendy, bustled into the ballroom with her mother, Lady Cranford, the pair of them gazing about with looks of seasoned outdoorsmen on the first day of hunting season.

Chapter Twenty-Eight

The last thing that Isobel saw before her vision blurred was North. The duke. *Jason.*

He'd broken away from his sister and was making his way to her.

She blinked, trying to clear the fuzz. Panic tangled her brain. Likely, her skin had turned one of the many improbable colors of her mother's dress. She was incinerating, burning alive.

She swung her gaze to the dowager. Lady Northumberland was oblivious, lecturing a footman.

She looked again to Lady Wendy. The younger woman was scanning the ballroom and caught sight of North. Making no effort to hide her scrutiny, the girl began sizing him up.

Georgiana had not yet reached Isobel—she was four feet away—but now she stopped, pivoted, and stared openly at Lady Cranford and Lady Wendy.

Isobel's first instinct was simply to run. To dart from the ballroom and leave all the remaining players to do their worst.

Her mother harbored an impulsiveness and an instinct for drama that thrived on large crowds and pageantry. Lady Cranford surely knew of her late husband's "other family" and would be vengefully bitter. Lady Wendy now watched Jason with the calculating purpose of a fox beneath the rabbit hutch.

Isobel's head swam with all the accusations, the *truths* that were about to be revealed.

Isobel Tinker is the illegitimate daughter of an earl.

Georgiana Tinker is an ostentatious actress.

Isobel was raised in Europe and had lovers and lost a baby and now peddles holidays to wealthy girls.

Isobel sailed, unchaperoned, to Iceland in the company of the duke and then traded herself to pirates.

Not all of it would be revealed tonight, Isobel knew. But some of it would be. There was no way around it. The rest would follow.

Insecurity and defeat fell like an avalanche; she couldn't breathe for the weight of it. What had she thought? That she could triumph at the ball of a duke? As his *betrothed*, for God's sake? To earn the approval of the dowager?

Meanwhile the approval of Wendy Bask was guaranteed. The girl needed only sail through the door.

Isobel felt hollow inside, light enough to float away.

This—after the dowager duchess had been so lovely.

After she'd squired Isobel on her arm and introduced her to her guests.

Now, Lady Northumberland and her daughters would be part of the gossip mill for weeks.

Worst of all, Jason would be lost.

She looked back to her mother. Georgiana was staring at Isobel. Her expression showed such deep, painful regret it pierced Isobel's heart. Isobel couldn't remember her mother ever looking so diminished.

Georgiana mouthed the words, *Oh God. I'm so sorry.*

Tears clouded Isobel's eyes. Slowly, she nodded. It occurred to her that Georgiana would *not* mount a confrontation. She was . . . she was . . .

. . . making her way to her.

Across the crowded ballroom, Wendy Bask and Lady Cranford had intercepted the duke. Wendy curtsied before him with the practiced grace of a dancer. Wendy's mother looked on fondly while a uniformed man facilitated an introduction.

Isobel glanced again at Georgiana. Her mother held out a hand, low with open fingers. The gesture was so foreign—almost nothing Georgiana did was low or discreet—Isobel almost didn't understand.

Without thinking, she reached for her mother. She could count on one hand the number of times that Georgiana had been present when she really needed her. But she was here now, and she wasn't causing a scene, and she didn't spoil for a fight. She was simply standing beside her, holding her hand.

Isobel felt a swell of love and gratitude for her mother. She was flushed with it; the hollowness inside began to fill.

"Proud smile," Georgiana whispered in her ear. "Chin high. Tits out. Which one is the duke?"

Isobel looked across the ballroom, and they saw North, yards away, bowing over Wendy's knuckles. The sight banished all thoughts of crying; now she wanted to shout. The outrage in Isobel's head took the form of four words: *He belongs to me.*

She opened her mouth to say it, but then suddenly the dowager duchess returned. Two of Jason's sisters joined her, and the three of them smiled in hopeful curiosity, their eyes darting back and forth between Isobel and Georgiana.

And now Isobel acknowledged that *running* had never been an option. It would only make matters worse and it wasn't her style. She was a realist, not a coward.

She cleared her throat. She sucked in two silent breaths and envisioned each vertebra of her spine fortified with iron.

"Your Grace," she said to the dowager, "I should like to make an introduction."

"Lovely," said the dowager, eyeing Georgiana Tinker's eye-wateringly bright gown, feathered headdress, and beautiful face.

"May I present my mother, Miss Georgiana Tinker."

The dowager blinked once, absorbing Georgiana's vibrancy. When she recovered, her smile was warm. "How do you do, Miss Tinker. I was so pleased you accepted our invitation on such short notice. We are delighted to have you to Syon Hall. Your daughter is a delight. And if I might say so, what a magnificent gown."

"Your Grace," said Georgiana in hushed, respectful tones. One of the things that made Georgiana the consummate professional was her triumph in a supporting role. She sank into a curtsy and clung to Isobel's arm.

After this, conversation dropped away. The moment took on an odd, expectant quality. Isobel and her mother turned in unison to track the movement of the Ladies Cranford.

"But have you seen a friend?" asked the dowager, following their gaze.

"Ah," said Isobel in the same moment that her mother said, "Yes."

Halfway across the room, Lady Cranford turned to stare directly, unerringly, at Georgiana and Isobel. The ice of her glare was like a snowball to the face.

"Oh no," groused the dowager, "is that Lady Cranford?"

Isobel didn't answer; she watched as her father's widow began a slow, determined march in the direction of Georgiana.

My God, Isobel thought in horror, *she's coming directly to us.*

Again Isobel felt the instinct to run. They could excuse themselves and slip away; they could cut their own path through the ballroom, marching to meet Lady Cranford halfway. She could whisper to her mother, *Do your worst, Mama*, and simply step back.

But then she looked at Jason. He was laughing at something his sister said, and looking pleasantly down at Lady Wendy. He appeared neither enchanted nor repelled; he was simply talking. Wendy related some anecdote with rapid movements of her small, gloved hands.

Without warning, he looked up and around, seeking out Isobel. If Lady Cranford's gaze had been ice, his was the sun. He smiled and gave her a wink. Ever so subtly, he affected a slight eye roll and nodded to Lady Wendy's flapping hands.

Isobel smiled, and the shimmers in her belly filled in all remaining hollowness.

She had the sudden thought, *I will try to salvage this.*
He is worth it.
I am worth it.

"Your Grace," Isobel said suddenly, turning to Jason's mother. "Forgive me, but my mother and I have an uncomfortable—dare I say, indelicate—association with the dowager countess currently making her way to us. I assume she is in your acquaintance. Lady Cranford?"

"Oh," sighed Lady Northumberland. "Lady Cranford."

Isobel pressed on. "I beg your pardon for—I . . . I find myself at a loss for what else I might say. I beg your pardon for our history and I beg your pardon for imposing this moment on you. And your daughters. Whatever it may entail."

She turned to Georgiana. "Shall we stay, or shall we go, Mama? I leave it up to you."

"I should go," said Georgiana quietly. "Salvage your future, Bell. I will perish if I ruin this for you."

"My future and our past are linked, and I thank God for it," Isobel replied. "No one will perish. Come what may. But hurry and decide. Stay or go?"

"*Stay*," whispered Georgiana, her voice as soft as a kiss.

Isobel nodded. She squared her shoulders and raised her chin and stared at the rapidly approaching dowager countess.

By the time Lady Cranford reached them, Isobel had schooled her face into aloof serenity. At her side, she gripped her mother's hand as if she meant to snap it off. She held her breath.

The dowager countess was prettier than Isobel had first thought. She was shockingly pale, but her features were delicate and her lashes long. She pinned Georgiana with a furious glare. She had the determined look of someone chopping off the head of a hysterical goose.

"Your Grace," Lady Cranford began, speaking to the dowager duchess in tight, clipped tones. "I must beg a word with you in private. Immediately. The matter is very urgent."

"Hello, Rosemary," drawled Lady Northumberland. "How purposeful you look. Will you not take some champagne? 'Tis a ball; it's meant to be a respite from 'urgent matters.' Surely you don't mean to pull me away from my guests."

"Your guests," ground out Lady Cranford, "are precisely the urgent matter I wish to discuss. There are . . . personalities present of whom you've not been fully apprised. You would not wish *dishonor* to fall upon this ball or this house or your daught—"

"Careful, Rosemary," cut in the dowager duchess, her voice calm but final, "before you invoke the names of my daughters—or any of my guests, for that matter. Not only do I eschew 'urgent matters' at my parties, I also forbid *slander.* I'll not stand for name-calling. Unless someone is brandishing a saber, I've no interest."

"But, Your Grace," said Lady Cranford stonily, her eyes lancing Georgiana with a hateful look. "This wom—"

Before Lady Cranford could finish, the dowager duchess swept a collective arm around Isobel and Georgiana and pivoted, effectively turning her back.

The cut direct.

Isobel had heard of this phenomenon but never witnessed it. Certainly if ever she imagined it happening, she saw herself on the receiving end rather than the beneficiary.

"Ah, Count St. Claire, there you are," called Lady Northumberland to a passing man. "Someone told me you've written a book. What is your passion? The history of . . ."

"The cistern, Your Grace," provided the man, clearly delighted.

"Yes," enthused the dowager. "I am fascinated. Will you tell us more?"

I love this family. It was Isobel's next thought.

I love this family, and I love the duke, and I have as much right to be a part of their lives as anyone else.

I fought pirates, for God's sake.
I speak seven languages.
I've traveled the world.
They see me.
I deserve to be seen and they see me.

Chapter Twenty-Nine

*W*ithin moments of the stupefying description of the cistern book, Jason appeared at Isobel's side. Isobel, still shaky and breathless from the near miss with Lady Cranford, had the extreme pleasure of introducing the Duke of Northumberland to her mother.

Jason said all the correct things, praising Georgiana's work as an actress and Isobel's skill as a cultural attaché. If he made no mention of their relationship, the possessive hand he settled on her lower back said more than words. And not simply to Georgiana. Bystanders craned to examine the duke's proximity to Isobel, his attention to her every comment, his possessive touch.

To her credit, Georgiana was careful not to upstage Isobel or flirt. Her radiant face was awash with love, and also with hopefulness. She was rapt, an audience member for once, desperate to see what delightful thing would happen next.

Ultimately, that thing was Jason pulling Isobel away.

"We've things of dire importance to discuss," he told their mothers and his sisters. "If you'll excuse us."

"Such an epidemic of dire discussions and urgent conversations at this ball," observed the dowager duchess. But she was already turning away, taking Georgiana by the arm to introduce her to a passing group.

Jason looped Isobel's arm beneath his and led her from the ballroom. The closer they got to the doors, the faster he walked. They were nearly running by the time he pulled her into a wide, shadowy corridor, vacant except for some distant guests.

Isobel laughed at his haste, looking behind her to see if the crowd had noticed their flight. When she looked back, Jason was reaching for her. Without breaking stride, he picked her up and whirled her into an embrace, burying his face in her neck.

"Is the ball over?" he breathed.

"Yes," she teased, "it is over and the house is deserted and now you and I and your sister may resume our work in your library."

"On second thought, it cannot end." He gave her a smacking kiss and set her down, recovering her arm. "Not yet. Not until I've made the announcement." He resumed their march down the corridor.

"What announcement?"

"Our betrothal. What else?"

Isobel missed a step. "Our—"

"Do not test me on this, Isobel. I've waited bloody long enough. I've a special license in my pocket. Calling on the archbishop was one of the few things I actually achieved in these last many weeks. If the vicar is still in attendance, we'll do the thing tonight."

"Do what 'thing'?" Isobel rasped, stopping in the middle of the hall.

Jason kept walking. "Prepare yourself, S'bell. My patience has run its course."

He turned to walk backward, facing her. From inside his coat, he pulled a tiny box. He flipped it in the air like one of his coins. Then he pitched it to her. Isobel was unprepared but caught it on reflex.

"But what is—?" She stared at the box in her hands.

"Jason?!" A head popped through a ballroom door. His sister Susana, her voice winded, like someone was chasing her.

"Not now, Sue," he ground out, not looking at her.

"It cannot wait," said his sister. "It's Reggie. He's delved into a political debate and offended someone's French relation. The man is threatening to call Reggie out. He's thrown his drink in Reggie's face. Mama is furious. She'll not have dueling at Syon Hall."

Jason closed his eyes and swore under his breath. He stared at the ceiling. "I swear, Reginald Pelham," he vowed, "for once could you imperil yourself without inconveniencing so many other people? Most of all, me?"

He pointed to Isobel. "Stay right here. Do not move. This will take ten minutes, no more." He strode in the direction of his sister.

"Are you certain I shouldn't come?" Isobel asked after him.

He was shaking his head. "Reggie's debt to you already extends two lifetimes."

Isobel watched Jason and his sister disappear into the ballroom.

She looked down at the small, leather box in her hands.

With trembling fingers, she slid the ebony latch and popped the lid. Nestled inside a froth of ivory velvet was a ring. The simple gold band was set with a swirl of stones in three shades of green—emeralds, peridots, and jade—interspersed with fiery white diamonds.

She looked up, staring through tears at the empty doorway. Her body pulsed from the inside with shimmering light. She sucked in a tearful breath.

"What a pretty ring," said a voice behind her.

Isobel turned.

Lady Wendy Bask trailed in from the ballroom, shoulders slumped, silk wrap sagging halfway down her back.

Isobel snapped the box shut.

"Oh," said Lady Wendy, "you're crying too. Excellent." A dramatic sniff. "I've reached the designated spot for weeping."

When the younger woman moved closer, Isobel could see splotchy cheeks and spiky lashes. Her eyes were red. But why would Lady Wendy Bask be crying? Had her mother harangued her and demanded they leave? Lady Cranford had vanished from the ballroom after she'd been cut by the dowager duchess. Or perhaps Wendy was upset because she'd seen Isobel disappear with the duke. Did the girl feel proprietary after only an introduction?

Even as Isobel tried to guess the source of the girl's tears, she found herself increasingly distracted by the close-up vision of her half sister. Here. Before her.

She had a small nose and bow lips that looked so very much like Isobel's. The resemblance was undeniable. Her hair was blond, darker than Isobel's by a shade. She was taller than Isobel (everyone was taller than Isobel), but something about the way she held herself was very familiar. Far too much about Wendy Bask felt eerily familiar.

Now the younger woman flapped a kerchief and blew her nose, watching Isobel over the top of the linen.

"I beg your pardon, my lady," Isobel began, dropping the ring box into her pocket. "I was waiting for—" She wasn't certain how to finish.

What honesty or civility did she owe this girl?

Could Wendy Bask truly have no idea who Isobel was? She appeared clueless. Young and distressed and a little bit self-involved. But clueless.

Isobel thought of that terrible day in the café, their only previous encounter. She had the vague memory of a sour child who'd stolen her father. In other words, her sworn enemy.

Isobel glanced at her again. The younger woman stared back with red eyes and an open, curious expression.

Isobel sighed and opened her mouth, trying to whip up that old resentment and envy. Instead, she felt . . . nothing.

Isobel was so very weary of being jealous and resentful, and Wendy Bask was innocent of their father's crimes. Honestly, she looked like any number of Isobel's fresh-faced clients—girls Isobel adored, girls for whom Isobel loved planning the holidays that would delight and enrich them.

"Was I weeping?" Isobel heard herself ask. "Forgive me. They were not unhappy tears. I'm . . . I'm waiting to be introduced to the duke's family and the guests . . . as . . . as the future duchess."

Resentful or not, Isobel wanted to make her attachment to the duke perfectly clear.

And it couldn't hurt to practice saying these words.

"Are you?" gasped Wendy, stepping closer. "But this is wonderful news."

It is? thought Isobel.

"Actually?" added Wendy. "I'll say it: *thank God!*" She clenched her fists before her like a boxer and then jumped up and down.

Isobel watched this, totally disarmed. With every

hop, the skirt on Lady Wendy's dress filled with air and expanded like an onion.

"Now perhaps my mother," sang Wendy, "can stop hounding me about the duke. And I can stop all the preening and pawing like a mare." She made a rather unladylike gagging noise and grabbed her own throat. "He's *so old*—"

Now the girl gasped, slapping a hand over her mouth. "Oh, do forgive me. I'm certain he is the perfect age for . . . you."

"Quite," managed Isobel.

"I am Lady Wendy Bask, by the way, and one thing you should know—"

"How do you do," said Isobel, her voice a little breathless.

"Oh yes, how do you do." Wendy bobbed a curtsy. "One thing you should know about me is that I have no desire to be married—not to anyone. But especially not to an aging duke who lives with his mother and fifty sisters."

And now Isobel was given no choice but to feel affection for the girl. The universe would allow nothing else.

"Have you," Isobel ventured, "another gentleman in mind, perhaps?"

Lady Wendy shook her head. "Not a man, a *vocation*." She lifted her hands like an archbishop on Easter. "*The stage*. I'm destined to be an actress. It is my only dream, and I intend to realize it. I don't care what my mother thinks."

Isobel blinked at her, trying to swallow the irony of this revelation. Lady Wendy began to smooth the lines of her dress.

"The great unfairness is that my late father would

have allowed it," Wendy declared, speaking to her skirt. "I am certain of this. But we lost him to a weak heart—may God rest his soul—and my brother is now earl, and my mother is a *tyrant*, and neither can be made to see how very essential this is to me.

"It doesn't matter," she finished, tightening her gloves. "I'll run away if I must. I need formal training despite being quite accomplished, even now. I'll perish if I cannot perform."

It was a mouthful of an admission, even without referencing their father.

Isobel thought she should feel something dark and spiteful, but she found only sympathy. Also, affection. Lady Wendy was too earnest and honest and impetuous not to like. And Isobel's fondness for actors was far more deeply ingrained than her distrust of half sisters.

"Enjoyed various theatrical productions, have you?" Isobel asked.

"Oh loads," assured Lady Wendy. "Whenever we are in Town. My brother ferries me to Drury Lane. We'll see whatever's on. Before that, my father and I were constant patrons."

And now Isobel did feel a pulse of something heavy and uncomfortable in the area of her heart. Their father had delighted in the theater; it was how he and Georgiana met. The connections felt too tight to be comfortable.

Even so, Isobel could not help but ask, "By any chance have you had the opportunity to travel, Lady Wendy? To see theatrical performances in Paris or Vienna or St. Petersburg?"

"No," breathed Wendy, "but I aspire to. I promised my mother I would participate in one London Season *if* she would accompany me to the great opera houses of Europe. She agreed, and I slogged through that terrible Season, only to have her retract the offer when it was all said and done. She thought I would enter into a courtship and forget about Europe. But I have an excellent memory. And *no intention* of being courted by anyone."

"Indeed," said Isobel, impressed. This was no trifling vow for a debutante.

"And *that* is why I intend to run away," Wendy continued. "And *that* is why I thank you. It'll be far easier now that I don't have to *pretend* to care about the Duke of Northumberland for a week, or a fortnight, or even a night. Now I can move forward with my—Oh!"

She slapped a hand over her mouth. "Why am I telling you this?"

"Your intentions are safe with me, my lady," said Isobel.

"Well, you have a kind face," Wendy theorized. "And you remind me of someone. I have a very bad habit of saying *too* much . . . to *familiar* people . . . with *kind* faces. Please, I beg you, tell no one? About my plans?"

"Never you fear," said Isobel. "The duke should be along any moment. However . . . I'd like to invite you to call to my travel agency in Hammersmith. Perhaps you've heard of it? Tinker's Travel?"

The girl shook her head, blond curls bouncing.

"Right. Well, if you convince your mother that she does, indeed, owe you a holiday, my shop can assist with all the arrangements. I've secured front-row seats at the finest theaters in Europe for other girls. I can even get you backstage to meet the players."

And now Lady Wendy was hopping up and down again.

"Consider it, perhaps, before you embark on any plan to run away."

Isobel was just reciting the shop name and direction when Jason strode into the corridor.

"Go," whispered Lady Wendy, frowning as she watched him approach. "Do us both this favor."

The girl was already backing away. "I will call on you in Hammersmith. Thank you, Miss Tinker!"

Isobel may have said, *Thank you*, or *Please do*, or she may have said nothing at all. Her eyes were fixed on the approaching duke, her insides filled with light.

"Where's the box?" he asked, coming upon her.

"Oh," said Isobel, fumbling in her pocket. "But what of your cousin?"

"Packed away in a carriage with his parents," he said, snatching the box from her hands. "The Frenchman mollified—if you can imagine—by your mother."

Isobel let out a laugh. "I can imagine. She is useful in mollifying Frenchmen."

He snapped open the box, plucked out the jewelry, and pitched the empty box into a plant.

"Take off your glove," he ordered.

Isobel peeled off the moss-green leather.

"Should we do this properly?" he asked, dropping to one knee. Isobel laughed. They were nearly alone in the hall. Only the occasional servant, distracted with the duties of the ball, hurried along the wall.

"You've been a stickler for propriety from the beginning," he said, looking up, reaching for her hand.

A second too late, he swiped his hat from his head and placed it over his heart. His hair was deliciously rumpled and she reached out to smooth it.

"Oh yes," she said. "A paragon, that's me."

"Isobel Tinker," he continued, "will you make my life

complete—after much, *much* excruciating delay—by becoming my duchess?" He slid the beautiful, glittering ring on her finger.

Isobel nodded, her voice too choked to speak.

"Brilliant," said Jason, vaulting up. "Let us hope the priest is still available."

Chapter Thirty

*P*ercival Toombs had been the parish priest of the Syon Hall vicarage for as long as Jason could remember. A kindly old man, considered a member of the family by his mother, Toombs was delighted at the prospect of marrying a Northumberland duke, rather than burying one. Jason had called on him earlier in the day to make the special request.

Toombs had shown less delight in the *timing* of the proposed matrimony, which Jason wanted to commence that very night. During the ball. Down the corridor from the dancing. Not only was this irregular, the vicar suggested that the duke's urgency might come off as a little . . . irreverent. And indecorous.

Jason did not care. He felt as if a blade had been yanked from his ribs. The pain was gone and he could look to the future with anticipation and not dread.

He would not be saddled with managing the dukedom alone.

His sister seemed truly relieved and happy.

Best of all, Isobel had come to him. And now that she was here, he would not let her go.

He told the priest the wedding time would be "cannot say for sure," and named the location as "I'll find you." The lack of a plan so distressed the priest that Jason promised *another* ball in the near future to properly celebrate the nuptials. Eventually Toombs relented, reviewing the special license and agreeing to make himself available. He clearly doubted the probability of an extemporaneous wedding but the old man never missed a party at Syon Hall and promised to bring his prayer book, just in case.

Now Jason stalked the ballroom, Isobel on his arm, searching for Reverend Toombs.

"But will you silence the orchestra," ventured Isobel, "to announce the betrothal? Or may we simply gather a small circle of family?"

"I'm less concerned about the announcement," Jason clipped, "and more about the *deed*."

Where was Percival Toombs? Jason began a wide circuit of the drinks carts.

"Deed?" she asked.

"The ceremony," he said, dodging a trio of giggling debutantes.

"Jason, I don't understand?"

"The wedding," he sighed. He spotted Percival's bald head bent over a tray of prawns. *Finally. Thank God.*

Isobel stopped walking, and he was yanked back. *Damn! So close.*

"Jason," Isobel whispered. "You cannot mean to conduct a wedding tonight. Here? In the middle of your sisters' ball?"

"That is precisely what I intend," he said. "Why not?"

They stood in the middle of the crowded ballroom. Revelers passed on all sides; servants offered libations. A footman passed with drinks on a tray and Jason snatched two of them.

"Well, because it's . . . it's not done," she explained weakly, taking a glass. "What of the legalities and the customs—what of a church?"

"We can be married here just as well as in the chapel. I've seen weddings happen on the field of battle and in a prison. Surely the Syon Hall conservatory will be a step up from these. And I assure you it will be perfectly binding and legal." He slid a packet of papers from his coat and unfurled them, showing her the special license he'd obtained from the archbishop.

"But when did you—?" she asked, blinking down at the paperwork.

"In London," he said. "After we made landfall. You'd sprinted away but I made this my first order of business. It was settled before I left London for Middlesex."

"You've had this for weeks?" she marveled. She put down her champagne to study the paperwork.

"Of course, Isobel. *I've been waiting for you.* The rest of my life has your name scrawled all over it. I want my name on yours. Look at us." He downed his drink and placed his glass beside hers. He took both of her hands in his own. "I've been privy to complicated marital relationships all around the world. I've seen everything from strong bonds like that of my parents', to 'understandings' that allow dalliances, to forced misery and everything in between. Only very rarely have I seen two people more perfectly suited than the two of us. Your strengths align with my frailties; your weak spots match up to my . . . my . . . charm and good looks."

She sputtered a laugh, her eyes swimming in tears.

"Please. Let me make you my wife. Without further delay. In other words . . ." he affected a pensive, faraway look, ". . . how can I say this?

"*Now,*" he finished, walking again, pulling her along.

"But—why?"

"Why do I want to marry you?" Jason sighed. "Or why do I want to do it as soon as possible?"

"Why . . . *tonight*?"

Jason stopped walking and turned to her. He leaned down to her ear. "Do you recall the state in which you left me at the thermal pool in Iceland?" he whispered. "On the last night? Have you not thought back, Isobel? Because it is *all I bloody think about.*"

She sucked in a little breath and nodded slowly.

"I have endured some measure of *that state* for nearly two months. Why now, you ask? *Now* we can finish what we started."

He raised up to give her a quick, hard kiss.

She stared up at him, her blue eyes wide, her creamy cheeks tinged raspberry pink.

He turned and pulled her along. "The priest agreed to marry us whenever the moment presented itself. I wanted you to have the ring obviously. I'd not planned for my mother to squire you around the room like a long-lost relation, but I'm happy the two of you get on."

Jason caught sight of Reverend Toombs again, now raising a toast to a neighbor and his wife. "*Caught,*" Jason mumbled, scooping Isobel in the man's direction.

They were so close—a line of dancers away—when Isobel dug in her heels and stopped walking.

Affecting a half pivot, she spun and freed herself, stepping to a shadowy alcove.

Jason swore in his head, watching her. "Let me guess. You have some romantic notion about a lavish wedding. Copious flowers and musicians and breakfast guests? Am I being a cad to keep these from you?"

She blinked twice, considering this, and shook her head.

"Because I *would* postpone my, er, enthusiasm if this is what you wanted," he said. "Please be certain—is that the wedding you want?"

"No," she rasped, "I don't suppose it is. I want only you."

"Excellent, we are in total accord."

She paced twice, back and forth, wiggling her fingers at her sides. "Stop."

"Stop asking you what you want or stop the wedding?"

"There is no *wedding*, Jason—who gets married in the midst of a ball?"

"*I* do. *You* do. Who pretends to *trade* the love of their life to pirates, her hands bound in ropes? Who abandons her with said pirates so she can fight her way free? *We do.* Please, for the love of God, let us finish this."

She made a sound of half laugh, half sob. "Yes," she said, "alright, let us finish it. But what is the need to sprint through it, Jason? It's not your nature. After all your talk of ambling about, learning the terrain, observing, not locking yourself in?"

"Bollocks to that; it doesn't apply. When I know what I want, I do not *amble*."

"Well, there is ambling and then there is some moderate pace, with a week to catch our breath. I understand that you are . . . that we are . . . desirous but—"

He let out a bark of a laugh. *Understatement, thy name is "desirous."*

"—but we are not children." She smiled a little, wiping her eyes. "We *can wait* until a proper wedding.

"Or," she challenged, "you could take me upstairs. Have your way with me. You've made your intentions clear. We needn't entertain pretense about the purity of anyone in this union. I am nearly thirty years of age. I've been around the world in every sense. I love you. You love me . . ."

She gazed down at the ring on her finger. She looked up and cocked an eyebrow. "We needn't be disrespectful to your mother, but surely there is someplace in this sprawling house we could slip away . . ."

Jason's body surged at the provocative look, but he forced out the word, "*No.*" He shook his head.

"You may stop trying to protect me," she said, laughing a little now. "It's sweet, and I'll cherish it all of my life. But I feel fully 'approved.' I feel 'accepted.' Truly. There's no need to—"

"My aim was never to have you know 'approval,' Isobel. I couldn't care less about that. What I want is for you to feel '*chosen*.' To *be* chosen. I choose you, love. And I pray God you will choose me."

"Yes. Alright." She sucked in a breath, the tears back in her voice. "You have burned me to the ground. In the very best, most necessary way. I am in ashes."

He leaned down to kiss her. "It was meant to be a dashing, romantic sort of gesture. Memorable and fun. But if you must view yourself in ashes, so be it."

She laughed and wiped her eyes again. "Now?" she asked.

"Right bloody now," he said. "I'll not risk losing you again, S'bell. I'm determined. Before you construct some other evasion."

"No evasion," she said, shaking her head. "I'm . . . I'm here. I came."

A tear slipped down her cheek. Jason kissed her again, sweeping her into his arms in the dim alcove. He breathed in the smell of her, kissed her neck, and looked out at the milling party guests and hustling staff and—

Reverend Toombs.

"There he is," Jason said, and they were off again, hand in hand, winding through the crowd. "It's on."

Chapter Thirty-One

 hey were married half an hour later in the candlelit conservatory of Syon Hall's east wing. The room was cold, the fires having been lit only ten minutes before. The floor-to-ceiling windows provided a moonlit view of the pond and pleasure garden but did little to forestall the October chill.

Jason felt no discomfort. Jason felt only relief and elation and anticipation. Underlying all of that, he felt blissful calm. No longer did he dread the future. He was free of guilt over his lapsed responsibilities as duke. He was so very grateful to his sister and to whatever convergence of luck, and the divine, and (remarkably) his cousin Reggie, that brought Isobel to him.

The service was brief. His mother was impatient to return to her guests and the Very Reverend Toombs had grown drowsy after too many glasses of wine. Isobel's mother, Georgiana Tinker, was also in attendance, as well as her clerk, Samantha, and all of Jason's sisters. There was no shortage of witnesses; so many, in fact, Jason thought perhaps they might forgo any future celebration that promised more guests and flowers and wedding finery. His mother disabused him of that idea in no uncertain terms, insisting that she would host a proper celebratory breakfast as soon as the arrangements could be made. Jason was to mention the party when he introduced the new Lady Northumberland to the ballroom.

He would have just as soon skipped this step—he was prepared to skip all steps that did not lead to a bed—but he knew he had a better chance of controlling the gossip surrounding a secret wedding if he and his family took ownership of the narrative.

"May I have your attention, please," Jason called out to the ballroom after the ceremony. He held a crystal goblet aloft and clanged it with a knife. The orchestra sat drowsily behind him, silent at last, and dancers began to drift toward the bandstand.

"The dowager duchess, my sisters, and I wish to take this moment to thank all of you for joining us at Syon Hall. As you know, the title of duke has fallen to me under tragic circumstances. May God rest the beloved men who came before me." He paused, unexpectedly choked up.

"In many ways," he went on, "I am still growing accustomed to the title." Another pause.

Behind him, Isobel placed a firm hand on his shoulder. He looked to her, took a deep breath, and raised his glass.

"However," he went on, clearing his throat, "when it comes to the role of *party guest*, I am as veteran as any of you—and my experienced eye informs me that everyone is having a jolly good time. Brilliant, and how very welcomed you are. Not to outdo any man here, but I should now like to lay claim to the very best time of all. But let me not get ahead of myself."

He cleared his throat. He smiled because most things went down more easily with a smile.

He paused again—why not build suspense?—and turned to beckon Isobel to step beside him.

She'd been smiling up at him, uncertain of what he would say, and now she blinked twice, looked to her mother, and then stepped forward. He clamped a hand around her waist.

"You lot," he said, pointing to the crowd, "are the very first to be introduced to my new wife, Lady Isobel Beckett, the Duchess of Northumberland. We married recently in a private family ceremony, and it gives me great pleasure to announce our nuptials publicly tonight."

His mother cleared her throat and whispered behind him.

"Oh yes," he continued. "And we invite all of you . . . and ten of your closest friends . . . to a more formal celebration of this happy news in coming weeks. Watch the post or for private messengers or homing pigeon or however it's done for an invitation."

And then, as a hundred stunned faces stared up at him, their eyes wide in unblinking shock, he raised a glass.

In the rear of the ballroom, someone started a rousing yell of, "Hip, hip, hooray! Hip, hip, hooray!"

It took two rounds before the crowd joined in, but then footmen descended with bubbling champagne flutes and the toast gained more momentum.

Jason couldn't have cared less. He signaled the conductor to resume the music; he shot the drink in his own glass, swallowing it in one gulp.

He turned to Isobel. "Your Grace," he said.

She fell into his arms, reaching up to grab him around his neck. Speaking softly against his skin, she repeated his own words from the heated pool the night of their betrothal.

"How do you want it?"

Jason made a growling noise and kissed her. He picked her up and whirled her around as a swarm of curious-eyed guests began queuing up to congratulate the happy couple.

She glanced at Jason, but he was already shaking his head: *Absolutely not.* He backed away, tucking her in front of him like a shield. His plan, it appeared, was to wind the two of them through the tightly packed orchestra to escape the crowd.

"Mama?" Isobel called, signaling her mother. Georgiana saw the problem immediately and stepped up, obscuring Jason and Isobel and asking the dowager to introduce her to "more of her lovely friends."

Georgiana's bright dress and brighter smile were an ideal interference, and Isobel pulled Jason from the bandstand. Moving quickly, eyes averted, *laughing*, they skirted the crowd, rounded the dance floor, and fled through the ballroom doors.

They didn't stop until they reached the giant, curved staircase. Breathing hard, they mounted the stairs hand in hand and hit the landing at a run. Isobel's hair broke loose and fell down her back. She kicked off first one shoe, and then the next.

When they reached the column that obscured the ground floor, Jason fell against it. Isobel continued on, but he gave her a yank, and she turned back. She was on his mouth in an instant, laughing as she kissed him.

He flattened himself against the marble, arms thrown back, allowing her to attack him. She came on like a swarm, grasping hands and swinging hair, stockinged feet climbing his body.

ISOBEL WANTED HIS evening coat *off*. She peeled her gloves and dug her fingers beneath the collar to roll away the heavy garment. He shoved up to allow it to fall to the floor. Without breaking the kiss, she attacked the buttons on his waistcoat, fingers working feverishly; it was the next piece to go.

He swore on a delighted hiss. "Damn, Isobel, I cannot keep pace." He reached for the buttons that marched up the back of her gown.

She didn't answer; her laughter faded away. She'd become so very focused. The culmination of weeks of wanting him suddenly felt near to bursting inside her. She slid his shirt from his trousers.

Jason groaned and picked her up by the bottom. She leapt up, straddling him, wrapping her legs around his waist. He shoved off the column and staggered on, not breaking the kiss.

"Where?" he gasped.

"Don't care," she panted, and it was true. He could take her to the laundry or the pantry or the potting shed. He could drop them to the rug and she wouldn't have cared.

His insistence on the wedding, here, now—*for her*, not for esteem or pomp or customs—had ignited something elemental inside her. She was overwhelmed with love, swamped by it. She was swimming in her love for him. And she'd never been more urgently aroused in her life.

"Bedchamber," he growled against her throat, staggering five more steps to fall against a thick oak door.

"Good—yes," she panted. In the back of her mind, it occurred to her that she'd never made love in a proper bedchamber before. Another new thing. Everything about loving him felt so very new. Stronger passion, deeper love, greater trust—*by far* the best technique.

And now a proper bedroom, with a proper marital bed. *Another new thing.* Her past experiences had been stolen or secret, on the fly, on the sly. Had she ever made love with the benefit of something as secure as a locked door? She couldn't remember. She didn't want to remember. She wanted only this.

Jason released her long enough to turn the knob. The door swung and they fell into the room. He kicked the door closed with his boot, and the strains of music and laughter were locked outside. The room was hushed except for their breathing.

Isobel opened her eyes, looking over his shoulder as they settled into a less frantic, deeper kiss. The chamber was cavernous. There were towering windows, steepled at the top with gothic arches. Moonlight spilled bright spears of silver across the stone floor. The only other light was a jumping fire in a massive hearth. Against the longest wall, between the windows was—

She blinked, squinting now.

A cot?

Yes, it was a cot. A rumpled, dingy cot, as flat and hard as a workbench.

Isobel broke off the kiss and leaned around him for a better look.

It was one of three forlorn pieces of furniture in the palatial bedchamber.

"What's the matter?" he asked, dropping kisses along her neck. His fingers found the buttons on the back of her dress and worked through them, flicking each one free with effortless proficiency.

"Well," she mumbled, scanning the room again. There were no linens, no tapestries, no rugs.

"Why is this room so . . . empty?" she asked.

Jason paused in the act of pushing her gown from her shoulders and looked around.

"*Bollocks*," he swore. He began to reverse the direction of her gown, pulling it back up.

"No. No. No. *No*," she chuckled, sliding it down. "It's not as bad as all that. I'm simply—It is not what I expected."

"This is the ducal bedchamber," Jason explained, kissing her between each sentence. "But I had the furniture of the previous dukes hauled away and bade the servants bring in whatever could be found in the attic." He left her mouth and attacked her neck with kisses. "Only until you arrived. I couldn't bear the other and I expected you'd have your own preference for the room."

He pulled away and frowned at the cot. "Poor planning," he said, turning back to stare at her mouth. "Extremely poor planning."

She laughed again. He cared, she could tell, although not so very much. He was not a man who stood on ceremony—and thank God.

And if it meant she could decorate the room however she liked . . .

Furthermore, if it meant she would share this room with him every single night?

She did not care. Not even about the cot.

She assured him with a deep kiss, and he answered her with a knee-weakening moan. Oh, how she loved the noises he made when she kissed him; he gave off a sort of animal enthusiasm, a relish.

His enthusiasm for her had never been in doubt—well, except perhaps for the four terrible weeks he had not come for her—beyond that, *when they were together*, he had never made her doubt.

How Isobel had longed to be free from doubt, to feel looked after, to look after someone in return, someone worthy of the effort.

She fingered the ring on her hand, relishing the cold pricks of each cut stone. It was so lovely to be *chosen*, just as he had said.

He gathered her around the waist and pressed her to him. She felt his arousal through the layers of skirt and shimmied *just so*, ramping up the exquisite pressure. He moaned again, kissing her.

"I've a bedroom down the hall," he said. "It's been mine since I was a boy. I meant to take you there, and then I . . ." he kissed her, ". . . forgot. There's still time."

Isobel shook her head, bussing him with a kiss and a lick with each pass. He allowed it until the third pass and then captured her mouth.

While he kissed her, she worked the gown from her arms and pushed it over her hips. It fell into a poof at her feet. She released his neck and worked her petticoats free, allowing them to fall the way of the dress. She broke the kiss and stepped from the circle of silks, standing before him in her corset and shift.

"No boyhood bedrooms," she whispered. "We're all grown now."

"Yes," he said, his voice choking a little. "So very grown."

He stripped from his shirt and tossed it. She blinked twice, very slowly, allowing herself to enjoy the sight of his broad chest, slim waist, and so many cleverly ridged muscles.

He put his hands on his hips and looked around. "Where shall we——?"

He made a raspy sound, half cough, half laugh. "I'm making a muck of this," he declared. He stooped to pull off his boots and stockings, flinging them over his shoulder.

"I'm not a virgin, I assure you," he went on. "I had every intention of seducing you properly but—"

"Oh, I'm seduced," she told him. "Just by the sight of you." She began a slow circle around him, looking her fill. "I've wanted you since the moment I saw you in my alley. I wanted you when you appeared in the tearoom with your aunt. I wanted you when I was ill on the brig, and every night in between. Just look at you."

Jason looked down at his body like a man searching for his lost spectacles, although . . . he knew. It was part of his charm. He knew he was tall and broad and handsome; he knew he was clever and in command.

And now all of that, she thought, *is mine.*

She walked to him, turning her back to offer him her corset strings. Jason, God love him, did not hesitate. The bindings flew, beginning at the top, and she felt immediate, tingling relief. The confining garment loosened, and Isobel tipped forward, pressing her bottom into his erection, allowing her breasts to spill free.

The position seemed innocent at first, accidental, like she was giving him more room, but the looser the ribbons became, the farther she tipped, eventually bent nearly in half, her bottom pressed against him.

Jason let out a wicked laugh and caught her around the waist, grinding into her. He flung the corset and leaned over her back, burying his face against her neck.

"There is so much I would do to you," he said, spanning his hands up her rib cage and cupping her breasts.

"We have all night," she whispered, breathing hard. "We have a lifetime. Thank God, we have a lifetime."

"*Now*," he countered, his voice a growl. He made a

thrusting motion, kissed her ear, and then fleeced her from her shift in one, swift movement.

Isobel closed her eyes and let out a little gasp. When she opened her eyes, he stood before her, his trousers and drawers gone.

"You're so beautiful," he whispered, kissing her. "You seemed too bright and beautiful ever to be contained by me or any man. But I wanted you; I wanted you any way that you would have me."

"Take me," she whispered, looking up at him. "Please."

He swept a hand beneath her knees and lifted her, carrying her in a naked bundle in his arms. He strode to the cot and she thought, *Alright, this really will happen on a—*

But he lingered only long enough to swipe a silky coverlet and then carried her to a deep window seat. The seat was cushioned with purple velvet, and he settled her in the center, tucking the coverlet between her and the cold glass of the window.

He fussed over her comfort, his face serious in the moonlight, while his magnificent body, hard and ready, strained against her.

She reached for him, stopping his ministrations, re-clining on the cushions, and pulling him down. They fell into a kiss; her legs rose on either side of him, her hands roved his back. All the parts she touched melded into a long, glorious, muscled exploration—hot and him. *Hers.*

His own hands found her center, felt her readiness, and he moaned.

"I cannot wait," he whispered, panting into her ear. "I'm sorry."

"Do it," she whispered back. "You promised."

He growled, rose up, and grabbed her by the ankles,

scooting her to the edge of the window seat. Isobel thrust up, raising her hips, seeking him.

His eyes flared when he saw her eagerness; he swore, and then he sank into her in a long, slow, deep thrust.

They both gave a shout, an exhalation of the long-awaited sensation of joining. They relieved sensual pressure at the same time they pitched it ever higher; it was everything at once, everything, everything . . .

Isobel almost forgot what came next, but Jason was seized by instinct. He began to move, driving into her with a force she should have expected but she did not, a force that thrilled her, that caused her to cry out in ever-escalating sounds of delight.

He kissed her, but it was too much; she needed to suck in breath, to shout. She turned her head to the side, and he dropped his mouth on her exposed ear and whispered, *"Yes, yes, yes, S'bell, yes . . ."*

She heard his words; she wanted to answer, but she was rising, rising, rising—

And then they launched.

His wrist was beside her lips and she whispered, "I love you," into his pulse point. Consciousness left her, flying out the window into the sky.

Above her, Jason thrust twice more and then spilled inside her with a guttural cry. She held to his shoulders, fingers digging into muscle, clinging for dear life.

Her eyes shot open at the sheer, concentrated force of the sensation, pleasure and sweetness, and love and heat. Her gaze fixed on the night sky, but her vision swam, and she saw flashes of the aurora borealis and the churning North Sea and the swiftly moving clouds of Middlesex. She saw her future, which looked oh-so-bright indeed.

Eventually, she saw Jason's hair, which flopped over her face in short, sweaty locks.

She heard his labored breath. She became aware of her own breathing. She heard a log in the fire disintegrate with a hiss and drop into the ashes.

"Have we survived?" she asked softly.

He didn't answer.

His arms tightened around her; he squeezed her until it was almost uncomfortable.

"Never leave me again," he said against her neck. "Never make me deny you to my family again."

She shook her head. "No. I promise. Never again."

He squeezed her once more, even tighter, and she let out a little squeak. He rolled from her, and she scooted against the window, making room. He gathered her into his arms and pulled the coverlet over the slick, naked tangle of their bodies.

"I love you, Isobel Beckett, Duchess of Northumberland," he said, kissing the top of her head.

For a time, they drowsed, sated and replete, and reveling in their love. A loud swell of music from downstairs roused Isobel, and she lay in Jason's arms, gazing at his sleeping face in the moonlight. With a gentle hand, she smoothed a tousled lock of hair from his brow.

He made a growling noise and nuzzled her hand.

"I cannot believe I came here to rescue you from your own . . . emotional drowning," she whispered, "and I became a duchess instead."

"Make no mistake, you did rescue me. Although my sister Ronnie claims it was only a matter of time before she took me in hand. But you rescued me in other ways."

"What will you do now?" she asked. "Now that Lady Veronica will manage the estate?"

"The notion is so new to me I hadn't thought," he said.

"I'll need to be present, I suppose, to be available and useful to Ronnie. My father sat in the Lords, as I've said. My brothers did not. If any part of the dukedom appeals to me, it would be government. I have something to offer, given my experience. What do you think?"

"I think it is an idea worth pursuing."

"What of your work?" he asked. " 'Tinker's Travel,' my spies tell me it's called. You'll carry on, I hope, despite being duchess. I cannot imagine my mother is entirely ready to give up running this house, unless you . . ."

He allowed the sentence to trail off. He was so very generous about her preferences and desires.

"I do wish to carry on working," she said. "I'll hire more help. I'll train Samantha to take on more responsibility. She has been asking, and she is ready. I want to be prepared if—"

And now she stopped. Without warning, her throat grew thick and painful with impending tears. Her eyes stung.

"If what?" he asked, listening carefully. He found her hand and interlaced their fingers.

"If we're blessed with a child," she finished on a rush, the tears impossible to hide.

"You would like to be a mother," he observed lightly, giving her time.

She nodded, tucking her face into his chest.

Against his skin, she whispered, "If I can carry a baby who will—"

She couldn't finish.

"We will try and try and try, Isobel," he assured her. "We will try in every room of this house, including on the rickety cot, and a million times in the bed that replaces it. You are young and I am virile."

She laughed. Only he would claim this.

"And perhaps you will be a mother. That is what I predict. And if not . . . it won't be for lack of trying—as I've mentioned—but we'll manage that too. Come what may."

She nodded again, squeezing her eyes shut. Tears rolled down her cheeks.

He jostled her closer, and her ear settled over his heart. She heard the heartbeats, fast and strong.

"And," she said, speaking to the dimness of the room, "I . . . I should like to travel."

He scuttled her up, settling her on his lap, facing him.

"I beg your pardon?" He raised one eyebrow.

She giggled, wiping her eyes. "It's true. I—I'm ready. I've missed it so. And how effective can I truly be as a travel agent if I've not set foot on the Continent in seven years?"

He exhaled heavily and dropped his head against the glass, staring at the sky. "Oh, brilliant, S'bell. The places I want to show you."

She took his face in her hands and guided it to hers. "On the contrary, the places I want to show you."

"We'll show each other," he said, kissing her.

And she laughed and fell against him.

And so began their very long, thoroughly fulfilling journey to happily-ever-after.

Author's Note

As with many Regency romances, *When You Wish Upon a Duke* walks a fine line between history and creative license. The themes I hoped to tease from the tradition of Peter Pan, especially those related to Tinkerbell, included travel, pirates, and the poor choices we sometimes make in fanciful men. These themes, as well as the 1817 timetable established in Book 1 of this series, informed the history I would use—that is, the history I would manipulate—to bring a Tinkerbell-inspired heroine to life.

The founder of Britain's first travel agency, Cox & Kings, got his start quartering English soldiers in India in the 1750s. In peacetime, Mr. Cox realized that the logistical experience he'd acquired while provisioning British troops could be useful to civilian travelers as well. Other travel agents followed and the business of packaging holidays, both domestically and abroad, began to crop up around London in the nineteenth century.

A shop like Hooke's Everland Travel could have existed in Mayfair in 1817, but that is where history leaves off and my fanciful story takes flight. The practice of respectable English women vacationing alone in Europe was unheard of before 1850. When women did begin to travel alone, they were almost always working as missionaries or nurses or in a secretarial role in a scientific expedition.

Likewise, the notion of a female travel *agent* is entirely the work of my imagination. Nordic pirates fall also into this category. I'll play the "fairy-tale card" for these and every fantastical detail in this series.

I can say that North's heroics in the Peninsular War and the state of Iceland in 1817 should be closer to accurate.

By design, all of my books are a wild ride, but this one is particularly over-the-top. Perhaps that's because it was written entirely in quarantine during the pandemic. I was isolated at home but sailed the North Sea to Iceland in my mind. Wherever you are when you read this book, I hope you have as much fun being swept away as I did.

Acknowledgments

Every author should have an editor as gracious, eagle-eyed, and intuitive as Elle Keck. I'm so grateful for her collaboration on this book and her faith in me.

The Usual Suspects helped me brainstorm throughout the nine months of writing this book. My buddies Lenora Bell and Cheri Allan kept me hitting all the beats. My teenagers made North's war stories truly heroic and pressed for Isobel to pose as North's captive instead of his fake wife. When I'm in too deep, it's such a gift to have outsiders swoop in and elicit an Aha-moment.

Finally, I'd like to thank Captain Ally of Island to Island Charters in Key West, Florida, for sharing with me her experiences camping across Iceland. The backdrop of this book was borne of that conversation.

Don't miss the first book in
Charis Michaels's Awakened by a Kiss series,

A Duchess a Day

An heiress with a plan . . .

Lady Helena Lark has spent years trying to escape
her wedding to the vain and boring Duke of Lusk.
She's evaded, refused, even run away. When her family's patience runs out, they pack her off to London to
walk down the aisle. But Helena has another idea: find
a more suitable bride to take her place, even if she must
look for a replacement duchess every day.

A bodyguard with a job to do . . .

Declan Shaw, better known as "The Huntsman," is a
mercenary who can pick and choose his clientele. After
his last job, escorting a young noblewoman to France,
landed him in jail under false accusations, he wants
nothing to do with aristocrats or women. But the law
isn't done with him, and if he agrees to babysit a duke's
errant fiancée, the payout could make his legal troubles
go away.

A most unexpected alliance . . .

When their worlds collide, Declan realizes that
containing his new client is only slightly harder than
keeping his hands off her. Helena senses an ally in
her handsome new bodyguard and solicits his help.
Together they must escape the forces that oppose them
and fight for the fairy-tale love they desire.

On Sale Now
From Avon Books

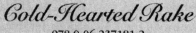